SILENT *in the* SANCTUARY

Also by

DEANNA RAYBOURN

SILENT IN THE GRAVE

SILENT *in the* SANCTUARY

A LADY JULIA GREY MYSTERY

DEANNA RAYBOURN

ISBN-13: 978-0-7783-2492-8
ISBN-10:   0-7783-2492-3

SILENT IN THE SANCTUARY

www.MIRABooks.com

Printed in U.S.A.

First Printing: January 2008
10 9 8 7 6 5 4 3 2

Acknowledgments

As ever, many thanks to my esteemed agent, Pam Hopkins, for all her hard work and support, for her unflagging optimism and for her ferocious devotion. Many thanks as well to my editor, the elegantly tenacious Valerie Gray, whose commitment to my writing has been truly humbling in the best possible way. My life and my work are the better for knowing both of you.

I am incredibly grateful to the MIRA editorial, marketing and PR teams for their enthusiasm and the exquisite care they have lavished on my novels. Particular debts of gratitude are owed to Cris Jaw and Julianna Kolesova for their stylish artistic contributions to this series. And many, many thanks to the unseen hands whose work is often unremarked, but so very essential, and much appreciated—the proofreading, production and sales departments.

Thanks also to my Jackson girls, as always, for all their love and support. Particular thanks to Kim Taylor, for going above and beyond the call of friendship, and all of those who have done more than I could ever have asked. It is a gift to know you and to call you friends.

And thanks most of all to my family; thanks to my daughter and my father for their many little kindnesses, and to my husband, for everything. As ever.

This book is dedicated to my mother,
Barbara Russell Jones, who has read every word
I have ever written, and loved them all.

SILENT *in the* SANCTUARY

THE FIRST CHAPTER
Italy, 1887

Travelers must be content.
—As You Like It

"Well, I suppose that settles it. Either we all go home to England for Christmas or we hurl ourselves into Lake Como to atone for our sins."

I threw my elder brother a repressive look. "Do not be so morose, Plum. Father's only really angry with Lysander," I pointed out, brandishing the letter from England with my fingertips. The paper fairly scorched my skin. Father's temper was a force of nature. Unable to rant at Lysander directly, he had applied himself to written chastisement with great vigour.

"The rest of us can go home easily enough," I said. "Just think of it—Christmas in England! Plum pudding and snapdragon, mistletoe and wassail—"

"Chilblains and damp beds, fogs so thick you cannot set foot out of doors," Plum put in, his expression sour. "Someone sobbing in the linen cupboard, Father locking himself in the study after threatening to drown the lot of us in the moat."

"I know," I said, my excitement rising. "Won't it be wonderful?"

Plum's face cracked into a thin, wistful smile. "It will, actually. I have rather missed the old pile—and the family, as well. But I shall be sorry to leave Italy. It has been an adventure I shall not soon forget."

On that point we were in complete agreement. Italy had been a balm to me, soothing and stimulating at once. I had joined two of my brothers, Lysander and Eglamour—Plum to the family—after suffering the loss of my husband and later my home, and very nearly my own life. I had arrived in Italy with my health almost broken and my spirit in a sorrier state. Four months in a warm, sunny clime with the company of my brothers had restored me. And though the weather had lately grown chill and the seasons were turning inward, I had no wish to leave Italy yet. Still, the lure of family and home, particularly at Christmas, was strong.

"Well, who is to say we must return permanently? Italy shall always be here. We can go to England for Christmas and still be back in Venice in time for Carnevale."

Plum's smile deepened. "That is terribly cunning of you, Julia. I think living among Italians has developed a latent talent in you for intrigue."

It was a jest, but the barb struck too close to home, and I lowered my head over my needlework. I *had* engaged in an intrigue in England although I had never discussed it with my brothers. There had been an investigation into my husband's death, a private investigation conducted by an inquiry agent. I had assisted him and unmasked the killer myself. It had been dangerous, nasty work, and I told myself I was happy to be done with it.

But even as I plunged my needle into the canvas, trailing a train of luscious scarlet silk behind it, I felt a pang of regret—regret that my days were occupied with nothing more purposeful than those of any other lady of society. I had had a glimpse of what it meant to be useful, and it stung now to be merely decorative. I longed for something more important than the embroidering of cushions or the pouring of tea to sustain me.

Of my other regrets, I would not let myself think. I yanked at the needle, snarling the thread.

"Blast," I muttered, rummaging in my work basket for my scissors.

"We are a deceptively domestic pair," Plum said suddenly.

I snapped the threads loose and peered at him. "Whatever do you mean?"

He waved a hand. "This lovely villa, the fireside, both of us in slippers. I, reading my paper from England whilst you ply your needle. We might be any couple, by any fireside, placidly whiling away the darkening hours of an autumn eve."

I glanced about. The rented villa was comfortably, even luxuriously appointed. The long windows of the drawing room overlooked Lake Como, although the heavy velvet draperies had long since been drawn against the gathering dark. "I suppose, but—"

What I had been about to say next was lost. Morag, my maid, entered the drawing room to announce a visitor.

"The Count of Four-not-cheese."

I gave her an evil look and tossed my needlework aside. Plum dashed his newspaper to the floor and jumped to his feet.

"Alessandro!" he cried. "You are a welcome sight! We did not expect you until Saturday."

Morag did not move, and our visitor stepped neatly around her, doffing his hat and cape. They were speckled with raindrops that glittered in the firelight. He held them out to Morag who looked at him as though he had just offered her a dead animal. I rushed to take them.

"Alessandro, how lovely to see you." I thrust the cape and hat at Morag. "Take these and brush them well," I instructed. "And his name is *Fornacci*," I hissed at her.

She gave me a shrug and a curl of the lip and departed, dragging the tail of Alessandro's beautiful coat on the marble floor as she went.

I turned to him, smiling brightly. "Do come in and get warm by the fire. It has turned beastly out there and you must be chilled to the bone."

He gave me a look rich with gratitude, and something rather more as well. Plum and I bustled about, plumping cushions and making him comfortable with a chair by the fire and a glass of good Irish whiskey. Alessandro had never tasted whiskey until making the acquaintance of my brothers, but had become something of a connoisseur in the months he had known them. To begin with, he no longer made the mistake of tossing his head back and drinking the entire glass at one gulp.

After a few minutes by the fire he had thawed sufficiently to speak. "It is so good to see you again," he said, careful to look at Plum as well as myself when he spoke. "I am very much looking forward to spending Christmas with you here." His English was terribly fluent, very much better than my Italian, but there was a formality that lingered in his speech. I found it charming.

Plum, who had poured himself a steady glass of spirits, took a deep draught. "I am afraid there has been a change in plans, old man."

"Old man" was his favourite nickname for Alessandro, no doubt for its incongruity. Alessandro was younger than either of us by some years.

The young man's face clouded a little and he looked from Plum to me, his silky dark brows knitting in concern. "I am not invited for Christmas? Shall I return to Firenze then?"

I slapped Plum lightly on the knee. "Don't be vile. You have made Alessandro feel unwelcome." It had been arranged that Alessandro would come to us in November, and we would all spend the holiday together before making a leisurely journey to Venice in time for Carnevale. There was no hope of such a scheme now. I turned to Alessandro, admiring for a moment the way the firelight licked at his hair. I had thought it black, but his curls shone amber and copper in their depths. I wondered how difficult it would be to persuade Plum to paint him.

"You see, Alessandro," I explained, "we have received a letter from our father, the Earl March. He is displeased with our brother Lysander and wishes us all to return to England at once. We shall spend Christmas there."

"Ah. How can one argue with the call of family? If you must return, my friends, you must return. But know that you will always carry with you the highest regard of Alessandro Fornacci."

This handsome speech was accompanied by a courtly little bow from the neck and a noble, if pained, expression that would have done a Caesar proud.

"I have a better idea, and a very good notion it is," Plum said slowly. "What if we bring Alessandro with us?"

I had just taken a sip of my own whiskey and I choked lightly. "I beg your pardon, Plum?"

Alessandro raised his hands in a gesture I had seen many Italians employ, as if warding something off. "No, my friend, I must not. If your father is truly angry, he will not welcome an intruder at this time."

"Are you mad? This is precisely the time to bring someone outside the family into the fold. It will keep him from killing Lysander outright. He will behave himself if we cart you back to England with us. The old man has peculiar ideas, but he is appallingly hospitable."

"Plum, kindly do not refer to Father as 'the old man'. It is disrespectful," I admonished.

Alessandro was shaking his head. "But I have not been invited. It would be a great discourtesy."

"It would be a far greater discourtesy for Father to kill his own son," Plum pointed out tartly. "And you have been invited. By us. Now I must warn you, the family seat is rather old-fashioned. Father doesn't hold with new ideas, at least not for country houses. You'll find no steam heat or even gaslights. I'm afraid it's all coal fires and candles, but it really is a rather special old place. You always said you wanted to see England, and Bellmont Abbey is as English as it gets, dear boy."

Alessandro hesitated. "If I may be so bold, why is his lordship so angry with Lysander? Surely it is not—"

"It is," Plum and I chorused.

Just at that moment, sounds of a quarrel began to echo from upstairs. There was a shout and the unmistakable crash of breaking crockery.

"But the earl, he cannot object to Lysander's marriage to so noble and lovely a lady as Violante," Alessandro put in, quite diplomatically I thought.

Something landed with a great thud on the floor, shivering the ceiling and causing the chandelier above our heads to sway gently.

"Do you suppose that was one of them?" Plum inquired lightly.

"Don't jest. If it was, we shall have to deal with the body," I reminded him. Violante began to shriek, punctuating her words with tiny stamps of her heel from the sound of it.

"I wonder what she is calling him. It cannot be very nice," I mused.

Alessandro gave an elegant shrug. "I regret, my understanding of Napolitana, it is imperfect." He dropped his eyes, and I wondered if he understood more than politeness would allow him to admit.

"Probably for the best," Plum remarked, draining the last of his whiskey.

"Do not finish off the decanter," I warned him. "Lysander will want a glass or two when they have finished for the evening."

"Or seven," Plum countered with a twitch of his lip. I gave him a disapproving look. Lysander's marital woes were not a source of amusement to me. I had endured enough of my own connubial difficulties to be sympathetic. Plum, however, wore a bachelor's indifference. He had never said so, but I suspected his favourite brother's defection to the married state had rankled him. They had travelled the Continent together for years, roaming wherever their interests and their acquaintance had directed them, exploring museums and opera houses and ruined castles. They wrote poetry and concertos and painted murals on the walls of ancient abbeys. They had been the staunchest companions until Lysander, having left his thirtieth birthday some years past, had spotted Violante sitting serenely in her uncle's box at La Fenice. It was, as the Tuscans say, *un colpo di fulmine,* a bolt of lightning.

It was also a bit misleading. Upon further investigation, Lysander discovered Violante was Neapolitan, not Venetian, and there was quite simply nothing about her that was serene. She carried in her blood all the warmth and passion and raw-boned energy of her native city. Violante *was* Naples, and for a cool-blooded, cool-headed Englishman like Lysander the effect was intoxicating. He married her within a month, and presented Plum and me with a *fait accompli,* a sister-in-law who smothered us in kisses and heady jasmine perfumes. For my part, I found her charming, wholly unaffected if somewhat exhausting. Plum, on the other hand, was perfectly cordial and cordially perfect. Whenever Violante stepped from a carriage or shivered from the cold, Plum would offer her a hand or his greatcoat, bowing and murmuring a graciously phrased response to her effusive thanks.

And yet always he watched her with the cool detachment one usually reserves for specimens at the zoological garden. I often thought there might be real fondness there if he could unbend a little and forgive her for coming so precipitously into our lives.

But Plum was nothing if not stubborn, and I knew a straight-forward approach would only cause him to dig his heels into the ground like a recalcitrant pony. So I endeavoured to distract him with little whims and treats, cajoling him into good temper in spite of himself.

And then we met Alessandro, or to be accurate, I met Alessandro, for he was a friend of my brothers of some years' duration. Rome had been too hot, too noisy, altogether too much for my delicate state when I first arrived in Italy. My brothers immediately decided to quit the city and embark on a leisurely tour to the north, lingering for a few days or even weeks in any particularly engaging spot, but always pushing on toward Florence. We settled comfortably in a tiny *palazzo* there, and I began to recover. My fire-roughened voice smoothed again, never quite as it had been, but not noticeably damaged. My lungs were strengthened and my spirits raised. Lysander felt comfortable enough to leave us to accept an invitation for a brief trip to Venice to celebrate the private debut of a friend's opera. Plum pledged to watch over me, and Lysander departed, to return a month later after endless delays and a secret wedding, his voluble bride in tow.

Alessandro had kept us company while Lysander was away, guiding us to hidden *piazze,* revealing secret gardens and galleries no tourists ever crowded. He drove us to Fiesole in a beribboned pony cart, stopping to point out the most breathtaking views in that enchanted hilltop town, and introduced us to inns in whose flower-drenched courtyards we were served food so delicious it must have been bewitched. Plum always seemed to wander off, sketchbook in hand to capture a row of cypresses, stalwart and straight as a regiment, or the elegant curve of a *signorina*'s cheek, distinctive as a goddess out of myth. Alessandro did not seem to mind. He talked to me of history and culture and we practiced our languages with each other, learning to speak of everything and nothing at all.

They were the most peaceful and serene weeks of my life, and they ended only when Lysander returned with Violante, bursting with pride, his chin held a trifle higher from defiance as much as happiness. With his native courtesy, Alessandro withdrew at once, leaving us to our privacy as a newly re-formed family. There were flinty discussions verging on quarrels, where we all went quite white about the lips and I could feel the heat rising in my face. Lysander had no wish to inform Father of his marriage, thinking instead to make a trip to England sometime in the summer, bringing his surprise bride with him then. Plum and I argued forcefully against this, reminding him of his duty, his obligation, his name. And more to the point, his allowance. If Father was made to look foolish, angered too far, he could easily slash Ly's allowance to ribbons or halt it altogether. Lysander was an accomplished musician, but he was a conductor *manqué*, a dabbler. He had no serious reputation upon which to build a career, and without a formal education, without proper connections, his situation was impossible. He relented finally, with bad grace, and Plum penned the letter to Father, writing in Lysander's name to tell him there was a new addition to the family.

The reaction had been swift—a summons to Lysander to bring his bride home at once. Lysander, in a too-typical gambit of avoidance, rented the villa at Lake Como, insisting we could not go home before Carnevale season and that we might as well spend Christmas in the lake country. But he had underestimated Father. The second letter had been forceful, specific, and brutal. We were expected, all of us now, to return home immediately. Lysander had masked his dread with defiance, dropping the letter on the mantelpiece and shrugging before stalking from the room. Violante had followed him, accusing him of being embarrassed of her, if I translated correctly. The Napolitana dialect had defeated me almost entirely from the beginning, and I think our inability to understand one another most of the time explained why Violante and I had learned to get on so well.

Suddenly, Plum cocked his head. "Listen to the silence. Do you suppose one of them has finally done the other a mischief?"

"Your slang is appalling," I told him, taking up my needlework again. "And no, I do not think one of them has done murder. I think they have decided to discuss the matter rationally, in a mature, adult fashion."

Plum snorted, and Alessandro pretended not to notice, sipping quietly at his whiskey. "Adult? Mature? My dear girl, you have lived with them some weeks now. Have you ever seen them discuss anything in a mature, adult fashion? No, and they will not, not so long as they both enjoy the fillip of excitement that a brisk argument lends to a marriage."

I blinked at him. "They are newlyweds. They are in love. I hardly think they need to hurl plates at one another's heads to enjoy themselves."

"Don't you? Our dear Violante is a southerner, who doubtless took in screaming with her mother's milk. And Lysander is a fool who has read too much poetry. He mistakes the volume of a raised voice for true depth of feeling. I despair of him."

"Do not worry, Lady Julia," Alessandro put in gently. *Giulia*, he said, drawing out the syllables like poetry. "To speak loudly, it is simply the way of the southerners. They are very different from those of us bred in the north. We are cooler and more temperate, like the climate."

He flashed me a dazzling smile, and I made a feeble effort to return it. "Still, it has gone too quiet," I commented. "Do you suppose they have made it up?"

"They have not," came Ly's voice, thick with bitterness. He was standing in the doorway, his hair untidy, his colour high with righteous anger, his back stiff with resentment. It was a familiar posture for him these days. "Violante is insisting we obey Father's summons. She wants to see England and to 'meet her dear papa', she says." He flung himself into the chair next to Plum's, his expression sour. "Hullo, Alessandro. Sorry you had to hear all of that," he added with a glance toward the ceiling.

Alessandro murmured a greeting in return as I studied my brothers, feeling a sudden rush of emotion for the pair of them.

Handsome and feckless, they were remarkably similar in appearance, sharing both the striking green eyes of the Marches and the dark hair and pale complexion that had marked our family for centuries. But although their features were similar, their clothes stamped them as very different men. Plum took great pains to search out the most outlandish costumes he could find, outfitting himself in velvet frock coats a hundred years out of fashion, or silk caps that made him look like a rather dashing mushroom.

Lysander, on the other hand, was a devotee of the spare elegance of Brummell. He never wore any colours other than white or black, and every garment he owned had been fitted a dozen times. He was particular as a pasha, and carried himself with imperious grace. When the pair of them went out together they always attracted attention, doubtless the effect they hoped for. They had a gift for making friends easily, and more times than I could count since my arrival in Italy, we had entered a restaurant or hotel or theatre box only to have my brothers greeted by name and kissed heartily, food and drink pressed upon us as though we were minor royalty. They could be puckishly charming when they wished, and delightful company. Until they were bored or thwarted. Then they were capable of horrifying mischief, although they had behaved themselves well enough since I had joined them.

I flicked a glance at Alessandro from under my lashes. He was still placidly sipping his drink, savoring it slowly, his trousers perfectly creased in spite of the filthy weather. He was an elegant, composed young gentleman, and I thought that with a little more time he might have been a noble influence on my scape-grace brothers.

I smoothed my skirts and cleared my throat.

"My dear," I told Lysander, "I think it is quite clear we must return to England, and you must face Father. Now, we can sit up half the night and argue like thieves, but we will talk you round eventually, so you might as well capitulate now and let us get on with planning our journey."

Lysander looked wonderingly from me to Plum. "When did Julia become brisk? She has never been brisk. Or bossy. Julia, I do not think I much care for this new side of you. You are beginning to sound like our sisters, and I do not *like* our sisters."

I said nothing, but fixed him with a patient, pleasant look of expectation. After a long moment, he groaned. "*Pax,* I beg you. I am powerless against a determined woman." I thought of his tempestuous bride, and wondered if I ought to share with her the power of a few minutes of very pregnant silence. But there was work at hand, and I made a note to myself to speak with Violante later.

"Then we are agreed," I said. I rose and went to the desk, seating myself and arranging writing materials. There was a portfolio of scarlet morocco, stamped in gold with my initials, and filled with the creamiest Florentine writing-paper. I dipped my pen and gave my brothers a purposeful look, the tip of my pen poised over the luscious paper. "Now, we have also had a letter from Aunt Hermia, and I have managed to make out that she is intending to hold a sort of house party over Christmas. We must not arrive without gifts."

"Oh, for God's sake," Lysander muttered. Plum had brightened considerably, thoroughly enjoying our brother's discomfiture. Clearly the return of the prodigal son as bridegroom was not going to be a quiet affair. Knowing Aunt Hermia, I suspected she had invited the entire family—a not-inconsequential thing in a family of ten children—and half the village of Blessingstoke as well.

"Come on, old thing," Plum said. "It won't be so bad. The more people there, gobbling the food and drinking the wine, the less likely Father is to cut off your allowance. You know how much he loves to play lord of the manor."

"He *is* the lord of the manor," I reminded Plum. "Now, I thought some of that lovely marzipan. A selection of the sweetest little fruits and birds, boxed up and tied with ribbons. I saw just the thing in Milan, and we can stop *en route* to the train station. That will do nicely for the ladies. And those darling little bottles of rosewater. I bought dozens of them in Florence."

I scribbled a few notes, including a reminder to instruct Morag to find the engraving of Byron I had purchased in Siena. It would make a perfect Christmas present for Father. He would enjoy throwing darts at it immensely.

Suddenly, I looked up to find my brothers staring at me with identical expressions of bemusement.

"What?" I demanded. "Have you thought of something I ought to have?"

"You have become efficient," Lysander said brutally. "You are making a list. I always thought you the most normal of my sisters, and yet here you are, *organising*, just like the rest of them. I wager you could arrange a military campaign to shame Napoléon if you had a mind to."

I shrugged. "At least I would not have forgotten the greatcoats on the Russian front. Now, Plum has proposed Alessandro join us in England."

Lysander sat bolt upright, grasping Alessandro's hand in his own. "My friend, is this true? You would come to England with us?"

Alessandro looked from Lysander to me, his expression nonplussed. "As I already expressed to your kind brother and sister, I am reluctant, my friend. Your father, the Lord March, he has not invited me himself. And this is a time of great delicacy."

"There is no better time," Lysander insisted. "You heard Julia. Father and Aunt Hermia are planning some bloody great house party."

"Language, Lysander," I murmured.

Naturally he ignored me. "Alessandro, our family home is a converted abbey. There is room for a dozen regiments if we wished to invite them. And do not trouble yourself about Father. Plum has invited you, and so have I. And I am sure Julia wishes it as well."

Alessandro looked past Lysander to where I sat, his gaze, warm and dark as chestnut honey, catching my own. "This is true, my lady? You wish me to come also?"

I thought of the weeks I had spent in Alessandro's company, long sunlit days perfumed with the heady scent of rosemary and punctuated with serene silences broken only by the sleepy drone of bees. I thought of his hand, warm on the curve of my back as

he helped me scramble over stone walls to a field where we pic-
nicked on cold slices of chicken and drank sharp white wine so
icy it numbed my cheeks. And I thought of what he had told me
about his longing to travel, to see something of the world before
he grew too comfortable, too settled to leave Florence.

"Of course," I said, with a firmness that surprised me. "I think
you would like England very much, Alessandro. And you would
be very welcome at Bellmont Abbey."

He nodded slowly. "Then I come," he said at last, his eyes lingering on me.

Lysander whooped and Plum poured out another splash of
whiskey into their glasses, calling for a toast to our travels. I
returned to my notes, penning a reminder to myself to send out
for a timetable. As my hand moved across the page, it shivered
a little, marring the creamy expanse with a spot of ink. I drew a
deep breath and blotted it, writing on until the page was filled
and I reached for another.

At length, the gentlemen left me, Plum to show Alessandro to
his room, Lysander to tell Violante the news of our imminent departure. I was alone with the slow ticking of the mantel clock and
the crisp, rustling taffeta sounds of the fire as it burned down to
ash. My pen scratched away the minutes, jotting notes to extend
our regrets to invitations, requests for accommodation, orders for
hampers to be filled with provisions for the journey.

So immersed was I in my task, I did not hear Morag's
approach—a sure sign of my preoccupation for Morag moves
with all the grace of a draught horse.

"So, we're for England then," she said, her chin tipped up smugly.

"Yes, we are," I returned, not looking up from my writing paper. "And knowing how little love you have for Italy, I suppose you are pleased at the prospect."

She snorted. "I am pleased at the prospect of a decent meal, I am. There is no finer kitchen in England than that at Bellmont Abbey," she finished loyally.

"I would not put the matter so strongly, but the food is good," I conceded. It was plain cooking, for Father refused to employ a French chef. But the food was hearty and well prepared and one never went hungry at the Abbey. Unlike Italy. While I had revelled in the rich, exotic new flavors, Morag had barely subsisted on boiled chicken and rice.

I returned to my writing and she idled about the room, poking up the fire and plumping the occasional cushion. Finally, I threw down my pen.

"What do you wish to say, Morag? I can hear you thinking."

She looked at me with an affectedly wounded expression. "I was merely being helpful. The drawing room is untidy."

"We have maids for that," I reminded her. "And a porter to answer the door. Why did you admit Count Fornacci this evening?"

"I was at hand," she said loftily.

"Ha. At hand because you strong-armed the porter, I'll warrant. Whatever you are contemplating, do not. I will not tolerate your meddling."

Morag drew herself up to her rather impressively bony height. "I was at hand." She could be a stubborn creature, as I had often had occasion to notice. I sighed and waved her away, taking up my pen again.

"Of course," she said slowly, "I could not help but notice that his excellency, Count Four-not-cheese, is coming back to England with us."

"Fornacci, *Fornacci,*" I told her again, knowing even as I did so I might as well try to teach a dog to sing. "And yes, he is coming to England with us. He wishes to travel, and it is a perfect opportunity for him to spend time in a proper English home. My brothers invited him."

"And you did not encourage him?" she demanded, her eyes slyly triumphant.

"Well, naturally I had to approve the invitation, as it were. It would have been rude not to do so."

I scrawled out a list of details that must not be forgotten before our departure. The heel of my scarlet evening slipper required mending, and I had left Plum's favourite little travelling clock with the watchmaker to have the hour hand repaired and the glass replaced. Violante had thrown it at Lysander and dented the hands badly.

Morag continued to loom over the desk, contented as a cat. I could almost see the canary feathers trailing from her lips.

"Morag, if you have something to say, do so. If not, leave me in peace. I am in no mood to be trifled with."

"I have nothing to say, nothing to say at all," she said, moving slowly to the door. She paused, her hand on the knob. "Although, if I *were* to say something, I would probably ask you how you think Mr. Brisbane will like the notion of you coming home with that young man."

A pause, no longer than a quickened heartbeat.

"Morag, Mr. Brisbane's feelings are no concern of mine, nor of yours. I shall retire in a quarter of an hour. See that the bed is warmed. It was chilly last night, and I shall blame you if I take a cold."

She made a harrumphing noise and left me then, thudding along the marble floors in her heavily soled shoes. I waited until she was out of earshot before folding my arms on the desk and dropping my head onto them. Nicholas Brisbane. The private inquiry agent who had investigated my husband's death. I had not thought of him in months.

Or, to be entirely accurate, I had suppressed any thought of him ruthlessly. I had smothered any thoughts of him stillborn, not permitting myself the indulgence of even the memory of him. There had been something between us, something indefinable, but *there,* I had been certain of it. But nearly five months had passed without word from him, and I had begun to think I had imagined it, had imagined the moments that had flashed between us like an electrical current, had imagined the one searing moment on Hampstead Heath when we had both of us reached beyond ourselves and clung to one another feverishly. There was only the memory of that endless kiss to comfort me, and the pendant coin he had sent me by messenger the day I had left England.

I drew the pendant from the depths of my gown, turning it

over in my palm, firelight burnishing the silver to something altogether richer. It was warm from where it had lain against my skin all these months, a talisman against loneliness. I ran a finger over the head of Medusa and her serpent locks, marvelling at the elegance of the workmanship. The coin was old and thin, but the engraving was sharp, so sharp I could imagine her about to speak from those rounded lips. I turned it over and touched the row of letters and numbers he had had incised as a code only I would decipher. I had felt a rush of emotion when I had first read it, certain then that someday, in some fashion I could not yet predict, we would find our way back to each other. *For where thou art, there is the world itself.*

And yet. Here I was, five months on, without a single word from him, his pendant now cold comfort for his indifference. I laid my head back down on my arms and gave one, great, shuddering sob. Then I rose and carefully placed the pen into its holder and closed the inkwell. I tamped the pages of my notes together and laid them on the blotter. I opened the morocco portfolio and dropped the pendant into it. Medusa stared up at me, expectant and poised to speak. I closed the portfolio, snapping the closure with all the finality of graveyard dirt being shoveled onto a coffin. Whatever had sparked between Nicholas Brisbane and I was over; a quick, ephemeral thing, it had not lasted out the year.

No matter, I told myself firmly. I was going home. And I was not going alone.

THE SECOND CHAPTER

Britain's a world by itself.
—Cymbeline

There are few undertakings more challenging than planning a journey for one's family. It is a testimony to my good nature and sound common sense that I arranged our return to England without resorting to physical violence. Violante, who had raged and howled against not being taken to England to meet her new family, decided she had no wish to leave the land of her birth and commenced to weeping loudly over each meal, watering her uneaten food with her tears. Lysander, always the softest and most malleable of my brothers, persuaded by a sister's single shimmering tear or outthrust lip, had grown a carapace of indifference and simply went about the business of eating, paying no more attention to Violante than he did the dozen cats who prowled about our *loggia*, purring for scraps.

Although Plum had joined enthusiastically into the scheme of Christmas at the Abbey, it suddenly occurred to him that he was leaving the fine northern Italian light indefinitely. He spent most of his time in the salon, painting feverishly and ignoring the summonses to meals, contenting himself with a handful of spicy meats tucked sloppily into a hunk of bread and a bottle of wine filched from the cellars. It was left to me to organise our departure with Alessandro's help. He was invaluable, cheerfully dashing off to deliver a message or secure another cart for our baggage. No task was too menial for him. He wrapped books and tied parcels with as much good humour as he had shown introducing us to the delights of Florence. I sorely missed him when he left us the day before our departure, promising to meet us at the train station in Milan. He was secretive and a little quiet, I thought, but he smiled and kissed my hand, brushing his lips not over my fingers, but across the pulse at my wrist. Before I could reply, Morag managed to drop an expensive piece of porcelain that belonged to the owner of the villa, and by the time I had sorted out whether or not it could be repaired, Alessandro was gone.

The next day we rose early and made the trip into Milan, Plum resplendent in a garish tasselled red fez he had purchased on his travels. Violante sobbed quietly into her handkerchief, blowing her nose every minute or so, and Lysander was busily tapping his fingers on the window, beating out the measures of a new concerto. The morning was brilliant, the rich white-gold light of Lombardy rolling over the landscape, gilding the scene in the style of a Renaissance masterpiece. Even the smallest detail seemed touched with magic. The humblest peasant on the road was magnificent, a gift to commit to memory and treasure on a bleak grey day in England. I sighed, wishing Italy had seen fit to give us a kinder farewell. It would have been easier to leave her in a rainstorm.

Milan at least blunted the edge of my regret. The railway station was thronged with people speaking dozens of dialects in four languages, and I knew I would not miss the chaos of Italian cities. There was something to be said for the orderliness of English society, I reflected, looking for the fourth time to the station clock. Alessandro had scant minutes to find us, I realised. I scanned the crowd anxiously for his tall, elegant figure.

"Perhaps he's been run over by a carriage," Morag put in helpfully. I fished in my reticule and extracted her ticket.

"Board the train, Morag. Your seat is in third class. I will see you in Paris."

She took the ticket, muttering in Gaelic under her breath. I pretended not to hear her and turned away, just in time to see Alessandro approaching. He was hurrying, as much as Alessandro ever hurried anywhere. His clothes were perfectly ordered, but his hair was slightly tumbled, and when he spoke his voice was faintly breathless.

"Ah! I have found you at last." He greeted my brothers and Violante, who wailed louder and waved her handkerchief at him.

"Come along, Alessandro," I told him. "We've only a moment or so to board."

"Then let us embark," he said, bowing from the neck. He offered his arm, and I noticed his other was carefully holding a basket covered with a damask cloth. Luncheon, I thought happily.

We were seated quickly in a surprisingly comfortable compartment. Violante and Lysander had begun an argument and were quietly hissing at one another. Plum took out his sketchbook to record a face he had seen on the platform. Only Alessandro seemed excited by the journey, his dark eyes flashing as they met mine.

"I have brought you a gift, a souvenir of my country," he said softly, placing the basket on my knees. I stared at it.

"I had thought it was luncheon, but as the basket has just moved on its own, I rather hope it isn't," I told him.

He laughed, a courteously modulated sound. Florentines, I had observed, loved to laugh but only modestly.

At his urging I lifted the damask cloth and peered into the basket.

"How very unexpected," I murmured. "And how kind of you, Alessandro. I don't suppose you would mind telling me what it is, exactly?"

This time he laughed fully, throwing back his head and revealing a delightful dimple in his cheek. "Ah, Lady Julia, always you enchant me. It is a dog, what you call in your country an Italian greyhound. Surely you recognise her. Her breed has been painted for centuries."

I peered again at the trembling creature nestled against a cushion. She was black and white, large patches, with a wet black nose and eyes like two bits of polished Whitby jet. She lifted her nose out of the basket and sniffed me deeply, then sighed and laid her head back onto her paws.

"Of course. I see the resemblance now," I told him, wondering how this frail, ratlike creature could possibly be related to the cosseted pets I had seen gracing the laps of *principesse* in gilded frames.

"*È ammalata,*" Alessandro said apologetically. "She is a little unwell. She does not like the travelling. I put her yesterday into her little basket, and she does not like to come out."

"Oh, that is quite all right," I said, hastily pulling the damask over her nose. "Perhaps she just needs a bit of rest. What is she called?"

"That is for you to decide."

I did not hesitate. "Then I shall call her after my favorite place in all of Italy. I shall call her Florence."

Alessandro smiled, a smile a nymph would envy, beautiful curved lips and even white teeth. "You pay the greatest honour to my city, my Firenze. I am glad that you like her. I wanted you to have some token of my appreciation for this kind invitation to your family's home."

Strictly speaking, the invitation had been Plum's and I noticed that there was no shivering, pointy-faced puppy for him. And as I clutched the basket and looked out of the window, saying my silent farewells to this country I had grown to love so well, I wondered what significance this present carried with it. Alessandro had implied it was a sort of hospitality gift, a way of thanking one's hosts for opening their home. Still, I could not help but think there was something more pointed in his intentions. And I was not entirely displeased.

Paris was grey and gloomy, sulking under lowering skies like a petulant schoolgirl. We had tarried a few days to shop and show Alessandro the sights, but none of us forgot for long we were being called home in disgrace. Lysander and Violante had made up their quarrel and spent most of their time cooing and making revoltingly sweet faces at one another. Plum, doubtless irritated at their good humour, sulked until I bought him the most outrageously ugly waistcoat I could find—violet taffeta splashed with orange poppies. He insisted upon wearing it with his fez, and wherever we went, Parisians simply stopped and stared. For his part, Alessandro was subdued. I had thought the glories of Paris would enchant him, but he merely regarded them and made notes in his guidebook. It was not until I found him murmuring Italian endearments to Florence that I realised the poor boy must be homesick. He had never left Italy before, and this trip had been a sudden, wrenching thing. There had been no pleasurable time of anticipation, no peaceful evenings by the fire with maps and guidebooks and lists at hand, no chance to dream of it. I think the reality of the cold grey monuments and the wet streets dampened his spirits as thoroughly as they dampened our hems. I promised myself that he would enjoy Bellmont Abbey and our proper English Christmas, even if it killed me. Of course, I had no way of knowing then that it would indeed kill someone else.

As a contrast to the dripping skies of Paris, London was lit with sunset when we arrived, the great gold light burnishing the dome of St. Paul's and lending a kindly glow to the chimney pots and brick houses stacked against each other like so many books in a shop. Even the air smelled sweeter to me here, a sure sign of my besotted state, for London's air has never been salubrious. I pointed out the important landmarks to Alessandro, promising him we would return after Christmas for a thorough tour. He sat forward in his seat, eagerly pressing his hands to the window, taking in the great city.

"It is so big," he said softly. "I never thought to see a city so large."

"Yes, it is. And filthy besides, but I love it dearly. Now, we will make our way to the Grand Hotel for the night, and tomorrow we will embark for Blessingstoke. The train journey is not long. Blessingstoke is in Sussex, and the Abbey is quite near to the village proper."

Plum leaned across Alessandro to take in the view. "God's teeth, it hasn't changed a bit."

"Plum, it may be Shakespearean, but it is still an oath. You know how Aunt Hermia feels about profanity."

He waved me off with a charcoal-smudged hand. "Auntie Hermia will be so happy to see her prodigal boys, she won't care if I come draped in rags and swearing like a sailor. I'll wager the fatted calf is being roasted as we speak."

On that point I was forced to agree. Our Aunt Hermia, Father's youngest sister, had come to live at the Abbey when our mother died from exhaustion. Ten children in sixteen years had been too much for her slight, graceful shape. Aunt Hermia had done her best to instill proper manners and a sense of decorum, but seven hundred years of March eccentricity was too much, even for her iron will. We were civilized, but the veneer was a thin one. In her later years, Aunt Hermia had even come to embrace her own peculiarities, and it was true that her drawing room was the only room in England where ladies were invited to smoke after dinner. Needless to say, Marches were seldom invited to Court.

"Speaking of returning home," Plum said, his expression a trifle pained, "I don't suppose we could stay at March House instead of the Grand Hotel?"

I blinked at him. "Plum, the arrangements have already been made at the hotel. I hardly think it would be fair to disappoint their expectations. Besides, Father is in Sussex. The house would have been closed up months ago, and I am certainly not going to simply turn up and expect the staff to scurry around, yanking off dust sheets and preparing meals with no warning."

"They are servants, Julia," Plum pointed out with a touch of exasperation. "They will be perfectly content to do whatever is expected of them."

I looked at him closely, scrutinising his garments. His coat buttons were loose, a sure sign he had been tugging at them in distraction. It was a nervous habit from boyhood. He dropped buttons in his wake as a May Queen dropped flowers. The maids had long since given up stitching them back on, and he usually went about with his coat flapping loosely around him. Yes, something was clearly troubling him, and I did not think that it was solely his irritation at Lysander's marriage. I suspected his pockets were thin—Plum's tastes were expensive, and even Father's liberal allowances only stretched so far.

Still, even if Plum was flirting with insolvency, there were other considerations. "It is impolite, both to the staff of March House, and the hotel," I told him. "Besides, I hardly think that it will help our cause with Father to have descended on March House with no warning and inconvenienced his staff and eaten his food. You know they will send the bills to him. Under other circumstances, I might well agree with you, but I think a little prudence on our part might go some distance toward smoothing matters for Ly," I finished.

Plum darted a look to the other part of the compartment where Lysander and Violante were huddled together, heads nearly touching as they whispered endearments.

"And we must do whatever we can for Lysander," Plum added, his handsome mouth curved into a mocking smile. He left as quickly as he had come, settling himself some distance away behind a newspaper. I turned with an apologetic glance to Alessandro, but he was staring out the window, his expression deeply troubled and far away. I did not interrupt him, and the rest of the journey into London was accomplished in silence.

The manager of the Grand Hotel, in an act of unprecedented kindness, assigned me a suite on a different floor from my family. There had been some difficulty with the arrangements, he said, fluttering his hands in apology, our letter had come so late, it was such a busy season with the holiday fast approaching. I reassured him and took the key, grateful for the distance from the rest of the party. Violante and Lysander had broken out in a quarrel again on the station platform, Plum was sulking openly, and Alessandro was by now visibly distressed. He only smiled when he noticed my trouble in coaxing Florence from her basket. She remained curled on her cushion, staring at me with the lofty disdain of a Russian czarina.

"Florence, come out at once. This is unacceptable," I told her. Alessandro smiled at me, a smile that did not touch the sadness in his eyes.

"Ah, my dear lady. She does not understand you. She is an Italian dog, you must speak Italian to her."

I stared at him, but there was no sign of jocularity in him. "You are not joking? I must speak Italian to her?"

"But of course, my lady. Do as I do." He bent swiftly and pitched his voice low and seductive. *"Dai, Firenze."*

The little dog leaped up at once and waited patiently at his heel. "You see? Very easy. She wants to please you."

The dog and I regarded each other. I had my doubts that she wished to please me, but I thanked Alessandro just the same and turned to make my way into the hotel. Florence sat, staring down her long nose at me.

I sighed. *"Andiamo, Firenze.* Come along." She trotted up and gave my skirt hem a deep sniff. Then she gave a deep, disappointed sigh.

"I know precisely how you feel."

The next morning I made my way down to breakfast in the hotel's elegant dining room, feeling buoyant with good cheer and a good night's sleep. Something about being on English soil again had soothed me, and I had slept deeply and dreamlessly, waking only when Florence barked out an order to be taken for a walk. I handed her off to a grumbling Morag with a few simple words of Italian, although I had little doubt Morag would simply bark back at her in Gaelic. But even Morag's sullenness was no match for my cheerful mood as I entered the dining room. I might have known that it would not last.

Resting against my plate was a hastily scrawled note from Lysander explaining that he and Violante had chosen to have a lie-in and would take the later conveyance instead of the morning train as we had planned. I wrinkled my nose at the note and crumpled it into my butter dish. A lie-in indeed. More like an attack of the cowardy-cowardy custards. Ly was nervous at the prospect of facing Father. The possibility of losing his considerable allowance, particularly with a wife to maintain, was a grim one. The notion of keeping Violante on the proceeds of his musical compositions was laughable, but also frighteningly real. Ly was simply playing for time, expecting the rest of us to journey down to Bellmont Abbey and smooth the way for him, soothing Father out of his black mood and making him amenable to meeting Lysander under happier terms.

It simply would not do. I applied myself to a hearty breakfast of eggs, bacon, porridge, toast, stewed fruit, and a very nice pot of tea. I enjoyed it thoroughly. The Italians, for all their vaunted cookery skills, cannot do a proper breakfast. A bit of bread and a cup of milky coffee is a parsimonious way to begin one's day. When I was well fortified, I had a quick word with the waiter and made my way to Lysander and Violante's rooms and tapped sharply on the door.

There was a sleepy mumble from within, but I simply rapped again, more loudly this time, and after a long moment, Lysander answered the door, wrapping a dressing gown around himself, his expression thunderous.

"Julia, what the devil do you want? Did you not get my note?"

I smiled at him sweetly. "I did, in fact. And I am afraid it will not serve, Lysander. We must be at the train station in a little more than an hour. I have ordered your breakfast to be sent up. I am afraid there will not be time for you to have more than rolls and coffee, but the hotel is packing a hamper for the train."

He gaped at me. "Julia, really. I do not see why—"

Violante appeared then, clutching a lacy garment about her shoulders and yawning broadly, her black hair plaited in ribbons like a schoolgirl's. She looked pale and tired, plum-purple crescents shadowing her eyes. I greeted her cordially.

"Good morning, Violante. I do hope you slept well. There has been a slight change in plans, my dear. We are all travelling down together this morning. Morag will help you dress. She is quite efficient, for all her sins, and the hotel maids are dreadfully slow."

"*Si*, Giulia. *Grazie.*" She nodded obediently, but Lysander stood his ground, squaring his shoulders.

"Now, see here, Julia. I will not be *organised* by you as though I were a child and you were my nanny. I am your brother, your elder brother, a fact I think you have rather forgotten. Now, my wife and I will travel down to Blessingstoke when it suits us, not when you command."

I stared at him, eyebrows slightly raised, saying nothing. After a moment he groaned, his shoulders drooping in defeat.

"Why, why am I plagued by bossy women?"

I smiled at him to show that I bore no grudge. "I am sure I could not say, Lysander. I will see you shortly."

I turned to Violante who had watched our exchange speculatively. "Remind me to have a little chat with you when we reach the Abbey, my dear."

She opened her mouth to reply, but Lysander pulled her back into their room and banged the door closed. I shrugged and turned on my heel to find Plum lingering in his doorway, doing his best to smother a laugh. I fixed him with a warning look and he raised his hands.

"I am already dressed and the hotel's valet is packing my portmanteau as we speak. I was just going downstairs for some breakfast."

I gave him a cordial nod and proceeded to my suite, feeling rather pleased with myself. An hour later the feeling had faded. Despite my best efforts, it had taken every spare minute and quite a few members of the hotel staff to ensure the Marches were ready to depart. Alessandro was ready, neatly attired and waiting patiently at the appointed hour, but two valets, three maids, and Morag were required to pack the others' trunks and train cases. A Wellington boot, Violante's prayer book and Plum's favourite coat—a revolting puce affair trimmed with coffee lace—had all gone missing and had to be located before we could leave. I had considered bribing the valet *not* to find Plum's coat, but it seemed unkind, so I left well enough alone. In the end, four umbrellas, two travelling rugs, and a strap of books could not be stuffed into the cases. We made our way to the carriages trailing maids, sweet wrappers, and newspapers in our wake. I am not entirely certain, but I think I saw the hotel manager give a heartfelt sigh of relief when our party pulled away from the kerb.

Traffic, as is so often the case in London, was dreadful. We arrived at the station with mere minutes to spare. A fleet of porters navigated us swiftly to the platform, grumbling good-naturedly about the strain on their backs. I had just turned to answer the sauciest of them when I heard my name called above the din of the crowded platform.

"Julia Grey! What on earth do you mean loading down honest Englishmen like native bearers? Have you no shame?"

I swung round to see my favourite sister bearing down on me with a porter staggering behind her. He was gasping, his complexion very nearly the colour of Plum's disgusting coat.

"Portia!" I embraced her, blinking hard against a sudden rush of emotion. "Whatever are you doing here?"

"I am travelling down to the Abbey, same as you. I had not planned to go down for another week or two, but Father is rather desperate. He has a houseful of guests already and no one to play hostess."

"Christmas is almost a month away. Why does he have guests already? And what of Aunt Hermia? We had a letter from her."

Portia shook her head. "Father is up to some mischief. There are surprises in store for us, that is all I have been told. As for Auntie Hermia, she is here in London. She came up to have a tooth pulled, and is still too uncomfortable to travel. Jane is looking after her until she feels well enough, then they will come down together. In the meantime, Father sent for me. You know the poor old dear is hopeless when it comes to place cards and menus."

She cast a glance over my shoulder. "Ah, I see Ly is here after all. I wagered Jane five pounds he would hide out until someone else softened Father up for him. Hullo, Plum! I did not see you there, skulking behind Julia. Come and give me a kiss. I have rather missed you, you know."

Plum came forward and kissed her affectionately. They had always been great friends and partners in terrible escapades, though they had not seen much of one another in recent years. Plum had travelled too much, and was faintly disapproving of Portia's lifestyle. For her part, Portia had embraced a flamboyant widowhood. She habitually dressed in a single colour from head to toe, and her establishment included a lover—her late husband's cousin as it were. His female cousin, much to the shock of society.

Today she was dressed all in green, a luscious colour with her eyes, but her beloved Jane was not in evidence. Plum kissed her soundly on the cheek.

"That's better," she said, releasing Plum from a smothering embrace. "How do you like Lysander's bride? She's a pretty little thing, but I fancy she keeps him on his toes. She is a Latin, after all. And who is *this*?" she asked, fixing her gaze on Alessandro. He had been standing a small, tactful distance apart, but he obeyed Portia's crooked finger, doffing his hat and sweeping her as elegant a bow as the crowded platform would permit.

"Alessandro Fornacci. Your servant, my lady."

Portia regarded him with unmitigated delight, and I could see her mouth opening—to say something wildly inappropriate, I had no doubt. I hurried to divert her.

"Alessandro, this is our sister, Lady Bettiscombe. Portia, my darling, I think we must board now before the train departs without us. The station master looks very cross indeed."

I looped my arm through hers and she permitted me to steer her onto the train. She said nothing, asked no questions, which made me nervous. A quiet Portia was a dangerous Portia, and it was not until we were comfortably seated and the train had eased out of the station that I permitted myself to relax a little. Alessandro and Plum had taken seats a little distance apart, and Lysander and Violante, after exchanging hasty greetings with Portia had moved even farther away. Lysander was still sulking over his enforced departure, and Violante was too indolent to care where they sat. A foul smell emanated from the basket at Portia's feet, and I sighed, burying my nose in my handkerchief. If I sniffed very deeply, I could almost forget the odor.

"I cannot believe you brought that monstrosity," I told her.

Portia gave me a severe look. "You are very cold toward Mr. Pugglesworth, Julia, and I cannot think why. Puggy loves you."

"Puggy loves no one but you, besides which he is half decayed."

"He is *distinguished*," she corrected. "Besides, I note that you have a similar basket. Have you acquired a souvenir on your travels?"

"Yes. A creature almost as vile as Puggy. She is temperamental and hateful and she loathes me. Yesterday she gnawed the heel from my favorite boot simply because she could." I nudged her basket with my toe and she snarled in response. "She only understands Italian, so I am trying to teach her English. Quiet, Florence. *Tranquillamente*."

"What on earth possessed you to buy her if you hate her so much?" Portia demanded, peering through the wickets of the basket. "All I can see are two eyes that seem to be glowing red. I should be very frightened if I were you, Julia. Sleep with one eye open."

"I did not buy her," I told her softly. "She was a gift."

Portia's eyes flew to Alessandro's dark, silken head, thrown back as he laughed at some remark of Plum's. "Ah. From the enchanting young man. I understand. Tell me, how old is he?"

"Twenty-five."

She nodded. "Perfect. I could not have chosen better for you myself."

I set my mouth primly. "I do not know what you are talking about. Alessandro is a friend. The boys have known him for ages. He wanted to see England, and Lysander is too much of a custard to face Father without some distraction. That is all."

"Indeed?" Portia tipped her head to the side, studying my face. "You know, dearest, even under that delicious veil, I can see your blushes. You have gone quite pink about the nose and ears, like a rabbit. I think that boy likes you. And what's more, I think you like him, too."

"Then you are a very silly woman and there is nothing else to say. It is overwarm in here. That is all."

Portia smiled and patted my arm. "If you say so, my love. If you say so. Now, what news have you had of Brisbane? I saw him last month and I know he has been a frequent guest at

Father's Shakespearean society of late, but I haven't any recent news of him."

"You saw him last month?" I picked at the stitching on my glove, careful to keep my voice neutral. "Then you know more of him than I. How did he seem?"

"Very fond of the Oysters Daphne," she said, her eyes bright with mischief. "He made me send along the receipt for his house-keeper. Julia, mind what you're doing. You've jerked so hard at that thread, you've torn the fur right off the cuff."

I swore under my breath and tucked the ragged edge of the fur into my glove. "You mean you had him to dinner? At your house?"

"Where else would I entertain a friend? Honestly, Julia."

"Did you dine alone?"

Portia rolled her eyes. "Don't be feeble. Of course not. Jane was there, and Valerius as well," she said. I relaxed a little. Valerius was our youngest brother and a passionate student of medicine. His favourite pastime was telling gruesome tales at the dinner table, not exactly an inducement to romance.

Portia poked me suddenly. "You little green-eyed monster," she whispered. "You're jealous!"

"Well, of course I am," I said, sliding my gaze away from hers. "I adore your cook's Oysters Daphne. I am sorry to have missed them."

She snorted. "Oh, this has less to do with oysters than with the haunch of a handsome man." She started laughing then, great cackling peals of laughter. I reached out and twisted a lock of her hair around my finger and jerked sharply.

"Leave it be, Portia."

She yanked her hair out of my grip and edged aside, a wicked smile still playing about her mouth. "You daft girl, you cannot possibly imagine I want him for myself."

I shrugged and said nothing.

"Or that he wants me," she persisted. Still I said nothing. "Oh, I give up. Very well, think what you like. Go on and torture yourself since you seem to enjoy it so. But tell me this, have you had a letter from him since you went away?"

I looked out of the window, staring at the houses whose back gardens ran down to the rail line. "How curious. Someone has pegged out their washing. See the petticoats there? She ought to have hung them inside by the fire. They'll never dry in this weather."

Portia pinched my arm. "Avoidance is a coward's tactic. Tell me all."

I turned back to her and lifted the veil of my travelling costume, tucking it atop my hat. "Nothing. I know nothing because he has not written. Not a word in five months."

My sister pursed her lips. "Not a word? Even after he kissed you? That is a shabby way to use a person."

I waved a hand. "It is all water down the stream now. I have done with him. I doubt I shall meet him again in any case. Our paths are not likely to cross. We have no need of an inquiry agent, and the only relation of his who moves in society is the Duke of Aberdour. And Brisbane has little enough liking for his great-uncle's company."

"True enough, I suppose."

I looked at her closely. "Do not think on it, Portia. It was foolish of me to imagine there was something there. I want only to put it behind me now."

Portia smiled, a smile that did not touch her eyes. She was speculating. "Of course, my love," she said finally. "Now I am more convinced than ever that you did a very wise thing."

"When?"

Portia nodded toward Alessandro. "When you decided to bring home that most delightful souvenir."

I slapped lightly at her arm. "Stop that at once. He will hear you."

She shrugged. "And what if he does? I told you before, a lover is precisely the tonic you need. Julia, I was gravely worried about you when you left England. You were ailing after the fire, and I believed very strongly that it was possible you might not ever recover—not physically, but from the trauma your spirit had suffered. You learned some awful truths during that investigation, truths no woman should ever have to learn." She paused and put a hand over mine. "But you did recover. You are blooming again. You were a sack of bones when you left and pale as new milk. But now—" she ran her eyes over my figure "—now you are buxom and bonny, as the lads like to say. You have your colour back, and your spirit. So, I say, complete the cure, and make that luscious young man your lover."

I laughed in spite of myself. "I am five years his elder."

"And very nearly a virgin in spite of your marriage," she retorted. I poked a finger hard into her ribs and she collapsed again into peals of merry laughter.

"Good God, what are the two of you on about?" Plum demanded from across the compartment.

Portia sobered slightly. "We were wondering what Father has bought us for Christmas."

Plum regarded her gloomily. "Stockings of coal and switches, I'll warrant."

Portia shot me an impish look. "Well, perhaps there will be other goodies to open instead."

This time I did not bother to pinch her. I merely opened my book and pretended to read.

THE THIRD CHAPTER

How like a winter hath my absence been from thee.
—SONNET 97

The journey to Blessingstoke was quickly accomplished. The tiny station was nearly deserted. As it was a Monday, and still nearly four weeks before Christmas, the village folk were about their business, although a peculiarly spicy smell hung in the air, the promise of holiday preparations already begun.

Father had sent a pair of carriages for our party, and a baggage wagon besides. There was a brief tussle over who should have custody of the hamper of food, but Portia prevailed, and I made certain to find a seat in her carriage. Somehow she managed to maneuver Alessandro into our small party, and Plum as well, leaving the newlyweds with the maids and the dogs. When Morag let her out of her basket, Florence perpetrated a small crime against Lysander's shoe, and I made a mental note to ask Cook to find her a nice marrow bone when we arrived at the Abbey.

No sooner had we left the station than word spread we had arrived. It was possible to watch the news travel down the road, just ahead of the carriages, for as we bowled past, villagers emerged from their cottages to wave. The blacksmith raised a glowing red poker in greeting, and Uncle Fly—the vicar and a very great friend of Father's—lifted his hat and bellowed his regards. There was a stranger with him, a handsome, well-groomed gentleman who eyed us with interest as we passed. He was soberly but beautifully dressed, and he swept off his hat, making us a pretty little courtesy. His eyes caught mine and I noticed a small smile, only slightly mocking, playing over his lips. His expression was merry, comfortably so, as if laughter was his habit.

"That is not a serious sort of person," I observed as we rounded the bend in the road, leaving Uncle Fly and his jocular stranger.

Portia snorted. "That is Lucian Snow, Uncle Fly's new curate. I made his acquaintance when Jane and I were down this summer."

"Surely you jest. I would never have taken him for a churchman."

"Father says Uncle Fly is having the devil's own time with him. He is always haring off to one of the other villages to 'minister to the flock'."

"Oh, dear," I murmured. "I do hope that is not the phrase he uses. How terribly earnest of him."

"Indeed. I imagine Father will have him to dinner whilst we are in residence. He will certainly invite Uncle Fly, and he can hardly fail to include the curate. Plum, I know you are an atheist, dearest, but do mind your manners and try to be civil, won't you?"

Plum, whose only interest in Italian churches had been the artworks they so often housed, gave a scornful look. "If Father is kind enough to supply me with game, it would be churlish of me not to join the hunt."

"That is a terrible metaphor. Mark what I said and behave yourself. Oh, look there. I see the Gypsies are in residence, just in time for the holiday."

Portia pointed to a cluster of brightly painted caravans in the distance. Tents had been pitched and cooking fires kindled, and at the edge of the encampment a bit of rope had been strung around to keep the horses penned. I imagined the men, sitting comfortably in their shirtsleeves in spite of the crisp air, mending harnesses or patching a bit of tin, while the women tended the children and the simmering pots. As a child I had joined them often, letting them plait flowers into my hair or read my fortune in the dregs of a teacup. But now the sight of the camp brought back other memories, bitter ones I wanted only to forget.

Deliberately, I turned from the window. "Alessandro, tell me how you like England thus far."

The rest of the drive was spent pleasurably. We pointed out local landmarks to Alessandro, and he admired them enthusiastically. It is always pleasant to hear one's home praised, but it is particularly gratifying from one whose own home is crowned with such delights as the Duomo, the Uffizi, and of course, *David*.

Our points of interest were somewhat more modest. We showed Alessandro the edge of the Downs, rolling away in the distance like a pillowy green coverlet coming gently to rest after being shaken by a giant's hand. We guided his gaze to a bit of Roman road which he complimented effusively—a bit disingenuous on his part, considering that Florence was founded as a siege camp for Caesar's army. We pointed out the woods—a royal hunting preserve for ten centuries—that stretched to the edge of the formal gardens of Bellmont Abbey.

Just past the gatehouse, the drive turned flat and smooth and I explained to Alessandro that this was where, as children, we had raced pony carts.

"All of you? The Lord March must have owned a herd of ponies for so many children," he teased.

"No, my dear *signore,*" Portia corrected, "you misunderstand. *We* were hitched to the pony carts. Father thought it a very great joke when we were behaving like savages to harness us up and have us race one another down the drive. It worked beautifully, you know. We always slept like babies afterwards."

Alessandro blinked at her. "I believe you are making a joke to me, Lady Bettiscombe." He looked at me doubtfully. I shook my head.

"No, I'm afraid she isn't. Father actually did that. Not all the time, you understand. Only when we were very, very naughty. Ah, here is the Rookery. This dear little house was originally built in the eighteenth century as an hermitage. Unfortunately, the sitting earl at the time quarrelled with his hermit, and the house was left empty for ages. Eventually, it was made into a sort of dower house."

"It is where we keep the old and decrepit members of the family," Portia put in helpfully. "We send them there and after a while they die."

"Portia," I said, giving her a warning look. Alessandro was beginning to look a bit hunted. She took my meaning at once and hastened to reassure him.

"Oh, it is a very peaceful place. I cannot think of any place I would rather die." She smiled broadly, baring her pretty, white teeth, and Alessandro returned the smile, still looking a trifle hesitant.

"There," I said, nodding to a bit of grey stone soaring above the trees. "There is Bellmont Abbey."

The drive curved then and the trees parted to give a magnificent view of the old place. Seven hundred years earlier, Cistercians had built it as a monument to their order. Austere and simple, it was an elegant complex of buildings, exquisitely framed by the landscape and bordered by a wide moat, carp ponds, and verdant fields beyond. The monks and lay brothers had laboured there for four hundred years, communing with God in peace and tranquillity. Then Henry VIII had come, stomping across England like a petulant child.

"King Henry VIII acquired the Abbey during the Dissolution," I told Alessandro. "He gave it to the seventh Earl March, who mercifully altered the structure very little. You'll notice some very fine stained glass in the great tracery windows. The Cistercians had only plain glass, but the earl wanted something a bit grander. And he ordered some interior walls put up to create smaller apartments inside the sanctuary."

Alessandro, a devout Catholic, looked pained. "The church itself, it was unconsecrated?"

"Well, naturally. It was a very great space, after all. The Chapel of the Nine Altars was made into a sort of great hall. You will see it later. That is where the family gathers with guests before dinner.

Many of the other rooms were left untouched, but I'm afraid the transepts and the chapels were all converted for family use."

Alessandro said nothing, but his expression was still aggrieved. I patted his hand. "There is still much to see of the original structure. The nave was kept as a sort of hall. It runs the length of the Abbey and many of the rooms open off of it. And the original Galilee Tower on the west side is still intact. There is even a guest room just above. Perhaps we can arrange to have you lodged there."

Alessandro smiled thinly and looked back at the towering arches, pointing the way to heaven.

"How wonderful it looks," I breathed.

"That it does," Plum echoed. He looked rather moved to be home again, and I remembered then it had been nearly five years since he had seen the place.

"*È una casa molto impressionante,*" Alessandro murmured.

The great gate was open, beckoning us into the outer ward. A long boundary wall ran around the perimeter. Original to the Abbey, it was dotted with watchtowers, some crumbling to ruin. Just across the bridge and through the outer ward was the second gate, this one offering access to the inner ward and the Abbey proper. The horses clattered over the bridge, rocking the carriage from side to side. Overhead, emblazoned on the great stone lintel was a banner struck with the March family motto, *Quod habeo habeo,* held aloft by a pair of enormous chiselled rabbits.

"'What I have, I hold'," translated Alessandro. "What do they signify, the great rabbits?"

"Our family badge," Plum informed him. "There is a saying in

England, a very old one, 'mad as a March hare'. Some folk say it is because rabbits are sprightly and full of whimsy in the spring. Others maintain the saying was born from some poor soul who spent too much time in the company of our family."

I clucked my tongue at my brother. "Stop it, Plum. You will frighten Alessandro so he will not dare stay with us."

Alessandro flashed me a brilliant smile. "I do not frighten so easily as that, dear lady."

Portia coughed significantly, and I trod on her foot. We passed through the second gate then to find the inner ward ablaze with the reflected light of a hundred torchlit windows. "Ah, look! Aquinas is here."

The carriage drew to a stop in the inner ward just as the great wooden doors swung back. Led by my butler, Aquinas, a pack of footmen and dogs swarmed out, all of them underfoot as we descended from the carriage. Aquinas had accompanied me to Italy but had returned to England as soon as he had delivered me safely into the care of my brothers. I had missed him sorely.

"My lady," he said, bowing deeply. "Welcome home."

"Thank you, Aquinas. How good it is to see you! But I am surprised. I thought Aunt Hermia wanted you to tend to the London house while they were in the country. I cannot imagine Hoots has been very welcoming." The butler at Bellmont Abbey was a proprietary old soul. He knew every stick of furniture, every stone, every painting and tapestry, and cared for them all as if they were his children. He was jealous as a mistress of anyone's interference in what he regarded as his domain.

"Hoots is incapacitated, my lady. The gout. His lordship has sent him to Cheltenham to take the waters."

"Oh, well, very good. He wouldn't be much use here, barking orders from his bed. I suppose you've everything well in hand?"

"Need your ladyship ask?" His tone was neutral, but I knew it for a reproach.

"I am sorry. Of course you do. Now tell us all where we are to be lodged. I am perished from thirst. A cup of tea and a hot bath would be just the thing."

"Of course, my lady."

The second carriage arrived then, followed hard by the baggage cart. There was a flurry of activity as I made the introductions. Plum and Lysander had met Aquinas in Rome, and Portia was a favourite of his of long-standing. But he seemed particularly pleased to meet his compatriots. He offered a gracious greeting to Alessandro and advised him that he had been assigned to the Maze Room, one of the best of the bachelor rooms.

"Oh," I said, turning to Aquinas, pulling a face in disappointment. "I thought Count Fornacci might have the room in the Galilee Tower. Quite a treat for a guest, what with the bell just overhead."

Alessandro shied and I gave him a soothing smile. "It never rings, I promise. It's just an old relic from the days of the monks, and no one has bothered to take it down."

Aquinas cut in smoothly. "I regret that one of his lordship's guests is already in residence in the Tower Room, my lady. I believe Count Fornacci will be very comfortable in the Maze Room."

I sighed. "Perhaps you are right. It's warmer at least."

Aquinas bowed to Alessandro. To Violante he was exquisitely courteous, and upon hearing his flawless Napolitana dialect, my sister-in-law embraced him, kissing him soundly on both cheeks.

"That will do, Violante," Lysander said coldly. She ignored him, kissing Aquinas again and chattering with him in Italian. Aquinas replied, then bowed to her and addressed his remarks to Lysander.

"Mr. Lysander, I have put you and Mrs. Lysander in the Flanders Suite. I hope you will find everything to your satisfaction."

Lysander gave him a sour look, collected his wife, and disappeared into the Abbey. Aquinas turned back to the assembled party. "Lady Bettiscombe, you are in the Rose Room, and Lady Julia is next door in the Red Room. Mr. Plum, you are in the Highland Room in the bachelors' wing. Signore Fornacci, if you will follow me, I will make certain the Maze Room is in perfect readiness for guests."

That was as close as Aquinas would ever come to admit to being unprepared. We had arrived with an unexpected guest, but Aquinas would forgo his own supper before he let it be known that all was not completely in order. We trooped into the hallway and Aquinas turned. "His lordship is in his study. He asked not to be disturbed and said he would see all of you at dinner. The dressing bell will sound in an hour and a half. I shall order tea and baths for your rooms. I hope that these arrangements are satisfactory."

He bowed low and turned to unleash a torrent of orders upon the footmen. In a matter of minutes we were whisked upstairs, separated according to our gender and marital status. Portia and

I were in the wing reserved for single ladies and widows. Formerly the monks' dorter, it was now the great picture gallery, with our rooms opening off of it. Dozens of March ancestors gazed down at us from their gilded frames, punctuated by enormous, extravagant candelabra and a number of antiquities, some good, some of doubtful provenance. There were statues and urns, one or two amphorae, an appalling number of simpering nymphs, and even a harp of dubious origin. No weapons though. Those were reserved for the bachelors' wing in the former lay brothers' dormitory. Their paintings were all martial in subject, with the occasional seascape or Constable horse to provide a respite from the bloodshed. Between them hung arquebuses and crossbows, great swords and axes for cleaving, and in between perched suits of armour, some a bit rustier and more dented than others. I preferred the ladies' wing, for all its silly nymphs.

Some time later, after I had enjoyed a hot bath and a pot of scalding sweet tea, I was sitting in front of a roaring fire, enjoying the solitude, too drowsy to rouse myself. Morag had gone to her room to whip the fur back onto my glove. I had bribed her with a plate of fruitcake to take Florence with her, and I was very near to dozing off when there was a scratch at the door. Portia entered, already dressed in a magnificent gown of heavy oyster satin trimmed in puffs of sable.

"Portia! You do look spectacular. You will put us all to shame as country mice. What is the occasion, pray tell?"

She flopped as far as her corset would permit into a velvet gilt armchair and pulled a face. "I am meant to be the hostess, remember? I have to look the part, and make certain I am the first one in the drawing room to welcome our guests."

"Thank heaven for that. I thought I had dozed off and slept through the dressing bell."

Portia waved a lazy hand. "You've ages yet. So, what do you think of our new sister-in-law? I think she is just what Lysander needed," she said, a trifle smugly. Lysander had been rather brutal in his criticism of Portia's marriage to Bettiscombe, a sweet hypochondriac nearly thirty years her senior. No doubt watching Lysander and Violante bicker from London down to Blessingstoke had been rather deliciously gratifying for Portia.

"Don't be so *cattiva*," I warned her. "We have all made mistakes." We were silent a moment—both of us, I imagine, thinking of our marital woes.

"I am rather surprised Father wasn't present to greet us," I put in finally, breaking the somber mood that had befallen us.

Portia shrugged. "You heard Aquinas. He is doubtless up to some mischief. I had a guest list from him in my room, so at least I know the names. Aquinas, bless him, had already ordered the meal and prepared the seating arrangements, so there was nothing for me to do but approve them."

"And with whom shall we be dining?" I asked, yawning broadly.

"Heavens, I do not know half of them. Uncle Fly, of course, and Snow, the curate. Oh, and Father has apparently decided to begin his Christmas charity early—Emma and Lucy Phipps are here."

"You are in a foul mood, dearest. Perhaps you'd better have some whiskey before you go down."

She tossed a cushion at me and I caught it neatly, tucking it behind my head. "Besides, I always liked Emma and Lucy. They were nice-enough girls."

"But so desperately poor, Julia. Did it never trouble you, the way they would simply stare into our wardrobes and fondle our clothes? And Emma always read my books without asking leave. It was *rude*."

"She is our cousin! And she was our guest, in case you have forgotten."

Portia gave a little snort. "I was never permitted to. Every Easter for a fortnight. The dreadful orphans come to gape at the earl's children like monkeys in the zoo."

"You are a dreadful snob. Their lives were appalling. Can you imagine what it must have been like to live with those terrible old hags?"

She shivered, and we fell silent again. Emma and Lucy's history was not a happy one. Father's youngest aunt, Rosalind, had been a great beauty, the toast of Regency London, showered with a hundred proposals of marriage during her season. But she had scorned them all, eloping in the dead of night with a footman. Proud as a Roman empress, she took nothing from her family, and suffered as a result. They were desperately poor, and a series of miscarriages left Rosalind in poor health, her body ailing and her beauty wrecked on the shoals of her pride. At last she had a healthy child, but poor Rosalind did not live to see it draw breath. Her three sisters swooped in and took the infant from its father, or to be entirely accurate, *bought* the child, for ten pounds and a good horse. They called her Silvia and raised her in seclusion, as they believed befitted the issue of such a scandalous marriage, and it was no great surprise to anyone when Silvia went the way of her mother. She married a poor man without the blessing of her family, and lived to regret it. Silvia, too, bore half a dozen dead children, with only Emma to show for it. Ten years later, Lucy was born, and Silvia was buried by her aunts who clucked sorrowfully and gathered up the motherless girls and took them home. Their father vanished from the story, although Emma, an inveterate teller of tales, claimed he was a pirate prince, sailing the seas until he had amassed enough treasure to bring his daughters home. I never had the heart to scorn her for the lie. The aunts took the girls in their turn, sending them to the Abbey every Easter, for what they called "their respite". I had had some idea that they had been educated for governessing or work as ladies' companions. I had not seen either of them in years, and I was curious as to what had become of them.

"What have they been doing these last years? I have not had news of them."

Portia shrugged. "Emma took a post some years ago as a governess. She has been with a family in Northumberland."

"Good gracious," I murmured. "One must pity her that."

"Indeed. And Lucy has been in Norfolk, looking after Aunt Dorcas."

I pulled a face. Aunt Dorcas was, in fact, Father's aunt, which made her only slightly younger than God Himself. She was one of the trio of frightening old aunts Father called the Weird Sisters.

These were the aunts that had had the raising of Emma and Lucy, and apparently Lucy had not yet managed to effect her escape.

"Poor child. Not much of a life for either of them, is it? Emma bossing other people's children about, and Lucy tending to that horrid old woman. I can't imagine which of them has the worst of it."

Portia arched a brow at me. "There but for the grace of God, dearest."

I nodded. "We are indeed the lucky ones. Now who else has been invited?" I asked Portia, stretching out my foot toward the fire.

"A pack of gentlemen I do not know, including Sir Cedric Eastley—I believe I have heard Father mention him, though I cannot recollect why—and a Viscount Wargrave, whoever he may be. Doubtless he will be a thousand years old and spend all of dinner leering down my décolletage. Then there is a fellow called Ludlow, and a Mrs. King, some relic of Aunt Hermia's, I'm sure. And of course, Aunt Dorcas."

I blinked at her. "You are joking. She must be nearly ninety."

"Nearer eighty," Portia corrected, "and with a host of indelicate habits, the likes of which I shall not alarm you with." She paused and her expression turned thoughtful. "Hortense is here."

"Is she? How lovely! She wrote the most delightful letters when I was abroad. I shall be exceedingly pleased to see her."

Portia's eyes narrowed. "You are a singular woman, Julia. I would have thought, given her notoriety, you might have found it a bit much that Father invited her."

"It seems a curious sort of hypocrisy to object to Hortense on the grounds that she was once a courtesan. Aunt Hermia has been rescuing prostitutes for years and forcing them on us as maids. Consider Morag," I reminded her. Morag had been one of Aunt Hermia's most doubtful successes. She was skilled enough, but entirely incapable of keeping a position with anyone who expected a conventional maid.

"Yes, but *Father.* He seems quite smitten with her. What if he marries her?"

"Then I shall give them a nice present and ask if I may be a bridesmaid."

"Ass. You are not taking this at all seriously."

"Because it is ridiculous. Father is nearly seventy, Hortense will not see sixty again. And she is delightful besides. Who are we to thwart their happiness?"

Portia nodded slowly. "I suppose you are right. Still, I would have thought you would have minded about her. Because of Brisbane."

She was watching me closely, and with some effort, I forced my voice to casualness. "The fact that she was Brisbane's mistress twenty years ago is no concern of mine. Their liaison ended decades ago. Besides, his affairs are his own business. I told you that on the train."

"I know what you *said,* Julia, but that is not necessarily what you believe. You are a faithful creature. I would be quite surprised if you were not still harbouring a *tendresse* for him."

"I thought you were the one encouraging me to molest our young houseguest with unwelcome attentions."

She snorted. "If you believe your attentions would be unwelcome, you are dafter than I thought. Do not think I failed to notice, dearest, you did not deny you still have feelings for Brisbane."

"Then let me do so now. Nicholas Brisbane is a person I will always think of with affection, for more reasons than I can enumerate. But as for any sort of future with him—"

The dressing bell sounded before I could finish, for which I was rather grateful.

Morag appeared then, and Portia tarried a few moments longer, bullying Morag into piling my hair onto my head. I had cropped it some months before, but had let it grow during my travels, and with a bit of artful pinning it looked quite becoming. Portia left as Morag was buttoning me into a severe crimson satin gown. There was not a ruffle or furbelow to be found on it, not the merest scrap of lace or tiniest frill. The simplicity was startling. I powdered my nose lightly and daubed a bit of rouge onto my cheeks, touching my lips with a rosy salve I had purchased in Paris. Morag grumbled about whorishness—a bit of duplicity, I thought, given her own past—but I ignored her and motioned for her to fix my earrings to my lobes. They were delicate things of twisted wires set with tiny seed pearls and bits of garnet. They were not costly, but they were very pretty and whenever I moved my head they glittered in the candlelight. I rose and instructed Morag to keep the fire hot to make plenty of coals for the bedwarmers. She trudged out, grumbling again, and again I ignored her.

I started from the room, then as an afterthought, Portia's words ringing in my ears, I hurried to my writing table instead. My morocco portfolio lay atop it, still clasped since I had last seen it in Italy. I snapped it open and scooped up the pendant Brisbane had given me. It took but a moment to secure it at the base of my throat. I paused to look at my reflection, surprised to see my colour was high. I must have over-rouged, I thought, wiping at my face with a handkerchief. I told myself I needed the pendant because the neckline of my gown was too revealing for a family dinner, but the truth was I had a dozen pendants more suitable, and scores of fichus and scarves that would have served just as well. If I had stopped to consider the matter, I might have realised I had put it on because now I was back in England what I longed for most was to see Brisbane again.

But I did not consider. I wore it as a curiosity instead, a piece of interest I might have bought in Italy. I could wear it among my family and no one save Portia would know it had been given to me by a man who had caused me more disappointment and more elation than any other I had ever known.

The dinner bell sounded as I left the room, and I hastened down the gallery. For all his eccentricities, Father disapproved of tardiness. I fairly flew down the staircase and along the corridor to the nave. From there it was some distance to the hall, but I could see the great wooden doors, fifteen feet high and propped open, light spilling over the great stones of the floor. Just outside the doors, in what had been one of the tiniest chapels, stood Maurice, the enormous stuffed bear one of our great-uncles had brought home as a trophy from a hunting expedition to Canada. He was a frightful old thing, with huge, sharp yellow teeth and claws that had terrified me as a child, and the bear bore him a striking resemblance. But now the bear was moth-eaten, and looked slightly embarrassed at the bald patches where we children had rubbed off his fur from too many games of sardines. I lurked behind him for a moment to catch my breath. The nave was deserted, the long shadows stretching empty up to the webbed hammerbeams of the ceiling. It appeared everyone else had already arrived. I took a slow, calming breath, then slipped through the doors.

As the Chapel of the Nine Altars, the hall had been built on mammoth proportions, and it had not been altered much over the years. A massive space, its walls were punctuated with nine curved bays that had once housed the altars of the most sacred place of the Abbey. The original stone had not been panelled, and the effect was impressively medieval. Tapestries warmed the stones instead—great, heavy things that told the story of a boar hunt in exquisite detail and rich colours that had grown gently muted over the centuries. Two of the bays had been converted to monolithic fireplaces, and in front of them wide Turkey carpets had been laid, although their silken pile did little to drive out the chill of the floors. Sofas and chairs were huddled near the hearths where fires blasted up the chimneys. In summer, lit with sunlight from the enormous tracery windows, the room was beautiful. On a cold winter's night, it was just this side of miserable. The other guests had already assembled, gentlemen doubtless grateful for their elegant coats of superfine, while the ladies shivered with bare shoulders. They were gathered near the hearths like wintering animals, and I saw Alessandro in particular looking rather pinched about the face. I noticed that Aquinas was moving about, pouring hearty measures of whiskey to ward off the cold. Portia's doing, no doubt.

She came toward me, her colour high and her eyes bright. "Dearest, where have you been? You've been an age. I was just about to go and look for you."

"The bell just rang," I began, but she was already towing me across the room to where Father stood in conversation with another gentleman whose back, in beautifully tailored black, was facing me.

"Julia!" my father boomed, in delight, I think. I kissed him, breathing him in as I did so. Father always smelled of books and sweet tobacco, a receipt for comfort.

"Good evening, Father. I was terribly slighted that you were not available to welcome me, you know," I teased him, smoothing his wayward white hair. "I might think you had forgotten I am your favourite." It was a joke of long-standing among us children to make him admit he loved one of us best. None of us had ever caught him out yet.

Father smiled, but I sensed somehow it was not at my little jest. There was something more there, some greater mischief, and I knew, even before the gentleman turned to face me, that I was the hare in the snare.

"Julia, my dear, I believe you already know Lord Wargrave."

And there in front of me stood Nicholas Brisbane.

THE FOURTH CHAPTER

Mischief, thou art afoot,
Take thou what course thou wilt.
—Julius Caesar

stood motionless for a lifetime it seemed, although I know it cannot have been more than a few seconds. I summoned a deliberate smile and extended my hand, forcing my voice to lightness. Rather unexpectedly, both were steady.

"Brisbane, what a surprise to see you. Welcome to Bellmont Abbey."

He shook my hand as briefly as courtesy would permit, bowing from the neck, his face coolly impassive as Plum's beloved Carrara marble. He was exquisitely dressed in evening clothes even Ly would approve, all black-and-white elegance, down to the silken sling that held his left arm immobile just above his waist.

"My lady. Welcome home from your travels."

My smile was polite, wintry, nothing more. Any observer might have thought us the most casual of acquaintances. But I was deeply conscious of Father and Portia watching us intently.

"Thank you. Did I understand Father correctly? Are congratulations in order?"

"The elevation is a very recent one. In fact the letters patent have not yet been read. His lordship is overhasty in his compliments," he said mildly, but I knew him well enough to know this was no façade of modesty. Brisbane himself would not care about titles, and I could only imagine he would accept one because it ensured his entrée into the highest circles of society—a useful privilege for someone in his profession.

For my part, I was impressed in spite of myself. I was one of the few people who knew the truth of Brisbane's parentage and upbringing. To rise from that to a viscountcy was little more than miraculous. It meant whilst I had been sunning myself in Italy, Brisbane had busied himself investigating something very delicate and probably very nasty for someone very highly placed.

"I did not realise you were staying at the Abbey, my lord. I confess I am surprised to see you here."

Brisbane's eyes flickered toward my father. "I might say the same of you, my lady. His lordship declined to mention you were expected to return home before next summer."

Father's eyes were open very wide, a sure sign he had been up to mischief. He was incapable of feigning innocence. I looked from him to Brisbane, fitting the pieces together swiftly. My appearance was as much of a surprise to Brisbane as his was to me. He was pale under the olive of his complexion, and I realised he was attempting to compose himself. Whatever he had expected of his visit to Bellmont Abbey, a reunion with me was no part of it.

I had just opened my mouth to tease him when he looked past me and beckoned sharply to a lady hesitating shyly on the edge of our circle. I had not noticed her before, but now I wondered how that was possible.

"My lady," Brisbane said smoothly, "I should like to present to you my fiancée, Mrs. King. Charlotte, Lady Julia Grey."

I know that I put out my hand, and that she took it, because I looked down to see my fingers grasped warmly in hers, but I felt nothing. I had gone quite numb as I took in the implication of what Brisbane had just said.

"Mrs. King," I murmured. Recovering myself quickly, I fixed a smile on my lips and repeated the greeting I had given Brisbane. "Welcome to the Abbey."

"And welcome back to England, my lady," she said breathlessly.

She was a truly lovely creature, all chocolate-box sweetness with a round, dimpled face and luscious colouring. She had clouds of hair the same honeyed red-blond I had admired on a Titian Madonna. Her eyes were wide and almost indescribably blue. She had a plump, rosebud mouth and an adorably tiny nose unadorned by even a single freckle. Only the chin, small and pointed like a cat's, belied the sweetness of her expression. There was firmness there, perhaps even stubbornness, although now she was smiling at me in mute invitation to befriend her. Unlike me, she wore widow's weeds, although touches of purple indicated her loss was not a recent one. The black suited her though, highlighting a certain fragile delicacy of complexion no cosmetic could ever hope to simulate. She was a Fragonard milkmaid, a Botticelli nymph. I hated her instantly.

"I am so very pleased to make your acquaintance, my lady,"

she was saying. "Lord Wargrave has told me simply everything about you. I know we are going to be very great friends." She was earnest as a puppy, and I had little doubt most people found her charming.

"Has he indeed? How very kind you are," I said, fingering the pendant at my throat. It had been an involuntary action, and I realised as soon as my fingers touched the cool silver it was a mistake. Mrs. King's bright blue gaze fixed on the piece at once.

"What an unusual pendant. Did you acquire it on your travels?" she asked, peering closely at the coin.

"No. It was a gift," I said, covering its face with a finger. I turned to Brisbane, who was watching our exchange closely. I nodded toward the sling. "I see you have managed to injure yourself, my lord. Nothing serious, I hope."

He lifted a brow. "Not at all. A nasty spill from a horse a fortnight ago, nothing more. His lordship was kind enough to invite me to recuperate here away from the bustle of the city."

"And you will be here for Christmas as well?" I asked, forcing my tone to brightness.

"As will my fiancée," he replied coolly, locking those witch-black eyes onto mine.

I did not blink. "Excellent. I shall look forward to getting to know her intimately." The words were blandly spoken, but Brisbane knew me well enough to hear the threat implicit within them.

His gaze wavered slightly, and I inclined my head. "I do hope you will excuse me. I must greet the other guests. Mrs. King, a pleasure," I said, withdrawing from the group. Father caught my eye, his own eyes bright with mischief. I turned my head, not surprised to find Portia at my elbow.

"Well done, dearest," she whispered.

"Whiskey," I hissed. "Now."

In another of the little altar alcoves a sideboard had been arranged with spirits of every variety. We made our way to the whiskey decanter and stood with our backs to the room. Portia poured out a generous measure for both of us and we each took a healthy, choking sip. I swallowed hard and fixed her with an Inquisitor's stare.

"I shall only ask you once. Did you know?"

She paled, then took another sip of her whiskey, colour flooding her cheeks instantly. "Of course not. I knew Father meant to invite him down for Christmas. I thought it might be a nice surprise for you. But I had no idea he was being elevated, nor that he had that…that *creature* with him. How could he?"

Portia shot Brisbane a dark look over her shoulder. "He kissed you. He gave you that pendant. I thought that *meant* something."

"Then you are as daft as I. Drink up. We cannot hover over the spirits all evening. We must mingle with the other guests."

She stared at me as though I had lost my senses. "But are you not—"

"Of course, dearest. I am entirely shattered. Now finish your whiskey. I see Aunt Dorcas mouldering in an armchair by the fire and I must say hello to her before she decays completely."

Portia's eyes narrowed. "You are not shattered. You are *smiling*. What are you about?"

"Nothing," I told her firmly. "But I have my pride. And as you pointed out," I said with a nod toward Alessandro, "I have alternatives."

Alessandro smiled back at me, shyly, his colour rising a little.

Portia poked me. "What are you thinking?"

I put our glasses on the table and looped my arm through hers, pulling her toward Aunt Dorcas.

"I was simply thinking what a delight it will be to introduce Alessandro to Brisbane."

Aunt Dorcas had established herself in the armchair nearest the fire, and it looked as though it would take all of the Queen's army to roust her out of it. No one would call her plump, for plumpness implies something jolly or pleasant, and Aunt Dorcas was neither of those. She was *solid,* with a sense of permanence about her, as though she had always existed and meant to go on doing so forever. Disturbingly for a woman of her size and age, she had a penchant for girlish ruffles and bows. She was draped in endless layers of pink silk and wrapped in an assortment of lace shawls, with lace mitts on her hands and an enormous lace cap atop her thinning hair. She wore only pearls, yards of them, dripping from her décolletage and drawing the eye to her wrinkled skin. She had gone yellow with age, like vellum, and every bit of her was the colour of stained ivory—teeth, hair, skin, and the long nails that tapped out a tuneless melody on the arm of her chair. But her eyesight was sharp, and her hearing even better. She was talking to, or rather *at,* Hortense de Bellefleur,

Father's particular friend. Hortense was stitching placidly at a bit of luscious violet silk. She was dressed with a Frenchwoman's natural elegance in a simple gown of biscuit silk, an excellent choice for a lady of her years. She looked up as we approached, smiling a welcome. Aunt Dorcas simply raised her cane to poke my stomach.

"Stop there. I don't need you breathing all over me. Where have you been, Julia Grey? Gallivanting about Europe with all those filthy Continentals?"

Her voice carried, and I darted a quick glance at Hortense, but she seemed entirely unperturbed. Then again, very little ever perturbed Hortense.

"Xenophobic as ever, I see, Aunt Dorcas," I said brightly.

"Eh? Well, never mind. You've put on a bit of weight you have, and lost that scrawny look. You were a most unpromising child, but you have turned out better than I would have thought."

The praise was grudging, but extremely complimentary coming from Aunt Dorcas. She turned to Hortense.

"Julia was always plain, not like Portia there. Portia has always been the one to turn men's heads, haven't you, poppet?"

"And some ladies'," I murmured. Portia smothered a cough, her shoulders shaking with laughter.

"Yes, Aunt Dorcas, but you must agree Julia is quite the beauty now," my sister put in loyally.

"She will do," Aunt Dorcas said, a trifle unwillingly, I thought.

I bent swiftly to kiss Hortense's cheek. "Welcome home, chérie," she whispered. "It is good to see you."

Simple words, but they had the whole world in them, and I squeezed her shoulder affectionately. "And you."

"Come to my boudoir tomorrow. We will have a pot of chocolate and you will tell me everything," she said softly, with a knowing wink toward Alessandro.

Before I could reply, Aunt Dorças poked me again with her cane. "You are too close."

I obeyed, moving to stand near Portia. "Portia tells me you have been staying here. I hope you find it comfortable."

Aunt Dorcas puffed out her lips in a gesture of disgust. "This old barn? It is draughty, and I suspect haunted besides. All the same, I think it very mean of Hector not to invite me more often. I am family after all."

I thought of poor Father, forced to face the old horror for months on end, and I hurried to dissuade her. "You would be terribly bored here. Father spends all his time in his study, working on papers for the Shakespearean Society."

"The Abbey is indeed draughty," Portia put in quickly. "And we do have ghosts. At least seven. Most of them monks, you know. I shouldn't be surprised if one walked abroad tonight, what with all of the excitement of the house party. They get very agitated with new people about. Do let us know if you see a holy brother robed in white."

Portia's expression was deadly earnest and it was all I could do not to burst out laughing. But Aunt Dorcas was perfectly serious.

"Then we must have a séance. I shall organise one myself. I

have some experience as a medium, you know. I have most considerable gifts of a psychic nature."

"I have no doubt," I told her, shooting Portia a meaningful look.

Portia put an arm about my waist. "Aunt Dorcas, it has been lovely seeing you, but I simply must tear Julia away. She hasn't spoken to half the room yet, and I am worried she might give offense."

Aunt Dorcas waved one of her lace scarves at us, shooing us away, and I threw Hortense an apologetic glance over my shoulder.

"I do feel sorry for dear Hortense. However did she get landed with the old monstrosity?"

Portia shrugged. "We have suffered with Aunt Dorcas for the whole of our lives. Hortense is fresh blood. Let her have a turn. Ah, here is someone who is anxious to see you."

She directed me toward a small knot of guests gathered around a globe, two ladies and two gentlemen. As we drew near, one of the ladies spun round and shrieked.

"Julia!" She threw her arms about me, embracing me soundly.

I patted her shoulder awkwardly. "Hello, Lucy. How lovely to see you." She drew back, but kept my hands firmly in her own.

"Oh, I am so pleased you have arrived. I've been fairly *bursting* to tell you my news!"

"Dear me, for the carpet's sake, I hope not. What news, my dear?"

She tittered at the joke and gave me a playful slap.

"Oh, you always were so silly! I am to be married. Here, at the Abbey. In less than a week. What do you make of that?"

She was fairly vibrating with excitement, and I realised I was actually rather pleased to see her. Lucy was one of the most conventional of my relations, a welcome breath of normality in a family notorious for its eccentricity. To my knowledge, Lucy was one of the few members of our family never to have been written up in the newspapers for some scandal or other. We exchanged occasional holiday letters, nothing more. I had not seen her in years, but I was astonished at how little she had changed. Her hair was still the same rich red, the colour of winter apples, and springing with life. And her expression, one of perpetual good humour, was unaltered.

"My heartiest good wishes," I told her. I glanced behind her to where the other lady stood, a quiet figure, her poise all the more noticeable against Lucy's ebullience.

"Emma!" I said, moving forward to embrace her. "I am happy to see you."

Emma was wearing a particularly trying shade of green that did nothing for her soft, doe-brown eyes, her one good feature. Her hair was unfashionably red, like Lucy's, but where Lucy's was curly and vibrant with colour, Emma's was straight and so dull as to be almost brown. She wore it in a severe plait that she wound about her head, pinned tightly. Her face was unremarkable; her features would have suited the muslin wimple of a cloistered sister. But she smiled at me, a warm, genuine smile, and for a moment I forgot her plainness.

"Julia, you must tell us all about your travels. We have just been discussing Lucy's wedding trip," she told me, motioning with one small, lily-white hand toward the globe. Flanking it were the two gentlemen, one the elder by some two decades, and clearly the other's superior in rank and wealth. His evening clothes were expensively made and the jewel in his cravat was an impressive sapphire. Lucy went to him and put her arm shyly in his.

"Julia, I should like to present my fiancé, Sir Cedric Eastley."

If I was startled, I endeavoured not to show it. Had I been asked to choose, I would have picked the younger man for Lucy's betrothed. He looked only a handful of years her elder, while Sir Cedric might well have been her father.

"Cedric, this is my cousin, Lady Julia Grey."

He took the hand I offered, his manners carefully correct, although not from the schoolroom, I fancied. There was the slightest hesitation in his gestures, as though he were taking a fleeting second to remember a lesson he had only recently been taught. He performed flawlessly, but not naturally, and it occurred to me this was a man who had brought himself up in the world, by his own efforts, and his baronetcy had been his reward.

Lucy gestured toward the younger man, a tall, slightly built fellow with a pleasant expression and quite beautiful eyes.

"And this is Sir Cedric's cousin and secretary, Henry Ludlow."

Unlike Sir Cedric's very new, very costly clothing, Ludlow's attire spoke of genteel poverty, but excellent make. Clearly he had come down in the world to accept a post in his cousin's employ, and I wondered at the vagaries of fate that had clearly elevated the one while casting the other down. I thought they should prove interesting guests and I turned to Lucy to inquire how long they would be with us at the Abbey.

"Until the new year," she announced. "Cedric and I will be

married here in the Abbey on Saturday by the vicar. Then we mean to stay through Christmas. It will be like the old times again, with all of the Marches together," she said, her eyes glowing with excitement. It seemed needlessly cruel to point out that her surname was not March and that she had in fact never spent a Christmas at the Abbey. I suspected she and Emma had yearned to belong to our family in a way that an Easter fortnight each year could simply not accomplish. Perhaps being married among us and spending her first Christmas in our midst would assuage some of that childhood hunger.

"Emma mentioned a wedding trip," I said, gesturing toward the globe. It was a sad affair, much mauled by us as children and by Crab, Father's beloved mastiff. She had taken to carrying it around with her as a pup, and by the time Father had trained her not to do so, the globe was beyond salvation.

Sir Cedric pointed to Italy. "We were thinking of Florence. And perhaps Venice as well, with a bit of time spent by the Tyrrhenian Sea in the summer. I know the loveliest spot, just here, below this fang mark."

I nodded. "Italy is a perfect choice. I understand the winters are not too brutal, and the scenery is quite breathtaking." I said nothing of the people, but I made the mistake of catching Portia's eye just as she was raising an eyebrow meaningfully toward Alessandro. I straightened at once.

Portia commandeered me again, excusing us from the little group and guiding me to where Violante and Lysander were standing with Alessandro. Violante was resplendent in a flame-

coloured gown, her expression sedate. Father had given her a noticeably wide berth, and I wondered if he had spoken to her at
all. I imagined he had given her a cursory welcome and then
excused himself to speak with anyone else. To make up for his
neglect, I addressed her with deliberate warmth.

"Violante, how lovely you look. That gown suits you. You
look like sunset over the Mediterranean."

She smiled, her slow, lazy smile. *"Grazie,* Giulia." She waved
her glass at me. "What am I drinking? It is very good."

I looked at her glass and grimaced. "That is Aunt Dorcas'
frightful elderberry cordial. I am surprised at Aquinas pouring it
for you before dinner."

"Plum, he brought it. I tell him I want something English to drink.
Lysander, he has the whiskey, but I am given this. It is very nice."

Well, Plum might have found her something more suitable, but
I was pleased he was making an effort to get on with Violante at
all. "Mind you don't drink too much of it," I warned her. "It is an
excellent cure for insomnia or incipient cold, but more than a tiny
glass will bring on the sweats."

She blinked at me. *"Che cosa?"*

I searched for the word, but Alessandro stepped in smoothly. *"La
suda,"* he said softly. She looked at him a moment, then shrugged.

Portia elbowed me gently aside. "Alessandro, have you met my
father yet?"

Alessandro shook his head. "I regret, no, my lady. His lordship
has been very busy with his other guests."

Even before she spoke the words aloud, I knew what she was

95

about. "In that case, Julia, you must perform the introductions. I know Father must be simply perishing to meet your friend."

I glanced over to where Father stood, still in conversation with Brisbane, then back to Portia. Her eyes were alight with mischief. Alessandro was regarding me with his customary Florentine dignity. "Ah, yes. I would very much like to pay my respects to his lordship, and thank him for his hospitality."

"Of course," I said faintly. "Portia, are you coming, dearest?"

"Oh, I thought I would get to know our delightful new sister-in-law," she said, delivering the *coup de grâce*. "But do not let me keep you."

"Come along, Alessandro," I said through gritted teeth. He cupped my elbow in his hand, guiding me gently—a wholly pleasant sensation, but I was still annoyed. I should not have been the one to make the introductions. He had been Plum's friend, and Ly's as well, before he had been mine. It had been their inspiration to bring him to England, but now that Father had to be dealt with, they were perfectly content to let me brave the lion's den on my own. Plum had made the acquaintance of Mrs. King and was busy giving her a tour of the room's beauties, and Lysander was too consumed with his bride to have a thought for anyone else.

And Portia was determined to stir the pot with Brisbane. I noticed his eyes sharpening as we approached, nothing more. There was no raising of his expressive brows, no naked curiosity, only the intense watchfulness of a lion lazing in the shade by a pond where the gazelle will drink.

"Father," I said, my voice a trifle thin, "I should like you to meet our friend, Alessandro. He came with us from Italy. Count Alessandro Fornacci. Alessandro, my father, Lord March."

Father turned to greet Alessandro, welcoming him with more warmth than I would have imagined. Alessandro accepted his welcome with exquisite courtesy, expressing his rapture at being in England and his extreme pleasure in sharing this most English of holidays.

"Hmm, yes," Father said, his eyes moving swiftly between us. Alessandro's hand had lingered a moment too long at my elbow, and Father had not missed it. "Your room is satisfactory?"

I suppressed a sigh. Father would not have cared if Alessandro had been lodged in the dovecote with only a blanket to cover him and a stray cat for conversation. He meant to detain him, to take the measure of him, and perhaps to let Brisbane do so, as well.

"My room is very nice. It overlooks a maze, very lovely."

"Excellent. You will want to see the maze up close, I'm sure. Mind you take a guide. Devilish tricky to get out of," Father said, laughing heartily. I stared at him. Father was never jolly. He was putting on dreadfully for Alessandro, and I was just about to send manners to the devil and lead Alessandro away when Brisbane put out his hand.

"Nicholas Brisbane."

Alessandro clasped his hand and bowed formally. "Mr. Brisbane." Father gave a guffaw. "Not just Brisbane anymore. He's a viscount any day now, my lad. Lord Wargrave."

"Milord," Alessandro amended.

Brisbane waved a careless hand. "No need to stand on ceremony. We are among friends here. Very good friends, I should
think," he finished with a flick of his gaze toward me.

"Quite," I said sharply. "Ah, I see Uncle Fly and his curate have
finally arrived. Come along, Alessandro. I should like to introduce you to my godfather."

Before I could manage our escape, Father caught sight of Uncle
Fly and bellowed out, "What kept you, Fly? Damned inconsid-
erate to make me wait for my dinner."

Uncle Fly laughed and clapped a hand to Lucian Snow's
shoulder. "Blame the lad. He was an hour tying his cravat. Doubtless to impress the ladies."

Father and Uncle Fly chuckled like schoolboys, and Lucian
Snow smiled good-naturedly. "Well, with such lovely company
a gentleman must trouble himself to look his best," he said,
sweeping the room with a gallant nod. A few ladies tittered, but
I realised Portia was not among them. She had taken herself off,
and I cursed her for a traitor that she had dropped me in it so
neatly and then fled.

But I had no time to consider her whereabouts. Uncle Fly
had made a beeline for me, Snow following in his wake. My
godfather smothered me in an embrace that smelled of cherry
brandy and something more—earth, no doubt. Uncle Fly was
an inveterate gardener and spent most of his time puttering in
his gardens and conservatory. No matter how often he scrubbed
them, his hands were always marked with tiny lines dark with
soil, like rivers on an ancient map. His fingertips were stained

green, his lapels dusted with velvety yellow pollen. And his hair, tufts of fluffy white cotton that stood out about his head where he had tugged at it in distraction, was usually ornamented with a leaf or petal, and on one memorable occasion, a grasshopper.

His curate could not have cut a more opposite figure. He was taller than the diminutive Fly by half a foot, and more slender, although one would never think him slight. His posture was impeccable; he was straight as a lance, with a slight lift of the chin that made it seem as if he were gazing at some distant horizon. But when the introductions were made and he bowed over my hand, his eyes were fixed firmly on mine. They were warm, melting brown, like a spaniel's, and they were merry. He twinkled at me like a practised rogue, and I found myself wondering how a man like him had come to hold the post of curate in an obscure country village. I introduced him to Alessandro, and Snow gamely attempted to greet him in Italian. It was laboured and wildly ungrammatical, but he laughed at his own mistakes, and Alessandro tactfully pretended not to notice.

Just then I saw Portia slip in, her expression smug. Before I could accost her, Aquinas entered and announced dinner. There was a bit of a scramble for partners, but since we were an odd number with more gentlemen than ladies, Portia insisted we dispense with etiquette and instructed each gentleman to choose the lady he wished to lead in.

To my surprise, Lucian Snow offered me his arm. "My lady, I hope you will do me the honour?"

I hesitated. Alessandro was hovering near, too polite to dispute with Snow, but a little dejected, I think. Just then Portia glided over, and slid her arm through Alessandro's.

"I do hope you will escort me, Alessandro. I simply couldn't bear to walk in on the arm of one of my brothers."

That was a bit thick, I thought. Lysander was already steering Violante to the door, and Plum was busy trying to lever Aunt Dorcas out of her chair. But Alessandro was too well bred to point this out. He merely bowed and smiled graciously at her.

"It would be my honour, Lady Bettiscombe."

I turned to Lucian Snow with a smile. "Certainly."

I took his arm, and he favoured me with a smile in return, a charming, dimpled smile that doubtless made him a great pet of the ladies. His features were so regular, so beautifully proportioned, he might have been an artist's model. One could easily fancy him posed in a suit of polished armour, light burnishing his golden hair, his spear poised over a rampant dragon. St. George, captured in oils at his moment of triumph.

"I must tell you, Lady Julia, I was not at all pleased at being invited here tonight," he said as we passed through the great double doors. Those warm spaniel eyes were twinkling again.

"Oh? And why not? Are we as fearsome as all that?"

"Not at all. But his lordship has been gracious enough to invite me to dine at least once a fortnight since I came to Blessingstoke, and I have gained half a stone. Another few weeks and I shall not be able to fit through that door," he said, his expression one of mock horror.

My gaze skimmed his athletic figure. "Mr. Snow, you are baiting me to admire your physique. It will not serve. I am an honest widow, and you, sir, I suspect are an outrageous flirt."

He laughed and gave my arm a friendly squeeze. "I know it is entirely presumptuous of me, Lady Julia, but I think we are going to be very great friends."

I raised a brow at him. Curates in country villages were not often befriended by the daughters of earls. But our village was a small one, and Father rarely stood on his dignity. He preferred the company of interesting people, and would happily speak with a footman over a bishop if the footman had better conversation. He must have made something of Snow for the curate to have been invited to dinner so often, and Snow seemed to be preening a bit under his favour.

The curate leaned closer, his expression mockingly serious. "I have offended you by my plain speaking. I am struck to the heart with contrition." He rolled his eyes heavenward, and thumped his chest with a closed fist.

"Gracious, Mr. Snow, are you ever serious?"

He rolled his eyes down to look at me. "On a very few subjects, on a very few occasions. I shall leave it to you to find them out, my lady."

He was an ass, but an amusing one. I primmed my mouth against the smile that twitched there.

"I shall look forward to the discovery," I said solemnly. We exchanged a smile, and I thought then that this might very well be the most interesting house party that Bellmont Abbey had seen since Shakespeare had spent a fortnight here, confined to bed with a spring cold. Of course, I was entirely correct about that, but for reasons I could never have imagined.

THE FIFTH CHAPTER

Let it serve for table-talk;
Then, howsoe'er thou speak'st, 'mong other things,
I shall digest it.
—THE MERCHANT OF VENICE

he dining hall was an impressive, handsome chamber carved out of the space of the north transept. It had been fitted with a tremendous fireplace and a table long enough to seat forty. We entered to find the seating arrangements at sixes and sevens. I blamed Portia. Aquinas, if left to his own devices, would have manfully struggled to create some order out of our uneven family party. But Portia had absented herself just before dinner, and the organisation of the place cards demonstrated a wicked sense of mischief afoot. Aunt Dorcas had been slotted between Plum and Ly, a move calculated to unnerve both of my brothers. Hortense was flanked by Father and Fly, both of whom doted on her outrageously. And I had been bookended by Alessandro and Lucian Snow, the two most eligible gentlemen present. In a final masterstroke, Portia had placed Brisbane squarely opposite me, where he could not fail to notice their attentions. Portia herself took a chair on the other side of Alessandro, doubtless with an aim to directing his focus wherever she fancied. It was Machiavellian, and had I not been at the locus of it, I should have admired it greatly.

As soon as we were arranged, Father took up his glass and the company did likewise. He raised his high in a patently theatrical gesture, and proclaimed in a resonant voice, "'Now good digestion wait on appetite, and health on both!'"

There was a chorus of "Hear, hear!", but as we drank deeply, I remembered that quote. It was from *Macbeth,* and I wondered with a shiver if that bloody play was an omen of things to come.

Just then Father's mastiff, Crab, pushed her way under the table, followed by her pack of pups. Mrs. King squealed—at a wet nose thrust under her petticoat to sniff her ankle, no doubt.

Father lifted the tablecloth, upsetting a few goblets and overturning a cruet of vinegar. "Down, you lot!" he thundered, and the dogs obeyed, settling themselves under chairs and onto feet, waiting docilely for a few titbits to be dropped. I smiled at how *normal* it all seemed. Well, normal for us in any event. I persuaded myself that I was being fanciful with my thoughts of omens, and I slipped a bit of lobster patty to one of the pups.

As we were finishing the fish course, talk turned to the wedding, and I heard Lucy chattering happily about the arrangements.

"Aunt Hermia has been an utter lamb. Before she left for London, she took me up to the lumber rooms to pillage the things that have been packed away. All the ladies came. We were the merriest party! Would you believe we found the most beautiful gown? Lyons silk, she told me. It must be quite seventy years old, but it is in very good condition. I imagine your mama must have worn it, Uncle March." Father lifted a brow at her, but merely continued eating his lobster patty. "And there was a bit of veiling from another bride, and a tiny wreath of orange blossom, fashioned out of silk. We took the things out for a good airing. Of course, there will not be flowers in the church. One forgets that an Advent wedding forbids it. I should have so loved to have carried even a bit of greenery, some holly, perhaps, tied with ribbons, with a few great buckets of it on the altar."

She was wistful, and Uncle Fly, who took a rather liberal view on church matters, waved his fish fork at her. "My dear girl, if you want flowers, have them. With the wedding here in the Abbey chapel and not at St. Barnabas in the village, no one is to know or care if you put a bit of nonsense here and there."

Lucy clasped her hands, her face alight with pleasure. "Do you mean it? Really? Oh, I should love that!"

Uncle Fly shrugged. "If you will come to the vicarage tomorrow, I will show you what I have in the conservatory just now. We can do better than a bit of holly, I'll warrant."

She was effusive in her thanks, but Uncle Fly merely nodded and applied himself to his fish. He was a great trencherman, and nothing pleased him more than a hearty meal from the Abbey kitchens.

"The pudding!" I said suddenly, and rather more loudly than I had intended. Conversation around the table stuttered to a halt, and everyone's eyes fixed on me curiously. "Yesterday. It was Stir-up Sunday, and Aunt Hermia was not here to make certain the puddings were stirred. And we were not here to make our wishes."

This was a calamity indeed. As long as Christmas had been

celebrated at Bellmont Abbey, the family had gathered in the kitchens after church on Stir-up Sunday to give the Christmas puddings a stir and make a wish. Traditionally, there had been one great pudding for the entire household, but with ten children, Father had quickly seen the wisdom in having Cook prepare a small pudding for each of us. We would stand in a row, swathed in aprons, some of us tottering on stools as we dragged the long wooden spoons through the heavy batter, chanting together the traditional rhyme:

> Stir up, we beseech thee,
> The pudding in the pot;
> And when we get home
> We'll eat the lot.

As we stirred, Aunt Hermia would peer over our shoulders, reminding us to make our wishes, and to stir from east to west in honour of the Three Kings. Then she would flap her hands, turning us from the room so she might add the charms to the puddings, a thimble for a lucky life, a ring to foretell marriage, a silver sixpence to betoken wealth to come. It was one of my favourite customs of the holiday, and not just for the festivity of the stirring-up. The puddings were heavenly, richly spiced and studded with golden raisins and currants and all manner of good things. But with Aunt Hermia in London, there was little chance the puddings had been made, and the notion of Christmas without our beloved puddings was unthinkable.

"Do not fret," Father said with a benevolent smile. "We have had a saviour in the shape of Mrs. King. She organised the stirring-up yesterday. She even made certain there would be extra puddings for those of you come lately."

I looked at Mrs. King who had coloured delicately, a light stain of rose across her round cheeks.

"You are too generous with your praise, my lord," she said. But for all her modesty, it was apparent she was quite pleased to be singled out for such approbation.

"How very kind of you," I said with deliberate sweetness, "to put yourself to so much trouble for strangers."

If she felt the barb, she did not show it. She merely shook her head emphatically.

"Not at all, my lady. His lordship has been so kind to me, and so very good to Lord Wargrave." She hesitated, darting a bashful gaze at her fiancé. "It was the very least I could do. The very least."

I gave her a bland smile and was greatly relieved when the footmen stepped forward to remove the fish plates. We moved on to the next course, and the conversation turned as well. I never knew who introduced the subject, but after a moment I realised Father and Mr. Snow were engaged in a rather brisk discussion of the Gypsies.

"But surely you must see, my lord, that permitting them to camp on your land only encourages their lifestyle," Lucian Snow was saying to Father.

Father regarded him with something akin to amusement. Father loves nothing better than a spirited debate, and I have often seen him adopt a contrary opinion in the company of like-minded people, simply for the sport of disputing with them. But on this issue, I knew his mind. He was not sporting with Mr. Snow; he was completely in opposition, and it was a position he would defend to the death, regardless of the rules of hospitality.

"Mr. Snow, are we not enjoined by the Holy Scriptures themselves to aid our brethren? Surely providing a bit of ground for their camp and a stick of wood for a fire to warm them is an act of charity."

"A misplaced charity," Snow replied earnestly, "for which the rest of the village will have to pay. Will you be responsible, my lord, when the shops are victims of thievery, when the farmers are victims of pilfering, when women are victims of—"

Emma gave a soft little shriek and raised her napkin to her lips. Father held up a hand. "That is enough, Snow. The Romany have camped on my lands as long as I have been lord of this manor. Never once have they repaid my hospitality with the ingratitude you have suggested."

"Nor would they," I put in swiftly. "To steal from their host would violate the very code by which they live their lives."

Mr. Snow turned to me, his expression sorrowful. "Your womanly compassion does you great credit, my lady, but I am certain you would share my opinion if you understood the depths of degradation to which these poor souls must sink. But I cannot bring myself to speak of such grim particulars to a lady."

Across from me, Brisbane continued to consume his dinner, looking supremely bored with the entire discussion. He seemed to be managing quite nicely in spite of his injury, and I wondered nastily if Mrs. King had cut his meat for him.

"What do you propose, Mr. Snow?" I asked him plainly.

Lucian Snow laid down his fork, clearly more enthused about the topic at hand than his dinner. It was a pity really. Cook had outdone herself with port sauce for the venison.

"There are those who believe that the children may be saved, my lady, if only they are removed from the influence of their parents' savagery at a sufficiently youthful age. I am one of those. I think if the children can be taken into good Christian homes, educated, taught their letters and numbers and basic hygiene, a skill or craft by which they may earn an honest wage, their lives may be immeasurably enriched. The poverty of their vagabond lifestyle is so wrenching, so contrary to morality and civility, that a complete break is the only way to save these poor lost children."

I blinked at him and laid down my own fork. "You advocate taking children away from their natural mothers? Away from the only family they have ever known? Mr. Snow, I cannot think that is the foundation of any useful programme."

I was deeply conscious of the rest of the party listening to our exchange. My family were accustomed to sparring with guests; debate had always been a bit of a blood sport for Marches, and Brisbane had never turned a hair at our escapades. But I noticed out of the tail of my eye the wide-eyed curiosity of Mrs. King, and the slightly shocked expressions of Sir Cedric and his young cousin. Alessandro was diplomatically quiet, doubtless wondering if it was the habit of English ladies to brawl with their guests at table.

"My dear lady," Snow was saying, "how can we possibly persuade them there is a better way unless they are given no opportunity to fall back on their own vile habits? I believe your own aunt, Lady Hermia, embraces a similar philosophy at her refuge in Whitechapel."

Hoist with my own petard. It was true Aunt Hermia kept the prostitutes secluded on the premises of her reformatory until they were well on the path to decency. She feared the lure of easy money would be too strong for them when they were first applying themselves to their new way of life. But I was not about to concede the point to Snow.

"Those women are adults, sir. They choose freely to come to the reformatory. It is only in the difficult first weeks, when they are being weaned off drink and a host of other vices, that she restricts their freedoms. And they are free to leave at any time and never return."

"My lady," Mr. Snow replied, "I can only put to you this question—what sort of monsters must these people be to deny their children a warm and safe home, without security, without education, without Christian principles?"

"In that case, why don't you just have done with it and drown the lot like kittens?" Plum put in. His face had gone a dull, angry red, and a lock of his hair fell over his brow. He was mightily outraged, and rather attractive with it. Mrs. King was staring at him, her expression rapt, her lips slightly parted. I could understand the allure. Plum was a very personable man, and in defence of his views, he could be as deliciously ruthless as any buccaneer.

In spite of his waistcoat—turquoise-blue taffeta splashed with pink peonies—he looked rather rakish as he turned the brunt of his wrath on Mr. Snow.

I opened my mouth to intervene with some inane, harmless remark, but Mr. Snow had the situation well in hand. He gave a quick laugh and flashed Plum a charming smile.

"Ah, you have been in Italy, Mr. Eglamour, where I will wager you learned a philosophy or two."

"Indeed not," Plum returned, his handsome mouth twisted with sarcasm. "I think little of a man whose morality may be swayed by his company. A man ought to think for himself and know what is right, and what I know to be right, Mr. Snow," he added with deadly precision, "is that those Roma have as much right as you or I to rear their families as they see fit."

I sighed. I had forgotten how rabid Plum could be on the subject of the Gypsies. He simply adored them. Once, when he was eight or so, and Father had confined him to his room for some transgression, he had packed his most treasured possessions into a tiny bundle and slipped out, scaling the Abbey walls with the aid of some helpful ivy. He had turned up at the Gypsy camp, thoroughly soaked from swimming the moat, and insisting defiantly that he would never go back.

The Gypsies dried his clothes and fed him, and when he was full and content, they brought him home, explaining patiently that if a lord's son was found among them, they would be taken in for kidnapping. Plum was an impetuous boy, but not a vicious one. He saw at once his new friends would suffer if he insisted upon staying. Reluctantly, squelching water out of his sodden shoes with every step, Plum returned. But he never forgot the kindness they had shown him, and whenever a question of Gypsy rights was raised, he was passionate in their defence. He made Father promise always to let them camp in the river meadow, and insisted the rest of us call them by their proper name, Roma. More than once as a lad he had engaged in fisticuffs when one of the village boys had taunted the Gypsies or thrown stones at them. I only prayed he would not brawl with the curate over the dinner table.

But Mr. Snow was determined to avoid a quarrel. He raised a hand, his expression genial. "Peace, Mr. Eglamour! I would no more spar with you than with your lovely sister. And indeed, who could be at odds when we have such good food, such fine company, and such a festive occasion?"

He raised his glass to us then, and we responded in kind, although I noticed Plum still looked faintly murderous.

Father settled back in his chair, clearly enjoying himself. "I propose a visit then. Tomorrow. We shall gather our party together and go to Blessingstoke. Fly can show off his church and his vicarage garden, what's left of it at this time of year at least. And we can call on the Romanies as well. The gentlemen can look over the horses, and what lady does not like to have her fortune told?"

There was a flash of excitement, murmurs from every quarter. Only Aunt Dorcas spoke audibly. "You oughtn't mix with them, Hector," she said to Father. "Some here might be unbelievers, and the presence of sceptics will disrupt the vibrations of their psychic gifts."

"For God's sake," I heard Lysander mutter, "has she been at the whiskey again?"

"Gin," Plum murmured back. "That was always her drink."

Unfortunately, Aunt Dorcas, like most of the aunts, had a tendency to tipple. None of them admitted to it, of course. Most of them sipped whiskey genteelly by the spoonful, claiming it was medicinal. Aunt Dorcas took a more forthright approach. She carried a flask, filled every morning by her devoted maid. For many years, the flask was tucked into her knitting bag, but when Plum was a boy he had poured out her gin and substituted vinegar instead. After that, she took to carrying it in her garters.

Aunt Dorcas opened her mouth again, but Father was too quick for her. "We shall make an outing of it. Any who do not wish to go may stay here, of course, but the rest of us mean to enjoy ourselves, vibrations be damned. Now, let us speak of something else. I am thoroughly bored with this subject. Mrs. King, have you read Lord Dalkeith's paper on the use of classical allusion in the sonnets of Shakespeare? It's rubbish of course, but I wondered what you thought of it."

Aunt Dorcas lapsed into furious silence, or rather into furiously muttering at her vegetables. But as her complaints were not audible to the rest of the company, we ignored her and turned our attention to Mrs. King.

She had ducked her head at Father's question and was blushing furiously, darting little glances from under her lashes. "Oh, your lordship, I hardly think I possess either the education or the natural intelligence to speak on such matters in such company. But

I did think Lord Dalkeith's point about the Parthenon to be very well-argued, did you not, my lord?" she asked, turning to Brisbane.

Brisbane, in the middle of a very fine gâteau, paused. "Naturally I would defer to Lord March's opinion. I believe he has already questioned Lord Dalkeith's sources, is that not correct, my lord?" he asked, returning the question neatly to Father. Portia had mentioned his recent attendance at Father's society meetings, but to my knowledge Brisbane had no great love of literature. The only books I had seen in his rooms had been of an eclectic and scholarly bent. There were volumes on the natural sciences, history, warfare, and—oddly enough—lives of the mystic saints, but no plays, no poetry, no novels. Why then this sudden attachment to Shakespeare?

I looked from Brisbane, newly enthusiastic on the scriptures of the Bard, to my father, their greatest prophet. And in between them sat Mrs. King, a picture of pink-and-white innocence, wearing a betrothal ring from Brisbane on her left hand and chattering happily with both of them.

And I wondered precisely what my father had been doing while I was away.

After the conversation about Shakespeare had wound to a close and the gâteau was thoroughly savoured, Portia rose and gestured for the ladies to follow. At Bellmont Abbey, ladies withdrew, but not in quite the same fashion as in other great houses. Here, ladies were taken to the lesser drawing room to drink their own spirits and smoke a bit of tobacco without the gentlemen present. Hoots always fussed about the smell getting into the draperies, but Aunt Hermia just told him to open the windows and sweep the carpets, that the dogs were worse. Usually, the ladies greatly enjoyed a chance to "let down their back hair", and even the primmest of women was seduced into conviviality by our habits. Confidences were exchanged, little jokes made, and many ladies later claimed that the evenings they spent at Bellmont Abbey were among the most amiable of their lives.

I, however, was in no mood to be amiable. I was tired from the journey, and more than a little eager to gain the privacy of my room and turn over the many questions that had been puzzling me all evening. But I did not have the energy to make my excuses to Portia. She could have taught Torquemada a thing or two about extracting information, and I knew I would not escape her without endless questions. It seemed simpler just to follow along and endure.

As we withdrew, I noticed Violante, lagging behind, her hand pressed to her stomach. I slowed my steps to match hers.

"Violante, are you quite all right?"

She nodded. "The English food. It is not very good. Heavy. Like rocks."

I bristled, but did not mention how perfectly inedible I had found gnocchi. "I am sorry you are unwell. Won't you join us for a little while? I can have Aquinas brew up a tisane for you."

She shook her head. "I have the fennel pastilles in my room. They make me right. *Buona notte, Giulia.*"

I kissed her cheek and sent her on her way, envying her a little.

The poor girl looked every bit as exhausted as I felt. But as I entered the lesser drawing room, I noticed an undercurrent that immediately piqued my interest. Lucy and Emma were seated on a sofa, their heads close together as they darted glances about the room and murmured softly. Portia was busy fussing with decanters and glasses, and Aunt Dorcas had entrenched herself firmly in the best armchair. Hortense had taken up a book and was reading placidly. It was left to me to entertain Brisbane's fiancée. I turned to her, fixing what I hoped was a pleasant expression on my face.

"And how are you enjoying your stay at the Abbey, Mrs. King?"

"Oh, it is an extraordinary place, my lady." She spread her hands, gesturing toward the single great column standing stalwartly in the centre of the room and the tapestries, older and smaller than those in the great drawing room, but depicting the same subject, a boar hunt. "This room alone quite takes my breath away."

I shrugged. "I suppose it is impressive enough on first viewing. This room used to be the chapter house, where the monks gathered for the abbot to read the Rule of the Order. The vaulting of the ceiling is quite remarkable, although in the family we think it's frightfully inconvenient. That central column is necessary for support, but it makes it devilishly difficult to arrange the furniture properly. Besides which, the room is draughty and the chimney never draws properly."

As if to prove my point, a gust of wind roared down the chimney, scattering sparks and ash on the hearth and a few bits of soot on Aunt Dorcas. If the night grew any windier, we should have to dust her.

"Well, perhaps it is not the most convenient of rooms," she temporised, "but the history, the very ancientness of the stones. I cannot imagine what they have seen. And the tapestries," she added, nodding toward the stitched panels. "They are enough to rival anything in a museum, I should think."

Portia joined us then, passing tiny glasses of port that shimmered like jewels in the candlelight.

"If you like the tapestries, you must ask Emma to tell you the story behind them. No one can spin a tale like Emma," Portia advised Mrs. King, gesturing with her glass to our cousin. "Emma, pay attention, my dear. I am telling tales out of school about you."

Emma started like a frightened pony, then relaxed, smiling at Portia. "What have you been saying to Mrs. King?"

"That you are a splendid spinner of stories, actually," I put in. "Mrs. King was admiring the tapestries, and Portia suggested you tell her the story behind them. She is quite right. No one does it as you do." I thought to raise her confidence a little. She had always been quiet, but there was a new shyness in her that troubled me. I felt Emma was in danger of becoming a sort of recluse, particularly now that Lucy was marrying. Emma had always lavished all of her attention on Lucy, and I wondered what would become of her once Lucy became Lady Eastley. It was to be hoped Lucy would repay her many kindnesses with a home when it was in her power to provide it. Emma could not be happy governessing in the wilds of Northumberland. It would be a poor showing on Lucy's part to leave her there.

"Come, Scheherezade, tell us a tale," I coaxed.

Emma flushed a little, not prettily as Mrs. King did, but a harsh red stain that tipped her nose and ears.

"If you really think that I should," she said, looking hesitantly at Lucy.

"You must," Lucy said firmly, and we added our voices to the chorus, insisting she take a chair nearer to the fire. She seated herself, turning so the light threw her face in sharp relief as she began to speak.

THE SIXTH CHAPTER

Her voice was ever soft,
Gentle, and low, an excellent thing in a woman.
—KING LEAR

"The story begins long ago," Emma related, her voice soft. We gathered around her, skirts billowing over each other like blowsy roses in a country garden. Aunt Dorcas had nodded off in her chair, and her little snores punctuated the tale. Emma paused and took a breath, heightening our anticipation.

"This abbey was once the home of an order of monks, holy men who passed their lives in contemplation and good works. They tended the crops and the flocks, minding both the animals and the souls of men, and they were much loved. But then Henry VIII directed his lustful gaze at Anne Boleyn, and the monks were doomed. During the Dissolution, these lands were taken from them, and they were cast out of this holy place to make their way in the world, penniless and without friends. One of them, the elderly abbot, who had known only this place as his home since boyhood, cursed it as he left, calling upon the very stones themselves to witness the injustice visited upon his order. He conjured a curse against the new owner, a courtier of the king's, crying out that the man should not live out a year in his ill-gotten home."

She paused again and I glanced at Mrs. King, not surprised to see her spellbound expression. Emma had always been an excellent storyteller. During their Easter visits we frequently abandoned our books and games and insisted she spin us tales instead. She always demanded a trinket for her troubles, but her stories were so enthralling we never minded parting with a doll or pair of shoes as the price of an afternoon's entertainment. I turned back to her, noticing that her eyes were shining now, brightened by her enthusiasm for her story. She would indeed have made a fitting bride for Shahriar, I thought as she picked up her tale.

"The new owner, the Earl March, laughed at the old man, and swept into the Abbey with his young countess. But his bride, a girl of seventeen, was not so insouciant as her lord and master. She feared the old abbot, for she had seen that he was touched with holiness, and every night when she made her prayers she begged God to spare her husband, for theirs was a love match.

"The months stretched on, and the seasons turned, and the young countess began to hope her husband would survive the curse. She doubled her prayers, and spent so much time on her knees that she wore holes into the silk of her gowns. Her husband mocked her, but still she would not cease praying for his deliverance. Until one day, when he grew impatient with her piety, and they quarrelled. To calm his temper he whistled for his horse and his hounds and he rode out to hunt boar. The countess fell to her knees in the chapel, vowing not to rise until her lord returned."

Emma paused and leaned very slightly closer. "They brought him home the next day, carrying him on a door, broken and bleeding from the tusks of his quarry. He died that night, in agony. His countess, fearing her husband's spirit could never rest in this place, raised a crypt in the village churchyard and buried him there. And after his funeral, she withdrew to the chapel and began to stitch. For nine years she worked, her fingers bleeding, her hands stiffening until she grew so withered she could no longer put down her needle. She told the story of that fateful hunt in silk and wool, stitching her grief until at last the story was complete."

Emma raised her eyes to the tapestries, nodding toward the last, a magnificent piece that depicted the broken earl being carried home, his hunter and dogs trailing sadly behind.

"In all those nine years, not a morsel of food passed her lips. Village folk said it was a miracle, that she lived on her grief and her tears, nourishing herself with pain until her task was complete. And as soon as the last stitch was set, she lay down on the floor of the chapel and died. She was buried next to her lord in the crypt, but the tapestries survive to tell us the story. And somewhere in the Abbey, there is still a door, stained with the blood of a proud young nobleman, and no matter how many times the wood is sanded or scrubbed, the blood remains."

Emma sighed, and in an instant, Scheherezade was gone, and she was my plain little cousin again, her hair too severe, her complexion too sallow for prettiness.

"That was beautiful," Mrs. King breathed. "What a tragic story, and how wonderfully you tell it."

Emma smiled. "Words are a cheap entertainment," she said softly, catching Lucy's gaze. The two of them exchanged a knowing look, and I wondered how many times Emma's stories had kept them from despairing. I could well picture them, approaching yet another aunt's door, hand-in-hand, ready to be taken in with little grace and no warmth. Perhaps Emma's imagination had warmed them when they were cold, and comforted them when they were sent to bed in strange new rooms, where unfamiliar noises could seem like spectres, and shadows could be goblins.

"Emma, you have always had a great talent, you ought to write a book. Heaven knows I've seen people with far less ability make a success of it," Portia suggested.

Emma shook her head. "Oh, I couldn't. The notoriety, the attention, I could not bear to be looked at like that, as if I were a circus animal. No, I should far rather keep a little cottage and a flock of chickens. That would suit me quite well."

"Besides, I mean to keep her quite busy with nieces and nephews very soon," Lucy put in, bouncing up to embrace her sister. "Cedric has said that I may have Emma with me, to act as my companion, and later as governess to our children. We need never be parted again." Emma put an arm around her sister and hid her face in Lucy's neck.

I avoided Portia's eyes, but I could guess her thoughts well enough. Sir Cedric, a wealthy and important man, had offered his impecunious sister-in-law a post, not a home. It spoke of a meanness in his spirit I could not like. It would have cost him little to keep Emma simply out of kindness. But she would work for her bread.

"To your very fecund future in that case," Portia proclaimed, raising her glass to Lucy and tactfully ignoring the subject of Emma's employment. We toasted the bride and spent a pleasant half hour discussing plans for the wedding. Lucy was a happy bride, thrilled with her betrothed, and content to hear our ideas for her nuptials. Our suggestions grew more and more outlandish as the port decanter emptied.

Finally, I rose and stretched and made my excuses. Portia put out her tongue at me.

"You know you are not supposed to retire until the gentlemen have joined us. It is rude to our guests," she said, putting on her severe elder-sister voice.

I covered my mouth, smothering a yawn. "Would you have me dozing on the sofa in front of them? I think that would be far more uncivil. Besides, poor Mrs. King is drooping in that chair. I think she would like to retire as well, only she is too polite to say it. Is it our fault the gentlemen have clearly lost sight of the time? Mind you poke Aunt Dorcas awake before you retire," I said with a nod toward the old woman.

Mrs. King protested genteelly, but I bullied her, and I fancied she looked a bit relieved as we quit the drawing room. Aquinas had anticipated me and was lighting chambersticks in the hall.

"My lady," he said, offering me one. "Mrs. King."

"Thank you, Aquinas. Good evening."

He bowed and wished us both a good evening. As we moved toward the great staircase, I caught Mrs. King hiding a yawn behind her hand.

"I do apologise," she said. "I am simply not accustomed to keeping late hours. It is silly, I know. I live in London and keep city hours. One would have thought coming to the country would mean early to bed and early to rise."

I gave a little snort of laughter as we started up the staircase. There were great carved panels of wood at the foot to keep the dogs out, or would have done if anyone had ever bothered to close them. A few of the puppies followed us up the stairs, lumbering along sleepily.

"You would do well to take one of the little brutes into bed with you. They haven't fleas, and the pups will be far cosier than any warming pan," I advised her.

She nodded, and for an instant her expression clouded.

"Mrs. King? Is everything quite all right?"

She hesitated, her pretty face drawn a little with an emotion I could not identify. Fear, perhaps? "Lady Julia, I do hope you will not think me terribly foolish, but—are there ghosts at the Abbey? I did not like to ask one of the gentlemen, they are so prone to think us ladies silly when we say such things." She gave me an apologetic little smile, but her lips trembled. "I just thought perhaps if I *knew*…"

I stroked a wriggling pup. "Well, I suppose there are a few old ghouls running about, and the odd monk here and there, but nothing you need trouble yourself with, my dear. Particularly the monks. Cistercians took vows of silence, you know. Our monks would likely just wave at you. Besides, these stones have been standing for more than seven hundred years. Naturally they would have acquired a spectre or two."

Her face fell, and for a moment I thought I saw moisture shimmering in her eyes. I would not have thought her so sensitive. I felt a stab of unwilling pity. "You must not worry about such things. I have lived here most of my life, and I have never seen a ghost. I do not think anyone has, not for ages." I was struck by a sudden thought. "But you have been here for some days. Why does this weigh on you now? Have you seen something?"

She bit her lip and darted a glance around, peering into the shadows at the end of the hall. "Last night," she whispered. "It was very late, but I was wakeful. I thought I heard a footstep, and yet not a footstep. It seemed to slither past my door. I could not move for a moment, I was quite paralysed with fear. And then, I do not know how I managed it, but I found the courage to open the door."

She paused, her eyes round. I realised my own heart was beating very fast. Even the puppy had gone quite still under my hand, as if hanging on her every word. "And then I saw it. Or rather the faintest impression of it. A swirl of grey and white, not quite a figure, and yet it was more than just a bit of mist. There was a shape to it. My breath caught in my throat, and it turned then, turned and looked at me, although it *had no face*."

"Good God!" I cried. "What did you do then?"

She shrugged. "What could I do? I slammed my door and locked it tightly. I burrowed under the bedclothes until morning. I did not dare to come out until the sun was up. I shall never forget the way it looked right through me."

I hastened to reassure her. "Mrs. King, I am so very sorry you were frightened. I can only tell you I have never heard of anyone in this house encountering a phantom in the whole of my life. And I have every expectation it will not happen again."

She smiled, and this time her mouth was firm. "You are very kind to reassure me. I know you will not mention this bit of foolishness to the gentlemen. I should so hate for them to think me foolish."

"Of course not. If anything else distresses you, you must come to me immediately. I insist. Now, I will wait here while you go to your room to make sure you are comfortably settled. If you require anything at all, just ring the bell. One of the maids will see to it, and I am but a few steps down the corridor in the Red Room. I will see you at breakfast, my dear," I said.

She bade me good night, and ducked her head shyly, as if embarrassed at her nerves. She clucked at one of the pups to follow her into her room and he did, waving his tail like a jaunty plume. My own puppy started to wriggle, and I gave him a little pat on the bottom to send him on his way. I stared at Mrs. King's closed door for a long moment, then passed to my room, humming a tuneless song as I went.

Once in my room, I disrobed quickly and attempted with no success to persuade Morag to take Florence again.

"I will not," she said, tucking my gown into the wardrobe. "She shakes like a poplar."

"That means she is cold," I told her in some exasperation. "She wants a little coat."

"She wants an exorcism," Morag muttered, slamming the wardrobe door. "If you don't want nothing else, good night."

I knew that tone well. It meant that I *daren't* want anything else. I climbed up into the bed, stretching my toes toward the warming pan, careful not to touch it.

"Remind me to have a word with Aunt Hermia about your grammar. It is a disgrace."

She said nothing, but poked up the fire and bobbed an exaggerated curtsey before taking her leave. I regretted my flippancy. Morag might be a creature of the streets, but she had her dignity, and she had worked terribly hard to raise herself from the squalor of her previous life. Her grammar had progressed substantially, and the worst of her brogue had been smoothed into something I could actually understand. It was wrong of me to needle her about it, and I made a mental note to apologise to her in the morning. I was far too cosy to leave my bed to deal with her at present. She had done a masterful job of warming the bed, and from the way Florence was snuggled into her basket, I suspected Morag had lined it with warmed towels. For all her sins, she was a thoughtful creature at times.

"Buone notte, Firenze," I said, with a nod toward the basket on the hearth. "Good night, Florence."

Florence growled in return, and I took up a book from the night table, determined to finish it. It was a rather spicy little novel Portia had given me, and I was in agonies of suspense as to whether the beautiful English captive would choose to stay in the *harim* of the sensual sultan or make her escape with the dashing Spanish buccaneer.

I must have dozed, for when I opened my eyes, the fire had

burned down and the book had slipped to the floor. I blinked for a moment, uncertain why I had awakened. Then I heard it, a soft slithering footstep just outside my door. I glanced to the hearth and saw Florence, sitting up in her basket, ears pricked up, lips drawn back.

"Shh," I soothed her softly. The hands of the clock on the mantel read two minutes past two. I considered the matter carefully. Violante and Charlotte had both been abed by the time I had retired. Portia would have rousted the ladies out of the drawing room and to their beds no later than midnight. I had heard a flurry of doors closing just about that time. So the ladies were accounted for, and even if the gentlemen had decided to play a game of billiards or retire to the smoking room, those rooms were on the opposite side of the Abbey. I thought of Mrs. King, her lips trembling as she spoke of what she had seen.

For what I did next, I can only blame my own unseemly reading habits. For years I wallowed in the unhealthy pursuits of Gothic heroines, tracing their footsteps as they wended their way through crumbling churchyards and decaying crypts. I walked with them into ghoulish dungeons hung with chains, and mouldering attics festooned with cobwebs. I thought them impossibly stupid, and yet when faced with the opportunity to chase a phantom of my own, I did not even stop to put on my slippers. I snatched a lace wrapper from the foot of my bed and hurried to the door, easing it open as silently as any practised burglar.

I slipped out of my room and into the shadows of the gallery. Bars of soft moonlight from the great Gothic windows illuminated the corridor, throwing the statues into sharp relief and casting sinuous, quatrefoil shadows over the floor. I peered one way, then the other, searching the gloom for anything out of the ordinary.

Nothing. I waited half a minute, willing myself to breathe quietly. Still nothing, and my feet were beginning to freeze on the stone floor. I had just turned to regain my room when I saw it, there at the end of the gallery, flitting past a statue of Diana.

It was a ghost, or at least something that looked very like how I imagined a ghost should look. It moved slowly, gliding soundlessly, perhaps a foot above the stone floor, and whiter than the marble of the goddess' motionless arm. The figure trailed ragged draperies behind it, foamy and billowing like fingers of damp fog on a moonlit night.

It paused then and so did my heartbeat. It was silhouetted against a tapestry of Venus and Adonis, silvered by the faint moonlight. I stared at it from my place in the shadows, suddenly horribly aware that in my white lace wrapper, I was as visible to it as it was to me. Before I could move, it gave a high, unearthly moan, then whirled and vanished, leaving behind nothing but a patch of shadow and the tapestry, stirring ever so slightly.

Before the tapestry had settled, I was back in my own room, door firmly locked, cowering under the bedclothes with a struggling Florence clutched to my chest. She kicked and fussed until I let her go, then marched to my pillow where she gave me a resentful look and promptly curled up with her tail over her nose and went to sleep. It was not much, but it was some comfort, and I put a hand on her silky back. She twitched, but did not move away, and after a long while I slept.

It was not until Morag unlocked the door with my morning tea, rousing me with malicious pleasure, that I realised what I should have known all along: that particular tapestry covered one of the hidden passages of Bellmont Abbey. The Abbey itself had been lousy with them as it provided the brothers an easy means of moving from place to place without disturbing one another or exposing themselves to inclement weather. Most had been blocked up or fallen into disrepair, but some remained, and a few were even used by the servants as service passages. And though I could not explain how a human being could levitate as perfectly as my phantom had done, it would be a very poor ghost indeed to require hidden passages to creep about the Abbey instead of walking through walls.

And if the ghost was not supernatural, then one of the inhabitants of the Abbey was up to something highly irregular and thoroughly interesting. An intrigue was afoot, and I was determined to unearth it.

I hurried through my ablutions, eager to begin investigating my little mystery. I was thwarted by Morag, who insisted on taking her time with my hair, and Father, who sent a note requesting my presence in his study after breakfast.

"Bother," I muttered, slipping the note into my pocket. The missive was perfectly courteous, but a summons from Father carried all the weight of a papal bull. "Finish, Morag. I've no more time to waste on your ministrations."

She jabbed the last pins in my hair with what can only be described as unnecessary force. I rose and hurried to the door, turning to smile sweetly at her. "Mind you walk the dog. And I was quite serious about a coat for her. I've a pretty little jacket Plum purchased for me in Milan. Persimmon is a frightful colour for me, but it should suit Florence nicely."

Morag crossed her arms over her chest and fixed me with a baleful stare. "I'll not be sewing for a dog."

I looked at her closely. Morag could often be cajoled into acquiescence, but once she had reached her limit, there was only one method by which it was possible to persuade her.

"I will pay you four shillings and will thank you for picking my pocket."

Morag was nothing if not avaricious. She gave me a thin-lipped smile and scooped up the dog, tucking Florence under her arm. "Come on then, ye wee rat. Let us take the measure of you and fit you for your wardrobe."

When I left the room, I took the opportunity to examine the spot at the end of the gallery where the ghost had disappeared. The egress was easy enough to find provided one knew where to look. The statue of Diana, poised on one foot, bow uplifted, obscured the view of the tapestry's edge. Not much, but enough to confuse the eye, particularly on a moonlit night with ghostly draperies fluttering about.

With apologies to Venus and Adonis, I slipped behind the

tapestry and found a solid stone wall, or at least the *appearance* of a solid stone wall. This was no simple case of a doorway that had been covered over for the sake of convenience. This was a proper secret passage, with a mechanism that had been oiled recently from the smell of it. I reached up to the single stone carved with the tiniest of March hares and pushed. The door swung back soundlessly. The passage beyond was black as pitch and freezing. I paused, listening intently, but of course I heard nothing. I stepped back and swung the door shut, moving out of the way as it slid into place.

I stood behind the tapestry, considering the matter carefully. The passage, although quite antique, had been well maintained, and the little hare had been carved by the family to clearly identify the key stone. Presumably the monks were cleverer than the Marches, and had found their way without such *aides-memoire*. The passage went some little way, then terminated in a flight of tight, twisting stairs up to a suite of lumber rooms. Originally a row of cells used as scriptoria by the monks, they were terribly useful for storage. The little passage itself had been occasionally used to move carpets or tapestries, but its dimensions had not permitted its use for anything more substantial. It was useful for the maids, for their rooms were in the attics, divided from the lumber rooms only by a short corridor. We children had used the passage when playing sardines or other such games, and I remembered sulking there once or twice when I did not wish to be found. I had not used it in a dozen years, and I did not think Morag even knew of its existence.

Who, then, did? My brothers, naturally, and Father and Portia.

But try as I might, I could not imagine any business that would necessitate any of my family wandering the Abbey in the guise of a ghoul. There was Aunt Dorcas, of course, but I snickered when I thought of her attempting to negotiate the snug little staircase with her bulk.

That still left the guests, any one of whom might have heard of the passage from a member of the household and decided to do a bit of exploring. Harmless enough, but why in the form of a spectre?

Interesting questions indeed, and I pondered them as I descended to breakfast. My little detour had taken longer than I thought, and by the time I reached the breakfast room, it was empty and most of the chafing dishes had been scraped clean. Aquinas entered with a steaming pot of tea and a rack of fresh, crisp toast as I peered at the sideboard, frowning.

"Do not tell me I have missed Cook's kedgeree," I said mournfully.

"I took the liberty of putting a bit back for your ladyship. I have been keeping it warm in the butler's pantry. I will fetch it now."

I seated myself and sighed. There are few greater pleasures in life than a devoted butler. I counted myself very fortunate to have secured Aquinas. I had offered him an outrageous sum to leave his previous employer, an act that had stricken me from that particular hostess' guest lists for eternity. It was a small price to pay for such competence, I reminded myself as he served a generous portion of the delectable kedgeree.

While I ate, Aquinas busied himself at the sideboard. I had

just popped the last bit of buttery toast into my mouth when I had a thought.

"Aquinas, did Uncle Fly and Mr. Snow spend the night, or did they return to Blessingstoke last night?"

He lifted my plate and whisked the toast crumbs into his little silver pan. "I called the carriage for them at midnight, my lady. His lordship offered them rooms for the night, but the Reverend Mr. Twickham was feeling a trifle unwell and wished to sleep in his own bed."

I looked up sharply. "Uncle Fly was ill? Nothing serious, I hope."

"Not at all, my lady. If I may speculate, I believe Mr. Twickham indulged himself a bit more than is his custom."

I burst out laughing. "He was drunk."

Aquinas looked mildly shocked. "I should be heartily sorry if I suggested such a thing, my lady. However, if I were to observe that he seemed to have a bit of difficulty putting on his coat, and that entering the carriage proved so treacherous he nearly ended up in the moat, these would not be exaggerations."

"Poor Uncle Fly. His head will be sore as a bear's this morning. And we lot are supposed to descend upon him for luncheon! How ghastly."

Aquinas agreed and removed my empty plate. I sat over the last few sips of my tea, making note of the fact that Uncle Fly and Lucian Snow could be eliminated from the list of possible miscreants who had donned the ghostly garb.

But instead of simplifying matters, it muddied them. Snow had a sort of puckish charm, and Uncle Fly had always been good for a joke, particularly of the elaborate and practical variety. If I numbered gambling among my vices, I would have wagered handsomely on one of them being our prankster.

Still, it left me with several interesting questions yet to be answered, including the one that intrigued me the most: what had Brisbane been doing when the clock struck two?

THE SEVENTH CHAPTER

O, that a man might know
The end of this day's business ere it comes.
—JULIUS CAESAR

The door to Father's study was closed, but I had no doubt he was within. I could smell his pipe tobacco, and if I pressed my ear quite tightly to the door, I could hear him talking. From the rhythm of his speech, it was apparent he was reciting one of his beloved soliloquies. Lear, no doubt. He was particularly fond of Lear.

I rapped sharply, and after a moment he called for me to enter. I felt a sense of peace descend as soon as I stepped over the threshold. Father's study held only the most pleasant connotations for me. Any childhood transgressions were dealt with as a matter of business, and lectures and punishments were meted out in his estate office where farmers and servants were given their pay or their notice. Here, there was only the memory of spending time alone with Father, a rare privilege in a household of ten children. It was in this room rather than in the schoolroom that each of us had learned our letters, following Father's finger as he traced out a line of Shakespeare and encouraged us to sound out the words. There was always a treat if we excelled—crumpets Father toasted over the fire, turning them on forks until they were brown and crisp.

There was a fire now, crackling away merrily on the hearth, the mastiff Crab stretched out lazily in front of it, her immense paws thrust into the ash for warmth. The walls were lined with books, none particularly valuable. The rare and costly volumes were shelved in the formal library where they were regularly dusted and rubbed with neats' foot oil. The study was the home of Father's private collection, the bulk of it devoted to Shakespeare, with some poetry and a bit of history as well. The tall Gothic windows were hung with claret velvet, and a pair of enormous thick silk rugs from Turkey warmed the stone floor. The furniture was lushly upholstered in more claret velvet. There were curiosities as well—an enormous armillary sphere, the stone wing of an Italian *putti,* a revolting stuffed monkey called Cyril that Father had won in a wager against the King of the Belgians—but it was a comfortable room, a gentleman's retreat. I remembered the hours I had spent in the window seat, secluded by those same velvet draperies as I read the books of my youth.

Father laid his book upon the desk. Bound in green leather and stamped with the March coat of arms, it was part of the set of Shakespeare that had been printed for him as a gift by the queen upon his accession to the earldom. I hazarded a glance at the cover as I took a chair opposite his. *King Lear.* I smiled to myself, but Father missed nothing.

"You seem in good spirits," he observed.

"I was merely thinking how nice it is that some things do not change."

He raised a silvery-white brow. "Like me? I shall never change. I am half as old as Methuselah and I mean to live forever. I shall point and laugh when Stonehenge crumbles to dust and I am still here."

"Just as well. I am told there is no more space left in the family crypt."

He pulled a face. "That may be, but when the time comes I shall make room for the old crone if I have to turn half the family out and sell their bones to make corsets."

"I presume you are referring to Aunt Dorcas?"

Father stretched his legs, wincing only slightly. I could only assume his rheumatism was paining him. His little twinges usually presaged a change in the weather.

"I had forgotten how awful she could be," he mused. "Hard to imagine now she was once the toast of the Regency and her sisters with her. All four of them were painted the year the elder two came out. The paintings are in the little alcove outside the music room. Striking girls, they were. All the bucks were in love with them."

"Even Aunt Dorcas?"

"Indeed so. An heir to a dukedom shot himself for love of her when she rejected his suit. They said she heard the news, then put on her prettiest gown and went to a ball where she danced every last dance, drank two bottles of champagne, and swam the pond on Hampstead Heath just to watch the sun come up."

I shook my head. It seemed impossible to reconcile that desiccated old toad with a ripe, nubile young woman who broke men's hearts as easily as one might crack an egg.

"I suppose time changes people," I hazarded.

"Time and regret," he corrected. "Dorcas and her sisters were outraged by Rosalind's elopement with a footman. They withdrew from society and refused to marry. They thought they were disgraced, as if marrying one's footman is any worse than the rest of the antics they got up to," he finished, reaching for the cup of tea on his desk. "They immured themselves in that old house in the Norfolk fens, and scarcely spoke two words to the rest of us for decades."

"How dreadful! To shut themselves up like that, with only each other for company. Why did we never visit them?"

Father shrugged. "They made it quite clear no one was welcome. They were content to fester in the country, quarrelling with one another and complaining bitterly about the pittance of an allowance they received."

This surprised me. "They were not given proper allowances?"

Father named a figure that made me gasp. "Generous enough, by anyone's standards," he commented dryly, and I was forced to agree. "Added to which, Grandfather settled the Norfolk house on them and paid for the maintenance. Their expenses were virtually nonexistent. I'll wager there is a small fortune stuffed under a mattress or behind a fireplace brick in that house."

"But I thought that side of the family was poor," I protested. "Emma and Lucy, always coming to us looking little better than charity children, complaining about cold-water baths and wearing the aunts' castoffs."

Father sipped at his tea. "Living in isolation can turn a person's mind, and their minds did not have far to turn," he said with a meaningful look over the rim of his spectacles.

"You mean they became *peculiar?*"

"In a word. They began to hoard things from the reports my father received. Money, newspapers, jars of jam. And never spent a ha'-penny if they could help it. Dorcas even had her sisters buried in paupers' graves in the churchyard in Norfolk to save a few pounds. She was certainly not going to spend her life's savings educating two girls she viewed as the fruits of sin."

"Their parents were married," I pointed out.

"Hmm. Yes, well, there was some confusion on that point."

I blinked at him. "Good heavens. Why did I never know any of this?"

Father shrugged. "Old family gossip. You were always burrowed somewhere with your nose in a book."

"And here I thought the family was in danger of becoming re-spectable." I still could not quite take it in. Lucy and Emma, bastards, and Dorcas and her sisters mad as hatters, after a fashion.

"But Aunt Dorcas' pearls and the lace," I began. Father shook his head.

"The pearls are glass beads, and the lace was her mother's. Her maid has been tearing it off and sewing it onto different gowns for fifty years. And what she has not hoarded, she has pilfered. Mind you lock up your valuables, I cannot vouch for their safety," he said with a sigh. "I could almost feel sorry for the old trout, but she is one of the most tiresome women I have ever known."

"Then why did you invite her for the wedding?"

Father's usual benign expression turned murderous. "I did not. That would be the handiwork of your Aunt Hermia, who I hope is suffering mightily from the pangs of her conscience as well as a toothache. She insisted if Lucy was to be married from here, Dorcas had to be present, and then she hared off to London while I have endured the old terror," he said with real bitterness.

"Aunt Hermia cannot help a toothache," I chided. "Besides, with so many other guests, you cannot be much bothered with her."

"Emma was not best pleased to see her," Father confided. "Although I imagine she has had an easier time of it than her sister. I would rather have the keeping of ten children than one old woman."

"You did have the keeping of ten children," I reminded him. "Now, tell me how it came to be that Lucy is to be married here."

Father shrugged. "Cedric is an acquaintance from the Shakespearean Society. Lucy was visiting London with friends. She called upon me, quite properly. I was just about to leave for a meeting, and the girl trotted along. Cedric was there, and I introduced them. He was instantly smitten, and since then they have been inclined to view me as something of a faery godfather. I have been told they mean to name their firstborn after me. It is all incredibly fatiguing."

"And Mrs. King? She is a member of the society also?" I asked carefully.

Father levelled his clear green gaze at me. "She is. As is Brisbane. They both began attending in September. I introduced them as well."

"You are a regular Cupid," I commented lightly. "You will want only a bow and arrow to complete the illusion." I chose my next words carefully. "I am surprised their courtship has progressed so quickly. Mrs. King does not strike me as the type of woman to become engaged to a man she has known but for two months, although perhaps I have misjudged her."

Father said nothing, but he sipped at his tea and his eyes slid away from mine. He knew something, and he was determined not to speak of it. And when Father made up his mind, it was pointless to attack him directly.

"What do you think of Violante?" I asked, and I do not think I imagined he looked relieved.

"I like her fine. She seems a rational sort of girl, from what I could determine with my faulty Italian. Pleasant enough, although with a beastly temper, I should think."

"Then you are not still angry with Lysander for marrying her?"

He set the cup into the saucer with a sharp rap. "Why the devil should I be angry? Ly has to live with her—"

Too late, he remembered the letter, the summons home with dire threats if we failed to obey. It had been a blind then, a lure to bring us back, for some other purpose entirely. But Father could hold his counsel well enough when he chose. If I wanted to know what he was about, I should have to lull him into security first.

I cut in smoothly. "I am so glad to hear it. She is indeed a delightful girl, and it is not kind to say it, but I think Lysander needs to be shaken up a bit. He is too tightly bound within himself. She is a tonic for him."

Father laid down his cup and smoothed his waistcoat, a fraying affair in aubergine stripes. His sartorial taste was frighteningly close to Plum's. "I am glad to hear it. Now, the reason I sent for you. Say hello to your friend. He has missed you, you know, and I don't mean to keep him forever."

He nodded toward the corner behind me. I turned to see a large, ornately wrought birdcage standing where a bust of Kean usually held court. Inside the cage was a bundle of sleek black feathers and a pair of intelligent jetty eyes.

"Grim!" I cried. I went to the cage and leaned near, careful to keep my arms behind my back. It would not do to have the tweed of my sleeves shredded by his sharp talons. He looked up at me, his head tipped quizzically to the side. After a long moment, he opened his beak.

"Good morning," he said cordially.

"Good morning," I returned. It was Grim's favourite greeting, no matter the time of day. I opened the cage door, and he bobbed his feathered head and hopped out. His wings were tucked behind his back, and he walked across the carpet with the dignified air of an elder statesman. Grim might have been a souvenir of the previous investigation, but he was also a great deal more. He had begun his life as a Tower raven, property of the Crown and petted darling of the Tower's inhabitants. I wondered sometimes if he missed the social comedown he had suffered when the Queen had made me a present of him.

I returned to my chair and Grim followed. Father passed me

a small box of sugared plums and Grim's eyes brightened. "That's for me."

"Yes, it is, Grim." I tossed a plum onto the carpet and averted my eyes. Grim was a lovely companion, but watching him eat even confectionery required a rather stronger stomach than I possessed.

Father rose and shot his cuffs. "I must take my leave of you, my dear. I have estate business to attend to before we depart for the village. Be ready in an hour."

There was a note of satisfaction in his voice. He sounded like a man about to effect an escape, and that only heightened my curiosity.

But this was no time to confront him. I merely smiled affectionately. "No matter. It will give me time to read the newspapers. I haven't had the English papers for weeks. I am frightfully out of touch."

Father paused. "I am afraid Aquinas is too efficient by half. He has burned them all. Read the latest *Punch* instead. It's just there on my desk," he prodded.

I picked it up and opened the cover. I waited until he had closed the door behind him, then counted to one hundred. When I finished, I tossed another plum to Grim and went to the lidded basket by the hearth where Father always stuffed newspapers he had not yet finished.

With apologies to Crab for disturbing her, I knelt and opened it. I was not surprised to find it was half full. Another mystery, and it was not yet nine o'clock, I mused. Quickly, I perused the pages, not quite certain what I was looking for. It was not until the second time through that I saw it: each bit of newspaper he had saved carried some piece on the same subject, a recent riot in Trafalgar Square, all written in the last fortnight.

When I was finished, I replaced the papers just as I had found them. Then I wiped my hands on my handkerchief and coaxed Grim back into his cage with the last of the sugared plums. This house party was proving intriguing indeed.

THE EIGHTH CHAPTER

If all the year were playing holidays,
To sport would be as tedious as to work.
—HENRY IV, PART I

he party that assembled in the hall an hour later was merry, but somewhat diminished. Violante was still unwell, and Hortense, who was fluent in Italian and not fond of the cold, offered to sit with her. Aunt Dorcas refused again to go, insisting the vibrations were bad and the weather would turn, her beady eye fixed firmly on Aquinas. I had no doubt she would insist on a hot tray for both elevenses and luncheon, and a fire in the library. From what Father had told me, it was apparent her food allowance did not extend to the luxuries one might find in the larders at Bellmont Abbey. No doubt when she left the house her trunks would be stuffed with vintage champagne and tins of caviar and lobster, but it would be rude to search them.

The rest of us made a picturesque group. The gentlemen were in country tweeds, even Plum, although he sported a velvet waistcoat in a particularly virulent shade of cerise. He carried his sketchbook, and his pockets bulged, doubtless with pencils and gums and grubby bits of charcoal. Brisbane too wore country attire, though his arm was confined in a black woollen sling now, and over his dark tweeds he had thrown an enormous black greatcoat. A man of lesser inches would never have carried it off, but he did so quite impressively. As usual, he was hatless, and as usual, his thick black hair was just unruly enough that I had to thrust my hands into my pockets like a schoolboy to keep from organising it.

In contrast, Father was dressed like a pedlar of dubious origin. His tweeds were thirty years out of fashion, and his shirt, though made for him by the finest tailor in London, had been stained with ink and tobacco until the cuffs were quite disreputable. He wore a cape one of the grandchildren must have unearthed from the dressing-up box, all bright red wool and braided gilt trim, like something out of Gilbert and Sullivan. To complete the ensemble, he had clapped a crumpled deerstalker on his head and wrapped a length of sky-blue velvet about his neck.

In comparison, the ladies were a vision of decorum. Lucy and Emma were nearly identical in grey flannel, serviceable as anything a governess might wear. Lucy had attempted to brighten hers with a jaunty green bow, to mildly depressing effect. Mrs. King, in simple black merino, and Portia, in green tweed with a dashing feather in her hat, were more decorative. My own costume, a delicious purple tweed edged in violet velvet, was not entirely unflattering, I decided, smoothing my cuffs.

"Do stop that," Portia muttered in my ear. "Yes, the fabric is divine and the cut is perfection. You needn't *preen*."

I put out my tongue at her only to find Brisbane's gaze on me, his expression thoughtful. It was not the first time he had witnessed such behaviour on my part, and I turned away, my face hot, as Father began ordering us about.

"All right, I make it twelve of us then. Can't all possibly fit in two carriages, so I have ordered horses for the gentlemen. Not you of course, Brisbane," he said with a chuckle. "I suppose you had best ride with the ladies." Brisbane did not smile.

In the end, Alessandro and Plum elected to ride with us as well, and after a short delay a second carriage was brought round. There was a jolly scramble for seats, and I was surprised to find myself sharing a carriage with Brisbane, Alessandro, and Mrs. King. I could not have engineered a more awkward arrangement, but when Portia winked at me as she hoisted herself into her own conveyance, I had little doubt she had had a hand in it.

"Oh, this is cosy!" Mrs. King declared as the footman slammed the door. The horses sprang and she gave a little shriek. Opposite me, Brisbane flinched, and I could not help but prod him a little.

"I do hope the motion of the carriage does not jostle your arm, my lord," I said. "I know how painful those falls can be. I remember a dozen devilish tosses when I was learning to ride. I was quite purple with bruises for the whole of that summer."

"I am perfectly well," he said blandly.

"I am glad to hear it," I replied, mimicking his tone. He shot me a black look, but I ignored it and turned to Mrs. King.

"Now, Mrs. King, you must tell me what you think of my home. But I warn you, I am quite partial and will not be swayed from thinking it the most perfect of spots."

"Oh, I quite agree!" she exclaimed. She proceeded to comment on everything we passed—the symmetry of the maze, the magnificence of the bell tower, the cleverness of the carp ponds.

And then she saw the gates. She went into raptures about the iron hares that topped them, the darling little gatehouse, the pretty shrubbery by the road. Another twenty minutes was spent on the straightness of the linden *allée,* and by the time we reached the village of Blessingstoke, my ears had gone numb with the effort of listening to her. Brisbane had spent the entire journey staring out the window, while Alessandro was fixed upon Mrs. King, regarding her with an expression of bemusement. He handed me out of the carriage on our arrival, and I asked him, *sotto voce,* if he was all right.

"So many words," he murmured. "I did not think one person could know so many words."

I patted his arm and made soothing noises at him until Brisbane poked him less than gently. "Terribly sorry, but would you mind?"

Alessandro stepped aside with a flurry of apologies as Brisbane climbed down from the carriage and extended his good hand to Mrs. King.

"Never mind," I told Alessandro, tucking my arm through his. "Let me show you Blessingstoke."

It had been arranged we would take luncheon with Uncle Fly once we had toured the village, and then pay our visit to the Roma camp. This pleased me, if for no other reason than it provided us with an opportunity to escape Mrs. King. Alessandro and I proceeded directly toward the village church of St. Barnabas, an elaborate confection of neo-Gothicism at its worst. It put me in mind of a great cake, frosted with sugar angels and roses and every possible embellishment the masons could imagine. Alessandro declared it was nothing to touch the elegance of the Abbey, and I smiled at him in approbation. I guided him through the tiny churchyard where a gloomy crypt stood watch over Marches who slumbered away the centuries beneath stones green with mould. I showed him the wishing well, just beyond the lych-gate, where legend told that wishes would be granted if two people sipped from the well at the same time. He made to unpin his sleeves to take up the bucket, but I stopped him, pointing out Mrs. King, headed in our direction, chattering as she clung to Brisbane's good arm. We scurried away in the direction of the baker's where we met Sir Cedric and Lucy, and Alessandro was introduced to the delights of a Bath bun and a glass of cider. We glimpsed Mrs. King once more, Brisbane in tow, but managed to avoid her by ducking into the linen draper's. I purchased a quantity of pretty silver ribbon, enough to trim a gown and Florence's coat as well, although I was quite certain Morag would charge me treble her fee when she saw it.

I had just concluded my transaction when the bell of St. Barnabas struck one, the appointed hour for luncheon. As we made our way to the vicarage, I noticed Alessandro seemed very quiet. I drummed my fingers lightly on his arm, and he smiled.

"I am not a good companion today," he said ruefully.

"You are woolgathering," I teased.

His expression clouded. "Woolgathering? I am no shepherd."

159

I laughed, but lightly so as not to hurt his pride. "Woolgathering is a silly expression. It means you are thinking of other matters, like building castles in Spain."

"Spain?"

I sighed. "Another one of our idioms."

"But why Spain? It is too hot, too rocky. If I were going to build a castle, it must be in Toscana."

"Yes, Tuscany is the best place for castles," I agreed solemnly.

He looked at me, his liquid dark eyes intent with emotion. "You think so? You would like to live in a castle in Toscana?"

Something had shifted between us, faintly, but the change was almost palpable. Our friendship had sat lightly between us, an ephemeral thing, without weight or gravity. Once, in the Boboli Gardens, under the shadow of a cypress tree on an achingly beautiful October afternoon, he had kissed me, a solemnly sweet and respectful kiss. But weeks had passed and we had not spoken of it. I had attributed it to the sunlight, shimmering gold like Danaë's shower, and had pressed it into the scrapbook of memory, to be taken out and admired now and then, but not to be dwelled upon too seriously. Perhaps I had been mistaken.

"Who would not?" I countered, a lightness to my voice I did not feel. I tugged at his arm. "Come now. We mustn't be late or they will begin without us."

We hurried along, Alessandro trailing a bit behind. He looked a trifle defeated, like a scolded puppy. As I had neither the time nor the inclination to coax him out of his melancholy, I did the next best thing, and seated him next to Portia at luncheon. She could be relied upon to flirt with him outrageously, and hopefully restore his good spirits in the process.

To my dismay, Uncle Fly looked worse than expected. His overindulgence had left him pale and not inclined to eat, although he waved us to the table and encouraged us to heap our plates. His cook was a local woman, very competent, and the food was almost as delicious as anything one could find at the Abbey.

Mr. Snow took the seat next to mine, and I was surprised to find I did not mind. His views on the Roma were simply appalling, but he was still a personable and charming man, and when the subject of the Gypsies was raised again, he merely shrugged and said pleasantly, "I am prepared to be educated."

This caused me to warm to him considerably, and altogether, luncheon was a thoroughly satisfactory affair. When it was concluded and the last plates had been scraped clean of apple cake and cream and the last cups of coffee drunk to the dregs, Uncle Fly waved us along.

"I mean to take to my bed. A bit of rest and I shall be right as rain. Snow can show you through the conservatory—mind you don't disturb my orchids," he finished with a severe look at Snow.

Snow's glossy gold brows drew together. "I am only too happy to guide our guests, but I shall worry for you, sir. Is there anything you require?"

Uncle Fly's expression was sour. "A glass of bismuth and a hot brick in flannel," he replied tartly. "Take a length of brown paper and a few buckets for Miss Lucy's flowers. She will want some for the altar as well."

Snow nodded and rose to hold my chair. We thanked Uncle Fly and flocked out of the snug vicarage and into the humid warmth of the conservatory. Lucy squealed in delight when she saw the profusion of white heather, a full month before one might expect to see it flowering on the heath. Uncle Fly had even managed to coax a few white violets to appear, and Snow wrapped those as well, careful to pack them in a bit of damp moss. A very polite argument broke out between Father and Snow as to whether the fragile blooms would survive until Saturday, but Lucy had fairly swooned at the sight of them, and Snow promised to look after them personally. In the end, two large buckets were filled with armfuls of heather, and the clumps of violets and a few other dainties were heaped carefully into a trug.

Snow and Mr. Ludlow carried them to the carriages, along with Snow's small travelling case. He was joining our house party to help with the wedding preparations and share in the festivities. And perhaps to perform the ceremony as well, if Uncle Fly was not better in four days' time, I thought ruefully. He rode with Emma, Lucy, and Portia to the Gypsy camp. It was a short journey, but long enough to send Mrs. King into raptures about the quaintness of the village, the picturesque beauty of the Gypsies, and the excellence of their site in the river meadow. The gaily painted caravans were particularly enchanting to her with their bowed tops. There were only a few of these. The majority of the Roma still lived in tents, and some of the caravan owners slept out in tents when the weather was holding fine.

We alighted and immediately were surrounded by a flurry of

activity. Children ran to us chattering excitedly, while their parents moved more sedately, the men to take the horses, the women to offer us the bitter tea brewed over their cooking fires. Although most strangers were treated with suspicion, we were greeted with affection because of Father. I noticed Snow, watching with a benevolent expression, and I wondered if he was indeed prepared to be of liberal mind. If any group of Roma was likely to change his views, it was this. Comprised of three families, all related in various degrees, they were flamboyant and emotional, but also easygoing and amiable. I had known most of them from childhood, and they greeted me now, embracing me fondly and asking after my health.

The spoke to us in English—Romany was not a gift they shared with outsiders—but I heard a thread of it carried on the wind as an elderly woman scolded her granddaughter for dropping a basket of washing. I flicked a glance at Brisbane. He gave every appearance of not hearing or understanding, but I knew he was drinking in every word and, moreover, that he knew I was watching. Romany had been his first language, taken with mother's milk, although he rarely spoke it, and few knew he was a half-blood. With his faint burr—a souvenir of his boyhood in Edinburgh—he passed as a Scot among Englishmen, although rumours still abounded that he was a Bonaparte, a bastard prince perhaps, who would look well in an emperor's robes. Others said he was a Spanish adventurer; still others claimed he was Turkish or Greek, with the blood of sultans or minor gods running in his veins.

But one only had to see him with his own kind to realise how absurd those stories were. No one could match the Roma for their proud carriage, the elegance of their walk. In Brisbane, the line of his profile, the smoothness of his gait, even the way he held his head, all betrayed him for what he was, and I was astonished the rest of our party did not see it at once.

I had not realised I was staring so long, but he turned his head then, just enough to catch my gaze. I knew he was think-ing of the other time we had visited a Gypsy camp together—the first time I had seen him with his own people, the first time I had heard him speak the language, the musical syllables spilling from his tongue like the sweetest wine, the first time he had kissed me.

First and most likely the last, I thought. A thick little lump of regret rose in my throat and I swallowed hard against it as he turned away, striking off from the camp on the path to the river. My fingers went to the pendant at my throat, warm even through the soft leather of my glove. It was useless to pine for what was not to be, I told myself severely, and I made up my mind to put the pendant aside once and for all when I returned to Bellmont Abbey.

At that moment, a woman unfolded herself from where she had been squatting, stirring her cooking pot. The smell of spices and savoury meat filled the air, clinging to her skirts and shawls and even her plaited hair as she came to us, but it was not the fragrance of her supper that startled me.

"Magda," I said, more loudly than I intended.

She gave me a sly smile. "Yes, lady. I am with my people again."

Magda had been my laundress for a time, taken in when her

own family had banished her for breaking one of their taboos. I had sheltered her and given her work, and she had betrayed me. An understandable betrayal, given the circumstances, and I had forgiven her. But I had not thought to see her so soon. The sight of her had taken me a little aback.

"I am glad. I hope you are in good health."

It was a foolish little speech, and pompous as well, but Magda merely nodded. "And also you, my lady." She glanced around at the rest of our party. "The gentlemen will wish to see the horses. My brother, Jasper, has few to sell now, but for the right price he might be persuaded."

The gentlemen, manipulated by her sly insinuation, hurried to where the small herd was staked, all except Plum, who made for a convenient outcropping to sit and sketch. Only the five ladies remained, and Magda turned to us with a knowing smile. "You wish to have your fortunes told. Cross my palm with silver, ladies, and I will reveal all to you."

She put out her hand and I stepped back sharply. "No, thank you." I turned to the others. "The rest of you do go ahead. Magda is quite good at that sort of thing. I am sure you will find it most interesting."

I turned and left them, chattering like magpies as they quarrelled genteelly over who should go first. Plum was already consumed with his sketching, and I knew he hated to be disturbed. I made instead for a little clump of trees some distance away where I spied a familiar figure. I waited until I was near to hail him.

"Not interested in horseflesh, Mr. Ludlow?"

Like Plum, Mr. Ludlow was attempting to sketch the scene, but his talents fell far short of my brother's.

"Say rather the situation puts me in mind of a child with his face pressed against the window of the candy shop without a tuppence in his pocket," he said with a rueful smile.

I motioned to his sketchbook. "I hope I am not interrupting you?"

He laughed, showing lovely, even white teeth. "I am but a dilettante, a hobbyist. It is an act of mercy to prevent me from putting pencil to paper."

He tucked the sketchbook and stub of pencil into his pocket. "And you? No liking for the prognostications of Gypsy witches?"

I shuddered. "I have had quite enough of those to last a lifetime, thank you. In any event, they always say the same things, don't they? Tall strangers, unexpected legacies, shipboard journeys. None of it ever comes true."

He dusted off a bit of fallen tree with his handkerchief and we sat. We were silent a moment, comfortably so, to my surprise. His posture was relaxed, but lightly, as if he were accustomed to holding himself in readiness. He had the bearing of an athlete, and it occurred to me he had probably taken a number of prizes at school.

"This is a peaceful spot," he said finally. "I can understand why they come back here every year."

"It is also very near St. Leonard's Wood, which is of course an attraction to them."

He turned to me with a puzzled expression. "St. Leonard's Wood?"

"Do not tell me you have not heard of it!" I cried. "You have been here some days, and no one has told you the tale? There is an enchanted wood, just the other side of that coppice. It is said that centuries ago a French hermit by the name of St. Leonard battled a dragon there, and slew it. But he was injured in the fight, and wherever his blood fell, there God raised white lilies to bloom every year. And in return for his bravery, God banished all snakes from the wood, and hushed the nightingales so that St. Leonard could meditate in peace."

Ludlow was smiling. "A charming story, but it seems a bit harsh on the nightingales."

"I thought so, too," I confided, "but you can well understand why the Roma would wish to camp where they would not be troubled by snakes."

"Indeed I can," he agreed. We fell silent again. It was a pleasant afternoon. The sun was low in the sky, casting long shadows over the scene, burnishing the Roma camp in its gentle light. It was a scene fit for a Romantic painter, and I wondered if Plum would be able to capture it. The ladies were apparently taking it in turns to enter Magda's tent and have their fortunes told. I knew the nuances of her performance, for I had seen it often enough.

First she would offer them a choice: cards, palms or leaves. Once they had chosen, she would compose herself, drawing inward as though straining to hear a voice from another world. After a long moment, when one's nerves were stretched and the hairs on one's neck were prickling, she would open her eyes and put out her hands. No matter the medium, her hands were always deft and warm. They moved through the cards quick as a conjurer's, or stroked one's palm with the same gentle firmness one would use on a cat.

The leaves were different. She kept a kettle of water hissing away by the fire outside, and when a visitor approached, she brewed the tea in a battered pot and poured it carefully into a chipped china Jubilee cup painted with the face of the queen. The tea was thick with leaves and never sweetened. It was quite a trick to strain the tea between the teeth as Russians do to keep the leaves in the cup. When the cup was empty, Magda tapped and swirled and inverted it, then turned it right again to scry the depths. Her expression never varied, nor did her tone. She spoke flatly of what she saw, relating the future as calmly as one might speak of the weather or the state of the roads. For her, nothing was yet fixed in stone. Choice and free will had as much to do with one's future as any fortune-teller's tricks. She told only of what might come to pass, not of what must be, and I had long suspected her of embellishing her fortunes slightly to suit her audience.

Now, for instance, Lucy was just leaving the tent, smiling widely and reaching out to embrace her sister. She was radiant with happiness, and I thought it very likely Magda had spied her ring and spoken cannily to her of wedding trips and babies to come. She might have mentioned a house as well, and a trunkful of pretty frocks. Lucy was a simple creature, and Magda knew well how to take the measure of a person, for good or ill.

Emma went next, reluctantly, I fancied, but Portia was in an organising mood and firmly motioned her into the tent. Lucy linked arms with Portia and Mrs. King and began to chatter, doubtless relating every detail of Magda's predictions.

I turned to Mr. Ludlow. "I wonder if you will think me very impertinent, but I should like to ask—will they be happy, do you think?"

Mr. Ludlow was a young man of sound common sense. He did not flinch or pretend to overly precious manners. The question was a serious one, and he regarded it as such.

"I believe they will, my lady. My cousin is a simple man, and from what I have been able to determine about Miss Lucy, she is a simple girl."

"And that is a simple answer," I teased.

He smiled again, a bit tiredly, I thought. "I meant only that most people get on well enough so long as their interests are compatible. He wants to live a luxurious, comfortable life and to have sons. She wants the same. I see no reason they should not be happy."

I nodded. "Where does Sir Cedric live?"

"He keeps a house in London, but I have been commissioned by him to find a country house. Kent, he suggested. Someplace with good, fresh air and plenty of grounds for exercise."

"For the children?" I hazarded.

"For the children." He paused and looked toward the cluster of gentlemen ranged about Magda's brother. They were examining a very fine hunter, chestnut brown with an elegant back. "He never thought to marry, you know. He shall not see fifty again. He will tell you quite freely he thought all that rubbish was behind him. And then he met Lucy and was, quite simply, bewitched."

I looked to where Lucy was sitting on a piece of carpet, nibbling at the fingers of her gloves, her expression sweetly vacant. "I do not see it," I said flatly.

Mr. Ludlow's mouth twitched. "He does, my lady. And who are we to judge her charms? She is pretty and pleasant, and he is growing old."

"I have been frightfully rude to ask such things, and it is very kind of you to pretend not to be shocked."

His eyes widened, and I noticed they were a rather subtly spectacular colour, brown and green and flecked with gold, like a cool country stream in the dappled light of a summer's afternoon.

"My lady, you have not asked anything that all of society has not asked. At least you asked directly instead of inviting me to supper to pretend an interest in my hobbies."

"Really, how appalling!"

He shrugged. "It has only happened twice, and since I refused to speak of the matter, I am certain it will not happen again. Word has got round that I am unforgivably silent on the subject, and people do not think to invite me for any other reason."

To express sympathy to him would have been insulting, even though I felt acutely sorry for him. He had clearly been raised a gentleman's son, perhaps with expectations. It seemed apparent some financial ruin had befallen his family, and now he must depend upon the kindness of his better-heeled relation to employ him. A man would have to exercise all his skills of diplomacy, purge himself of pride, to accept such a position.

I nodded toward the horse. "What do you make of that creature? He seems sound enough from here."

Ludlow did not hesitate. "He is too nervous. You can just see the white of his eye all round. Sir Cedric will tell you he is spirited, but Cedric knows steamships, not horses. That animal would throw you at the first gate and happily leave you to limp home. Why do you smile, my lady?"

"Because that was my brother Benedick's horse. He sold him for precisely that reason. I do hope Father does not buy him again."

"Again?"

I nodded. "Father has purchased him three times, and sold him on every time because he cannot be controlled. Then he forgets how awful the beast was and buys him back again. It's really quite foolish of him."

Ludlow and I shared a smile. It occurred to me then that some men demand a second glance, others require it. Ludlow was the latter, nondescript and calm as a millpond, but calmness has its own attractions. "May I dare to ask a further impertinence?"

He bowed gallantly from the neck. "Of course."

"What will become of you now that Sir Cedric means to settle in the country?"

Ludlow stretched his long legs out in front of him, crossing them at the ankle. "I shall remain in London, I daresay. His investments are diverse. It takes a man quite in the thick of things to handle the correspondence. Sir Cedric thinks he can manage very well spending most of his time in the country. I shall travel down to Kent as needed to receive instructions, and the London office will be under the supervision of his director. And, of course, he must be in London during the Season. He has many interests in Parliament, and must be in attendance when it is sitting."

"He sounds quite the magnate," I said lightly.

"That he is, and entirely self-made, although he does not much care for people to know it."

"I hold the American view that self-made men are the most worthy," I told him. "If a man can better himself through his own gifts, his own native wit and determination, why are we so quick to think the worse of him for it?"

Ludlow considered this for a moment. "Perhaps because we have a thousand years of history instructing us to the contrary. We are taught that a man is born to his place, and in his place must he die," he finished, with the faintest edge to his voice.

"You must be quite invaluable to him, that he would entrust such responsibility to you."

A fleeting wistful smile touched his lips. He nodded toward Snow, who stood just at the fringes of the crowd gathered round the hunter. Snow had doffed his hat and was raising his face to the fading sunlight. He looked like a man thoroughly contented with his lot in life, his expression one of perfect contentment.

"That gentleman has the life I would have chosen for myself."

"Really? I should think you would have made an excellent curate. You have a soothing voice. One does not like to hear about damnation from a man who sounds as if he were pronouncing a sentence from the Queen's Bench."

Ludlow laughed. "I was reared for it. My mother and Sir Cedric's were sisters, daughters of a vicar with a country living. Sir Cedric's mother married a miserly merchant who died when Cedric was but a lad. Cedric was brought up in poverty. He was apprenticed at the age of seven, if you can imagine it. My lot was quite different. My mother married a gentleman, the fourth son of a baronet. It was always hoped I would be given the living attached to the baronetcy's estate."

"And you would have been happy there?"

He closed his eyes briefly. "It is the most sublime place I have ever seen. It is in Cornwall, sheltered in a valley so beautiful, it must have been wrought by the hands of angels. I went there only once, but the memory of it lives with me still. The rectory was small, a doll's house, but perfect in every detail. There was a rose garden and a chicken house and a nuttery and every last gift that nature can offer."

He sighed, and in that one small exhalation I heard a lifetime's anguish. "My father quarrelled with his brother, the current baronet. They did not make it up before my father died, and though I tried to apologise and make amends, my overtures were not received with approval. I was given to under-stand my father's sins would not be forgiven, nor mine for being his son. It was up to me to make my way in the world, as best I could."

I shook my head. "I cannot approve this system we have of keeping young men on leashes to be led about by their betters. My sisters and I are settled with some degree of independence, but my brothers feel the weight of my father's authority, even as grown men. And my father has been the soul of liberality. Any other man in England would have thrust my brothers into the church and the army and the navy just to be rid of them, whether they had any vocation for those institutions or not."

Ludlow gave me a look of approbation. "Most ladies would have no sympathy for impecunious gentlemen, tossed by fortune's whims."

"Mr. Ludlow, I like to believe I would have sympathy for anyone thwarted in his happiness."

He smiled, the first genuine smile I had seen from him. The corners of his eyes crinkled; he looked younger suddenly and almost content.

"My lady, I may at least lay claim to being useful. Believe me when I say that service has its own rewards."

I thought of my own exhilaration when I embarked upon the investigation into my husband's murder, and the killing boredom when it was finished, the restlessness that came with stitching cushions and pressing flowers day after monotonous day.

"On that point, Mr. Ludlow, we are in complete agreement." I rose, and he jumped to his feet. "No, no. Stay where you are, I insist. I mean to walk a bit and admire the scene. Perhaps you will make that sketch after all."

He laughed, a light, pleasant sound, and reached for his sketchbook. "I may at that, my lady."

I left him then, and turned my steps toward the path to the river and Brisbane.

THE NINTH CHAPTER

You would look up to heaven, but I think
The devil, that rules i'th'air stands in your light.
—The Duchess of Malfi

walked nearly to the river before I spied him, his good shoulder propped against an ancient willow. He was staring at the dark water as a soft river breeze ruffled his hair. He did not turn, even when I drew close enough to touch him.

"Curiosity is a character flaw, and a dangerous one," he remarked in an acid tone. "Or didn't your father teach you that?"

"He tried," I said cheerfully. "But I am afraid that lesson, like so many others, simply did not take."

He turned then and looked directly at me. I had forgot how singularly intense his focus could be. He had a trick of staring quite through me, stripping me bare while revealing nothing of himself. There had been moments, only a few, when he had been unguarded with me, giving me the smallest glimpse into the man behind the impenetrable façade. This was clearly not to be one of them. He kept his arms folded over the breadth of his chest, and I wondered if the gesture was meant more to contain himself or to keep me at bay.

With some effort, I was able to breathe evenly, and when I spoke, my voice was steady.

"I do hope you are enjoying your stay at the Abbey. Have you been in Sussex long?"

He ignored my opening gambit. "I will not tell you anything," he said flatly.

I opened my eyes very wide and blinked at him. "Of course you mustn't. I should not expect it of you. You are a professional, after all."

He ground his teeth together in a manner I knew only too well. "On that point, I must request your discretion."

"Why, Brisbane, are you suggesting that your fiancée does not know what you are? I am astonished. A gentleman should be more forthcoming with his intended. How is she to know if you can support her adequately if you do not share these things?"

He took a step closer, using his height to great advantage. The breeze had risen, whipping his greatcoat about him like great black wings, and he loomed over me like some sort of fallen angel. "Are you enjoying yourself?" he demanded.

I nodded. "Oh, immensely! And you must promise to invite me to the wedding. I shall be bereft if I cannot wish you well on your nuptial day. I think I shall wear green. Not fashionable for weddings anymore, but during Tudor times it was just the thing. I believe it has some connotations of pagan fertility, but we shall draw a veil over that."

His jaw tightened a bit more. "I will not discuss this with you.

Not Charlotte, not my profession, and not my presence here at Bellmont," he repeated.

I fluffed the velvet trim on my cuffs and adopted a tone of supreme indifference. "So you have said, and I agreed with you. Really, Brisbane, you do not listen at all. You shall want to remedy that before you take a wife. A lady likes to be listened to. Tell me, as we are friends, what became of Mr. King? She did not murder him, did she? I shall feel quite nervous for you if you marry a murderess."

His hand twitched, and though he did not reach for me, I knew I had prodded him too far. Teasing Brisbane was not a sport for the faint of heart. It was only slightly safer than baiting bulls. I could not help myself. Perhaps I wished to punish him for the long, lonely months without word. Perhaps I wished to punish him for forcing Charlotte upon us. I only knew I wanted to hurt him, not deeply, but the temptation to twist the knife was irresistible.

"Honestly, Brisbane. You cannot seriously expect me to believe you intend to marry her. She is ridiculous. She would bore you to sobs in a fortnight."

He opened his mouth, to say something vicious I have no doubt, but I held up a hand. "No, you mustn't tell me. I would rather not know." I tapped the black sling firmly. To his credit he did not flinch. "I do hope you are convalescing well. The air here is quite restorative."

"I am fine, thank you for your concern," he ground out, his lips stiff with anger.

"Excellent. And how is Monk? Keeping well, I trust?" Monk

was his majordomo, as well as a sometime operative in his investigations. I had only the vaguest theories as to Brisbane's activities whilst I had been away, but I knew whatever they had been, Monk would have been at the thick of them.

"Monk is in London. And since you will learn of it as soon as you speak with Valerius, I will tell you he is looking after Monk while he recovers from a broken leg."

I gaped at him. This was most unexpected. "Valerius is treating him? But he is a student. He is not qualified—"

"Under Mordecai's direction," he amended. That eased my mind a little. Mordecai was Brisbane's oldest friend. An excellent physician, he had taken my wayward younger brother under his tutelage. Father would never consent to let Valerius establish his own consulting rooms, but with Mordecai's help, he could do some real good in the slums that festered behind the elegant quarters of London.

"When did he break his leg?" I asked suddenly. The speed of the attack caught him off his guard.

"A fortnight ago," he replied, and I had little doubt if he had thought on it, he would have given me a lie.

"A fortnight ago," I repeated innocently. "The same time you fell from your horse. How very unlucky. And how very fortunate that neither of you were near Trafalgar Square. I understand there was a terrible riot there, just about a fortnight past. Why, either one of you might have been injured much worse."

"I read of it in the papers," he said smoothly, refusing to rise to the bait.

"As did I. Just this morning. The stories were utterly appalling. Ten thousand people marching to register their protest at the treatment of the Irish, and two thousand soldiers beating them back. I understand some poor souls were left with broken bones, and shots were even fired. So barbaric."

I paused, holding the eyes that never left mine. "Well, I must be getting back to the others. You should come along and watch them conclude the deal for the horse. It should be most entertaining. Oh, I am sorry, I forgot," I said, with a meaningful look at his sling, "you do not ride." I spun smartly on my heel and started down the path.

"Julia—"

I turned back in surprise. He had never once called me by my Christian name. Emotions warred on his face, feelings I could not identify as I waited, only an arm's length from him, expectant, hoping for some word, some declaration.

But he simply stood staring at me, locked in a silence he would not, or could not, break, and after an endless moment I let out a ragged little breath that sounded almost like a sob.

"You know, Brisbane, if you thought to rouse my jealousy by bringing her here, you have failed. Abjectly. She is welcome to you, with my blessing."

He spoke then, something profane, but he did not follow me as I walked away.

After my tête-à-tête with Brisbane, I felt thoroughly exhausted, drained of all feeling and numb with cold and a bit of misery as well as I retraced my steps to the Gypsy camp. I had not been gone a very long time, but it was sufficient for the ladies to have finished their fortunes. Emma and Portia had joined Lucy on her bit of carpet by the cooking fire, and were sipping at chipped mugs. More of Magda's dreadful tea, no doubt, but at least it would keep the rising chill from one's bones.

The gentlemen were still haggling, though they had been joined by Plum and Mr. Ludlow. Mrs. King was some little distance apart, attempting to converse with a charming little girl whose glossy black plaits swung to her waist. Next to the child's exotic charms, Mrs. King looked like a fragile Dresden shepherdess. I thought of warning Mrs. King it would be prudent to keep an eagle eye upon her valuables, and to count the coins in her reticule when the child left, for there was no knowing if the girl was old enough to realise we were friends and not to be stolen from. But just then she looked up and waved at me, her betrothal ring from Brisbane sparkling on her finger, and I held my tongue.

I made for the knot of gentlemen instead, meaning to join them when a figure swayed out from behind the nearest tent. "You do not wish me to tell your fortune? I am never wrong, lady, as you well know."

I sighed. "No, Magda. Thank you. I trust the ladies paid you sufficiently for your services?"

She shrugged. "Is there enough silver in the world to exchange for knowing what the future holds?"

"Probably not. In that case, I shall leave you to it."

I made to step around her, but she stood in my path, not touching me, but making it impossible for me to pass.

"What do you want?" I demanded.

Magda shook her head, rattling the coin-bedecked chains at her ears and throat. Roma woman often dressed thus, carrying their life's savings on their person for safekeeping. "You were kind to me once, lady," she said, pouting a little.

"For which you repaid me in ways that would have bought you a gibbet if I had gone to the authorities. Instead I arranged for you to leave London, at great personal cost to myself," I reminded her. "Do not think to win me with your petulance. It is a child's trick."

She curled her lip at me and tossed her head. "Very well then. But I will tell you this for free—that one still walks with the dead," she whispered, nodding toward the dark figure slowly walking toward us from the river path. She grasped my arm fast in her bony fingers. "I told you once before the screams of the dead echo in his steps. You did not believe me, and you nearly died. Do you believe me now?"

I wrenched my arm free. "That is a faery story meant to frighten children. What did you tell my cousin Lucy? That she would marry and take a shipboard voyage?"

Magda looked at me in surprise. "Of course I did. That is what she wished to hear, and it was the truth. And I tell you the truth as well—that man is like the raven. His shadow speaks of death to come."

"Enough!" I cried, and pushed past her.

"Tell me, lady, has he ever told you the truth about Mariah Young?" she called after me, laughing her harsh, grating laugh.

I stalked off, refusing to turn and address her. The question she asked had nagged at me since I first heard the name Mariah Young. I knew little about her, save that she had some attachment to the Roma, and some connection to Brisbane as well. And that she had been murdered. Beyond that I knew nothing. I had asked Brisbane only once, and he had refused to speak of her. The fact that Magda knew I would have asked, and that Brisbane would not have confided in me, confirmed she knew both of us better than I could have wished.

The gentlemen were just concluding the deal when I approached, with much slapping of hands and laughter and no doubt a few ribald jokes as well. They had dispersed to join the ladies, all save Sir Cedric who remained, stroking the hunter's nose with an air of proprietary satisfaction.

"Ah, Lady Julia!" he cried as I approached. "Congratulate me, if you please. I have just become the owner of this magnificent animal."

I peered at the hunter's face, noting the edge of white showing cleanly around the entire eyeball. I smiled.

"Congratulations, indeed, Sir Cedric. I hope Mephistopheles will make you an excellent mount."

His hand paused. He looked at me, a trifle uncertainly. "Mephistopheles? Like the devil?"

"Yes, but I am certain it is a term of opposite affection. As one will name a black kitten Snowflake, that sort of thing."

His expression eased and he went on petting the animal's nose. It was the first opportunity I had had to assess Lucy's fiancé in any sort of detail. He had removed his gloves to better acquaint himself with his purchase. His hands were manicured, but all the creams and unguents in the world could not erase the patchwork of scars and calluses formed from many years of hard labour. His tweeds were well-cut and almost alarmingly new. They bore the hallmarks of good tailoring, doubtless from the finest shops in Savile Row. Beneath his hat, a few stray locks of silvering blond hair curled to his collar. His whiskers were the same odd mix of silver and gold, and with his ruddy complexion and tawny eyes, the whole put me greatly in mind of an aging lion. His physique was powerful and sturdy, though he lacked Brisbane's inches.

"Well, what do you make of the old boy then?" he asked, and I turned my attention to the horse.

"A very fine hunter. Perhaps he needs a bit of training to settle his nerves, but with the proper handling—"

"Not the animal," he corrected. "Me. Shall I pass muster to marry Lucy? Or am I too rough a creature to be connected to the Marches?"

He spoke lightly, with a chuckle underscoring his words, but I fancied I heard something else there, the faintest note of resentment.

I reached out and stroked the horse's nose. He flared his nostrils at me, but ducked his head to be rubbed again.

"Sir Cedric, you have met my father's Aunt Dorcas. The fact that we still own her as one of ours should speak volumes on the subject."

He nodded. "She does seem a bit of a Tartar, that one. There is not much love lost between her and Emma and my Lucy."

I hesitated. If our dirty linen was pegged out, the line would stretch from Brighton to Newcastle. And yet, Sir Cedric was not yet kin. I did not like to air too many of our troubles before him.

"I think many young ladies of spirit resent the hand that curbs them," I temporised. "You needn't have her to stay once you are settled. She will expect it, of course, but Father will make certain she is cared for."

Sir Cedric drew back, a trifle affronted, I think, his colour rising. "Lady Julia, I hope I shall always do my duty by my relations, both by blood and marriage."

"Of course you will," I hastened to soothe him. "I had a very nice chat with Mr. Ludlow earlier. I know you gave him a place when he was left to make his way in the world. Very commendable."

His face relaxed, the swift ruddy colour abating a little. I had not thought him so easily vexed, but it appeared he had the temper to match his complexion. I only hoped Lucy knew how to manage him.

"I did. He is a clever boy, and I could have searched the City twice over and not found his match. He can tally a ledger page just by running his eye over the figures, and he can write a perfect letter the first time through, with nary a blob or smudge. Any employer would be lucky to have got him, but he is mine and I mean to keep him."

A peculiar turn of phrase, I thought, and I wondered briefly if he thought the same about Lucy.

I smiled. "Well, I will leave you to your acquisition, Sir Cedric. I wish you every happiness with him."

I gave the horse a final pat and turned in the direction of the ladies and their little tea party on the carpet.

As I moved away I heard Sir Cedric give a sharp exclamation. "He bit me! Here, sir, I shall not want this horse. The damned thing bit me!"

I covered a smile with my hand and hastened my steps. Retrieving his money from Jasper's pocket would be a frustrating and ultimately futile exercise. Watching him try would have been tempting, but there was other game afoot.

As I neared the ladies, Mrs. King approached me, having abandoned her efforts at conversation with the Gypsy child.

"My lady!" she called. I waited for her, and she hurried, her face a trifle pale.

"Mrs. King, are you quite all right?"

She paused, biting at her lip. "I do not know. My lady, can you tell me if that woman—Magda, I believe her name is—can you tell me if she is quite truthful?"

I shrugged. "She is as truthful as any of her race."

Mrs. King blinked at me. "I thought you were their champion. I am surprised to hear you speak thusly."

For some unaccountable reason I felt cross with her, and I did not trouble to hide the edge in my voice. "Mrs. King, I am no one's champion. I hope the Roma may be treated with respect and compassion. But those hopes do not prevent me from seeing them as they are. They have been greatly persecuted by our laws for centuries. Duplicity is simply their means of surviving in an unjust world. If I say they lie, I mean it as a statement of fact, and only because they are forced to it, as you or I would be in the same circumstances."

She shook her head. "I do not mean to quarrel with you about the Roma. But I must know if this woman speaks truly. Does she have the sight?"

I tipped my head to the side and looked at her carefully, from the pale complexion to the tiny lines sketched at the corners of her eyes. I had not noticed them before. "She frightened you, didn't she? When she told you your fortune."

Mrs. King dropped her eyes, but not before I saw them fill with tears. "She touched my betrothal ring at first. I thought she was going to give me a fortune like Miss Lucy's. I expected her to speak of wedding trips and trousseaux. Instead she dropped my hand and stared straight through me. She bored into me with those black eyes. I felt quite faint for a moment, but I heard her distinctly. She warned me about ghosts. She said I was in danger, if I did not leave the Abbey, some terrible fate would befall me."

I nearly snorted, and to cover the sound, I coughed behind my glove. Mrs. King clapped me heartily on the back.

"Are you quite all right?"

I waved her away. "Perfectly, I assure you."

Magda, for all her faults, could occasionally perpetrate an act of genius. Doubtless she had heard through the grapevine of village gossip that Mrs. King was betrothed to Brisbane. And though she liked to utter her Cassandra-like warnings about him to me, she also knew I harboured a *tendresse* for him. Magda and I had had our troubles, but she would always be loyal to me, in her own fashion.

I touched Mrs. King's arm. "I should not worry if I were you, my dear."

Mrs. King clutched at me. "She said I should retire early, bolt my door, and not stir until morning," she whispered.

Gently, I detached her fingers. "Excellent advice. The Abbey is full of odd little staircases and twisty corridors. One might take a nasty tumble in the dark. Far better to stay safely in your room."

She nodded, clasping her hands together. "I must warn the others though. It would be selfish of me not to do so."

I raised my hand to pat her again, then thought better of it. "Do whatever you think is best, my dear."

She thanked me, and I think would have even tried to embrace me, but Brisbane had spotted us together and was moving rapidly in our direction.

"Ah, here is your fiancé now. I am sure he will be only too happy to allay your fears. If you will excuse me," I murmured, making a hasty retreat.

When I was a safe distance away, I hazarded a glance back over my shoulder. Mrs. King was turned away from me, her face buried in Brisbane's shoulder. He was staring over her head at me, his expression unfathomable.

Then I remembered the lesson of Lot's wife, and hurried on my way.

THE TENTH CHAPTER

Men should be what they seem.
—OTHELLO

The rest of the afternoon idled pleasantly by. The Roma provided us with a simple tea—just thickly-cut bread with fresh butter—but, sauced with the lovely view and the brisk air, it was utterly delicious. Father managed to avert a disaster by purchasing Mephistopheles from Sir Cedric himself, and Plum completed a rather superb series of sketches from his vantage point on the little outcropping. Mrs. King insisted upon telling the party of her ominous fortune, and though the ladies responded with murmurs of sympathy, the gentlemen jollied her out of her fears by telling the most outrageously silly ghost stories. Father went to great lengths to soothe her worries by insisting the ghosts of Bellmont Abbey were of the very best sort, and terribly friendly as well.

"That is precisely what I am afraid of," she pointed out, and the entire group broke into laughter. She laughed as well, and after that seemed much more at her ease.

Alessandro was prevailed upon to tell us tales of Tuscan *strega,* and Mr. Ludlow and Mr. Snow made their contributions as well, relating folktales of their travels to India and China. Then Jasper was persuaded to bring out his guitar and sing a few Gypsy songs. Several of the children had crept quite close to hear the ghost stories, and they sang along with Jasper's melodies, a high, sweet chorus, not as pure as any in Westminster Abbey, but just as engaging. They were enchanting, and it was not until the sun had sunk completely below the horizon that Father rose to his feet and motioned toward the gathering darkness.

"It will be full dark soon, and I do not like the look of that sky. The temperature is falling as well," he added, rubbing his hands together briskly. "I think we shall be in for a bit of snow from the look of the cloud just over the Downs." Naturally the gentlemen had to spend another quarter of an hour debating the weather as the ladies stood shivering, Portia rolling her eyes at me behind Father's back. In the end, they all agreed that, yes, it was indeed growing colder and darker and we ought to depart at once for the Abbey.

"Thank God for that," Portia muttered, thrusting a hand into the crook of Alessandro's arm.

We made our thanks to our hosts and pressed coins upon the children. As we picked our way to the carriages, Mr. Snow fell into step beside me.

"What think you now, Mr. Snow?" I teased gently. "Do you have a better liking for our travelling friends? Or do you still mean to reform them?"

He smiled and took my elbow in his hand, guiding me over stones in the dusk. "They do seem happy enough, I grant you. But it will be cold tonight, bitterly so, and I cannot help but think of them, shivering in their caravans, huddled together for what meagre warmth they can find."

I glanced ahead to where Brisbane strode, tall and strong, a far cry from the starveling child he had once been.

"If today teaches you anything, Mr. Snow, let it be this—you must never underestimate them. No race on earth has a greater capacity for survival."

Mr. Snow sighed theatrically. "It is difficult for a man to admit his errors, my lady, but how can he resist so lovely a teacher?"

This gallant speech was accompanied by a lightly mocking smile. I fixed him with my sternest expression.

"You are outrageous."

"You are not the first to say so. And since you have seen this leopard in all his spots, let me say further that I am extremely pleased to have been invited to join this happy party, if only because it means I shall be in proximity to the most enchanting lady I have met in a very long time."

His charm was thick as treacle and just as cloying. He could be a merry companion, but I was in no danger of falling prey to him.

"Tell me, what led you into the church? Did you always have a vocation for the religious life, or were you converted in a brilliant flash of light, a new St. Paul on the Damascene road?"

If he was disappointed his attempt at flirtation had fallen flat, he bore no grudge. He relaxed then, and I decided I liked him better when he was at his ease.

"I was in the army, that last great hope of all second sons. My father was a knight, and a poor one at that. My elder brother inherited a crumbling estate in Surrey and four sisters to keep. I was bought a commission and sent into the world with a pat on the head and one good suit of clothes." I slid a sidelong glance at the suit he wore now. Well-cut and fashioned of quality tweed. His tastes were beyond the reach of a curate's meagre compensation, and I wondered idly how he managed.

"And did you like the army?"

"I did, actually. I found I was terribly competent at standing in a row and marching where I was told. I was even rather good at shooting. I did, however, find it quite disturbing when my opposite number in a skirmish decided to shoot back at *me*."

"I can well imagine," I murmured.

"I was lightly wounded, not enough to maim me forever, but enough to permit me to leave the army without lifting eyebrows. My brother prevailed upon connections of his to find me a living, and so I entered the church. This is my third parish, and I must say, it is my favourite thus far. I find I am suited to the contemplative life."

He was smiling again, that small smile that hinted at some greater amusement and invited me to smile with him. He seemed to take nothing too seriously, including himself. We had reached the carriages by then, and he handed me in, leaving his hand in mine a trifle longer than strictly necessary. I watched him as he strode away. He reached his conveyance just as Emma moved to enter the carriage. She stepped back shyly, but he put out a hand, smiling as winsomely as he had at me. She laid her tiny hand in his gloved palm, darting a tremulous glance at him from under her lashes, and I sighed. It was a pity that something as mundane and dull as money should prevent a marriage between otherwise suitable partners.

As we rode back to the Abbey, Brisbane again stared out of the window, and Alessandro was a captive audience to Mrs. King's prattling, leaving me free to think on Mr. Snow. He was mischievous and gallant, and I would wager there was a fair bit of roguish Irish blood in him. But I knew better than to think his attentions were reserved for me alone. I had observed his flattery toward Portia as well, and it was not difficult to understand him. An impoverished younger son with a sybarite's tastes, his way in life would be greatly eased by the acquisition of a rich wife. He had scarcely spoken two words to Emma, not out of any inherent unkindness, I decided, but simply because she was poor, and a poor lady could do nothing but weigh him down, like stones in a drowning man's pocket. No, his charm had been directed solely at the unattached ladies of means—or at least the ladies he *thought* were unattached. It seemed impossible he could have failed to hear the gossip that followed Portia, and he had even met Jane, although it was possible he had not guessed the precise nature of their relationship. Or perhaps he had and was prepared to be a liberal husband about such matters. After all, the Duke of Devonshire had entertained a similar arrangement between his wife and her best friend, I mused. Of course, the lady in question had shared her bed with the duke as well as his wife, but for all I knew that might have been an attraction to Snow.

"Penny for your thoughts," Mrs. King said suddenly, smiling winsomely at me.

"Not for a pound," I replied tartly. "Look there, the Abbey. How lovely it is, blazing with lights! Quite the faery palace."

We were silent the last few moments of the drive, and matters quickly fell to chaos when we alighted. There was much calling back and forth, noise from the dogs, orders being shouted to the footmen and grooms, and it was some minutes before everyone was sorted.

Just as I was about to step inside, I realised Mrs. King had lingered in the inner ward, hanging back as the carriages were driven away and the gates were rattled into place for the night, locking us in as effectively as any prisoners. The inner ward was deserted except for the small, lone figure in black. She stood perfectly still, staring up at the stone walls of the Abbey and did not stir, not even when I went to her.

"Mrs. King? If you stay out here, you will take a chill, and as I must stay with you out of politeness, I shall take one also, and I would very much rather not."

For a long moment she did not look at me, but when she did, her expression was one of awe. "I wonder, my lady, I do wonder if you realise how lovely it all is."

I blinked at her. "I beg your pardon?"

She sketched a broad gesture with her arm, sweeping from the courtyard cobbles to the great iron bell of the Galilee Tower, encompassing all of it, from moss-slick stones to the crooked little watchtower that looked as if it might well have been laid by a slightly inebriated mason.

"All of this. This place, your family. I wonder if you know how perfectly wonderful it all is."

I thought on it for a moment. "I don't suppose I do. It is all I have ever known," I told her, a trifle apologetically.

She nodded, her lips pursed. "Yes, that makes sense. I don't imagine Parisians go around marvelling at how wonderful Paris is either."

"But Paris is not wonderful. It is appallingly filthy. Of course, it is a garden compared to Rome. Now Rome—"

She laid a finger on my arm, tipping her head slightly as a kitten will when it is being especially appealing. "Thank you, my lady. I have never been so warmly welcomed, nor so kindly treated as a guest."

"Ah, well, we do try. It is a draughty old place really, and with Aunt Hermia gone I cannot entirely vouch for the maids. Aquinas does his best, but he is far too soft with them. And just so as not to catch you unawares, I must warn you that arguments will erupt. It is not a March family party until something is broken," I said, with an attempt at lightness.

Mrs. King shook her head, her face sweetly serious. "I still think it is wonderful—so natural and unaffected. I really do not think you realise how extraordinary your upbringing has been. To be raised with such liberality, such freedom."

I was surprised she thought so. Most people were horrified by our upbringing, and Father had received regular letters from clergymen and meddling society mothers detailing how we were being ruined. I felt a rush of genuine, if somewhat tepid, affection for Mrs. King.

"How very kind of you to say. It puts most people off terribly, you know. We are scarcely received in society at all. I love my family dearly, but we hardly know how to *behave* properly." That was appallingly true. Our manners had changed little from my grandfather's day, when gambling and drinking to excess were the norm, and duelling and philandering were the sports of kings. I had elderly aunts who still turned quite misty with nostalgia whenever the scandals of the past were raked over again. They complained bitterly that society had all but ended with the Regency, and that the queen was nothing more than a dull German *hausfrau*. They mourned fancy-dress balls that lasted a week, and affairs with lords and their valets alike. Their adventures were the stuff of legend, and few of us managed to equal them. My own murdered husband and burned house were the merest peccadilloes in comparison.

I smiled at Mrs. King. "We cannot even manage a simple dinner without throwing the table of precedence completely out of order. But we mean well enough."

She hesitated, nibbling at her bottom lip. Then, in a rush, "My lady, I wonder if you might call me Charlotte."

I hesitated and she hurried on. "No, I am sorry. It is a presumption. Please forgive me."

I put a hand to her sleeve, giving her a sweetly duplicitous smile. "Of course it is not. You are betrothed to Brisbane, and I like to think I shall always count him a friend. I must think of you likewise. I should be very pleased to call you Charlotte."

The lovely lips curved into a seraphic smile, and her entire face seemed illuminated with pleasure. "And may I call you familiar as well?" she asked shyly.

"I should be disappointed if you did not," I told her. I looped my arm through hers. "Now, let us go inside. We haven't much time until the dressing bell, and I do not mean to be late for dinner. I have it on good authority that Cook has roasted ducks in perry tonight."

She followed me in, but just as we were about to mount the stairs, I spied Lucy, staggering under the weight of one of the great buckets of heather. I sent Charlotte along and hurried down the nave.

"Dearest, one has footmen for this sort of thing," I reminded Lucy, taking up one handle of the bucket.

She heaved a sigh of relief and straightened. "Bless you, Julia. I know the footmen are supposed to carry these, but they managed to drop the first one and crush half the heather! It simply will not do," she said, and for an instant I was reminded of the stubborn child she had once been. She had always been more obviously willful than Emma, although she was often the one made to give way. Emma had a gift for getting what she desired without ever appearing to want it at all. Lucy, on the other hand, was more forthright in her demands, and was just as often punished for her acquisitiveness.

Still, every bride wants her little pleasures, I reminded myself, and perfect flowers were a small enough thing to ask. We carried them to the chapel, the one part of the great Abbey that had remained completely untouched after the Dissolution. Virtually nothing had changed in the three hundred years since the monks had fled.

Except for the bucket of sodden heather on the floor, I thought sourly. I righted the bucket and began stuffing the crushed blooms into it.

"I shall have one of the footmen fill the bucket and attend to the spilled water. It has done no damage, except to the flowers, poor things."

Lucy left the altar and spun slowly on her heel, taking in the shadowy chapel. It was chilly in the darkness with only the great iron candelabra on the altar for warmth.

"I've never been in this part of the Abbey. It is so cold here. How did they bear it?" she asked, rubbing her arms.

"I suppose they were accustomed to it. None of the Abbey was heated, you know. The monks used to complain that the ink in the scriptoria froze when they were trying to copy manuscripts."

Suddenly, her eye alighted on something, an iron ring fixed to the wall. The iron plate behind it was wrought in the shape of a mask, like some gruesome relic of Carnevale. It looked like a throwback to pagan times, like some wicked creature out of myth, its hair wrought into the rays of a burning sun, the empty holes for its eyes staring in sightless menace.

"What is that?" she demanded, moving closer to it in the flickering shadows.

"A sanctuary ring. This was the Galilee when the Abbey was still a church, a sort of vestibule where the faithful would gather before the mass. We are just below the bell tower here. It was consecrated ground, and the ring was put there for the use of felons who might claim sanctuary from the law. The bell rang out whenever the right of sanctuary was invoked."

She touched it lightly, then turned to me. "What became of them? They stayed here? Forever?"

I thrust the last sprig of heather into the bucket, snapping it in two as I did so. Lucy did not seem to notice. Hastily I shoved it behind the others.

"No. A felon being pursued by the law could, if he reached that ring, claim sanctuary for forty days. At the end of that time, he had to turn himself over to the authorities for trial or confess his guilt and be sent into exile."

Lucy turned back to the ring. "Astonishing. And people actually did that here?"

"Naturally," I said. "Murderers, thieves, heretics, they all came here and clung to that ring, invoking the right of sanctuary." Lucy showed no inclination to leave, but from far away I heard the familiar chime of the dressing bell. I moved toward the great oaken doors leading to the nave. "If you are really interested, you must ask Father. There is a book somewhere in the library. It lists the criminals, with all the ghoulish details. You would enjoy it thoroughly," I finished in a brisk, nursemaidy tone. "Now if you will excuse me, I must dress for dinner."

"Oh, Lord! That was the dressing bell, was it not? I must fly!"

She gathered her skirts in her hands and dashed out, hurtling down the nave. I followed, feeling a hundred years old and wishing Sir Cedric the very best good luck. I had a suspicion he was going to need it.

* * *

Once in my room, I had very little time to dress, and everything seemed to conspire against me. Florence was sitting up on a hearth cushion, yapping at nothing in particular while Morag bustled about, dragging things from the wardrobe and shoving them back again.

"No, not the black. The décolletage is too severe without a sizeable necklace, and I've nothing that will do. Fetch the bottle-green velvet. That will serve."

Morag heaved a sigh. "I have only just sponged it."

I dared another look at the mantel clock, then began shoving pins into my hair myself. "The dark pink satin then."

She folded her arms over her chest, puckering her lips. "I have not yet finished whipping the hem."

"Whyever not, for heaven's sake?" I jammed another pin into place.

"Perhaps because I spent the better part of the day playing dressmaker to that wee beastie," she countered, pointing at Florence. The dog, sensing we were talking about her, fell silent and cocked her head. She put me greatly in mind of Charlotte King just then.

"Then the black will have to do."

Morag shot me a darkly triumphant look and spread the heavy black satin onto the bed, smoothing it with a proprietary hand. When she was finished, she pointed to a box on the dressing table that, in my haste, I had not seen.

"Mind you don't forget to open that. Mr. Aquinas was very

specific. He brought it up after breakfast and said to be certain you opened it before you went down to dinner."

I tucked the last pin into place and took up the parcel. It was wrapped in brown paper and secured with a bit of ordinary tape such as solicitors use. There was a small piece of card tied to it, penned with two words in my Father's hand: *Wear me*.

"What the devil is he up to now?" I muttered. Father adored little japes of any sort, but I was in no mood to play Alice. I wrenched the wrappings free and found a box—a familiar box of dove-grey velvet.

"It cannot be," I said softly. I stared at it a long moment.

Morag came to peer over my shoulder. "Well, it is. When did you see them last?"

I did not open the box. "Before Edward's death. They were still in the bank vault when he died, and I did not wear them during my period of mourning. I had half-forgot they were there."

Still I made no move to open it. Morag finally gave me a little push, and I flicked open the clasp. Another moment's hesitation, and I opened the lid.

There, nestled against a bed of black satin, was the most perfect collection of grey pearls in England. Even the queen had nothing to touch them. They had been assembled at great effort and expense, by Edward's forebears. Known as the Grey Pearls, they were a sort of gemological pun. They had been given to each Grey bride on her wedding day. My own mother-in-law had bitterly resented giving them up, and it had taken every bit of Edward's considerable powers of persuasion to convince her to part with them. I had worn them that day, but I had never liked them. I always associated them with Edward's sour mother. Much later someone mentioned to me in passing that for every pearl a bride wears she shall shed one tear. They had been only too prophetic in my case.

But even I was forced to admit they were magnificent. I stared down into the box where they nestled like pale sleeping serpents. There was a great collar, earrings, and matching bracelets. The collar was fastened with a heavy silver filigree clasp, worked with an Imperial eagle, the red eyes of its double profiles a pair of winking rubies. The bracelets had been copied from the collar; the earrings were simpler. There was a final piece as well, an enormous rope of pearls that, when hung straight from the neck, reached to the knees. Every pearl in the set was enormous, and perfectly matched to its brothers.

I turned over Father's note, but there was nothing else. He had gone to some trouble to remove these from the vault in London—not in accordance with proper bank policy, but then there were advantages to being an earl—and by the time I had puzzled out his motives, dinner would be a distant memory.

"Fine. I will wear them. They will suit the black in any case," I said finally, thrusting the box at Morag. She clipped and fastened and looped until I was weighed down like a Michaelmas goose.

Just as she clasped the last piece into place, I gasped. "You've scratched me."

She peered at the collar. "Not I. One of the eagle's heads is bent. His beak has nipped you, it has."

She reached to meddle with it, but I waved her away. "I've no time to bother with it now. I will wear them tonight, and then send them to the jeweler to be mended."

Morag fetched my slippers then, dainty things of thinnest black kid, overlaid with exquisite Spanish lace and perched on black velvet heels. I had paid a fortune for them, and was giving serious thought to having all of my evening gowns shortened by an inch to show them off to best advantage. I wriggled my feet into them and tucked a handkerchief and small box of violet cachous into the tiny pocket sewn into the seam of my gown. Morag reached for a small fur tippet, and as she scooped up the bit of fur, Florence began to howl.

Morag had the grace to look abashed. "She thinks it is her friend. They've spent the afternoon together, and Florence has grown rather attached."

I took the fur from her and dropped it in the basket. "Then she may keep it. It smells of dog now, in any case."

Morag snorted indignantly. "It does not. That dog is as clean as you or I."

I had little doubt the animal was as clean as Morag, but I knew it was more than my life was worth to say so.

Florence grabbed at the tippet with her tiny teeth and dragged it farther into her basket, growling happily.

Morag leaned over and clucked at her. *"Haud yer sheesht, wee a body."*

I stared at her. "Have you gone completely daft? You cannot teach that dog Scots."

She rounded on me, hands firmly at her hips. "I certainly can. You are teaching her English, and Scots is just as good a language."

I opened my mouth to reply, but she held up a hand. "You will be late for dinner, and I've had a long day. I am in no humour to be hauling trays up at midnight because you've not had enough to eat. Off with you."

I took my leave, grumbling under my breath. Between my family, my maid, and my pets, my life was clearly no longer my own.

THE ELEVENTH CHAPTER

Yet men will murder upon holy days.
—THE EVE OF ST. AGNES, KEATS

*D*inner was a spirited and lively affair. Conversation and wine flowed in equal abundance, and everyone seemed in high spirits with only a few exceptions. Violante sat next to Father, nibbling at pickled chestnuts and bestirring herself only to reply to questions. She kept her hand firmly at her belly, and I began to wonder if there was not perhaps a happy event in her future.

Hortense had survived her day with Violante and Aunt Dorcas and was seated at Father's other hand, coolly elegant in ice-blue satin trimmed in silver ribbon. She looked like a pale snow queen, rimed in frost, a few tasteful diamonds winking out from her hair. Emma and Lucy were dressed in the same gowns they had worn the previous evening, as was Charlotte, although she had added a scrap of purple lace to the bodice, a perfect foil for her roses-and-cream complexion. Portia was resplendent in jade green, her wrists heavy with carved jade bracelets purchased from the hold of a Chinese merchant ship. My jewels were by far the most extravagant, and as the soup course was served I began to feel a little embarrassed by them. Father had shown no flicker of recognition when I entered the room, and if he had heard the exclamations of delight by the ladies, he betrayed no sign of it. For his part, Brisbane flicked one glance at the spectacular jewels draped over my skin and turned back to his whiskey.

We talked of many things that night at dinner: our venture to the Gypsy camp (which caused Aunt Dorcas to shudder into her consommé muttering about vibrations) and the Irish question (a subject Father changed as quickly as possible) among them. Alessandro was prevailed upon to answer questions about Italy, and from there the conversation turned to travel.

Sir Cedric had chanced to mention his excursions in Kashmir, enthusing about the natural beauties of the place.

"In fact, I am of a mind to take Lucy there after Italy," he finished. "Italy is all well and good, but it takes a half-savage place like India to know you are truly alive."

Mr. Snow gave a little grimace of distaste. "If by 'alive' you mean tortured by insects, heat, filth, and disease, then I will grant you are correct, sir. Not to mention the difficulties between the races. My posting to India was the most trying of all my time in the army. No, I am afraid I must dispute with you. It is a place where the hardiest man may be well and truly tested. It is no place for the gentler sex."

"On the contrary," Lucy put in brightly, "Emma was there some years ago, and she found it most enchanting."

Portia and I exchanged quick glances. Emma's foray to India

with Aunt Gertrude to find a husband had not been a success, and it was less than discreet of Lucy to mention it. Poor Emma had returned from India after a single season, as unattached as the day she arrived there, and it was this failure to find a husband that had forced her into service as a governess.

Brisbane turned to Emma. I could not see his expression, but his tone was one of sincere interest. "Most ladies find it a challenge. Did you not mind the climate? The language difficulties?"

"Oh, no, my lord," she said quietly, her expression earnest. "I found it paradise. The climate was quite exhilarating, and the native people, so warm, so friendly and artless. I would go again tomorrow if I were able." There was a wistfulness about her I found oddly touching, and I felt suddenly sorry for her, constrained by her station and her lack of income to suffer the whims of others. She could travel only by invitation, on the largesse of another.

As if cued, Lucy cried out dramatically, "Then you must come with us!" She was sitting across from her sister, and she looked from Emma to Sir Cedric, imploringly. He hesitated for the barest moment, and before he could speak Emma did so.

"No, Lucy," she said gently. "I am sure Sir Cedric wishes to make his wedding trip without accompaniment. There will be other travels. Perhaps in a few years, when there are children who might benefit from a little supervision from their Aunt Emma," she finished with a smile. Sir Cedric threw her a look of pure gratitude, and Lucy blushed deeply at the mention of children. Snow was watching Emma with a warm gleam in his eyes, and I wondered again if something might be done to nudge them toward a match.

Conversation turned again, this time at Portia's behest, and a spirited debate broke out on the subject of trout, for reasons I never clearly understood. I was too busy watching Father, who had been noticeably quiet that evening. His eyes darted over the company ranged at his table. He was keenly watchful, as though he expected something to happen, but what, and by whose hand, I could not imagine.

After dessert the ladies adjourned briefly to the lesser drawing room. I was not surprised my pearls drew their attention as flame will draw moths. They gathered round for a better look—even Portia, who had seen them often enough. Only Mrs. King hung back, her expression pensive.

Violante pronounced them *molto bellissimo,* though Aunt Dorcas merely rolled them in her palm, dropped them with a decided sniff and took her chair by the fire. I glanced at Hortense, who had suffered Aunt Dorcas for the better part of the day. She was concentrating intently on her needlework, but her lips twitched with suppressed laughter. Lucy was the most appreciative. She ran her fingers over the pearls at my wrists, sighing softly.

"Cedric has promised me pearls for a wedding gift, but I cannot think they will be as fine as these," she remarked. Lucy was nothing if not practical. "How long have they been in the Grey family?"

I shrugged. "Ages. The clasp is a double-headed Romanov eagle, perhaps a sign they were fashioned for Russian royalty. The Greys always liked to claim they belonged to Catherine the Great herself." I furrowed my brow. "Now that I think on it, I should probably send them to Edward's heir."

"Whyever so?" Portia demanded as she lit a thin Spanish cigar. "The pearls are yours. Edward's will was quite specific."

"Yes, but I never wear them. Besides, his cousin has the estate and not enough money to keep it. Perhaps he could sell them. It is a hard thing to inherit an enormous beast of a house and no funds to maintain it. Pity it's entailed. He cannot even sell it to recoup his losses. I imagine the pearls would go quite a long way toward refurbishing Greymoor."

The estate was not far; in fact its eastern border was the western property line of Bellmont Abbey. It had been a nice-enough house when Edward's father was alive. But his untimely death, coupled with Edward's neglect, had wreaked havoc on the property. Edward's distant cousin had inherited the old wreck, and though he had a comfortable income, he had nearly bankrupted himself simply trying to keep a roof on it. It would have been wiser to abandon the old place and buy a nice sturdy new house, but he was stubborn. Turning the pearls over to him might make quite a difference to his gently impoverished family. Viewed in that light, letting them moulder in a London vault seemed a rather criminal act.

Portia drew deeply on her cigar, puffing out a perfect ring of blue smoke. I sniffed appreciatively at the aroma of it as she fixed me with an indulgent smile. "God, you are sentimental."

Mrs. King moved forward then, throwing Portia a look that might almost have been reproachful. "I think it is a truly admirable sentiment, Lady Julia," she said quietly.

"Yes, well," I said briskly, "they are only bits of oyster grit after all. I far prefer rubies. Now, I should like to hear more about India. Emma, I had forgotten you were there. Will you oblige us with a story?"

Emma hesitated, but the others gathered around, murmuring encouragement and settling themselves comfortably. She gave me a shy smile, then took a tiny sip of the port Portia had pressed upon her.

"I suppose what I remember most clearly are the gardens, in particular the moonlight garden of the Amber Palace."

"Oh, how romantic!" breathed Charlotte.

"It was. The garden had been commissioned by a prince as a wedding gift for his bride. You see, this prince was very strict, and followed the customs of his Mohammedan overlord. His wives and concubines lived in seclusion, locked away from the world so long as the sun shone. But once dusk had come, and darkness had fallen over the land, the royal ladies were permitted to stroll in the gardens. Out of his love for his bride, the prince constructed this particular garden to be at its most spectacular by moonlight."

Her eyes took on a faraway gleam, and I knew that Emma no longer saw the stone walls and tapestries of an English drawing room. She saw only India, with all of its exotic beauties, and she brought us with her by the magic of her words.

"There were jasmines, of course, and tuberose, filling the air with such strong perfume that the ladies wore no scent because they knew they could never compete. There was a formal parterre, which was completely cleared and replanted several times each year so the garden would always be perfect. In the center of the parterre was a fountain of gold, fed by a stream that ran through the garden which the servants called the Stream of Paradise. At one end there was a throne where the prince could sit and watch his ladies enjoy the pleasures of the garden, and above the throne was carved the words, 'If there be paradise on earth, it is this, it is this, it is this…' And along each side ran colonnades, the columns so thick with bougainvillea and jasmine that you could not see the marble for the flowers. It was truly an enchanted place."

"How did you come to see it?" Portia ground out her little cigar in a china dish and waved her hand to clear the air. I stared at the slender stub and realised suddenly where I had seen that particular variety of cigar before. Reluctantly, I turned my attention to Emma.

"The prince loved to entertain. He often gave dinners for the regiments and the English diplomats. He always toasted the queen and insisted his children be brought out to mingle with the guests. It was important to him that they learn English. He believed the future of India lay with England, and he wanted his children to be forward-thinking." She hesitated, ever the consummate storyteller, the pause heightening our interest. "And yet, even as we ate his food and listened to his talk of progress and the modern age, I always thought of the ladies, locked behind marble walls until the moon rose and they were freed, like enchanted princesses under the spell of an evil queen. I liked to imagine them dancing to their strange, sad, quavering music, dancing through the columns and the fountains and the parterres, and out of the gates, leaving him behind forever."

"Would they do such a thing?" Charlotte asked.

Emma gave her a sad smile.

"No. For much the same reason that Julia's pet raven does not leave her, although his cage is seldom closed. Sometimes captivity is a comfortable place."

I would have liked to have heard more—if nothing else the condition of women in the East was an excellent subject for brisk debate—but the gentlemen joined us then, and an exuberant discussion broke out over how we should amuse ourselves. I listened as the others bantered, edging around the group to Portia's chair. I leaned close enough to brush her ear with my lips.

"Tell me, dearest, how long have you been smoking Brisbane's cigars?"

Portia waved a lazy hand. "He sent a box of them after the last time he dined with us. I had invited him to smoke after dinner and admired the scent of them." She slanted me a wicked look. "I thought you were not jealous."

"I am not. I was simply going to offer you a pastille to sweeten your breath. I'm sure it smells vile after that cigar."

She laughed then and gave me a little push. I looked up to find Alessandro watching us, his dark eyes unusually brilliant. I gave him a small smile and he returned it warmly, suggestively even. I dropped my eyes then and we turned our attention back to the question of amusement. Charades was suggested and mercifully rejected. Someone else put forth the idea of word games; another made an argument for a theatrical, and Aunt Dorcas suggested a séance. Mrs. King blanched visibly and the proposal was quickly abandoned.

Finally, the notion of sardines was bandied about, and found to be agreeable to everyone. After another lengthy discussion concerning rules and procedures, it was established we should each play alone, and that the upper floors would be considered out of bounds for fair play, as well as the servants' accommodations and offices so as not to disturb the staff. Aunt Dorcas insisted upon remaining in the lesser drawing room beside the fire, and Hortense nobly offered to sit with her and keep her company. To my surprise, Violante joined our merry group, her olive cheeks flushed with hectic colour.

Aquinas was summoned to supply each guest with a candlestick and lit taper. As Father had never bothered to install gaslights or proper heating on the main floor, it would be dark and chilly hunting one another.

Amid much laughter, we drew lots to see who would hide, and Charlotte King was the chosen one. She clutched her candlestick nervously, perhaps a bit timid at having to brave the darkened Abbey alone to hide. She hesitated at the door, looking tremulously back at the group of us, but someone—it might have been Portia—called a little word of encouragement and she seemed to take heart. She slipped out, and the rest of us joined in a circle and began to count.

When we reached one hundred, we broke apart and took up our candlesticks. I heard Lucy's high laugh, and Sir Cedric's answering chortle. It occurred to me then that although we had agreed to hunt alone, the game was a perfect opportunity for the betrothed couple to steal a few kisses. The thought was not an appetizing one.

As soon as we left the drawing room, the group scattered like startled birds, some flocking down the side of the cloister toward the library, others taking the opposite tack and exploring the approach from the nave that led to the great drawing room. I decided to take a more thorough approach. There were few better hiding places than the shadows behind Maurice the bear. I slid into the space behind him, holding my candle aloft, careful not to singe his shabby fur. I had just decided that Charlotte must have chosen another place for her concealment when a hand clamped down upon my bare shoulder.

I gasped and turned on my heel, but before I could speak, the hand moved to my waist, drawing me hard against a masculine form and bold lips searched out my own.

With a bit of effort, albeit belated, I pushed with my free hand against the hard, muscular chest under my fingertips.

"Alessandro, really!" I licked my lips. He had tasted warmly of brandy.

He drew back, breathing heavily, a single lock of dark, silky hair spilling over his brow. He kept one arm locked about my waist, his other holding his candle high. The shadows threw his face into the sharpest *chiaroscuro,* and for a moment he seemed a stranger to me, harder, more forceful. Then he spoke, and the illusion faded.

"*Il mio* Giulia *caro,* I can hold my tongue no longer. My heart, it is so very full."

"Oh, dear," I murmured.

"Please," he said urgently, "I must speak. For months I have known you as the sister of my very dear friends. I have honoured you as the greatest lady of my acquaintance. But now I must tell you that I wish you to return to Italy. With me."

I blinked at him and pushed at his arm so that I could breathe.

"But Alessandro, there is every possibility I shall return to Italy. Plum and I spoke of that the night we invited you to come to England. Do you not remember?"

He shook his head, his glossy hair gleaming in the candle-light. "No. Just this evening, Lysander tells me Violante is expecting a child."

"Is she! How wonderful for them. I suppose that explains the pickled walnuts," I mused.

"Yes, and I am happy for my friend. But he wants the baby to be born here. And wherever Lysander goes, there goes Plum as well. I know you will not return to Italy alone." He grasped my hand in his. "So come with me."

I swallowed hard. "Alessandro, my dear boy…" I began.

He raised a hand to silence me. "No, say nothing now. Now you will refuse me. I can see this. You must think on it." He pressed his lips to my fingers ardently, then disappeared as quickly as he had come. I counted to twenty, waiting until I was certain he had gone. I slid out from behind Maurice, giving the old dear a pat as I did so. I wondered how many other such scenes he had witnessed.

I had not gone four steps when I collided heavily with another figure, bouncing ever so slightly off a solidly muscular form. The other player's candle was held just at my line of sight, dazzling my eyes.

"I do hope I didn't interrupt your interlude with Count Fornacci," Brisbane said nastily.

"Lower your candle, you've half-blinded me."

He placed it on a table, and I could just make out his face, inscrutable in its fitful light. There were times I understood him better than most, I liked to think. Other occasions, I found him as difficult to comprehend as ancient Greek.

"If you mean Alessandro, I can only say you are being absurd. He is a boy."

Brisbane arched a brow at me. "You are ungenerous. I would have called him a man fully grown."

I tapped the toe of my slipper on the carpet. "I will not quarrel with you, Brisbane. Besides, we are meant to be playing sardines, and I have not yet begun to hunt properly."

"Do not bother with the dining room. I have already been there."

"How kind of you to share your intelligence with me. Now, if you do not mind—"

Brisbane turned, maneuvering me down the hall toward the nave. "I thought we should try the billiard room."

"We are not supposed to work *together*," I reminded him.

He ignored me, and it occurred to me then that he had some ulterior purpose in seeking me out. For an instant, I thought of Alessandro's declaration and wondered if Brisbane had something similar in mind. Immediately, I rejected the notion and cursed myself for a fool. He was betrothed to Charlotte King, and although I was certain the engagement would come to nothing, he insisted upon maintaining the fiction of their relationship. No, Brisbane wanted me with him for some other reason, but I could not yet work out what it might be.

Grumbling, I allowed him to lead me to the billiard room.

We searched the shadows, and I found it curious how the near-darkness heightened my senses. I could hear my pearls click softly in the silence and the hushed rustle of my taffeta petticoats. I was conscious too of Brisbane, never more than a few feet from me. I caught the scent of him, his shaving lotion—something herbal, with a hint of spice, and something else, something indefinable but essentially Brisbane. It was a distinctive scent, and had I been blindfolded and asked to choose him out of a thousand men, I should have done so without hesitation.

I shook myself from my fancies and moved away to look behind the heavy draperies at the window, but Brisbane followed me. He was casual about it, lazy as a panther stalking a deer, but just as effective.

"There is no one here," I said finally. "I mean to try Father's study."

"A fair idea," he said smoothly, opening the door for me. He had taken it as understood I would not question his accompanying me again, and it is a credit to how well he knew me that I did not. He could be silent as a tomb when he chose, and nothing would pry him open.

I preceded him to the study, and after a lengthy conversation with Grim, we searched it, turning up nothing. My gaze lingered on the box where Father kept the newspapers, the ones that told of the vicious riot in Trafalgar Square. Questions trembled on the tip of my tongue, but I did not ask them. We were at last forced to admit defeat and moved on, closing the door softly behind us.

A few shadows flickered in the nave, a few glimmers of light glowed from under closed doors, but there was no one about. I had just begun to wonder if we were entirely alone in this part of the Abbey when the silence was shattered by a broken scream.

It faltered, then started again, over and over, until I thought I should run mad from it.

"The chapel," Brisbane muttered. He grabbed my hand, crushing it in his, and began to run. I dropped my candle along the way, glancing back only once to make certain the flame had not sparked the carpet.

I dropped the candlestick and pressed my free hand to where a pain stabbed my side. "Brisbane, I am tightly laced. I cannot run so quickly."

If he heard me, he did not care. He did not slow his pace until we reached the great oaken doors of the chapel. One was closed; one stood open a scant few inches. Light spilled across the carpet of the hall, and yet I was as reluctant to enter the chapel as I would have been to cross the very threshold of hell.

The screams had stopped, and there was only a tense, expectant silence as Brisbane pushed open the door and we stepped inside. The scene before us was like something out of a nightmare.

Lucian Snow was lying on the cold stone floor just in front of the altar, his neck twisted so that he faced us, his eyes wide open and staring.

And above him stood Lucy, clutching an iron candelabrum that dripped slow, heavy drops of crimson blood onto the floor.

THE TWELFTH CHAPTER

Most sacrilegious murder hath broke ope
The Lord's anointed temple…
—MACBETH

*I*n an instant Brisbane was beside her, but before he could pry the candelabrum out of her fingers, she dropped it. It made a horrendous clatter on the stones. She flinched and turned her face up to Brisbane's, her eyes rolling back white. He caught her with his good arm before she could slide to the floor. He looked at me over his shoulder, and I stepped quickly over Snow's body to retrieve the candelabrum.

"Put it aside, out of the way," he instructed me softly. "I shall wish to examine it later." It was typical of him to worry about the evidence before the girl.

I carried the candelabrum at arm's length, mindful not to disturb the blood or other, nastier bits. I tucked it behind the altar and hurried back to help Brisbane lower Lucy carefully to the floor a little distance away. She opened her eyes and Brisbane spoke calmly to her, but she made no reply. Her gaze was fixed on Lucian Snow's broken head.

I heard Brisbane tell her she should stay where she was and not move, then he joined me at the body.

"I suppose it is quite certain he is dead?" I asked faintly.

"There are bits of him stuck to your shoe," he remarked, rather unhelpfully. I felt instantly sick, but I swallowed hard, forcing the sensation down. Brisbane was making a quick study of the body, noting its position and the arrangement of the clothes, as well as the scene. I knew better than to interrupt him. Brisbane did not take kindly to distractions whilst he was working. Instead I moved to where Lucy was sitting.

Her shoulders shook as if she were sobbing, but there were no tears, and not a sound escaped her lips. Impulsively, I put my arm around her.

"It is all right, Lucy. I am here with you. You are not alone." If she heard me, she did not give any sign of it. She simply sat, her shoulders shuddering as if with extreme cold. I noticed then that her hands were wet with blood. She held them open in her lap, staring at her red, sticky palms.

I rose and went to Brisbane. "Your coat. Lucy needs it."

His eyes did not leave the corpse. He had thrust his good arm into the sleeve of his fine wool evening coat; the rest of the coat was simply draped over his other shoulder like a cape. He stripped it off without hesitation. "That is good of you," I whispered as he thrust it into my hands.

He nodded absently, still scrutinising the body. I turned to Lucy, but before I could reach her, Father appeared in the doorway, Portia just behind, Ludlow hard on her heels.

"We heard screams. What is wrong?" Father demanded.

His gaze moved from the broken, bloody body on the floor to Brisbane, to me, to Lucy and her hands wet with blood.

"Oh, Miss Lucy, what have you done?" Ludlow murmured mournfully. Lucy roused then, looking from Ludlow to Father to Brisbane. Then her eyes lit on the iron ring in the wall, and somewhere in the sluggish depths of her shocked mind, something must have stirred.

She rose and staggered toward Father. Her face pale as moonlight, her steps unsteady as she held out those gore-stained hands in front of her.

"My lord! In this holy place, I claim the right of sanctuary!" Her voice was shrill, her eyes burning with emotion. The phrase, the gestures, were the grossest of melodrama, but Father did not laugh. He looked down at her, his expression grave.

"Child, what have you done that you would invoke sanctuary?"

The rest of them, Cedric, Charlotte, Plum, Ly, and Violante, arrived just in time to see Lucy throw herself to her knees, her white face upturned to my father's.

"My lord, I claim sanctuary. You cannot take me for murder. Under the law I am given forty days. You cannot take me," she repeated. There was a gasp from the doorway, and I glanced up to see that Emma had arrived, pushing past the others to witness her sister's declaration.

Father reached out to Lucy, but she drew back in terror, her eyes rimmed in white. Suddenly, she rose and ran to the wall, wrapping her fingers about the hideous iron ring, clutching it like a drowning woman. Her hair had come loose from its pins, and she bore a striking resemblance to another Lucy, the mad, blood-stained Bride of Lammermoor.

At that moment pandemonium broke loose. Emma fell into a swoon. Cedric caught her, cursing. Violante began to shriek; Plum pushed Ly who supported her and urged her away. Henry Ludlow was deathly pale, but maintained his composure. Charlotte went very white to the lips, and seemed to stagger a little. Plum reached out to steady her, his expression grim.

I still stood clutching Brisbane's coat, but I made no move either to return it to him or give it to Lucy. Portia went to Lucy and put her hand on the poor girl's shoulder, shaking her a little.

"Lucy, what are you saying? You could not have killed Mr. Snow."

Father flicked his eyes toward Brisbane. Lucy shook off Portia's hand and tightened her grasp on the sanctuary ring. "I invoke the right of sanctuary. I cannot be compelled to leave this place, by force or persuasion. I am protected by God and the law."

Brisbane looked incredulous, but to my amazement, Father held up his hand. "You have my word, Lucy. You have invoked sanctuary and sanctuary you shall have. We shall not remove you."

I could hear Brisbane's jaw grinding from where I stood, but he did not speak. Sanctuary laws had been repealed under the Stuarts. The law had every authority to remove her from the chapel and interrogate her given the circumstances. But Father clearly had his own reasons for acquiescing to Lucy's bizarre request, reasons to which none of us would be privy until Father had a mind to tell us. In the meantime, there was much to be done.

First, Father ordered Sir Cedric to take Emma and Charlotte to the lesser drawing room. Ly had already removed Violante, probably to the drawing room as well. Emma had revived from her swoon, but she was frightfully pale. Charlotte had recovered herself and stood a trifle closer to Plum than propriety permitted. His hand hovered at her elbow, ready to support her should she have need of him. Sir Cedric, his ruddy face drained of colour, looked back for a long, lingering moment at Lucy, his expression anguished. Then he seemed to fold in on himself, his shoulders sagging as he turned and left the chapel, his mouth working furiously though he said nothing. Father gave Portia a significant glance, and she accompanied them. I had no doubt by the time everyone was settled in the drawing room, she would have poked up the fire and rung for brandy. Portia was not a particularly nurturing sort of person, but she was very efficient in a crisis.

Wordlessly, Brisbane took his coat out of my hands and draped it around Lucy's shoulders. She slumped against the cold stone wall, but in spite of Father's reassurances, she would not relinquish her hold on the ring.

Brisbane and Father went to study the body, and I stepped near, shielding Lucy from the sight of it.

"We must remove the body, my lord," Brisbane said *sotto voce*. "If you mean to keep her here—"

"I know you do not approve, my boy. But you will simply have to trust me. I must have a care here."

The tension in Brisbane did not ease, but he relented. "If you

233

wish, my lord," he said finally, the syllables clipped. "But the body must be attended to. And the candelabrum."

Father's brows rose a little. "Ah. Is that what it was? I suppose you have put the weapon aside for safekeeping?"

"Just behind the altar," I whispered. "I took care not to disturb the, erm, matter on the base of it."

Father nodded. "Julia, my dear, will you fetch Aquinas? Tell him what has happened here and that Brisbane and I will require his assistance. I want him to prepare a suitable resting place in one of the offices." He brightened a little. "The vegetable larder, you think?"

I felt a lurch in my stomach and I suddenly regretted the second serving of duck I had eaten at dinner. "I hardly think so, Father. The food…"

"Ah, quite right. Any room without a fire will suffice. They are all cold enough to serve our purpose. Tell him to use his best judgement. And we shall require a footman, I suppose, to help us shift the body."

Brisbane was regarding my father with an approving glance. His eyes moved to Lucy, and Father, taking his meaning, nodded. "Someone must sit with Lucy. She should not be left here alone. And tell Aquinas we will require a sturdy footman to keep watch outside the door. I would not have her try to leave us. Also, a sheet for poor Mr. Snow, I think. We may give him that dignity at least."

"What of Uncle Fly? He must be told, and it would be horrid for him to learn of this from the servants. You know how they gossip."

Father stroked his chin thoughtfully. "I will send a note. Best wait until morning. No point in rousing his entire household this time of night."

To my surprise, Brisbane spoke up. "I will go myself, if you like."

Under other circumstances, I might have thought it curious Brisbane had volunteered to deliver the note instead of asking a footman, but I knew him better than that. He wanted a chance to play the sleuthhound around before news of the murder spread. Snow had boarded with Uncle Fly, and it was entirely possible his staff could shed some light on why my cousin would have found it necessary to murder him. Lucy herself seemed in no condition to speak of it. She kept her grip on the ring, eyes closed, keening softly.

I took one last look at the battered remains of Lucian Snow and left the chapel.

I met Aquinas just outside the door and blessed Portia's efficiency in sending him along.

"Aquinas, I am afraid the Reverend Mr. Snow has died suddenly."

Aquinas was a superior servant; he betrayed little reaction to the news that there was a corpse in the chapel. He merely blinked once, slowly, and then crossed himself.

"I do hope it was not the duck, my lady."

My stomach lurched again. "No, nothing like that. Mr. Snow was murdered. Mr. Brisbane, that is, Lord Wargrave is attending him now. If you could find someplace suitable to er, *store* Mr. Snow, I think that would be best."

"Of course. One of the larders, I expect, will serve nicely."

"Father said the same thing. It seems terribly unhygienic, what with the food and all. And I cannot think that Cook will appreciate having a dead man in the larder when she is trying to feed a house party," I objected.

"Of course, my lady, but he must be kept in a place sufficiently cool enough to retard decomposition—"

I held up a hand. "I do *not* wish to know. Father is expecting you," I finished, gesturing toward the chapel. He bowed apologetically.

Leaving him to it, I hurried upstairs to my room, poking Morag awake from where she was dozing by the fire. As quickly as possible, I sketched the evening's events. She gave a little scream, then shoved her fists into her mouth to stifle it.

"Murder? Here at the Abbey? We will all be killed in our beds, we will!"

"Do not be an ass. Now, Lucy must not be left alone in the chapel. She is quite fragile right now, and there is no one else to sit with her. Emma is too distraught at present. Lucy needs someone of sound common sense, and you will do, provided you do not start wittering on about murder."

Morag's eyes were round with terror. "What if she tries to kill me?"

"Morag," I said through gritted teeth, "there will be a footman at the door should you have need of him, but you will not. The girl is quite overcome. What she requires now is compassion. Take your needlework and a few coverlets, for you and for Lucy. It is chilly in the chapel."

"Shall I bring a weapon, just to defend myself in case of murderous attack?"

"By all means," I said brutally. "Bring your embroidery scissors. You can cut her hair if she threatens you."

Morag obeyed, but sulkily. She took her time gathering her things, and I used the opportunity to remove the pearls. I had a wretched headache from their weight and a sore spot on my neck where the twisted beak had pecked me. It was a relief to be rid of them.

Morag was still muttering sourly under her breath, and I followed her to the chapel myself to make quite certain she carried out my instructions. The body was gone and a quick glance behind the altar revealed the iron candelabrum had been removed as well. Chairs had been brought, hard, pitiless things from the corridor. Lucy was sitting on one, slow tears dripping down her face. Someone must have brought a basin, for her hands were clean now and faintly pink, as if from hard scrubbing. She had been persuaded to release the sanctuary ring and sat with her hands resting in her lap. She looked very small, and quite vulnerable. At the sight of her, Morag's demeanour changed.

"Poor little poppet," she said softly. She moved the other chair to sit beside Lucy, folding a woollen coverlet over the younger woman's shoulders. "Now, Miss Lucy, you know me, don't you? I am Morag, Lady Julia's maid. I've come to sit with you for a bit. You won't mind that at all, will you?"

Lucy shook her head and turned, burying her face in Morag's shoulder. Morag patted her awkwardly, crooning something soothing in Gaelic. She waved me away and I slipped out, closing the heavy doors behind me. A footman had taken up his post outside and he stood up as I passed.

He was pale and wide-eyed, and I wondered exactly how useful he would be in a crisis.

I paused by his chair, looking at him closely. He could not have been more than twenty. "Which one are you?" I asked him.

"William IV, my lady," he answered immediately. This was one of Father's little whimsies. Unable to remember the names of the dozens of young men who had served as footmen at the Abbey, he had taken to calling them all William, using numerals to distinguish between them. I gave him a reassuring smile.

"I am sure you will do quite fine, William. Just mind the door, and do not let anyone in or out without his lordship's permission. Have you a weapon?"

"A—a weapon, my lady?" he stuttered.

"It might be useful, should matters get out of hand," I mused. "Still, you are a sturdy lad. I'm sure you can handle any trouble that arises with your fists."

I smiled again, but he merely nodded and murmured, "Yes, my lady," his expression worried.

I hurried to the domestic offices, not entirely certain where I would find my father and Brisbane. I finally ran them to ground in the game larder. It was a suitably grisly place, any number of dead feathered and furred things hanging from steel hooks in the ceiling. There were a few other lumps of meat, things I could not immediately distinguish, and my thoughts went at once to my Aunt Lavinia who had adopted a ferociously vegetarian diet. The notion seemed oddly attractive to me now.

The worktable had been cleared of all foodstuffs, all the little pots of paté and forcemeats, and Lucian Snow had been arranged atop it. He was decently draped in a sheet, and at his head the iron candelabrum lay as a sort of macabre decoration. I glanced from my father to Brisbane.

"Well, it did seem the best place after all," Brisbane began defensively. "There is a proper table and it is very cold."

I shuddered, and Father gave a brisk nod. "He will do well enough in here for tonight. There is not enough light to do any sort of proper examination. Perhaps in the morning…"

I stared at him, not quite comprehending his meaning. "But Father, you must summon the authorities. We cannot deal with this as a private matter. A man has been murdered in our home."

"Do you think I am not aware of that?" he demanded. His lips thinned, and his eyes were hard with anger and grief. "Child, I *am* the authority in this part of Sussex, or had you forgotten?"

"Of course not, I simply meant—"

"I know well enough what you meant. You think I ought to summon the coroner, that there should be an inquest, neat and tidy, and with what result? My own niece sent to be hanged?"

"Surely they will not hang her."

His anger ebbed then, leaving him spent. He rubbed a hand over his face. "That is the difficulty. They will not hang her. They dare not because she is of my blood. And yet, how can I ever look any man in the eye after that and pronounce justice if I will not seek it for my own?"

Brisbane remained silent, his good arm folded over the sling at his chest.

"What do you mean to do then?" I asked softly.

"I must send to London tomorrow. The Metropolitan Police may be depended upon to be discreet and to be impartial."

I did not like to point out to him that no one was likely to be impartial when an earl was involved in a murder investigation. Instead I nodded. "Very well. And what of this examination?"

Brisbane spoke up. "Much may be learned from studying the corpse, but it must be done quickly. In the morning we can go into Blessingstoke and telegraph Scotland Yard, though it is anyone's guess how long it will take them to dispatch an investigator. In here, he will be quite cool and fresh whenever their man arrives. I mean to examine the victim first and make very certain they miss nothing."

Already he was thinking of Snow as the corpse, the victim. It was astonishing to me how quickly Brisbane could slip into the role of investigator, but even as I looked at him I could see his eyes were bright, his jaw set, his very mien one of intense excitement.

I sighed. Between the pair of them they had decided on a course of action I could not entirely approve. The villagers were accustomed to thinking of Father as little less than a demigod. Yet I could not help but wonder how they would like having their minor county officials passed over entirely in favour of London investigators. They would very likely be affronted, and to add insult to injury, I was not completely certain what Father was proposing was legal. But the point was not worth arguing. The combination of Father's very deep pockets and very blue blood was a potent one.

"There are no windows. There will not be ample light," I pointed out, hoping to dissuade them on the grounds of practicality. Father waved a dismissive hand.

"With a few mirrors and enough lamps, I believe we can illuminate the room sufficiently."

"Not to mention all of the helpful kitchen maids and scullery maids and pot boys. Really, Father, there is no hope that this will go unnoticed."

"I am aware of that, Julia," Father said with some asperity. "I am also aware I must bear the responsibility of the reckoning of this crime. Every decision I make will be scrutinised and found to be lacking. That is why I must have your help, both of you."

He sighed heavily and ran a hand through his thick white hair. "Brisbane, you will have to gather the evidence and prepare the reports. With Julia's help."

I felt a hot rush of triumph. Brisbane did not even look my direction. "I am prepared to do what I can for you, my lord, but surely there is no need to involve Lady Julia."

"There is," my father put in wearily. "She knows the family and the Abbey. She can give you information, and she will be invaluable in dealing with the ladies of the party. I know the wretched girl has confessed, but I wish every provision for her innocence to be explored." He shook his head. "I can only think that her mind must have been quite deranged for her to have done this terrible thing."

"Very well," Brisbane said, grudgingly. "Lady Julia and I will work together."

"Good," Father replied. "Now, we will seal this room, and address the rest of them."

"What will you say to them?" I asked as we filed slowly out of the game larder.

Father shrugged, his upright posture failing him only a little. "I cannot imagine. But I shall think of something."

THE THIRTEENTH CHAPTER

The game's afoot!
—HENRY V

s I made my way from the game larder to the lesser drawing room, I realised the lights, doused for the game of sardines, had been lit. Every sconce, lamp, and candelabrum blazed, banishing the shadows. It was little consolation. The very air of the place felt different to me now that murder had been done here, and I wondered if I would ever feel quite as I once had about my home.

Just as I approached the drawing room, the door was flung open and Alessandro bolted out, his face twisted with emotion.

"Ah, Julia!" he cried. He rushed to me, but before he could engage in any impropriety, I raised a hand. He stopped in his tracks, scant inches from me. He took my hand in his.

"Alessandro. I see that you have heard about Mr. Snow. It is a terrible thing."

He shook his head. "Julia, I do not understand this. I knew nothing until Lysander came and found me. I was on the other side of the Abbey, in the room with all of the plants. I cannot think of the word."

His brow furrowed in concentration, or perhaps in frustration.

"The conservatory?" I hazarded.

"*Si*, conservatory. I was there, and Lysander came to look for me. He said that Signore Snow has been murdered in the chapel, and that Miss Lucy, she has confessed to this horrible thing."

I could feel the confusion emanating from him. I had left Father and Brisbane to finish their preparations in the game larder, and I knew I had but a moment until they appeared. For either of them to find me in a tête-à-tête with Alessandro was not a complication I relished.

I adopted my most soothing tone. "Yes, it is frightful. And what Lysander told you is correct. But my father has matters under control, and we must soldier on."

He started, his skin going quite pale under its usual olive cast. "Soldiers? There will be soldiers here?"

"No, my dear. It is simply an expression we English use. It means we must do our duty and not give way to emotion."

Alessandro blinked at me, and I realised then how impossible it would be to explain the concept of a stiff upper lip to an Italian.

I turned him and prodded him toward the door. "Come now. Father wishes us all gathered in the drawing room, and he will be along any minute."

He cast a doubtful look at me over his shoulder, but he went without a murmur. If only every man in my life were so biddable,

I thought ruefully. He paused at the door to permit me to enter first, and I made at once for the chair nearest Portia.

In the drawing room, the assembled company was solemn. Brandy and tea had been supplied, but no one seemed very inclined to partake. Cups and glasses were clutched in pale, nerveless fingers, and Charlotte for one, trembled so badly I thought her cup would shatter in its saucer. Plum stood by the window, glowering at the blackness beyond. Violante was grasping Ly's hand so tightly their fingers had gone white.

"Where is Aunt Dorcas? And Hortense?" I whispered to Portia.

"Bed," she murmured. "The old fright was tired, so Hortense saw her up to bed. Then she told Aquinas she was retiring herself. Something about a headache. They would not have heard the screaming, and I thought it best to let them be."

I nodded. "Time enough for them to hear of it tomorrow."

By way of reply, she took a deep swallow of whiskey, closing her eyes for a long moment. I could just see the fine lines at their corners, newly incised from fatigue. I felt a rush of affection for her then, and covered her hand with my own. She grasped it, and a ghost of a smile touched her lips.

Portia looked up in relief a moment later when Father entered, but it was Emma who rose, deadly pale but composed.

"My lord uncle!" she cried, her lips trembling. She bowed her head and raised a handkerchief to her mouth.

Father patted her back, a trifle awkwardly. "There, there, my girl."

"What happened?" she asked him, simply, as a child might have done.

Father shook his head. "I do not know, save that Mr. Snow is murdered, by her hand, Lucy claims. She refuses to leave the chapel, and I have respected her wishes."

"But why?" Emma demanded, pulling away. "It is so cold there. Why can she not go to her room?"

"My dear," Father said, moving to take a chair by the fire, "I would have been perfectly willing to confine her to her room if she had wished it. She remains in the chapel by her own choice."

"Confined to her room?" Emma followed him, sinking to a needlepoint hassock at his feet. "Why must she be confined at all?"

Sir Cedric interjected, his face stormy, "I imagine his lordship feels he has no choice." His voice shook, as though he held the reins of his emotion, but only lightly.

Father said nothing, but merely looked at Emma, waiting for her to comprehend. Portia handed him a whiskey, and he gave her a feeble smile in thanks.

Emma shook her head slowly. "You cannot believe it of her. She could never have done this."

Father took a sip of his whiskey. "Child, there is a dead man in my house, and a girl who claims to have killed him. I am compelled to believe her."

Emma gave an anguished sob and tore at her handkerchief, shredding the fine lawn with her nails. "No! I will not believe it."

The rest of us were silent as Emma gave vent for a moment to her emotion. Charlotte and I caught one another's gaze, and I was moved to see she looked quite devastated by our family's tragedy. Portia went to pour whiskey for Brisbane and myself, while Sir

Cedric sat, his face betraying his disquiet. He seemed to be struggling, and I wondered if he doubted Lucy. They had known each other a bare two months. Was he pondering now if the girl he loved so passionately was capable of bashing a man over the head with a candelabrum?

Henry Ludlow simply stared into the depths of his teacup as though scrying for answers. His eyes were shadowed, and he looked desperately tired. Perhaps he felt guilty for his outburst in the chapel, condemning Lucy as she stood, her hands wet with the blood of Lucian Snow. Or perhaps he was relieved to think his kinsman had been spared marriage to a woman capable of such atrocity.

From the window, Plum moved to stand behind Charlotte's chair, his face pale in the shadows. She did not turn to look at him, but her back relaxed a little, and I noticed that Brisbane watched the pair with as much interest as I did.

After a moment, Emma composed herself, wiping her eyes and smoothing her hair. "So she must be turned over to the assizes?"

Father shook his head. "Tomorrow I will send to Scotland Yard for an investigator and hand this matter over to the proper authorities. Any local justice will be seen as tainted."

Emma's face fell, and I knew she must be thinking of the little girl whose plaits she wove with ribbons when they were children, the little girl she comforted with bedtime stories. Father looked at her, his eyes warm with sympathy. "We have this short time until the investigator arrives to gather any evidence that the courts may take into consideration when choosing to exercise leniency."

His tone, however, left small doubt that he considered leniency an unlikely prospect.

I had thought she would weep afresh at this, but she merely nodded and resumed her seat next to Sir Cedric.

Sir Cedric rose, his face purpling with rage. "I have heard quite enough. I will not have my future wife treated like a common criminal. She will be released now, and I will take her away from here myself."

Father rolled his glass of whiskey between his palms. His voice was deadly pleasant. "I think not, Cedric. This is my home, and the girl is my relation. You are not yet married, therefore you have no rights in the matter. If you do not care for my management of this affair, you are free to go. But if you stay, you will not question me again."

For a moment I thought Sir Cedric might actually have an apoplexy on the spot. He raised a shaking finger at Father. "How dare you, sir! Your high-handedness is not to be borne. I will not have her treated with such suspicion."

"She will be treated with suspicion the whole of her life if you do not do as I say!" Father roared, slamming his whiskey glass onto the table. "Do you not see that, man? Everywhere she goes, whispers will follow her. Everyone she meets will wonder, *did she get away with murder?* The taint will live with you forever, poisoning your lives, and it will poison your children's lives as well. Is that what you want?" Father demanded brutally.

Sir Cedric opened his mouth, then closed it again, gaping like a newly caught fish. Finally, he gave up the fight and dropped heavily into his seat. "I will put all of my resources at her disposal," he said hollowly. "I will do everything in my power to secure her freedom."

Emma murmured her thanks, and I caught Brisbane's glance. I believe in that moment we were thinking the same thing: for all Father's breeding and Sir Cedric's money, Lucy had confessed to murder. It seemed rather a good bet she would swing for it.

Father cleared his throat. "I have asked Lord Wargrave, as he has some experience in these matters, to prepare the reports and statements the courts will require. You will all cooperate with him fully, should he choose to avail himself of your assistance."

Father's tone left no room for misinterpretation: this was an order. The rest of us, accustomed to such directives, merely nodded. But Charlotte King dropped her teacup. The delicate handle snapped and tea splashed over her pretty slippers.

"Experience?" Her eyes flew from Father to Brisbane. "My lord, what can his lordship mean?"

Brisbane regarded her coolly. "His lordship means in my capacity as a private inquiry agent."

Charlotte clutched at the saucer. Her complexion was noticeably paler, and I wondered for a moment if I should ring for a vinaigrette.

"My lord, you astonish me. I had no notion you were in trade," she said, her voice flinty. "I think we must speak of this when we have more privacy."

Brisbane inclined his head, and I smiled to myself. Behind her, Plum's expression had turned decidedly smug.

Father issued a few more instructions then, most notably that no one was to approach the chapel without his permission, nor were messages to be sent to Lucy that he had not first approved. Emma asked if she might go and sit with her now that she was in command of herself, and he agreed. She also received permission to bring her sister a few articles she might require for her comfort.

Father then bade the party good-night in a clear gesture of dismissal. First to leave was Charlotte King, sweeping out without a word of apology for the broken cup or a glance for her erstwhile fiancé. Plum trailed behind her and Portia followed with Emma. Ly and Violante walked out slowly, murmuring softly in Italian. Alessandro followed them, casting bewildered glances at me as he left. I lingered with Brisbane, watching Sir Cedric and Henry take their leave.

Father stretched his legs to the hassock. His rheumatism was doubtless playing up again as a result of the cold. He showed no sign of stirring. I laid a hand on his shoulder.

"Are you coming, Father?"

He shook his head. "Not quite yet. I mean to finish this rather excellent whiskey and have a bit of a think. Good night, both of you. There will be much to do tomorrow."

Brisbane and I bade him good-night and left him. Much to my surprise, Brisbane escorted me up the staircase and through the long gallery of the dorter toward my room. It was a breach of propriety for him to do so, but I did not think anyone would trouble about it under the circumstances.

Before we reached my room, Brisbane took my elbow and turned me to face him.

"I realise his lordship has sanctioned your involvement, and I do not deny you could be quite helpful in the present circumstances," he began. I bit back a retort. "However," he went on, "I will reserve the authority to remove you from this investigation at any time should I feel your safety may be in jeopardy."

I could not help it. I laughed.

"Brisbane, you must be joking. That is quite possibly the most pompous thing you have ever said to me."

His grip tightened. "I am not in the mood for jokes, my lady. I meant precisely what I said. If at any time I think there is even the merest possibility of danger, I will have you out of here if I have to throw you over my shoulder and carry you out on my back."

The image was a delicious one, but I pushed it aside. I could feel the warmth of his palm even through the heavy satin of my sleeve. "But we were partners together—we solved a murder between us, or had you forgotten?"

"I have forgotten nothing," he ground out. His eyes dropped for an instant to my lips, and I knew he was thinking of that reckless kiss on Hampstead Heath. He dragged his gaze back to mine, his eyes suddenly cool and pitiless. "Most particularly, I have not forgotten that I bungled that investigation so badly you nearly died."

I paused. It was true the investigation had ended badly. But that had been due as much to my own foolhardiness as anything else. In fact, Brisbane's timely intervention had saved my life. I could not believe he thought otherwise.

I shook my head slowly. "No," I whispered, "all those months in Italy—not a word from you. It was not because of that. Not even you could be so willfully, blindly stupid. You saved my life."

"I nearly cost it," he countered. I searched his face, but it was implacable, cold and white-lipped as marble.

He dropped my arm, and I stepped back. His fury was almost tangible as it crackled in the air between us.

I swallowed hard, forcing my voice to evenness. "I have as much right to investigate this murder as you. This is my home, my family, and it is my father who has lent his authority to my involvement. So do not think that I mean to step aside simply because you click your fingers at me. We are partners again, whether it pleases you or not. Besides," I finished with a malicious smile, "someone will have to make inquiries while you settle matters with Charlotte. I rather think your engagement is at an end."

I hurried down the corridor to my room. I hazarded a glance behind me as I gained my room, and was not surprised to find Brisbane staring after me with a baleful expression.

As I undressed, I realised my hands were shaking, an inconvenience without Morag to assist me. But eventually I fought my way out of the gown and went to stand in front of the looking-glass. Where Brisbane had grasped my arm there were bruises rising, faintly violet in the candlelight. The sleeve itself was crushed, and no amount of sponging would salvage it. I thrust the gown into the wardrobe and closed the door. I would not wear it again.

THE FOURTEENTH CHAPTER

Who dares not stir by day must walk by night.
—KING JOHN

In spite of the evening's events, I drifted off to sleep rather quickly. I had thought the image of Lucian Snow's shattered head would stay with me, but even that horror was not able to blunt the dullness of the volume of Plutarch I had taken to bed. I fell asleep with it draped over my chest and woke some time later to find the candle guttered and the fire nearly burned down to ash. It was chilly in my room despite the tapestries and thick carpets, and I rose to poke at the fire, wrapping myself in a coverlet from the bed. Florence was slumbering away in her basket, only her nose poking out from the fur tippet.

I jabbed at the fire a bit and tossed a shovelful of coal onto the grate. It caught, and I sat for some minutes, warming myself and thinking of Lucian Snow. He had been an attractive and charming man and a confirmed flirt, that much was certain. But what about him had driven Lucy to murder? Had he flirted with her, then scorned her? The notion was laughable. I had a suspicion Lucian Snow reserved his attentions for wealthy, unattached ladies of good family. Lucy was betrothed, decidedly not wealthy, and though she was a March, the connection was a slender one. Of course, he was younger and much more personable than Cedric, and there was always the possibility he might have seduced Lucy away from her bridegroom. She was young and impulsive to the point of recklessness at times. It would not be difficult for a persuasive and passionate man to open her eyes and awaken her sensuality, I mused.

But no, Lucian had seemed to have more of an eye to the main chance than that. I thought of our conversations, his warm eyes and lingering fingers. He had been laying the groundwork for a courtship, I was certain of it. He had nocked his arrow toward something more profitable than an impoverished virgin.

But if he had no interest in Lucy, then what was her interest in him? He was worldly and whimsical and no doubt irreligious, all qualities to be deplored in a curate, but who among us had not met a dozen such like him before? Fortune was not always kind to second and third sons. With no solid expectations, the church was often the only means of a comfortable living. More than one churchman had been made of a dissolute rogue. Clearly, this had been Lucian's lot, but how did it touch Lucy?

Asking her directly was out of the question. She was in a state, and I had no doubt it would take all of Father's considerable powers of persuasion to convince her to abandon sanctuary and give herself over to the authorities. I had little confidence she would stand up to their questions; I was not prepared to subject her to mine.

But I knew I would not sleep again without attempting to find some answers. I rose from my seat by the fire and found my slippers and a heavy velvet dressing gown. I relit my chamberstick from the fire and fixed it firmly into its holder. Silently, I slipped from my room and made my way down the gallery of the dorter, across the landing, and down another corridor until I reached the turning I wanted.

I peeped around the corner, scanning the bachelors' wing for any sign of activity. Formerly the lay brothers' dormitory, the bachelors' wing was comprised of a broad corridor with windows overlooking the central cloister spanning the length on one side, and a chain of bedchambers on the other. The wing ended at the door to the guest room in the Galilee Tower. In that room a tiny spiral stair rose to the bell tower itself where the great bell rested in silence. I thought of Lucy grasping the sanctuary ring with blood-slicked hands and shivered. The bell ought to have rung for her, but it had remained silent, perhaps rusted mute after centuries of disuse. Deliberately, I pushed aside such morbid thoughts and tugged my dressing gown about me more tightly as I moved into the bachelors' wing.

The clock had just struck two, and all was perfectly still in that part of the Abbey. A faint moon, very nearly full, shed its pale silver light through the bank of graceful leaded windows. Hastily, I blew out the chamberstick. The moonlight was just enough illumination for my purpose.

Holding my breath, I crept along the corridor, careful to keep to the middle of the way where the stone floor was thickly carpeted. The bars of dull silver moonlight gave just enough light to read the cards slotted by each door. I squinted at the names. *The Honourable Eglamour March,* Plum, as he was known in the family. He was sleeping in the Highland Room, a smallish bedroom, charmingly furnished with tartans and antlers. The door was closed, and though I paused a moment I heard nothing. Beyond lay the Maze Room—so named for its perfectly framed view of the Tudor maze in the garden—and Alessandro. All was silence there as well.

I moved on. *Sir Cedric Eastley.* Aquinas had put him in the Yellow Room, the best of the bachelor rooms with its primrose taffeta hangings and a pair of Gainsboroughs flanking the bed. Strictly speaking, the room ought to have gone to Brisbane as the ranking bachelor, but Aunt Hermia had probably devised the sleeping arrangements before she left for London. She never did manage to work out such details properly.

I had passed Sir Cedric's door and had almost reached the Tower Room when I felt a rush of air against my face. I opened my mouth to exclaim, but before I could do so, a strong hand clamped about my wrist and dragged me into the room. The door was closed behind me and I was pushed up against it, the hand now firmly pressed over my mouth.

I shoved it away. "Brisbane," I hissed, "what do you think you are about? If you wanted to speak to me—"

"Do shut up," he whispered harshly. I shivered as his lips grazed the curves of my ear. "You are not the only person about."

I pushed his hand aside and caught my breath. "Who?"

"I do not know yet. I was just about to find out when you came blundering along."

"I do not blunder," I began, but a single firm finger laid over my lips silenced me. I was acutely conscious then of my state of relative undress, and his. He was still wearing his evening trousers and a fine, heavy white linen shirt, but this last garment had been casually opened almost to the waist, and topping the ensemble was a long robe of handsome dark red silk, flung over his injured shoulder to dashing effect. His hair was a trifle more unruly than usual, and the faint smell of sweet Spanish tobacco clung to the finger that still touched my lips.

His strong form pressed me to the door, and I began to be aware of a somewhat breathless sensation, quite like the one I had experienced during my trip to Florence upon first seeing Michelangelo's excellent rendering of *David*. I had spent rather a long time admiring the perfect symmetry of the statue's musculature, the way the breadth of his shoulders and the arrogant stance of his legs had countered the elegance of his profile and the sleekness of his flanks. It occurred to me, pressed as I was between Brisbane and the door, that Brisbane himself seemed to have almost precisely the same proportions as that exquisite work of art.

"Stop wriggling," he growled, his breath warm on my neck.

I cannot recall precisely what happened next. I must have said or—rather more likely—done something which conveyed the direction of my thoughts, for the next thing I knew, he was kissing me with thoroughness and enthusiasm. It was highly gratifying.

I had just begun to apply myself to a response with complete abandon when a faint noise distracted me. It took some seconds to place the sound, and several more to get Brisbane's attention. His focus was quite masterful. In the end, I was obliged to use rather forceful measures.

He swore and broke off, rather short of breath and rubbing his shin. "You kicked me! What the devil was that for? For the love of God, Julia, if you did not want me to kiss you, you should never have—"

I broke in swiftly, untwining my fingers from his hair. "I heard a noise, a door closing in the corridor." It only occurred to me later I should not have interrupted him. It might have been highly useful to know what action on my part had prompted such an uninhibited response.

Brisbane's eyes glittered in the feeble moonlight and he swore again, which I must admit rather pleased me. I too was rather regretting the end of our interlude. But the investigation must necessarily take precedence, and I primly removed his good hand from my person. He stepped back, and I patted my garments into place, giving a little sigh of impatience.

"Brisbane, you have ripped my favourite nightdress."

He showed not the slightest remorse. "I will buy you another," he muttered, pushing me aside and kneeling to peer out the keyhole.

"You most certainly will not. Of all the wildly inappropriate—" I let my voice trail off as I glanced around the room. It was round, as all tower rooms should be, the narrow lancet windows fitted with stained glass depicting the March hares. The draperies and bedclothes were bottle-green velvet edged in gold, enhancing the medieval atmosphere. I was not surprised to see that Brisbane had already put his stamp upon the place. He did not so much stay in a room as *inhabit* it. A pair of boots stood upon the hearth and a stack of books teetered on the bedside table, each of them marked with a playing card to hold his place. A telescope perched on slender legs at one of the windows, a chart of the stars unfurled beside it. His discarded silk neckcloth was draped carelessly over his pillow, doubtless where he had tugged it off as he began to disrobe. I looked hastily away, noting the half-empty glass of whiskey and the nearly full decanter on a little inlaid table that stood beside the velvet armchair by the fire. There was a cushion squashed into the depths of the chair and his black greatcoat shrouded the back of it, a comfortable place to while away a cold winter's evening with a good book. Toilet articles—combs, clothes brushes, and a wickedly sharp razor—were neatly arranged on the washstand, and I wondered how he managed his ablutions with his injury.

"Brisbane," I whispered. "How do you shave yourself? You've only the one good arm. I should think it frightfully awkward to manage."

"It did not seem to hamper me a moment ago," he returned mildly.

Whether he was making reference to his abduction of me or to what followed, I could not say. Before I could speak, he had sprung to his feet and was easing the door open.

The corridor was empty.

I prodded Brisbane. "If you heard something, we must investigate."

"I know that," he said through clenched teeth. "Would you kindly remove your finger from between my ribs?"

I obliged him and we slid out into the corridor, moving swiftly as we dared. When we reached the end of the corridor, Brisbane flung out his arm, pressing me flat against the stone wall and knocking the breath out of me.

"Ooof," I said, gasping a little. He shook his head, frowning at me. It was on the tip of my tongue to tell him what I thought of his methods, but by that time he was edging his head around the corner to determine if the staircase was clear. He gave a little exhalation of disgust and dropped his arm. I took this as a sign I was free to move and stepped around him into an empty gallery. There were perhaps a dozen doors that led off of it, and at the end the main staircase, leading to the other floors and a hundred other rooms.

I stepped back. "If there was indeed a phantom, we have lost him. He might have gone anywhere, and if we attempt to follow him now, we shall doubtless rouse the entire household. Shall we search Mr. Snow's room instead?"

Brisbane gave me a piercing look. "Why?"

I sighed. "Because he is the victim. Perhaps among his possessions lurks some clue to why Lucy did this terrible thing. Perhaps even some mitigating factor can be found that might sway the judges to clemency."

Brisbane shot a quick look back down the gallery, then took

my elbow and led me to Lucian Snow's room. Father had taken the precaution of having it locked, but such an inconvenience was of no consequence to Brisbane. From the pocket of his dressing gown he extracted two slender steel picks. He handed one to me. "Put this into the lock and hold it steady," he instructed. He knelt, his thigh brushing my leg, and slid its mate into the lock. He kept his eyes closed, working by touch, and as his hand grazed my fingers, I had the oddest sensation that this was somehow even more intimate than the kiss we had just shared. He had the lock sprung in a brief moment, and we were inside, the door closed behind us.

The room was gloomy. A cloud had passed over the moon, throwing the room into deep shadow. Brisbane went to the bedside table, swift and sure-footed as a cat, and struck a match to the candle, illuminating the room passably well. I glanced about, not entirely surprised to find that Lucian Snow was not a particularly tidy person. A discarded shirt and neckcloth were draped at the foot of his bed, and the writing table was a litter of books and papers. He had been given the Blue Room, a small but elegant chamber, with dark blue and silver hangings and a rather nice suite of mahogany furniture. There was a bottle of excellent port on the table, as well as a humidor filled with expensive cigars. The air was thick with the acrid smell of stale smoke.

I glanced around, taking quick inventory of his belongings. There was a small toilet case, and a portfolio of fine morocco on the writing table. I searched them both, paying particular atten-tion to the letters in the portfolio. There were only two, pleas from his sisters for money, and nothing of any interest whatsoever in the toilet case. His brushes were not as clean as they might have been, but were exceptionally fine quality, as was the ivory razor slotted neatly into its case.

"Mr. Snow did appreciate nice things," I murmured. When Brisbane did not reply, I looked up to find him standing as I had left him, propped against the door. I would have thought him bored with the entire endeavour, save that his expression was one of expectation, as though he were waiting for something.

"Do you not mean to help?" I demanded.

He shrugged his good shoulder, the candlelight playing off the planes of his face, throwing the tiny scar on his cheekbone into relief. It was a small, perfect crescent moon and I wondered, not for the first time, on which of his travels he had acquired it. "You seem to have the matter well in hand."

"Don't be obstructionist. We are supposed to be investigating Snow's death. It seems logical enough to begin here if we mean to understand why Lucy killed him."

"She has confessed it. The motive is largely immaterial."

I snapped the case closed and straightened, fixing him with a basilisk stare. "You gave Father your word you would investigate. You know perfectly well the courts may grant her leniency should there be cause for it."

"Yes, and she is the proper one to supply it. Sniffing through Snow's things will not tell us what we need to know to save Lucy from the noose."

"You are a brute," I told him. I moved to the wardrobe and eased it open. Snow had been a bit more careful with his clothes than the rest of his things, or at least the footman who had unpacked for him had been. The garments were neatly hung, and his shoes were arranged on the floor of the wardrobe with precision.

"I do not understand you," I complained, feeling the pockets of Snow's clothes for anything unexpected. "Were you not the one who preached to me that stones must never be left unturned in an investigation?"

"Yes, if one has nothing more pressing."

I ducked back out of the wardrobe to look at him. "It is half past two in the morning. What engagement can possibly be more pressing than searching Snow's rooms?"

He said nothing, and after a moment, it occurred to me he had not heard me at all. His eyes had a faraway look, and it was apparent he was listening closely to something on the other side of the door.

I felt a quick, sharp lance of misery. Surely he could not have a liaison planned with Charlotte? She had been icy and aloof when she retired for the evening. She had neither looked at him nor spoken to him after it was revealed that he was an inquiry agent. But what if he meant to cajole her, to soothe her to sweetness, affection even, with an explanation? If any man could do it, it was Brisbane. I had more cause than most to appreciate the devastating effect of his charm when he chose to employ it.

Before I could ask what he was about, Brisbane eased open the door and slipped out, closing it silently behind him.

"Men," I muttered, returning to the wardrobe. I continued to complain to myself as I searched. I did not relish putting my hands into the pockets of Snow's clothes, or into the toes of his shoes. The only time I had ever handled Edward's clothes had been after his death when, as a good widow, I packed up his belongings and sent them to charity.

I was just about to admit defeat when I thrust my hand into the last shoe and my fingers touched something hard and lumpy. I turned the shoe over and emptied it into my palm. It was a handkerchief, knotted securely. It took some minutes to release the knots, but I did so, careful not to damage the fabric. Inside, I found a tiny collection of jewels. There was a string of amber beads, a bracelet of flowers fashioned out of coral, a brooch set with turquoises and seed pearls. And in the midst of them sat a clever little jade monkey, his tail curved like a question mark.

I looked over each piece carefully, making note of the engravings. They were dainty, delicate things, suited to a lady's boudoir, and I could not imagine how Snow had come by them. I wrapped them carefully in the handkerchief, touching the embroidered monogram lightly with a finger as I slipped the little bundle in my pocket. There were two mysteries to solve now, I reflected. First, why had Lucy killed Lucian Snow? And why were my Aunt Hermia's jewels in his possession when he died?

THE FIFTEENTH CHAPTER

We that are true lovers run into strange capers.
—AS YOU LIKE IT

*D*espite my iron resolve to search Snow's bedchamber thoroughly, the room was growing colder by the minute, and I was uncomfortably aware that I had not yet solved the mystery of the phantom. I knew it for pretense, of course, a childish trick to alarm the superstitious. But I could not like the idea of someone playing tricks when there were other, more sinister events afoot. A man had been murdered in my home, and it was not impossible that his death had some connection, however tenuous, to our spectre.

Certainly, the costume of a phantom could be assumed for entirely innocuous reasons. An assignation, for one. Not only would a spectral disguise keep people at a distance if one happened to be spotted, it also rather neatly preserved one's incognito. Certainly it might have been Sir Cedric, but I had little doubt Lucy intended to hold him at bay until she was properly married. Given her mother's sad history, Lucy would have marked her lesson well and insisted upon a ring before submitting to the ultimate caresses.

But Sir Cedric was not the only gentleman with a lady love at Bellmont Abbey, I realised with a start. Father had brought Hortense under his roof, a notion that did not bear thinking about, I decided with a shudder. I liked Hortense very well, but the idea of Father playing the Casanova was faintly distasteful. Besides which, Father would never think it necessary to don a disguise to pay a nocturnal visit to his *inamorata*. He would be discreet, I was certain, but haunting his own hallways was carrying things a bit too far.

That left Brisbane. Instantly my mind whipped back nearly two years in time, to a conversation I had had with Portia as we strolled in Hyde Park. I had just met Brisbane for the first time, and Portia was entertaining me with tales of his exploits, both as a fighter and a lover. *He uses disguises sometimes in the course of his investigations…for discretion…he came to her once dressed as a chimney sweep. Quite invigorating, don't you think?*

Ruthlessly, I pushed the memory aside. I refused to torment myself with thoughts of him and Charlotte. He did not mean to marry her, and whatever his game with her, I meant to discover it.

And then there was Plum, I thought, dread rippling in my stomach. I had seen him once or twice watching Charlotte with some warmth. Her manner toward Brisbane had been correct and deferential, but not affectionate. Perhaps, for her part, the marriage to Brisbane was a means of securing her future. And if her heart was not involved, she might well permit herself to engage in a dalliance with Plum. For Plum's part, he was a great admirer of beauty, and not overly scrupulous if the beauty belonged to another. The fact that donning ghostly draperies and lurking in corridors was just the sort of lark Plum would find hilarious did not comfort me.

I shook myself, ashamed of my doubts. Plum's amorous exploits in Italy—and they had been legion—had been restrained compared to most of the travellers we had encountered. Everyone went to Italy to dally with the *signorinas*. Holiday romances were one thing. To assume he would interfere with a betrothal was another, and I resolved to put the notion from my mind.

I extinguished the light and crept to the door, easing into the corridor. There was no one about. Brisbane had disappeared, and in spite of his twitchiness, there was no sign of the spectre. On a whim, I turned my steps to the staircase and made my way silently downstairs. It was slow going, for the moon had disappeared entirely, and I had to hold the banister, feeling each step carefully beneath my slipper before I descended another tread. At the bottom a lamp glimmered faintly, the night-light that Aquinas always left lit—a single brave little flame, wavering in the chilly draughts. It threw shadows down the main corridor, but I steeled my resolve and made my way toward the chapel. At the opposite end of the nave I could just make out Maurice, his claws and teeth terrible in the half-light.

Another turn and I was at the chapel, the doors firmly closed, William IV asleep at his post. His head was sunk low on his chest, bobbing heavily with each slow breath.

I clicked my tongue at him. "Really, this won't serve. Do wake up," I said, poking at his shoulder. Suddenly, he gave a great shudder and slid down in the chair. He gave a deep, resonant snore and muttered in his sleep.

I bent swiftly and smelled his breath.

"Dead drunk," I murmured. He smelled strongly of brandy and there was a faint, seraphic smile curving his lips.

I stepped over him and put my eye to the keyhole of the great doors. The key had been lost ages ago and never replaced. Now the enormous keyhole was a tidy little window on the chapel and its erstwhile inhabitants. Not surprisingly after her ordeal, Lucy was curled onto a crude pallet of blankets, sleeping deeply, her mouth agape, one hand flung above her head. Emma was slumped next to her, a hand tucked in Lucy's. The tableau touched me. I was close to my own sisters, Portia in particular, and I could only imagine the anguish Emma must be feeling at the possibility of losing her beloved girl to the hangman's noose.

It seemed like an intrusion to spy upon her grief. I turned to leave then, and saw something gleam out of the tail of my eye. I peered closer and realised it was a brandy bottle, tipped on its side and quite empty. I looked at the slumbering footman and bent swiftly to look under his chair. No bottle or glass there, I observed. How then did he manage to become intoxicated?

Nibbling my lower lip, I turned the heavy knob of the chapel door, easing it open just enough to slip inside. I tiptoed to where my cousins slept. I picked up the bottle and sniffed it. Brandy, yes, but something more, a shadow of something bitter.

I leaned over Emma, listening to her quiet, even breathing. It was so soft I could scarcely hear it, and when I pressed a finger to her wrist, I felt the merest flutter. Frightened now, I put my hand to her heart. The beat was faint and slow. I paused only to touch the pale skin at Lucy's wrist. It was as weak as her sister's. I took to my heels, bottle in hand, fairly flying up the stairs and down the dormitory wing to the Tower Room. I was careful to keep to the carpet, my slippers noiseless, and when I reached Brisbane's room, I scratched softly, muttering prayers as I did so.

He opened the door at once and I pushed inside. He closed the door behind me and turned, his back to it as if to shield me from whatever had caused me to take flight.

"What has happened?" he demanded. The bedclothes were askew and the bed still bore the impression of where he had lain, but the lamps were lit and he held a book in his hand.

"It's Emma and Lucy. I think they have been drugged, and the footman as well," I told him, holding out the bottle.

He took it, sniffing deeply. "Brandy, but it has been tampered with." He sniffed again, then touched his tongue to the rim of the bottle.

I snatched it from him. "Are you quite mad? You do not know what may be in there."

He shrugged. "It is laudanum, quite a lot of it, I should think. How are they?"

I spread my hands helplessly. "Senseless. They seem to be sleeping, but I can scarcely feel the pulse at their wrists, and their heartbeats are slow and heavy. The footman has been drugged as well, but he seems less affected."

"He is taller than either of them by a foot and doubtless

heavier than either by an hundredweight," he commented, moving to the wardrobe. He flung open the door and pulled out a small leather case.

"Brisbane, you cannot mean to physic them yourself. They need a doctor."

"Look outside," he ordered. "The snow has begun, and it will only get worse. It would take more than two hours to fetch a doctor from Blessingstoke and they haven't that long if we mean to keep them alive."

"Oh," I said faintly. I drew myself up to my full height and squared my shoulders. Whatever horrors the night would bring, I was prepared to face them.

Brisbane turned at the door, the case tucked under his arm. He nodded toward the washstand. "Bring the basin. This is not going to be pleasant."

I gulped and nodded, snatching up the basin and following him to the chapel.

The next hours were not ones I can remember with any pleasure. It began with a vicious argument between Brisbane and myself as to whether the rest of the household should be roused. He insisted we should deal with the situation alone, maintaining that until he knew how and why the girls had been drugged, he did not want to alert the malefactor who had attempted to harm them. I flew at him, accusing him of suspecting a member of my family, which he coldly affirmed, and matters deteriorated from there. We were hardly speaking by the time we reached the chapel. Brisbane knelt swiftly over William IV, palpating his pulse and counting.

"He will be fine. His heartbeat is strong. Roll him onto the floor and let him sleep it off," he ordered.

I did as he bade me, swearing fluently under my breath the entire time. William IV was a substantial lad, and it took all of my strength to wrestle him off of the chair and into a more comfortable position on the floor. By the time I reached Brisbane in the chapel he was already finishing his examination. The crimson dressing gown was pooled at his feet, the leather case open beside it. I could just make out an assortment of lethal-looking instruments and small, smoked-glass vials tucked inside.

He glanced up at me, his eyes boring into mine. "They have not been drugged," he said, rising to his feet. "They have been poisoned. We must get them moving and we must dose them with stimulants. Fetch Aquinas and have him bring tea, pots of it, as hot and sweet as he can manage."

I nodded and moved swiftly to the door. I paused the barest moment, glancing back at him. He was on his knees, draping Emma's arm over his good shoulder, levering her to her feet. Her head lolled back against him, her features peaceful and immovable. There was an expression of grim determination on his face and I could hear him talking softly to her, demanding she open her eyes and respond to him. I blinked back sudden tears and left them. It was in God's hands now, God's and Brisbane's.

I rapped lightly at Aquinas' door. He roused at once and answered the door wearing a dapper dressing gown of striped China silk over his trousers.

"My lady?" he inquired, as brightly awake as if I had rung for him at teatime.

"Brisbane needs you. He is in the chapel. Someone has poisoned Miss Emma and Miss Lucy with laudanum. He said to bring tea, masses of it, as hot as you can."

"And sweet," Aquinas said knowingly. "The sugar will help with the shock."

I blinked at him. "How do you—never mind. I do not wish to know. Bring enough for William IV. He has been dosed as well, but Brisbane says he is not as unwell as the ladies. Mind you are quiet. Brisbane does not wish to rouse the household."

I scurried back to the chapel, and in a remarkably short time, Aquinas appeared, bearing quantities of hot coffee and tea, both liberally sweetened. The three of us took turns for the next few hours walking the girls, slapping lightly at their faces and ladling hot drinks down them. They vomited often, but Brisbane merely commented that this was good and encouraged it. William IV slept on, rousing only to take a few cups of tea before resuming his slumbers. Aquinas hefted him onto his back and carried him to his own room, reasoning that the boy would have more privacy in the butler's room than the footmen's dormitory. Some hours before dawn something turned, and both Emma and Lucy seemed suddenly stronger. Their pulses were even now, and stronger, and Brisbane let Emma slide gently to the floor. "They are sleeping," he told me. He stretched then, like a bear rousing itself from winter sleep.

"This cannot have been good for your shoulder," I said softly. "You must be in pain."

He shrugged.

"I have methods," he said blandly. "The ladies ought not stay here," he observed. "It is too cold, and they will be vulnerable to a chill. Aquinas, you take Miss Lucy and I will carry Miss Emma. They will do well enough in their own room."

Aquinas moved quickly to take up Lucy as Brisbane hefted Emma up once more. I remained behind to clear up the traces of the unpleasantness, bone tired and moving as slowly as an old woman. It would be dawn in a few hours and the household would begin to stir. I washed the basin in the butler's pantry and realised I must return it to Brisbane's room before the gentlemen rose.

Once more I traversed the dormitory, scratching lightly at Brisbane's door. After a long moment he answered, still wearing his dressing gown and trousers.

"I have brought your basin."

He took it, but to my surprise, stepped aside. I moved wearily into the room and sank down into one of the armchairs by the fire. "So we may presume they were drugged intentionally. To what purpose?"

Brisbane took the chair opposite me. "Perhaps because they wished to escape the inevitable."

I stared at him. "I do not think I comprehend you. I am stupid with tiredness. Do you mean to suggest they took the laudanum *on purpose?*"

He shrugged. "Possibly. But unlikely. I could believe it except for the footman. If Emma had brought the drugged brandy into the chapel for the purpose of destroying herself and her sister, how did the boy come to drink it?"

I said nothing, but merely nibbled at my lip. It was a dreadful but alarmingly possible theory. Emma was just devoted enough to take Lucy's life to save her from the horror of a state execution. Naturally she would take her own life as well. I hated to admit it, but Brisbane might well have deduced it.

He passed a hand over his brow. I looked at him sharply.

"Headache?"

He smiled, a thin, wry twist of the lips. "Not yet. I have managed to keep them at bay for some time."

"A new medicine?" I asked hopefully.

"Of a sort."

I had discovered during our last investigation that Brisbane was prey to violent headaches, migraines of the most virulent type. After employing traditional medicines to no avail, he had been driven to more exotic methods.

He rose and rummaged in the wardrobe for a moment, returning with a peculiar piece of apparatus he placed on the floor in front of him. It was a tall, slender glass vessel, reaching as high as his knee and divided into a few chambers. Into one he poured some water. Then he fiddled with a live coal and a bit of silver paper and a small greenish-brown brick of some substance I did not recognise. There was a tube attached to the vessel ending in a carved mouthpiece. Brisbane put his mouth to it and drew in a breath. He did this a few more times, and after a moment I could detect a heavy, sweetish smell, very unlike his usual tobacco.

"I know what that is!" I cried suddenly. "It is a hookah!"

"And you know this from your many nights spent in opium dens?" he inquired blandly.

"*Alice in Wonderland,* actually," I admitted. "The caterpillar. '*You are old, Father William.*'"

Brisbane said nothing but drew in a deep, languid breath. He held it in rather a long time, then exhaled slowly, letting a thin, sinuous plume of smoke curl over his head.

"That is not your usual tobacco," I pointed out.

He took another slow, sensual draw off the pipe. "It is called hashish. It is widely used in the East. In small doses it relieves pain and acts as a mild intoxicant."

"And in large doses?"

Brisbane shrugged. "Hallucinations, if one is stupid enough to take too much."

I was silent a moment, thinking of the one time I had seen Brisbane in the throes of a sick headache. Absinthe had been his drug of choice then, leaving him prey to hallucinatory stupors. The experience had been disturbing.

But as he smoked, I realised the hashish seemed to have no effect beyond a mellowing of his temper. He smoked slowly, and as I watched, his pupils dilated and he relaxed visibly. His posture eased, and his eyes, always expressive, seemed to take on a Byzantine slant. It was oddly fascinating. He might have been a sultan at his ease in a *harim,* and I his trembling concubine. The thought was a diverting one, but this was no time to pursue it.

He said nothing for a long while, then he removed the mouthpiece and held it out to me. I swallowed hard, then reached out and took it. His eyes never left mine as I pulled in a modest breath of sweet, heavy smoke. I coughed and my eyes watered, but by the second draw I was comfortable and by the third I held it, then blew the smoke out slowly between my lips.

He pulled the pipe out of my hands. "That is enough. I shall not be responsible for your corruption."

I opened my mouth to remonstrate, but he waved me to silence.

"Now," he began, more briskly than I had expected, "let us theorise for a moment on why anyone else would wish to harm Lucy and Emma."

"Because they saw or know something they oughtn't," I said promptly.

"And who would wish to do that?"

I shrugged. "Poisoning is a woman's method. We must look to the ladies of the house."

"Not necessarily," he began to argue.

I persisted. "I think it was a woman. Moreover, I think she masquerades as a ghost." I paused, then took a deep breath. "I saw a phantom last night, at the end of the ladies' wing in the dorter. It was at least a head shorter than six feet, and the draperies were filmy stuff, wispy, like fingers of fog."

To his credit, Brisbane did not doubt me.

"What did it do?"

"It did nothing. It seemed to look at me, then it vanished."

He looked at me severely. "I would thank you to save the nursery stories for Charlotte. What did it do?"

"I simply mean it was there one moment, and not the next. It slipped behind a tapestry concealing a hidden passage. That particular passage leads to the lumber rooms in the scriptoria, and from there, one might go anywhere in the Abbey. The ghost might have been about some nefarious business. We have, after all, had a murder and two attempted murders since it appeared."

Brisbane shook his head slowly. "It is too early to theorise. We must know more. When the ladies have awakened tomorrow, they must be questioned, and the footman as well. And there is still a corpse to examine and the Reverend Twickham to call upon with the news of his curate's murder."

I gave him a smug smile. "That ghost is somehow connected to this ghastly business. And you will have to admit that I am right."

Brisbane said nothing, but resumed his pipe. The smoke curled around his head, thick and sweet. I felt suddenly light as a feather.

"Brisbane, honestly. I do not see how you can stand the smell of it. It makes me feel quite queer."

He gave me an enigmatic smile and regarded me through half-lidded eyes.

"You'll get used to it in time."

THE SIXTEENTH CHAPTER

Murder, though it have no tongue, will speak
With most miraculous organ.
—HAMLET

For the remainder of the night—what little there was of it—I slept as one dead. I do not know if it was due to the effects of Brisbane's exotic smoke, or simply fatigue from a broken night's rest, but I rose with a slight headache and heavy-lidded eyes. My first thought was of Aunt Hermia's jewels. I had hidden the lumpy little bundle under my pillow for safe-keeping. I felt a stab of guilt when I realised I had forgotten to show them to Brisbane. Then I remembered his occasionally high-handed behaviour and smothered it. It would give me great pleasure to present him with the jewels *and* a reason for their presence among Snow's belongings.

I rose slowly, stretching and yawning widely enough to crack my jaws. Florence was lethargic as well, barely opening her eyes when Morag brought my morning tea. I waved scraps of buttered toast under the dog's nose, but she turned away, burrowing into the fur tippet with a sad little moan.

"Morag, I think Florence is ailing. Ask Cook for some beef tea.

If she drinks that, then an egg, softly cooked, or a bit of chicken and potato."

Morag grumbled at the extra work, but dressed me quickly in a thick gown of black merino edged in velvet ribbon. When she turned back to the wardrobe, I tucked the bundle of Aunt Hermia's jewels into my pocket.

"And my boots. I may step out after breakfast," I told her, making up my mind then that I would accompany Brisbane when he called upon Uncle Fly to break the news of Snow's death.

"You'll not stir a foot outside," Morag said roundly. She went to the draperies and flung them back, rattling the rings on the pole. I went to her side and gasped.

"Heavens, it must have snowed all night."

"As near as. The moat is iced, but not solid enough to walk upon, and the gates are frozen shut. We'll none of us be leaving the Abbey today, not even poor Mr. Snow," she said, her expression mournful.

I stared out at the sullen winter landscape. I did not recognise the view at all. Rather than the sweep of lawns from the moat's edge to the formal gardens and woods, and then to the rolling Downs beyond, there was only softly billowing white, like a great pale ermine mantle draped over the landscape. The distinctive architectural features of the grounds—the statues and staircases, gates and urns—were shapeless white lumps. Beyond the formal gardens, the trees were black against the bleak grey sky, their bare branches encased in ice, like so many gnarled skeleton fingers. Just below my window, the waters of the moat moved black and fathomless beneath a paper-thin sheet of ice. Morag was unfortunately and entirely correct. We were housebound at Bellmont Abbey.

And Morag, who loved nothing better than a good disaster, smiled.

As soon as I left Morag, I made my way to Hortense's chamber. Mindful of Brisbane's instructions not to speak of Emma and Lucy's ordeal, I went to her only for comfort. Hortense's presence was a balm to the most wounded spirit, and I had neglected her terribly since I had returned home. She had been given the Empire Room, perhaps as a compliment to her native country. It was elegant in its simplicity and perfectly suited to set off Hortense's serene beauty. The walls were hung with lily-strewn striped silk, pink and white, and the floor was warmed with an Aubusson, a relic from Madame de Pompadour's apartment at Versailles, if legend was to be believed.

Hortense opened the door at once, her lovely face wreathed in smiles.

"Julia! How lovely to see you. I was just having my morning chocolate. You must have a cup." She was dressed in a morning gown of lilac velvet with a little frill of silver lace at the neck. She resumed her seat and patted the sofa beside her. I sank onto it gratefully.

"We have had so little time to speak, my dear," she chided gently. She poured a cup of thick, frothy chocolate and I sipped at it, feeling the warmth of it clear through to my bones.

"I know. I have missed you as well. And you have been an angel

291

to take on Aunt Dorcas. She is the most terrible old fright, and you are a guest. You should not have to sit with her and pretend to enjoy it."

Hortense did not settle back into the sofa as I had. Even at sixty her posture was exquisite. She perched on the edge, her spine straight as a dancer's. When she reached for her cup, it was like something out of a ballet.

"My dear, it is nothing. She is not such an ogre, you know. She still has some scandalous gossip, though how she manages, living in such isolation, I cannot imagine."

"Well, you are a better woman than I."

We fell quiet a moment, companionable in silence as we sipped at our chocolate.

"I do hope you've given Aquinas your receipt. This is divine," I told her finally.

"I shall do so before I leave, I promise you. And now I know what to give you for Christmas. I've far too many chocolate pots and some of them are very pretty. You must choose your favourite."

I did not insult her by protesting. Although she lived like a lady of means, in truth Hortense's funds were rather thinly stretched. A number of her former lovers, Brisbane included, provided her with annuities, but the sums were not great, and she performed little economies from time to time, such as passing along a treasured possession rather than shopping in the costly establishments on Bond Street. As her things were invariably expensive and her taste was exquisite, I did not mind.

"He is looking well," Hortense said softly. I wondered if thinking of Brisbane had conjured the idea of him.

"Absolutely. Pity about his shoulder, but I am sure he will be perfectly recovered soon enough."

"I was very surprised to hear of his elevation."

I shrugged. "It is not so uncommon. It is the Prime Minister who decides such things. If Brisbane was useful enough in diverting some scandal or righting some wrong, he would wish to show his gratitude."

Hortense was pensive, but even in thought, she was careful not to furrow her brow. Years of strict discipline had kept her face unlined and smooth as a girl's. I tried once to copy her. For an entire day I neither smiled nor frowned. By teatime, I had a vicious headache and resigned myself to wrinkles.

"Still, Nicholas is not so very highly born."

"Not on his mother's side, no. But his father is the grandson of a duke, and his great-uncle, the present duke, still has considerable influence. If he decided to press for the honours, the Prime Minister might well oblige him."

"Perhaps. Your cup is empty, *chérie*. May I pour for you again?"

I held out my cup, watching her slim, elegant white hands as she poured. I had accused her once of using witchcraft to keep her beauty, and it did not seem an entirely ridiculous notion. She was lovelier at sixty than any woman of my acquaintance half her age. Even her hands bore little trace of her years. They were smooth and unblemished, as fine as the porcelain she held.

"Do you look for a ring?" she teased.

"No, of course not," I lied, taking my cup and drinking deeply to cover my confusion. I scalded my tongue.

Hortense smiled at me in spite of herself. "I am not betrothed to your father, you know. And I never will be."

"Hortense, I am sorry. It is none of my concern."

She waved a hand. No jewels sparkled there, but at her wrist she wore a lovely cameo set with diamonds that seemed vaguely familiar.

"Of course it is, my dear. Nothing would give me greater pleasure than to be your stepmama. But to do so, I would have to marry your father, and that is something neither of us has a mind to do."

I set the cup into the saucer carefully. "Then you've spoken of it?"

She lifted a velvet-clad shoulder. "*Naturellement.* But I am a woman very much in love with my freedom, and Hector is a man very much in love with his wife."

I blinked hard, and when I spoke my voice sounded thick to my own ears. "He still loves Mother?"

Hortense's smile was patient as a Botticelli Madonna's. "He is a very loyal man, your father. He has a great heart, and there is a tiny corner of it for me. That is enough for both of us."

I sipped at my chocolate, feeling suddenly very relieved. "You really do not wish to marry him?"

Hortense's eyes danced with mischief. "And have to endure his family? Absolutely not. You are all quite mad."

She winked at me and laughed her sweet, silvery laugh. When she sobered, she wagged a finger at me.

"I should be very cross with you. Never once in your letters did you mention the delicious Conte di Fornacci. I think you are the black horse."

I blinked at her. "Ah. Dark horse. Yes, I suppose. It was all very simple really. He is a friend to Lysander and Plum. He very kindly showed us all over Florence, and when we moved on to Lombardy, it seemed quite natural to invite him along."

"Hmm." That one little syllable held a world of meaning within it.

I gave her a severe look. "He is a friend."

"And do you mean to return to Italy with this friend?" she asked, drawing out the last word ever so slightly.

My cheeks were hot again. "I do not know. It was discussed, but circumstances may have changed now," I replied, thinking of Violante's new expectations. "He has asked me," I mumbled into my cup.

Hortense tipped her head and gave me a long, thoughtful look. "You should take a lover."

I choked on my chocolate, and it was a long moment before I regained my composure. "How precisely did we move from you possibly becoming my stepmother to advising me on my *amours?*"

She tapped my knee. "I am a woman of the world, *chérie.* There is nothing I have not seen, and very little I have not done. Think on what I have said."

"I imagine I should have trouble forgetting it."

Hortense pulled a face. "Now you will be English and proper again. We are not supposed to speak of such things.

Very well. I too can be English. We shall talk about the weather. It is cold."

In spite of myself I laughed. "You are very silly, Hortense. And very good to care what happens to me."

For an instant, the cool mask slipped, and I saw real affection in her eyes. "I like to think if I had ever had a daughter, she might have been something like you."

I reached out and took her hand. It was smooth and supple in mine, and smelled of summer roses.

"Of course, she would dress better. That gown," she said, clucking her tongue. "So severe, so masculine in the cut."

I wrinkled my nose at her. "I happen to like this gown. I bought it in Milan. It is very smart."

Hortense gave me the gently raised eyebrows that indicated disagreement, then squeezed my hand. "You used to call me Fleur, like my closest friends. You must do so again or I shall think you are cross with me."

I rose and dropped a kiss on the top of her beautifully coiffed head. "I could never be cross with you. Now I must fly. I have nearly missed breakfast altogether."

I moved to the door, but before my fingers touched the knob, she spoke. "He does not love her, you know. He never did."

I went quite still, my back turned to her. "It is his own affair, Fleur. I am no part of it."

"Still, I thought you should know. He has said nothing to me, of course, but I have known him since he was a boy. He has not changed so much that I cannot read him."

A flash of memory from the previous night, his lips, his hands, his breath coming hard and ragged after he kissed me. Then I thought of Charlotte and the burden of guilt he still carried from our first investigation.

Ruthlessly, I pushed the thought of him away and reached for the knob.

"As I said, it is no affair of mine."

She made no reply. I did not blame her. It was a foolish lie. It did not deserve a response.

As soon as I left Hortense's room, I met Portia just coming from her room. Outwardly unruffled, her eyes were snapping and the tiny jet drops at her ears trembled violently.

"Oh, dear. Whatever is the matter?"

We fell into step as we descended the stairs.

"What isn't? Aquinas has informed me that none of the staff from the village will be able to make it in today, so we are lacking two footmen, four maids, and a boot boy. Dear brother Benedick trudged from the Home Farm to shout the news that the telegraph line at Blessingstoke has collapsed under the snow, so I cannot send to London for anything we should require. And, no great surprise, Cook is threatening to quit because there is a dead man in the game larder. As an interesting side note, Violante has packed her bags and is demanding to be taken to the station at once and put on the first ship back to Italy."

"Pressing problems indeed," I agreed.

"And one of the cats has given birth, quite nastily, in the linen cupboard."

"How sweet! Which one?"

She gave me an arch look. "Christopher Sly. Which is all rather odd, as Father was quite certain he was a tom."

"Hmm. Well, I suppose the most immediate concern is Violante. Is she still upset?"

Portia shrugged. "How the devil should I know? I coaxed her back to her room and sent for Lysander to manage her, but she kept babbling on about dead men in the game larder and how such things aren't done in Italy."

I tipped my head, musing. "I wonder where they house their murder victims then? In the scullery? Or perhaps the laundry? No, altogether too hot there, I should think."

"There is no cause for flippancy, Julia. I have a headache that has begun at my knees and gone right over the top of my head and back down again. I do not look for improvements as the day goes on."

As we reached the bottom of the stairs, I patted her arm. "I shouldn't worry about the staff. They will be snug enough in the village, and heaven knows we've plenty of hands to keep this place running without them. And don't mind too much about Violante. I have no doubt it's her pregnancy making her hysterical."

Portia sighed heavily. "I suspected she was breeding. I have never seen anyone eat so many pickled chestnuts. Her fingers were quite shrivelled from them. I suppose I had best go speak to Cook and make certain we've plenty more of them."

"While you're about it, assure her the body will be removed as soon as possible. And tell Aquinas to make certain the staff are given black armbands to wear as a token of respect for Mr. Snow."

Portia put her hands on her hips, giving a perfect impression of one of the maids in a pet. "Any more instructions, missus?"

"Do make certain the linen cupboard door is kept shut. I shouldn't like Florence to get a taste for kittens."

She put out her tongue at me and moved to turn away.

"One last thing, dearest. Do you know where Aunt Hermia keeps that funny little jade monkey Uncle Leonato brought her from China?"

Portia threw up her hands in exasperation. "Really, Julia, of all the impossibly stupid things to wonder about." She paused and thought, clicking her tongue against her teeth. "Oh, very well. The last time I saw it, she kept it on her night table."

"And the amber beads from Russia?"

"In a box next to the monkey." She started to tap her toe on the carpet.

"And the coral bracelet from the Java Sea?" I pressed.

"In her knickers."

I gave her a sour look. "You might be a little more helpful, Portia."

"Well, honestly. She isn't even here. Why you would ask about her little trinkets is beyond me. If you are so keen on them, have a look for yourself. You know she would not mind. Now, I really must go and find something for my head."

"Ask Brisbane," I called after her sweetly. "He has a new cure I think would suit you perfectly."

* * *

In the end, I had no time and little stomach for breakfast. I had thought to make a dash into the dining room for a bit of toast, but the notion of Lucian Snow, lying cold and possibly bloated in the game larder put me firmly off the idea.

The game larder itself had been fashioned into a crude sort of laboratory. A stone counter ran the length of the room. On it, propped against the walls, was a quantity of mirrors, from tiny things fit for a lady's reticule to enormous looking-glasses taken from the dressing rooms. In front of these were as many lamps as the counter could hold. The effect was dazzling, so bright I blinked as I entered the room.

Brisbane was already there, dressed in shirtsleeves and making an adjustment to one of the lamps. He grunted when I came in but did not look up. I turned my gaze firmly away from the sheet-draped figure on the table. I noticed a small table had been brought in and laid with a clean white cloth. Brisbane's leather case was there, and a book with a mouldy green cover. A few instruments such as tweezers and scissors had been arranged neatly on the cloth. I did not look further to see what else might lurk there.

"There are aprons on the hook behind the door," Brisbane said finally. "Put yours on and bring the other for me."

I put out my tongue behind his back and went to the door. The aprons were not the dainty pinafores the maids wore, but the thick white canvas affairs the footmen donned for the most menial chores. It was not until I was halfway back, aprons in hand, that I realised what he had said.

"Brisbane, surely I do not need an apron. I mean, I won't be—"

He turned, raising a brow coolly at me. "Of course you will. I have one good hand and his lordship is not at liberty to assist."

He put out his hand for the apron.

"What do you mean Father is not here? What else could he have to do?"

Brisbane's nostrils flared in impatience. "He was speaking with Miss Lucy and Miss Emma. I rose early this morning and told him about the drugged brandy. But now I believe he is searching for Lady Dorcas. The upstairs maid says she has disappeared."

I stared at him, clutching the aprons in nerveless fingers.

"Disappeared? Are you quite serious?"

"As the grave. My apron?" He put out his hand again and I thrust it at him, my mind whirling.

"Where could she have gone? The gates are frozen shut and the moat is covered in ice. She cannot have gone far."

"Then she is probably quite safe."

Brisbane whipped a quick knot into the strings at the neck of the apron, then looped it over his head, mussing a lock of hair onto his brow. He reached his good arm behind his back, then gestured for me to help him. I crossed behind him, reaching around him for the strings. For such a large man, his waist was narrow, and I crossed the strings, moving in front of him to tie them securely. He said nothing, but I glanced up to see the hint of a smile flicker at the corner of his mouth.

"Brisbane, how can you be so calm? She is an elderly lady, and that was a killing storm. She might be frozen in a snowdrift for all we know."

Brisbane moved to the little table and opened the book. "Put on your apron. This might prove a little unpleasant and that is a very nice gown."

I obeyed him, my fingers stiff with cold and dread. When the apron was secure, I went to his side, peering over his shoulder at the book. I was instantly sorry.

"I haven't given up on the subject of Aunt Dorcas," I warned him. "But this is a more immediate problem," I said, waving a hand from the hideous plates in the book to the motionless figure on the table. "I do not think I can do this."

Brisbane looked at me severely. "Did you not insist to me just last evening that you would have your part in this investigation?"

I clamped my lips together against the faint smell emanating from the body. I nodded.

"Very well. This is part of an investigation. That body may hold information for us, and if it does, I mean to find it."

I swallowed hard, terribly grateful I had eschewed breakfast. "But you cannot possibly, that is to say, those pictures are quite specific and very, erm, thorough. I really think only a trained physician should make such an extensive examination. And don't you think the authorities will notice if you cut him like that?"

Brisbane looked back at the book. After a moment he nodded, reluctantly, I fancied. "They might at that. Very well. I shall not perform a proper post-mortem. But I will do everything else. Now, you must be my hands."

For the next hour I did as I was told. I started by unpinning my sleeves. When I rolled the first above my elbow, Brisbane's eyes lingered for the briefest moment on the soft white skin at my wrist. I glanced up when I turned back the second, but his gaze was firmly fixed on the book in his hand, and from that moment on his manner toward me was coolly proper.

"Begin by drawing back the sheet," he instructed quietly. "Fold it down all the way, and mind you don't disarrange anything further."

I reached a hand to touch the sheet, then drew it back sharply. "I know it is just a fancy, but I thought it moved."

Brisbane looked up from the book. "If this is too much for you, I can ask Aquinas."

I shook my head, forcing myself to take in one slow breath, then release it calmly. "No. If you can do this, so can I."

I would have expected a tiny spark of admiration in his gaze for that little speech, but his nose was buried in his book again, and I rolled my eyes. This time, I approached the sheet and removed it, as crisply as any housemaid about her chores.

Following his explicit instructions, I loosened Mr. Snow's clothing, removing his evening jacket, waistcoat and neckcloth. I felt them carefully, but the pockets were empty. I laid them aside and steeled myself for what must come.

"Wait," Brisbane said, bending swiftly over the body.

"What is it?" I demanded, elbowing Brisbane a little. His expression was grim. "There."

He pointed to Lucian Snow's neck. Bruises blossomed around the throat, heavy blackish-purple things, livid against the pale skin. It was clear, even to my amateur's eyes, that they were finger marks, borne in with great pressure.

"What fools we have been," Brisbane muttered.

I stared at the bruises, my mind working furiously. "Lucy could not have done that."

Brisbane rose, stroking his jaw. It was darkly shadowed, as if he had shaved quickly and without particular care that morning. It was oddly attractive.

"No, she could not. And those bruises would not have shown half so violently if he had been strangled after death." Brisbane took his good right hand and fitted it to the bruises, his own handspan matching the marks nearly perfectly. I could almost see the crime in my mind's eye, the murderer, facing Lucian Snow, bearing down upon him, crushing the life out of him as they stared into each other's eyes.

Abruptly, Brisbane moved to Lucian's head. Before I could look away, he had turned the head and was probing the wound gently. I swallowed hard, refusing the heaving insistence of my stomach. After a moment, Brisbane drew back his hand and shook his head.

"There is a bit of a depression here where the bone was broken, and a fair amount of blood matted in his hair."

"He was struck down before he was strangled?" I asked.

Brisbane nodded. "A fair hypothesis, I think. Had he been struck after death, there would have been very little blood."

"To what purpose?" I asked.

"To incapacitate him," he replied. "A blow there would have

rendered Snow unconscious, an easy victim for his killer. And that would explain why there is only one handprint," Brisbane added. "The murderer did not require both hands to subdue him."

I looked at Brisbane's left arm, firmly strapped to his chest and blinked. He marked the glance.

"Yes, my lady, I am the obvious suspect," he said, a trifle acidly. "Is my word good enough, or would you care for an alibi? I seem to remember I was with *you* when Snow was murdered."

"Sorry," I mumbled. I ducked my head to hide my blushes.

"The question is, if the girl could not have killed him by strangulation, and the blow struck with the candelabrum was landed *before* he died, what did she see?"

I began to pace the room, putting a little distance between myself and the gruesome relic on the table.

"Either Lucy was an accomplice, perhaps striking the blow with the candelabrum herself, remaining behind when her partner fled…" I began.

That mesmerizing pair of eyes fixed on me intently. "Or she did not touch him, but is taking the blame upon herself for another's crime," I finished.

I could not imagine Lucy creeping up on a man and striking him viciously with a candelabrum. Of course, until the previous night, I would have thought her incapable of any violence at all. I was rapidly revising my opinion of her. My first investigation had taught me the unlikeliest of suspects may be the most culpable.

"It may have all happened quite quickly," Brisbane said. "The murderer strikes Lucian Snow with the candelabrum, then finishes him off with a carefully placed hand to the throat. He is free to leave, perhaps without a spot of blood upon him. He might have slipped past Lucy in the darkness, or if he heard her coming, he had only to duck into one of the empty rooms along the nave and wait until the hue and cry was raised when the body was discovered. In the meantime, Lucy could have entered the chapel, found the body and, with a striking lack of good sense, picked up the candelabrum and implicated herself in a murder."

"Or," I said slowly, "Lucy might have been there all along. She may have seen the strangler at work, and stayed behind to make certain the deed was finished with a savage blow of the candelabrum once the murderer departed."

I looked up to find Brisbane regarding me with a curious mixture of distaste and admiration.

"That is the most gruesome notion yet. And it took a woman to think of it. No, it will not signify. I still maintain the blow with the candelabrum was struck before he died. The coroner may have a different opinion on the matter, but I am convinced."

The rest of the examination was swiftly carried out. I obeyed Brisbane's instructions dispassionately, as though I was comfortable handling lifeless things. To my everlasting relief, Brisbane at least observed the propriety of not having me strip the body completely. He asked me only to remove Snow's shirt. I busied myself tidying Snow's things while Brisbane examined the torso beneath the flannel undergarment. It was over more quickly than I had expected, and the conclusions were inescapable: Lucian

Snow had been, to all appearances, a healthy man, killed in his prime by strangulation.

Brisbane's eyes were alight with an enthusiasm I knew well. Rather than a straightforward murder, this crime was something more puzzling. There was a challenge here, and Brisbane loved nothing more than a knotty problem to untangle.

"I suppose the first order of business is to speak with Lucy and Emma," I said at length.

"Indeed," Brisbane said, "although I suspect they will not have much to contribute. Still, there may be something useful there. I will take the footman."

"You mean you do not object to my questioning Lucy and Emma?" I asked, astonished.

He gave me the slow, lazy stare one might give to a backward child. "I cannot. They are unmarried ladies confined to their bedchamber."

It was on the tip of my tongue to point out that my undressing a dead man could hardly be considered proper, but I did not. It was enough that he had acknowledged the necessity of my role in the investigation. In truth, I felt a little deflated. He had capitulated so easily. I had girded myself for a fight.

I looked at Brisbane. He was gazing down at the body of Lucian Snow rather thoughtfully. Then he reached out and twitched the sheet over the still, white face.

He turned to me, his eyes quite black in the magnified light of the mirror-lit larder. "You must find out everything that they might try to conceal. Be ruthless. Leave them no secrets to cling to, use whatever tactics you must. No man deserves that fate," he finished with a flicker of his gaze toward the shrouded form.

I glanced from Lucian Snow's remains to Brisbane's implacable face. "I will not fail," I told him firmly.

THE SEVENTEENTH CHAPTER

Truth will come to sight, murder cannot be long hid.
—THE MERCHANT OF VENICE

I was surprised to find Sir Cedric standing outside Lucy and Emma's door, shouting at the footman who barred his way. Sir Cedric was clearly in a temper, his usually ruddy complexion dark red at the ears and nose. The footman, William V, I think it was, looked at me with something like desperation.

"Good morning, Sir Cedric," I greeted. "Is there something I can do for you?"

He looked from the footman to me with narrowed eyes, silent for a moment as if he were trying to place an unfamiliar face. Tiny flecks of saliva had gathered at the corners of his mouth, and I felt a little rush of pity for Lucy.

"Lady Julia. I have a mind to see my fiancée, but this buffoon will not open the door to me."

I cleared my throat gently. "Well, it is rather inappropriate under the circumstances."

His complexion darkened further still and I began to fear he would have an apoplexy, an eventuality too gruesome to consider. To begin with, there would be no place to store another body.

"The circumstances are, my fiancée is ill, and no one will give me news of her and she will not see me."

I gave him my most winsome smile. "How terribly frustrating for you. Why don't you go and have a cup of coffee, or perhaps a nice cigar? I will speak with Lucy and bring you news of her straightaway."

The narrow eyes relaxed a little. "Will you? Straightaway?"

I patted his arm, drawing him away from the door. The footman seemed to sag a little in relief. "I promise. Sometimes ladies do have these little indispositions. I am sure it is nothing for you to concern yourself about."

"She better not have taken a chill in that chapel last night. I warned March not to leave her there, and if she falls ill from it, I shall know who to blame," he warned me.

I smiled again. "Lucy has suffered a very great shock, and we all want what is best for her. Now, you go and make yourself quite comfortable and I will do what I can."

He thanked me grudgingly and took his leave, glancing back once or twice darkly at the footman. When he had rounded the corner of the dorter, the boy leaned against the door.

"Oh, thank you, my lady. I could not make him understand that Lord March said to admit no one except yourself or a maid. I thought I would have to hit him, and I do not think his lordship would have approved of that."

I smiled at his earnestness. "You might be surprised, William. Has anyone else attempted to see the Misses Phipps?"

He thought for a moment. "No, my lady. The maid brought them a tray for breakfast, and Lord March was here very early to look in on the ladies."

"Very good. And how long have you been here?"

"Mr. Aquinas fetched me out of bed a few hours before dawn to keep watch and let no one past. He said it was on Lord Wargrave's orders, and when Lord March came he said that Lord Wargrave had been quite right."

I nodded. "Excellent. You were perfectly right to refuse Sir Cedric."

He blushed with pleasure. "Thank you, my lady." He stepped aside smartly and opened the door for me.

The room was warm and quiet, and I moved inside, motioning for William V to close the door softly behind me.

"Julia," came a feeble voice from the bed. I approached, surprised to find Emma awake. Lucy slumbered on, curled as tightly as a puppy against her sister. Emma held out her hand to me and I took it. It was cool and light as a bird.

"How are you feeling?" I asked her in a whisper. Lucy stirred but did not wake.

Emma gave a short shake of the head. "As well as one may expect. Uncle March was here earlier. He explained about the laudanum in the brandy."

Her eyes shimmered with unshed tears, and I tightened my hand over hers. She smiled mistily at me.

"Julia, I cannot imagine who would do such a thing to us."

I hesitated. I did not like to pose such a question, but it must be asked. "Then you did not…" My voice trailed off.

She shook her head, almost angrily. "Of course not. How could I do such a thing to my Lucy?" She turned her head on the pillow to look at her sister nestled against her.

"I am sorry, Emma. It was a possibility, you know."

She closed her eyes. "I know." We sat in silence so long I began to think she had drifted into sleep. But then she opened her eyes and looked at me.

"That would have been the coward's way, and I am no coward," she said, more to herself than to me.

Before I could reply, Lucy stirred and raised herself a little. "Lie down, dearest," Emma told her. "You must not tire yourself."

Lucy obeyed, and I moved around to her side of the bed. She turned, giving me a sad, sleepy smile. "Hullo, Julia."

I moved straight to the heart of the matter. "Lucy, I know this has been a terrible shock for you, but you must know that your family stand with you. We know you did not do this thing."

She laid the back of her arm to her brow, staring up at the ceiling. She made no reply, and I went on. "Lucian Snow was not killed by your hand. We know this for a fact. The evidence says he died of strangulation, by a hand much larger and stronger than yours."

Without preamble, a sob erupted from her, tearing from her throat. She folded in half, her face to her knees, keening. Emma started for her, but I put an arm about Lucy's shoulder.

"I do not know why you claimed you did this, but we know you did not. And we will make certain the authorities know it as well."

Suddenly, Lucy stumbled from the bed to the washstand and began to retch. She had eaten nothing, but she doubled over, heaving until the spell passed. Emma went to her and stroked her back, murmuring soothing things until she finished. Then I handed her my handkerchief to mop her face. When she was done, she looked a great deal more lucid than she had since we had discovered her bending over Lucian's body.

She returned to the bed, and when Emma had tucked the coverlets firmly about her, Lucy clutched at my hand, pressing it to her hot face. "Oh, Julia, I do not know what happened. All I remember is leaving the drawing room to play sardines, then a great blackness. There is simply nothing there until I came to when you found me, standing there…" She broke off, her voice catching, but with a great effort of will she mastered it. "I have thought and thought, but I cannot retrieve any memory of the time between. I only know that I saw him there, broken, and I knew I had struck him. I knew that I must have done something unspeakable."

I thought of the Easter holidays Lucy and Emma had spent with us as children, of the little nothings that sometimes went missing, children's trinkets, but usually something of sentimental value. I thought of how Lucy's nose always itched when she lied about whether she had seen them. Always, that telltale little twitch, giving her away. I watched her now, pressing the handkerchief hard against the tip of her nose.

"Did you see anyone when you were playing sardines?"

Lucy shrugged helplessly. "I do not know. I have no memory of it." She scrubbed at her nose. "It is so cold here," she said apologetically, not quite meeting my eyes.

We talked for a long time. Emma said nothing. Perhaps she knew how important it was for the questions to be asked, and answered. I questioned Lucy by every possible method, but her answers were always the same. She had quit the lesser drawing room alone. From the time she left until the time Brisbane and I had discovered her with the candelabrum, she had no memory whatsoever—not of sound or sight, nor even scent. After awhile she began to droop, and I took pity on her.

I rose and Emma threw me a grateful look. "Lucy, you must eat something. You also, Emma. It's very important to keep up your strength. I promise you, we will discover the truth."

Emma smiled her thanks, but Lucy was not looking at me. She was staring at the ceiling again, her eyes fixed once more on the slender web of hammerbeams that hung above her head.

Luncheon was an understandably solemn affair. Father had said nothing about Aunt Dorcas, but to my astonishment, he seemed angry rather than worried. Violante sulked openly while Lysander chewed his fingernails and did not even pretend to eat. Plum pushed the food around his plate as he shot significant glances at Charlotte King. That worried me a trifle. Plum was subject to occasional fancies, not the least of which was a penchant for the role of Galahad. He loved nothing better than to rescue damsels in distress, and Charlotte bore all the hallmarks of a lady in need of a knight. She was a comely, vivacious widow whose engagement was likely at an end, marooned in the middle of Sussex with a houseful of people she scarcely knew and a murderer. Even more worrisome, she did nothing to discourage Plum. Instead she alternated hurt, puzzled looks at Brisbane with gazes of mute longing toward my brother. With such a performance, it was a wonder she was able to eat at all, but I noticed she managed to tuck away three helpings of the curried lamb. If she was not careful, she would soon have to let out her stays, I thought spitefully.

For his part, Brisbane was entirely indifferent. He too ate three helpings of the lamb, as well as a sizeable portion of roast potatoes and an enormous plate of cherry tarts with almond cream. Father managed a bit of everything, but he seemed distracted, putting mustard on his peas and salt on his dessert. He ate it anyway, and I noticed Hortense doing her best to amuse him. From time to time he smiled wearily at her, and I looked away, not wishing to intrude on their intimacy. It was apparent to me now that he needed her, and I was pleased to find that I was comfortable with the notion. I turned to Alessandro then, sorry to find him quiet and withdrawn. The murder had upset him terribly, and from the hollow look about his eyes, I thought it entirely possible he had not slept at all the previous night. I did my best to entice him into conversation, but his replies were succinct to the point of backwardness, and after a few minutes I gave up.

Understandably, Sir Cedric and Henry were quiet, eating

stolidly, without contribution to the conversation or any apparent pleasure in their food. I had not yet had a chance to speak with Sir Cedric about Lucy, and he spent most of the luncheon hour shooting me significant glances. I tried giving him a reassuring nod, but he simply redoubled his efforts. I ignored them and toyed with my food, too often putting my fork down still laden; the image of Snow's cold corpse was yet too vivid and too many unanswered questions lingered in my mind. Portia heroically took on the chore of steering the conversation, butterflying from subject to subject, skillfully avoiding any topics which might be awkward. I suppose that is how we arrived at the subject of Christmas again, and Charlotte's role in the stirring up of the puddings.

"So very kind of you to lend a hand," Portia finished brightly.

I speared a bit of potato and pushed it around the plate.

"My dearest mama always taught me, 'One must lend a hand wherever one can,'" Charlotte put in earnestly.

I threw Brisbane a hateful look. I still could not quite believe he had taken the trouble to propose marriage to her. She was ridiculous, with her cloying sweetness and her silly platitudes. She could not have held his attention for the duration of a fish course, much less the rest of their lives.

Lysander roused himself then. "Who is expected for Christmas? I am rather surprised we have not seen Benedick and his brood yet."

Benedick, perhaps the favourite of my brothers, lived on the Home Farm, the other side of the Abbey from Blessingstoke. He had been conspicuously absent of late. I missed him, and his de-

lightful wife. My nieces and nephews were another matter altogether. They were like very good, aged cognac: delicious, but only
in very small doses.

"Benedick's lot are in quarantine," Portia advised him.
"Measles. They look to be recovered by Christmas, but if they
come, Olivia and her family will not."

I blinked at her. It was not like Benedick to be at odds with
any of our siblings. Most of us quarrelled with one another from
time to time, but Benedick was usually the only one on speaking
terms with everybody.

"Olivia's children infected his with measles," Portia explained.
"Benedick made some remark about the stupidity of taking one's
children visiting when they've come out in spots, and she took
it rather badly."

"I see," I said, poking at a piece of lamb. "What of the rest of
them?"

Portia laid down her fork and began to tick them off on her
fingers.

"Bellmont is in London for the little season. He has parliamen-
tary duties and cannot get away. Olivia and Benedick we have
spoken of. Nerissa is unwell," she said with a lift of the brows. I
took her meaning instantly. Unlike most of our sisters, Nerissa
did not bear children easily. For every healthy living child, there
had been a handful of miscarriages. She had adopted the habit
of taking to her bed during each pregnancy, and if she was
breeding again, we would not see her again until the child was
christened.

"Lysander, Plum, you, and I are here, Julia," she said, nodding at me and continuing to tick off her fingers. "Beatrice is being set upon by all of her husband's family. They are descending to Cornwall *en masse* for the holiday, and there is no chance of her escaping them. That leaves only Valerius, and he has not yet made up his mind whether to spend Christmas in the bosom of his family or dosing the lower orders in Whitehall."

"So many Marches," Violante murmured.

"Indeed," Father replied. I did not know if Lysander had informed him yet of Violante's expectations, but from the kindly way Father was regarding her, I suspected he had. Father adored grandchildren, and the only thing that made him happier than being covered in them was escaping them and spending an afternoon locked in his study while they overran the Abbey like savages.

At least that was one family matter settled, I thought as I stared irritably at my peas. I could not imagine why I should feel so twitchy, so bad-tempered. I could have cheerfully thrown my cutlery at someone's head, and it was only when the dessert dishes were being cleared that I realised it was because I was frustrated. Luncheon, a lengthy family affair, had interrupted my burgeoning investigation, and what I wanted most, what I *craved,* was time alone to puzzle over the pieces I had collected and fit them together.

The coffee was replenished, and I had just made up my mind to excuse myself when Aquinas entered, Morag hard on his heels. Aquinas' expression was as carefully schooled as ever, but his wiry grey hair was ever so slightly dishevelled, and his cuffs were not shot. Morag looked faintly deranged.

Aquinas made straight for my father, bent to his ear, and whispered. Father listened, then murmured, half to himself, "Good God, not this too."

He waved a hand. "Tell Lady Julia. Something ought to be done to recover them." He covered his face with a hand.

Around the table, cups and spoons stilled, conversation halted. Every face swivelled to face Aquinas expectantly. He cleared his throat.

"I regret to inform you," he began, but Morag interrupted, her bony cheeks hot with indignation.

"Something of great value is missing in this house!" she announced to the assembled company. She paused, glancing slowly around the table, holding everyone's gaze in a gesture Sarah Siddons would have envied. When she had circled the entire table, her eyes flashing, she lifted her chin and proclaimed, "The Grey Pearls have been stolen!"

THE EIGHTEENTH CHAPTER

All that you meet are thieves.
—TIMON OF ATHENS

To say that pandemonium broke out would be an understatement of the grossest kind. Naturally, I blamed Morag.

I rose and took her by the elbow, dragging her toward the potted palm in the corner. "What do you mean by coming in here and making an announcement like a character in a melodrama? What must our guests think?"

She wrenched her elbow from my grasp and folded her arms over her chest. "There is a dead man stinking in the game larder," she reminded me sourly. "I hardly think a few missing pearls will be the ruin of this house party."

"He does not stink," I told her severely. "At least not much."

A mêlée had erupted at the table behind us. Sir Cedric had apparently tired of holding his temper and was shouting at Father, calling him Fagin and asking what sort of house he kept where innocent men were murdered and ladies' jewels went missing. Father shouted back, calling him a jumped-up boot boy (a barbed reference to the fortune Sir Cedric made in selling cheap shoes to the working classes) while Hortense and Ludlow were busy coaxing them apart. Meanwhile, Violante was scolding Lysander in her native language in extremely colourful terms if Alessandro's expression was any indication, and Plum had taken advantage of the pandemonium to cover Charlotte's hand with his own.

Brisbane left them all to it and joined me. Morag bobbed him a clumsy curtsey, but her expression softened a touch. She would never admit it, but she was fond of Brisbane—for his slight Scottish burr, if nothing else.

"M'lord," she murmured.

"Morag, always a pleasure," he said as if he meant it. "When did you notice her ladyship's jewels were missing?"

"Just now. I went to do her chamber—"

"You *just now* went to do my chamber?" I interrupted. As my lady's maid, it was Morag's duty to bring my morning tea, help me dress, then tidy the room and prepare my clothes for the afternoon. The fact that she had not touched my room until luncheon was highly unusual.

"I had to tend the wee doggie," she informed me loftily. "She would only sip at the beef tea. Three trips I made to the kitchens for food for that animal. And then she had to—" She broke off, colouring slightly as she glanced at Brisbane. "She had to *you know,* and I took her to the courtyard, only she would not put a paw on the snow. She kept rolling over and staggering until I finally scraped the snow out of one of those great stone boxes and found some greenery. I put her there and she did what nature expects."

I rolled my eyes heavenward. "That bit of greenery was Father's prized hare topiary."

"Was it so? It did have a look of a rabbit, now that you mention it," Morag mused.

Brisbane cleared his throat. The muscle in his jaw was not yet jumping, but it was twitching ever so slightly.

"Morag, kindly tell his lordship everything he needs to know about the pearls."

The chaos behind us had eased to a mild roar, and it appeared Father and Sir Cedric were organising a truce. Father had stopped shouting and Sir Cedric had resumed his seat, his colour still alarmingly high.

Morag clucked her tongue, thinking hard. "Well, this morning, after I tended the wee doggie, I realised I had best look sharpish about finishing Lady Julia's room because luncheon was nearly over. I went in with a bit of underlinen—" she whispered the word "—and that was when I realised the pearls were not on the dressing table."

"What do you mean they were not on the dressing table? You did not put them away first thing this morning? They ought to have been locked up as soon as you finished dressing me."

She pursed her lips. "And how was I supposed to do that and tend to Florence? You said to take care of the doggie."

"Because I thought you understood the pearls were to be taken care of immediately."

"But you did not *say* so," Morag countered, her expression triumphant.

"I did not think I had to," I said through gritted teeth. "I assumed you knew a parure of pearls worth thousands of pounds would be of a higher priority than ministering to the needs of a dog."

"And you are quite certain the pearls were there this morning?" Brisbane cut in smoothly.

Morag and I paused, staring at one another.

"Now that you mention it…" she began.

"Oh, *no,*" I moaned. I had removed the pearls myself the previous evening, dropping them onto the dressing table when I had collected Morag to take her to the chapel to sit with Lucy. I could not say with certainty I had seen them since.

Morag shook her head. "No, m'lord. They were gone when I brought the tea things this morning."

Brisbane's eyes narrowed. "You are quite certain?"

She nodded. "I am. I remember now. I did not have to move them aside to put down the tea tray. Lady Julia put them square in the middle of the table last night. If they had been there this morning, they would have been in my way."

Brisbane thought for a moment. "That will do for now, Morag."

She bobbed another curtsey and fled, giving me one last nasty look over her shoulder.

"I cannot believe they are gone. So careless," I fretted.

"Perhaps not gone. Just mislaid," Brisbane said, his expression thoughtful. He was staring at the luncheon guests, and in that instant, I knew he suspected someone in particular of having stolen them. But he said nothing.

Involuntarily, my hand went to my pocket, feeling the outline of the knotted handkerchief with its cache of Aunt Hermia's humble jewels. It was on the tip of my tongue to tell him what I had discovered in Snow's room, but as I watched him stare at the assembled company, his expression smugly satisfied, I realised he had no intention of including me in his triumph.

He turned to me. "My lady?" He looked at me quizzically, inviting me to speak.

I smoothed my skirts. "Nothing, Brisbane. I am sure the pearls will turn up eventually."

One development of that harrowing lunch party was the revelation to the company at large that Aunt Dorcas was missing. Father made the announcement after coffee, rather offhandedly, in my opinion.

The reaction was predictable. Sir Cedric flew into a rage again, and it took all of Henry Ludlow's considerable powers of persuasion to settle him down. Portia and Plum fired questions at Father until he raised a hand for silence.

"A poor choice of words on my part. She is not missing. She is elsewhere, and I am assured she is in perfect health," he finished smoothly, but there was an edge to his voice and I knew he was not as satisfied with the matter as he pretended.

The rest of us stared at each other in bewilderment.

"Such an unusual household," Charlotte King murmured finally. "First jewels disappearing, now people. I begin to think I am in a faery story of the most fantastic kind." Her lips trembled a little, and I almost felt sorry for her. "Perhaps we ought to look for her," she ventured.

"Unnecessary," Father cut in sharply. "Amuse yourselves as you will this afternoon. I shall be in my study and I do not wish to be disturbed unless God Almighty himself comes to call."

He rose and threw down his napkin, stalking off, Crab and a few of her pups trotting closely behind.

Charlotte, perhaps chagrined at being dismissed so brutally, bit her lip. Plum leaned near and murmured something that brought a sudden smile to her face. Through it all, Brisbane appeared thoroughly disinterested. He merely sipped at his coffee as though waiting for something to happen.

For my part, all I could think on was the pearls and what Father had said of Aunt Dorcas' penchant for pocketing little trinkets she admired. Was it possible she had taken my pearls and then fled with them? But the weather would have made that impossible, I reminded myself.

"Perhaps then a walk on the battlements of the boundary wall," Charlotte said. "I should so like some fresh air."

"That sounds delightful," Plum said, his fez fairly quivering with anticipation. They made to depart, and I signalled to my brother.

"Plum, a word, dear. Mrs. King will want to fetch her warmest things if you mean to venture onto the battlements, and this will only take a moment." He agreed, with bad grace, and we watched as Violante rose quickly, with Hortense's gentle support. She had soothed the girl and promised Lysander she would look after her and sit with her while she rested. Lysander gave her thanks, but grudgingly so. In spite of himself, he was beginning to like Father's *inamorata*.

Sir Cedric and Henry Ludlow excused themselves next, Ludlow moving quickly to keep up with his volatile kinsman. I had been correct in my initial estimation of Sir Cedric: he was only lightly civilised, as his behaviour of late had shown. He could play the gentleman well enough, but when provoked by circumstances, he reverted to the slum-born starveling. He had come so far from the poverty and degradation of his upbringing, I reflected, but I wondered if he had come quite so far as he pretended.

And as I regarded Sir Cedric, a horrible thought rose in my mind. If Lucy had indeed taken the blame for another's crime deliberately, as well she might have, what man would she have better reason to shield than her own fiancé? Remembering the bruises on Snow's neck, I glanced at Sir Cedric's hands. The fingers themselves were not long, but his palms were broad as an ape's. His handspan would fit the bruises perfectly. I looked from his sturdy hands to his supple wrists. It had been a mistake to look at this man and see only the web of wrinkles at his eyes, the mane of hair shot with silver. I had ignored the strength left in him, the savagery that might well lurk just below the surface. What would it take to rouse it? I wondered.

"I have to speak with Cook about tea," Portia announced. "That seed cake she served yesterday was appalling, and if she sends up wine biscuits one more time…of course she is very sensitive. She might just as well throw a cleaver at my head as give me a ginger biscuit."

She rose and looped her arm through Alessandro's, pulling him to his feet. "I know. I shall bring her this delicious young man as a peace offering."

Alessandro seemed to struggle to find the proper words. "My lady, I would be very happy to accompany you, but Lady Julia's pearls. Perhaps we ought to search for them."

Portia smiled at him fondly. "Yes, and as soon as I have spoken to Cook, we will poke around belowstairs and see if we can find them. Perhaps Morag forgot what she was about and left them in the pantry."

Alessandro threw me a pleading glance, but I pretended not to see it. As much as I enjoyed his company, and as much as he deserved to be rescued from my sister, I was acutely aware of his intentions after his declaration of the previous night. I had no wish to be alone with him until I had formed an answer to his question. At present, I could give him none. The investigation, with all its winding paths and blind alleys, demanded my full attention.

Finally, only Plum, Brisbane, and I remained in the dining room. I excused myself, dragging Plum into the transept while Brisbane savoured his coffee. I glanced around to make quite certain we were alone.

"What is it, Julia?" Plum asked, folding his arms over his chest.

"It is Alessandro. You've been frightfully negligent hosts, you and Ly both. You must do something with him this afternoon."

"Like what? In case you have failed to notice, the Abbey is inescapable."

"Not for Aunt Dorcas," I muttered.

He rolled his eyes. "Aunt Dorcas is famous for disappearing when there is trouble because usually she is the cause of it."

I poked his chest as hard as I could, pressing hard on one of the tourmaline buttons of his waistcoat. "I hardly think she is responsible for the murder of Mr. Snow."

"Ouch. I meant the theft of your pearls. She's a terrible old cat about pearls, you must know that."

"Father did say something to that effect," I admitted. "But how did she leave the Abbey? And where is she now?"

Plum shrugged. "She might have gone to the village to call upon Uncle Fly. She might have taken the train to London. She might have gone home for all we know."

I blinked at him. "I had not considered that. I suppose she might have left before the snow was too thick to travel. But *how?*"

"Julia, Father said not to worry. He has had word she is all right. She is probably sitting at the Home Farm, warming herself by the fire and driving Benedick to madness."

I remembered then what Portia had said about Benedick braving the snow to come up to the Abbey and shout news to Father.

"Of course. I am just being silly. I'm sure she is perfectly fine. But about Alessandro—"

He groaned and raised his hands. "Very well. I promise to entertain him properly. But not now. Charlotte is waiting."

A warning trembled on my tongue, but I swallowed it. Plum was a man fully grown. He would not thank me for interfering in his *affaires du coeur.*

"Thank you, dearest. Mind you include Ly. He is looking frightfully peaky."

Plum rolled his eyes again and left me, and I was glad of it. He had been in a frightfully bad temper for months, and his mood seemed to have darkened since we returned home. I trailed slowly back into the dining room and joined Brisbane at the table. I picked up my cup and put it down again. I had no appetite for cold coffee.

"What did you discover from Lucy?" he asked finally.

I pulled a face. "Nothing. She claims she has no memory whatsoever from the time she left the drawing room, until we found her, standing over Snow's body, clutching the candelabrum." A sudden thought occurred to me. Brisbane had a working knowledge of mesmerism. "Perhaps Lucy had been influenced by someone who knew how to wield the prodigious powers of the mind. Is that possible?"

Brisbane ran a hand over his temple. "Possible, but entirely too convenient for my taste."

"Agreed," I said briskly. "So the question is, whom is she protecting? Sir Cedric is the obvious choice."

"Actually, Emma is the obvious choice," Brisbane countered.

"Yes," I said impatiently, "but we have already established, that is, *you* have already established, this murder was done by a man."

"True enough," he said, far more amiably than I expected.

"So Sir Cedric is our most obvious candidate for murderer," I finished. "We must search his rooms."

"I will search his rooms," he corrected. "It would be highly inappropriate for you to do so."

I felt a little thrill of pleasure at this demonstration of his regard for me. "You mean because a lady should not be present in an unmarried gentleman's bedchamber," I teased, thinking of the many trips I had made to his own chamber the previous night.

"No," he said slowly, his eyes warm with amusement. "I mean it must be done properly and by a professional. You, my lady, are still an amateur."

He was still laughing when I left him.

THE NINETEENTH CHAPTER

He who would search for pearls must dive below.
—ALL FOR LOVE, JOHN DRYDEN

e had not gone five feet outside the dining room before Brisbane struck out on his own without a word. I cleared my throat. He turned, his brows knit with concentration.

"Yes?"

"I thought we were meant to search together," I told him, reaching for the ragged edges of my patience.

His stance was arrogant, legs wide apart and firmly set. He did not even have to speak to expose his stubbornness; I could read it in every line of his body. "I do not see why that should be necessary."

"Because we are investigating this murder together." There was a tart edge to my voice, even to my own ears. Brisbane ignored it.

He shrugged. "I do not require your assistance to search Sir Cedric's room. Go and have a poke around the lumber rooms. Perhaps your pearls will turn up. At the very least, you can have a look through Snow's portmanteau. I presume that is where it was stored."

My hands fisted at my sides. I forced them to relax, and gave Brisbane my sunniest smile.

"What an excellent notion. I shall go there at once."

He turned on his heel and left me then, but not before I saw an expression of relief flicker over his features. He was pleased to be rid of me, but why? I had known as soon as Father instructed us to work together that Brisbane opposed the idea, but this was more than simple obstinacy. Brisbane had some deeper purpose in keeping me at bay, and I knew the only way to discover it was by stealth. He was a complicated riddle of a man, but puzzling him out was a task to which I felt more than equal.

Determined to solve at least one of the mysteries afoot in the Abbey, I made my way up the staircase to the dorter. On impulse, I paused at Emma and Lucy's door. William V nodded at me genially and I tapped.

Emma called for me to enter, and I was pleased to see that she was sitting in a chair by the fire, wrapped in a dressing gown, a luncheon tray balanced on her knees. There were a few little dishes of invalid food, a bit of soup, a blancmange, a compote of softly stewed fruits.

"I am glad to see you eating," I remarked, taking a chair beside her.

She gave me a gentle smile. "I cannot manage much, but I must recover my strength. Lucy will need me," she added, glancing at the bed. Lucy still slept, bundled in coverlets, her hair spilling across the pillow.

I turned back to Emma. Her eyes were still resting upon her sister's sleeping form. Her face puckered, and for a moment I thought she was going to weep. But her eyes remained dry, and I took the opportunity to study her. The horrors of the night were clearly marked upon her face. Her eyes, usually her best feature, were sunk and darkly rimmed. A few threads of grey I had not seen before wove through her dull hair. Her thin face was pale, and her hands trembled a little as she dipped a spoon into the blancmange. She brought it to her lips, then laid it down untasted, her expression apologetic.

"It is difficult to manage anything. I just kept thinking of where we were, what awful thing Lucy had confessed to. And then the brandy. It seemed quite unreal."

"I know," I told her, my voice warm with sympathy. "But there is hope."

Her eyes lit with the fervour of a mystic saint. "What hope? Julia, you must tell me. If there is any chance, however remote, that my dearest sister may be saved, comfort me with it."

I patted her arm. "I cannot speak of it, but know this—the evidence clears her name. What other troubles she may still face, I cannot say, but of murder she is innocent."

Emma's eyes closed and her head drooped on her slender neck, as a flower nodding on a stem. When she looked up, tears sparkled on her lashes, lending a sudden brilliance to her eyes.

"Bless you. I cannot tell you what this means to me." She hesitated, then rushed on, the words spilling out of her quickly. "The maid who brought the tray said Aunt Dorcas has gone missing. Is this true?"

I nodded. "I am sorry to say it is. But everything that may be thought of to recover her is being done."

"That poor old woman," she murmured.

I hastened to reassure her. "Do not worry, I beg you. She cannot have gone far. There are no tracks in the snow, so she must be here in the Abbey somewhere."

Emma clutched at the neck of her dressing gown. "I never spoke of this, but I am sorry to say she is prey to odd turns from time to time."

"Odd turns? Of what sort?"

"When Lucy and I lived with her, occasionally she wandered off, sometimes even overnight. It used to frighten us terribly, but always she was found, wandering and confused." Emma paused, as if steeling herself, then hurried on, perhaps hoping to confide before her courage deserted her. "Often, when we found her, there would be a trinket, sometimes a jewel, in her pocket. We never spoke of it, of course. Oh, Julia, you mustn't tell anyone what I have said. She always recovered quickly enough once she was home again. She would be furious if she knew I told anyone. But to think of her, so old, so vulnerable—" She broke off, fresh tears coursing down her cheeks. She dashed them away quickly with the back of her hand.

"We have only to find her. A rather sizeable needle in a fairly small haystack," I finished with an attempt at jollity. "Besides,

Father says he has had word and she is quite safe. Just off for a bit of an adventure."

She shook her head. "I cannot bear to think of it. She could be stern, you know. I cannot say that I ever liked her. But she did her duty by us. She took us in when we were motherless. I will pray for her, and Lucy will as well."

"I am certain your prayers will be effective," I said, almost meaning it. Personally, I preferred more immediate action than petitioning the Almighty, but I tried very hard not to think less of those who believed differently.

We parted then, and I made my way up the tiny, twisting stair, the soles of my shoes scraping lightly the stones that so many sandaled monks had trod before me. The lumber rooms, formerly the scriptoria where manuscripts were copied, were every bit as cold and miserable as I had expected. Frost rimed the tiny windows under the eaves of the larger of the two rooms, permitting only the faintest light to penetrate the shadowy corners. I scurried around, lighting lamps and banishing the gloom, and gathering quite a collection of cobwebs with my hems. Hoots never allowed the maids entrée to the lumber rooms, preferring to dust them himself. He claimed it was because there were too many objects of value tucked away up here, but everyone knew better. Hoots had made himself a rather cosy nest, far away from his butler's pantry and bedchamber. Furnished with a cast-off velvet recamier and a few excellent bottles of Bordeaux, the little corner under the eaves was a perfect bolthole. Father never minded—the Bordeaux was his traditional Christmas present to

Hoots—and Aunt Hermia always said Hoots worked harder than twelve men and deserved whatever rest he could snatch.

Now the little couch looked forlorn, and the Bordeaux was far too cold to drink with any pleasure. Poor Hoots. He would miss Christmas at the Abbey terribly. I made a note to remind Father to send him a hamper of delicacies, crowned with the best bottle of wine in the cellars. Perhaps his doctors would make an exception and permit him a thimbleful in honour of the season.

I took up one of the lamps and walked slowly around the room. Most of the contents were as familiar to me as my own face. We had played here as children, exploring each trunk and hatbox, prying open crates to peer at the treasures within, dressing ourselves up in shredded velvets and Prince of Wales feathers that had once graced noble brows during Court presentations. Those little attic rooms echoed with our games and silly songs of our own invention. Eventually we outgrew our Cavalier plumes and Regency silks, letting them fall where we tired of them. It was left to Aunt Hermia to pack them tenderly away in tissue and lavender, and the scent of the herb lingered still, stale and sharp in the cold air. Holding the lamp high, I looked carefully at each trunk, touched the crumbling frames of decaying paintings. I traced the spiders' webs and the dust, and noted the lack of footprints and smudges. This lot had not been disturbed. No one had been here since Hoots had last enjoyed his wine, and I was careful to blow out the lamps, taking one with me to light my way to the lesser lumber room.

This room told another tale as soon as I opened the door.

While the larger room was used to hold the Abbey's more important unused treasures, the smaller was the repository of more humble items. The castoffs of daily life found their way here. Instead of court trains and Tudor lace, this room held neglected toys and clothes long out of fashion, pieces we had used for our amateur theatricals. There were my brother Bellmont's school-books in a teetering stack in the corner, nibbled by mice and smelling strongly of mould. A crate by the door held a service of china Aunt Hermia had been given as a gift and hated on sight. And on the opposite side were bags, the trunks and portmanteaux of the houseguests, mine included.

The baggage told an interesting story of its own. Portia and I used similar trunks, of excellent make and quiet colour, discreetly marked with our ciphers. Sir Cedric, on the other hand, had an enormous boat of a bag, peacock-blue leather stamped with his monogram in gilt letters six inches high. Ludlow's was a sober affair of brown calf, a small portmanteau barely adequate for a gentleman's wardrobe. It was mute testimony to his poverty, but at least he had a portmanteau at all. Lucy and Emma had nothing here, I realised as I searched. I had seen them thus far in only two dresses each, and it occurred to me then that was likely all they had. Plain, sober colours for evening, and serviceable wool for day. With a pair of stout walking boots each and a pair of evening slippers, this was their wardrobe. I glanced again at Sir Cedric's exotic baggage and shrugged. I could well understand Lucy's attraction to him. He had spent more money on that single trunk than Lucy had seen in her entire life, I would wager, and when she married him, she would command a sizeable part of that fortune. Such a man would wish his wife to be dressed in the first rank of fashion, noticeably, gaudily even. After a lifetime of living in the shadows, dependent upon the charity of others, the prospect of such riches would be heady.

I moved to Charlotte's trunk. It was small and fashioned of pale kidskin and completely empty, as were the others I searched. I even poked through my own and those of the rest of the party who had come from Italy. I had a notion Alessandro would mind terribly if he found out, so I searched his quickly and closed it with a stab of guilt. I could not truly suspect him of any villainy, but that was the difficulty with murder. It took more than a life; it killed trust as well. I now looked more closely at everyone, scrutinising those I had known well, wondering what secrets lay hidden that friendship or family bonds could not penetrate.

And what of other, deeper and more abstruse emotions, I wondered, staring at Brisbane's bag. That he felt some attraction to me, I had no doubt. Neither did I doubt he was fighting it with every weapon at his disposal. He claimed to blame himself for the calamitous end to our first investigation, for the danger to me, but I felt in my bones there was more to his aloofness. I ran a hand over the soft black kidskin, as if touching his possession could teach me about the man himself.

I suppose I could justify opening the trunk on the grounds that I meant to search all of the bags in the lumber rooms, but the truth is far simpler: I wanted to know more of him, and I thought there might be the slightest chance some article left behind in the bag could give me some enlightenment. As if a bottle of toilet water or a spare comb could interpret a character as complex as Brisbane, I thought bitterly as I threw back the lid, cursing my own foolishness even as I hoped for some bit of illumination.

What I found was no bottle of toilet water, no broken comb or discarded pair of boots. It was a gown, a white gown of sheerest gossamer laid over silk, trailing fingers of cloudy white like fog on a windy night.

I stared at it for a long moment, scarcely believing my eyes. I reached into the trunk cautiously, as if expecting it to move of its own accord. The silk was cold to the touch, and when I lifted it, it foamed up, springing to life. I jumped back, then approached it again, poking at it with a nervous finger. Something sharp jabbed into my flesh and I jerked it back, staring at the bright bead of blood welling on my fingertip. I wrapped my handkerchief carefully about my finger and inspected the dress more closely. Each layer was fitted with a thin bit of wire at the hem, a wire that could be bent to one's whim. The layers could be made to trail out, even when the wearer was quite still, and the effect would be one of ghostly movement.

I laid it aside and removed the rest of the contents. There was a bit of black veiling, sheer but without sheen or pattern. A headdress of sorts followed, more of the white silk overlaid with gossamer tissue. And below this was the most interesting find of all, a pair of pattens. I had not seen them since I was a girl. They were for country-dwellers, an apparatus to strap over the shoes on muddy days. Put simply, they were soles on high iron rings, lifting the wearer out of the muck. They made a tremendous clanging sound as one walked, but as I inspected the bottoms, I realised these would be perfectly silent. They had been fitted with black felt soles, rendering them noiseless, even on the stone floors of the Abbey.

I sat back, staring at the bizarre collection before me. Individually, the pieces were unusual enough; together they made a ghost, dressed in trailing white draperies, features obscured by a bit of black veiling, pattens to make it seem as if the spectre were floating above the floor.

Somewhat against my will, I was forced to admire the ingenuity behind the costume. I realised as I looked closely, it had been assembled from bits and pieces found at the Abbey. The white costume was one Aunt Hermia had worn to a midsummer masked ball. Titania, I think she was. The pattens had been long discarded. Old-fashioned and ungainly, they had been decaying in the lumber rooms for years. I remembered them from my childhood. The bits of black veiling and felt were easily explained as well—a mourning bonnet stripped of its veil, a wide hat cut into soles. The whole had been cleverly done, and all of it from here in the smaller lumber room. It would not have taken more than a quarter of an hour to effect the necessary modifications, and hey, presto, a phantom was born.

But who? And why hide the costume in Brisbane's trunk? The latter question was easier to answer. Brisbane was clearly too large to be the ghost. If a white gown was found in his trunk, it might occasion some snickering, but no real danger to him. It was a nasty prank on the part of someone who did not wish him well, but it would not do him any lasting harm.

The greater question was who? And as I packed the costume carefully back into the trunk, I realised there was but one way to find out.

Feeling pleased with myself in spite of the meagre results of my search—Snow's bag had been empty as well—I hurried down the stairs. I had just crossed the gallery with the intent of meeting up with Brisbane in the bachelors' wing when I happened to glance down the gallery toward the ladies' bedchambers. A flicker of movement caught my eye as Charlotte's door opened and a familiar black head edged out.

Just then, I heard a footstep rising on the stair and leaned over the banister to see who approached.

"Charlotte!" I cried, rather more loudly than necessary. From the tail of my eye I saw the black head disappear and the door to her room close swiftly.

Charlotte nodded at me as she gained the gallery. She looked rosy from her outing on the boundary wall, her hands still tucked into a dainty muff of squirrel fur.

"I hope you have had a pleasant walk," I said, my eyes lingering on a hairpin dangling just above her ear, the curl above it threatening to escape.

She did not flush, but I noticed her lips were pinkly moist and a little swollen. She licked them before she replied.

"Very pleasant, thank you."

I dared not let my gaze slide past her shoulder for fear she would turn. I detained her for a moment, asking inane questions about her comfort—Had she enough to eat at luncheon? Was her bedchamber warm enough?—keeping my eyes firmly fixed on her face. She replied that she was quite comfortable, and we exchanged pleasantries.

A few minutes' worth of imbecilic conversation was all the situation required, I decided, and I was just about to take my leave of her when she laid a hand on my sleeve. Her expression, sweetly placid before, had taken on an anxious cast. Her eyes darted about, as if she feared to speak freely.

"My lady, I wonder…" She broke off, worrying her lip with her tiny, pearly teeth.

"Yes?" I prodded. The great irony of Charlotte King's character was that when one craved silence, she chattered like a monkey, but when one wished her to speak, she was silent as an oyster. I gave her an encouraging smile, determined to pry her open.

She twisted her hands together. "I feel a vile creature for even suggesting such a thing, but I did wonder—the death of the curate, the disappearance of Lady Dorcas, the theft of the Grey Pearls—these terrible events might possibly be connected."

I resisted the urge to pinch her for pointing out the obvious. It was unfair to expect her to handle these developments with any sort of equanimity. Those of us born into the March family enjoyed a long and illustrious heritage of drama and disaster. I endeavoured to explain this to Charlotte.

"My dear, of course they are connected. They all happened

here, in our family home. But you must realise such things have been happening to us for more than three hundred years, and for four centuries before that prior to our taking up residence in the Abbey. One has only to read a history of the March family to see that we are an unprincipled, unpredictable lot. There have been beheadings and elopements, abductions and accidents. We are rather too accustomed to such things, I suppose."

Charlotte shook her head, the loosened lock of silky primrose-yellow hair falling free over her shoulder. "You misunderstand, my lady. I do not refer to the past history of the March family. I speak only of the present." She leaned closer, and I smelled fennel seed on her breath. "I speak of your present connections."

I held my breath for the space of a heartbeat. Surely she could not mean Brisbane?

"The Gypsies," she whispered, her voice urgent.

I laughed. It was impolite, but I could not stop myself. She was so earnest, so determined to help.

"My dear, it is not possible."

She tightened her grip on my sleeve. "Are you quite certain? Think on it, my lady. Mr. Snow was adamant in his condemnation of them. He proposed taking their children away and putting them into orphanages. They might well have heard of his views and took steps to ensure he could not see them to fruition."

"Mr. Snow revisited those thoughts after we called upon their camp," I protested.

She shook her head, dropping her lashes to fan her cheeks. It was a lovely, sorrowful expression and I rather thought Plum ought to paint her thus. He could title it *Beauty Grieves*.

"He did not change his mind, not truly," she told me. "If you thought so, it was because he believed it prudent to be polite to his hosts. He admitted as much last evening before dinner. We spoke of it, just before we withdrew to the dining room."

I said nothing, and she pressed her advantage. "And what of the pearls? Surely so great a treasure would be an impossible temptation to those already accustomed to thieving?"

"And Lady Dorcas?" I asked, not bothering to blunt the edge to my voice. "Even if you could persuade me the Gypsies had reason to slay Mr. Snow and to purloin my jewels, you cannot possibly conceive any reason they would trouble themselves to *steal* a portly old woman."

Charlotte shrugged. "They would if she had seen what she ought not. And who else would be so cunning as to send a message that the lady is well? Lord March would not question such tidings from them. And all the while she may be among them, in distress, in need of our aid, never realising *it will not come*."

I gaped at her. "Are you seriously suggesting the Romanies trespassed into the Abbey, murdered Mr. Snow, hid themselves for some time, then crept upstairs and stole the pearls from my dressing table, unseen by anyone except Aunt Dorcas? And then to cover their crimes, they abducted their only witness, into the snow, over a distance of *miles*, without leaving a single track outside the Abbey?"

She raised her chin, summoning her dignity. "I think it a

likely solution, yes. And if you are not afraid of them, I am not ashamed to say I am. They are a ruthless, vicious people, and I for one will be glad when I am gone from this place and away from them."

She tipped her nose into the air and took her leave, banging her door behind her. I stood for a moment, lip caught between my teeth as I worried the notion like a dog at a bone. That the Roma were capable of less than impeccable behaviour, I was fully aware. I had seen examples of their cunning and their duplicity with my own eyes.

But I had never seen them behave maliciously. They could be terrible foes if they decided to revenge a wrong, but they were peaceable to those who treated them with courtesy, and my father had been a patron of sorts to them for many years. It was the grossest violation of the Roma code to betray the goodwill of one's host, and murder was an unspeakable crime to them. Neither would they steal from me. As the daughter of my father and a friend to them, I was always treated with respect. And the notion that Aunt Dorcas would have been stolen away to preserve her silence as a witness was laughable. She was old, but age had done nothing to impair her volume. She was capable of shouting down the rooftops if she wished, and if anyone laid hands on her, I had little doubt the villagers down in Blessingstoke would have been roused from their peaceful slumbers.

No, it was a pretty, tidy theory for Charlotte, who liked pretty, tidy things. Unfortunately, it crumbled beneath the smallest scrutiny. I wondered if she had expounded her theory to Plum.

With his devotion to the Roma, he would have put such a flea in her ear their budding friendship would have withered on the vine. But the smell of fennel seed on her breath had convinced me they had gotten up to more than conversation. Plum always chewed the vile things, claiming they sweetened his breath. I hated them; their hard striped backs put me too much in mind of little insects. He might have offered her a few from the gilt snuffbox he carried in his pocket, but there was something indefinable about her, some self-satisfaction she carried this afternoon I had not seen in her before that convinced me otherwise. An interesting notion, if it were true. I had always suspected Brisbane's attentions to her were manufactured, but I also believed he would not break with her until it suited him. I wondered how well he would like it if she threw him over for more amiable company first.

Dismissing Charlotte from my thoughts, I entered my room, closing the door softly. The fire was banked up and Brisbane was seated near the hearth in an armchair, Florence tucked in his lap as he stroked her head. Morag was nowhere to be seen.

"This is a cosy scene," I commented, drawing up a chair for myself. Florence protested with a growl, but I put out my tongue at her and she laid her head down again on Brisbane's thigh, content to let him fondle her ears. He said nothing for a long moment. He simply sat, petting the pup's silky head in long, supple strokes that never varied in their rhythm.

"You've very nearly put her to sleep," I commented.

He raised his good shoulder in a shrug, careful not to

disturb Florence as she dozed. "It would not be difficult. She has been drugged."

"I beg your pardon?"

Lifting her carefully with his good hand, he settled her into her basket and tucked the fur tippet gently about her. She gave a little sound that might have been a purr had she been of another species, and settled in for a nap.

"What do you mean she has been drugged?"

"Some narcotic, perhaps laudanum as well, certainly an opiate. When I ducked in here, Morag mentioned she had trouble rousing the dog. I had a look at her, and when you consider what happened in this room, it is perfectly logical."

It spoke volumes about the unconventional nature of our relationship that Morag did not question his presence in my room. Fortunately for me, Morag's penchant for gossip was entirely one-sided. She might carry tales to me, but she was a gorgon when it came to protecting my privacy.

I suddenly realised what Brisbane had just said. "What happened in this room?"

"The theft of your pearls," he said patiently. "Everyone knows Florence stays in your chamber. Anyone wishing to purloin the pearls would have come prepared to silence her. By the way, rather quick thinking out there with Charlotte. I was not so careful as I ought to have been," he finished with a rueful grimace.

"You are welcome. But as I rescued you, I think I am owed a forfeit. Did you speak to William IV this morning?"

He made a moue of disgust. "I did. The boy doesn't have the

intelligence of a sponge. He swears blind he did not leave his post except to follow a ghost."

I sat up quite straight. "A ghost? Did he describe it? Where did he see it?"

"At the far end of the nave, walking toward the vestry."

I tipped my head to the side, considering. "Walking? Ghosts don't walk."

"This one did. Apparently it had a slow, lumbering gait, and the boy, after several minutes of terrified debate with himself, decided to follow it."

"And?"

Brisbane shrugged. "It had disappeared. William searched the vestry, the cloister, even the kitchen passage, but it had vanished."

I could have screamed in exasperation. "The fool! Did he not remember that the vestry has *two* doors, one from the cloister passage and the other directly beside the chapel?"

"No, not even when he returned to his post and discovered a bottle of brandy, with a tag neatly inscribed for Miss Emma and Miss Lucy."

I groaned. "So close, and he did not have the wit to use the other door. It never occurred to him that the ghost was simply a ruse to lure him from his post?"

Brisbane shook his head. "I think if he had reasoned that out for himself, he might have been prudent enough not to drink from the bottle. He said he took a sizeable swallow or two, then sealed it up again and took it inside to the ladies. He returned to his post, and sitting down in his chair is the last thing he remembers until he awoke this morning in Aquinas' bed. That required a bit of explaining as well," he finished blandly.

I gave a great sigh and slumped back in my chair, drumming my fingers on the arm. "Sir Cedric's room?"

"Nothing of interest. He has appalling taste in books, but other than that, I can find no crimes to lay at his door."

"Pity," I mused. "I think he would make a proper villain."

Brisbane quirked one glossy black brow at me. "Have you not yet learned that villainy is not written on the face, but the heart?"

I said nothing for a long moment, thinking of my husband's murderer, and the sweet, gentle face I had loved. At length I cleared my throat and changed the subject.

"What of your expedition to Charlotte's room? What did you find?"

Brisbane gave me a bland smile. "Nothing."

"Let me amend that. What did you *hope* to find?"

He paused, then looked at the fire. "I cannot say." He glanced back at me. "You needn't grind your teeth at me. I cannot say."

"So be it. We will simply each of us have our secrets then."

His eyes narrowed sharply. "Do not think of withholding anything from me. I am in deadly earnest, my lady. You were of use in the first investigation, I do not deny it. And I am keenly aware that his lordship has ordered your involvement this time. But do not think I mean to make you an equal partner in this. I work best alone."

I blinked slowly at him, a trick I had learned from Portia. Most men find it devastatingly disarming.

"Have you something in your eye? A cinder perhaps?"

I sighed in disgust. "No. I am perfectly well."

"And what did you discover in the lumber rooms? Did you search all of the bags?"

"Yes, captain," I said, larding my voice with sarcasm. "And I found nothing in the other guests' bags at all. They were empty as the tomb on Easter Sunday." Quite deliberately I did not mention his bag. But then, he did not ask.

Brisbane quirked a brow at me in surprise. "It is not like you to blaspheme. Have you been gambling and keeping low company as well?"

"I have. I am toying with the notion of taking up hard drinking directly. Father has an excellent cellar."

He stared at me a long moment, those astonishing black eyes searching mine. Finally, he shook his head. "You are up to something, but I cannot make out what and I do not have the time at present to compel you to speak."

I snorted. "Compel me indeed! I think you know me better than that. I should like to see the man who could *compel* me to do anything I did not wish." That little speech surprised even me. I had come far from the quiet little dormouse I had been before my husband's death. Widowhood had been the making of me, I decided.

But before I could admire myself too thoroughly, Brisbane leaned forward in his chair, pinning me once again with his gaze, but softening it somehow, and in the process drawing me in until I could see myself reflected in the inky depths. There was something other-worldly about that gaze, something oblique and unspoken, and yet it held all the sensual promise of a courtesan's smile.

"Do you not think I have other methods to compel you?" he murmured.

My corset felt suddenly too tight. My breath was coming far too quickly as I thought of what methods he might employ. Methods such as those he had used to such effect the previous night, perhaps? I felt dizzy at the prospect, and violet spots danced in front of my eyes. A dozen pictures flashed through my mind: Brisbane dragging me into his room in the low hours of the night, kissing me until I could not speak or think. I thought of my response to him, so unaffected, so impossible. I had always believed myself cold, unbreachable. And yet my defenses always fell to Brisbane, usually when he needed to breach them the most. How convenient for him, I thought bitterly.

My throat felt thick, and when I spoke, my voice was like honeyed whiskey. "Brisbane," I said softly. Holding his gaze, I slid to my knees, coming to rest between his booted feet. I heard his breath catch, and a noise in the back of his throat that might have been a stifled groan.

I held up my own hand teasingly. "A question first, my lord."

I dropped my hand to his boot top. It rested there a moment, my fingers just below the curve of his knee, before I slid it with deliberate, teasing slowness down the supple leather to his foot. He exhaled slowly through flared nostrils, his eyes never leaving mine.

Suddenly and without warning, I grabbed the boot hard and swung it up. He pulled back, swearing fluently in Gaelic, but I had caught him by surprise. I clamped onto the boot with both hands and held it.

"Your boots were wet last night when you dragged me into your room. That is why they were sitting on the hearth. And your greatcoat was draped over the armchair to dry. That is why you kissed me and then pretended to hear a ghost in the corridor. You thought I was coming to see you, and you could not afford for me to know what you had been about. You wanted to distract me so I would not realise you had been abroad in the night."

He stopped cursing and lapsed into furious silence. I dropped the boot and resumed my chair, wiping my hands disdainfully on my skirts. The little skirmish had roused Florence and she sat up in her basket, weaving a little, but watching with interest, her ears pricked at a quizzical angle.

"I note you make no attempt to deny it. Very sensible." I nodded toward his boots. "The watermarks are still present on the leather. You ought to have Aquinas tend to them before they are ruined, you know."

Still he said nothing, the little muscle in his jaw twitching madly. Perhaps he thought to draw me out by his silence, to learn precisely what I knew by refusing to admit or deny anything himself.

Unfortunately, all that I knew I had already revealed. From the boots drying on the hearth and the faint smell of wet wool, I had deduced that he had left the Abbey some time after the snow had begun to fall. For what purpose, I could not imagine.

But as I stared at his lowering brow, his lips thinned with displeasure, I realised I did in fact have one more arrow in my quiver.

"Come, Brisbane, let us not quarrel. We must be friends again. I will tell you what I found in Mr. Snow's room after you left, if you will tell me what you have done with Aunt Dorcas."

THE TWENTIETH CHAPTER

To do a great right, do a little wrong.
—THE MERCHANT OF VENICE

*I*f I expected Brisbane to reveal all, I was destined to be thwarted. He shot the cuff of his injured arm, studying his nails with affected nonchalance.

"I can only tell you what I have already told your father—your aunt is perfectly safe."

I puzzled this over for a moment, not knowing quite where to begin. "That is impossible. You left no tracks in the snow."

"I was back before the snow began to fall," he said grudgingly. He did not like to explain the matter, that much was apparent. But perhaps he hoped a little information would throw me from the scent.

"Then how did your boots come to be wet?"

"I was careless. I stepped on a patch of ice. It was not fully frozen yet, and my boots broke through to the puddle beneath. The hem of my greatcoat was fully soaked."

No matter how much I prodded, he told me nothing more, except to reassure me Aunt Dorcas was well. I was surprised at how much I worried for her. I had not thought myself fond of the old toad, but I would have been genuinely sorry if any ill had befallen her.

"Now," he said severely, "what did you find among Snow's things?"

I tipped my head to the side. "You still have not told me what you thought to find in Charlotte's room."

He fixed me with a stare so intent, I felt the room falling away, blackness creeping along the edges of my vision. I swallowed hard, sliding my gaze away from his. "Goodness, Brisbane, if Mesmer had had a stare like that he mightn't have needed a pocket watch. Very well, you do not mean to tell me. I can guess for myself. You hoped to find the Grey Pearls in her room."

His lids dropped and he reached a lazy hand to pet the dog. "And what led you to that conclusion?"

"A clever jewel thief would never have hidden the jewels in his own room. They might easily be discovered by a diligent servant. Now, anyone would realise there is no point to searching the Abbey—it is far too large and there are nooks and crannies and secret passages God Himself does not know of. Any of them might serve as a hiding place, but how much better to put the pearls in Charlotte King's room and throw suspicion on her? If they were discovered among her things, she would have a difficult time explaining how she came by them. Jewels found in the public rooms of the Abbey carry a mystery with them, jewels found in Charlotte's room breed a scapegoat. She might well be arrested and bound over for trial, and no one else would be under the slightest cloud of suspicion."

"An interesting theory," Brisbane said slowly. His fingers twitched, and I wondered if he was longing for his pipe. "Now, back to the matter of Snow's room."

My fingers went then to the small bundle still nestled in my pocket. I debated fiercely with myself about whether or not to disclose it. Finding it had been rather gratifying. I still did not know what it signified, but I did trust Brisbane to do what was best for my family. I did not believe Aunt Hermia had given the trinkets to Snow herself. Indeed, if I believed that I would have kept them and confronted her with the collection myself. But determined as I was to solve these little mysteries myself, there were few things I could refuse Brisbane.

I drew out the bundle and handed it to him. He turned it over, peering at the monogram worked in silk thread, the tiny design of flowers twining through the letters. After he had committed every detail of the handkerchief to memory, he untied it and took out the pieces one by one, turning them over and marking them carefully. When they had all been considered, he handed them back. I wrapped them and knotted the handkerchief, pocketing the little bundle.

"And you actually found these in Snow's room?"

I nodded and said nothing.

"The handkerchief is, I suppose, Lady Hermia's? And the jewels as well?"

"Yes. I asked Portia about them. She said Aunt Hermia kept them in a little pasteboard box on her night table." Brisbane had begun to glower, so I hastened to reassure him. "You needn't look so murderous. I did not tell her where I found them."

His expression was thoughtful. "Snow did not arrive as a houseguest until yesterday, well after Lady Hermia departed the Abbey for London. A box of trinkets on her night table would be easy enough for anyone to pilfer. Snow, or another, had only to make certain the corridor was empty, creep inside and pocket the jewels. It is interesting to note that nothing of real value was taken."

"The important pieces are all locked in Father's safe or in the vault in the bank in London. Aunt Hermia keeps out only the things she wears often, those little baubles, a ruby brooch, a few rings, and her chains of sapphires. I am quite certain she would have taken those with her to London."

"So we have here a crime of opportunity."

"Tied to Snow's murder?" I asked. Brisbane shook his head slowly.

"It would be premature to say. He seemed perpetually short of money, if his sisters' letters are to be believed. Perhaps it was simply too easy for him, a few trinkets that could be pawned in the city. By the time Lady Hermia missed them, it would be far too late to lay the blame at his door. Perhaps one of the maids would be blamed, perhaps even dismissed over it. In the meanwhile, Snow has a little money and no suspicion falls on him."

"That is reprehensible," I told him, "and yet entirely plausible." There was another possibility that was plausible as well: Aunt Dorcas. Father and Plum, as well as Emma, had mentioned her penchant for taking things that did not belong to her, usually of the sparkly variety. What if she had nipped into Aunt Hermia's room and helped herself to a few of the prettier trinkets? But why hide them among Snow's things? From the stories I had heard, she had seldom troubled to hide her crimes in the past. Usually the odd little jewel had actually been found on her person. If nothing else, the jewels would be difficult for her to retrieve from Snow's room. It seemed the little bundle had raised more questions than it had answered.

We were silent a moment, locked in our thoughts. Florence had settled back into her basket and was snoring peacefully. I thought of what Brisbane had suggested, that someone had crept into my room and drugged the poor little thing to keep her quiet while they took my pearls. The very idea made me shatteringly angry. I did not actually like the animal, but she was helpless, a baby really. I made a note to tell Morag to give her more beef tea for her supper.

I turned to find Brisbane regarding me. I had not realised he was staring, and his scrutiny flustered me. I smoothed my skirts again. It was becoming something of a nervous habit.

"I think you had better keep a shorter rein on your fiancée," I said lightly. "She seems overfond of my brother's company. Perhaps you ought to have a word."

Brisbane reached into his coat pocket and withdrew something. He opened his hand to show me a diamond ring sparkling on his palm.

"Charlotte broke our betrothal before breakfast this morning. I have no fiancée."

He held the ring up to the firelight, watching the light bend and shatter into a tiny rainbow as it played over his hand. "Pity. It is a lovely ring."

"Very well done of her to return it since she has no intention of marrying you," I said, my voice husky with pent emotion.

He watched the play of light a moment more, then dropped the ring back into his pocket.

"I am rather relieved to be rid of the charade, truth be told," he said finally. "I tired of playing the intended bridegroom."

"I knew you could not mean to marry her!" I cried, triumphant. "I cannot believe anyone would think you a couple."

"Well, when I embarked upon this sham betrothal, I never expected to have to convince you of my sincerity," he admitted. "But I am glad to be done with it. I have no wish to be betrothed, in pretense or otherwise."

I wagged a finger at him playfully. "Now, Brisbane, you mustn't talk like that. You will lead people to believe you have no mind to marry at all."

"I do not," he said. He turned to the fire, and I had the most curious conviction he was doing so because he could not speak the next words directly to me. "I could never marry a woman like Charlotte."

"You mean a silly woman?" I asked teasingly.

"No, a wealthy one," he returned quietly.

It is astonishing how words can cut one to the quick and yet leave no outward trace. One would have expected a lash like that to leave a mark.

But pride, though deplorable as a vice, can be a worthy ally at such times. It was pride that lifted my chin and lent a note of lightness to my voice.

"Ah, a confirmed bachelor, like the noble Duke of Aberdour," I said.

"I am nothing like my great-uncle," he replied, his voice laced with bitterness. There was no pragmatic reason I could imagine for his opposition to marriage. His business was a profitable one, his lineage—though spotted with less than elevated blood—was illustrious enough for all but the most fastidious of brides, and now his achievements were to be crowned with title and an estate. He could even retire from his work as an inquiry agent if he wished and live a life of leisure. People would whisper about his having been in trade of course, but it had been my experience that with sufficient time and a healthy fortune, such a shortcoming could be deliberately overlooked.

But opposed he was, and from the set of his jaw, I did not imagine his position was one he had taken lightly or would relinquish easily. Pride was an expensive commodity, and his was easily wounded. It was a very great irony that the fortune my husband had left me should prove such an impediment to my happiness.

"Well, you needn't marry," I said finally. I was determined to be reasonable, as coolly logical as he. "You have your work to divert you, the excellent Monk to assist you, and Mrs. Lawson to manage your domestic affairs. What more may a man need?"

"What more indeed?" He looked at me then, a look I knew I should never forget, and a thousand things lay unsaid between us.

"I do not mean to marry again myself," I said suddenly and with conviction.

"Do you not?" he asked softly, and I wondered if he were thinking of Alessandro. Ah, Alessandro. Such a delightful companion, and yet when I thought of him I felt a hundred years old.

"I made a mistake the last time I married. I should not like to do so again."

"Then you and I understand each other perfectly," he said, his demeanour suddenly brisk. "And we cannot sit idly by gossiping like old maids. We have a murder to solve."

It was a testament to his distraction that he included me in that last statement. Or perhaps he was so eager to leave off the subject of marriage he did not mind returning to the safer ground of murder. In either event, it did not matter to me. As we rose and made our way downstairs, I realised that some small, cherished hope within me had gone very still. It was not entirely lost, but I reminded myself sternly Brisbane was a partner in detection and nothing more. If only I could make myself believe it.

We met Father in his study for a little council of war. I fussed over Grim, smoothing his feathers and feeding him from the box of sugared plums, while Brisbane and Father exchanged information. There was little to say. Brisbane had already informed him Aunt Dorcas was safe, but from the cool touch of frost in Father's manner, I could only deduce he was not pleased with Brisbane's role in the affair, nor in his refusal to send for Father when Emma and Lucy had fallen ill. The pearls were missing, and no clue had been discovered in the murder of Mr. Snow, save my little cache of jewels.

Father turned them over in his hand, his face stony as he touched a finger to the trinkets. Suddenly, he shot Brisbane a piercing glance. "Do you believe these are related to your other matter?"

Brisbane did not look at me, but he shifted in his seat, averting his profile as if to exclude me from the conversation.

"I do not," he said, his voice pitched so low I very nearly did not hear him at all. Instantly I left Grim to his sweets and took the chair next to Brisbane, looking with interest from him to my father.

Brisbane's cheek twitched a little, and I knew he was thoroughly annoyed, but with Father or me, I could not decide.

Father gave the bundle a searching look and placed it on the desk. "In that case, I do not think we need concern ourselves with this. I will see to it that it is returned to Lady Hermia's room."

"My lord, I would rather keep the evidence myself," Brisbane began. Father waved him off with a peremptory hand.

"I see no need. You know what was found and where. Surely keeping it in your possession is not necessary."

Brisbane did not argue, but I could feel the irritation emanating from him. He was a man seldom thwarted, but then so was my father. What had begun as a small territorial skirmish between them was rapidly deteriorating into a formidable battle of wills.

Father exerted his command over the situation by changing the subject. As it would have been a breach of etiquette to return to a topic once he had abandoned it, this was a gambit he used when it suited him. I always found it illogical that a family so willing to throw off society's greater constraints would abide by the lesser, but we were nothing if not inconsistent.

"Where are we then, with this business of Snow? Lucy is resting, claiming she knows nothing of it, and we have no clue save the bruises, which tell us a man must have been involved? And someone wishes to put her and her sister out of the way."

"Succinct, and correct," Brisbane replied. "We have discovered no reason for Miss Lucy to have wished Mr. Snow ill, nor have we discovered a reason for her to have been willing to take an accomplice's guilt on her own shoulders."

Father considered for a moment, running his hands through his silver-white hair. "I think she must have told Julia the truth. She is innocent in every possible way of this atrocity and remembers nothing. Someone is preying on her now, gambling everything on her inability to remember what she has seen."

Brisbane's eyes narrowed. "It does explain the attack on Miss Lucy and her sister. Were I the villain, I should not like to stake my chances on escaping the gallows on the slender hopes that a young and healthy girl will not recover her memory. If I were cold-blooded enough to murder once, I should do so again, very soon and without compunction."

"And the attack on Emma as well?" I asked.

Brisbane shrugged. "They are close as two sisters can be. If Miss Lucy took anyone into her confidence, it would be her elder sister. Whoever poisoned Miss Lucy either did not care if Miss Emma died as well, or hoped that she would."

Father nodded. "We will keep a footman on watch, for their protection."

"Agreed," I said. "But we must consider the possibility that Lucy is in league with the murderer as well. Father, I know you wanted us to find some proof, some shred of evidence to speak in her favour and keep her from the hangman's noose, but I cannot be persuaded she is entirely innocent."

Father reached for the snuffbox on his desk and began to fidget with it. It was a nervous habit of long standing. He flicked the lid open with a thumbnail, then snapped it closed. It was a practice that annoyed Aunt Hermia to no end. If he indulged the habit in front of her, she usually snatched it out of his hand or snapped it closed on his finger.

Now he opened and closed it, rhythmically, like a metronome keeping time. I suspected it helped him to think. He finally snapped it closed and sat up in his chair, rather more energetic than I had seen him since Snow's broken body had been discovered the night before.

"I know you suspect Cedric, Julia. But I wonder, a girl like that, on the verge of marriage to a man so much her elder. She has seen nothing of the world, had no experience. I must wonder if she decided to indulge in a liaison before she married."

"I did wonder," I admitted, "but it seemed so diabolical. Suppose she did decide to take a younger lover. Could it have been Snow? Cedric might have murdered him in revenge," I mused.

"I think his lordship is thinking more abstractly," Brisbane put in. Father regarded him coldly, doubtless resenting Brisbane for speaking on his behalf. I smothered a sigh. There were enough currents and eddies of tension within the household without the two of them at each other's throats. Brisbane continued, oblivious to Father's annoyance. "Cedric is the obvious choice for the murderer if Snow was her lover. But what if Snow discovered her affair with another and demanded a price for his silence? That would make him a blackmailer, and there is already evidence he was."

I blinked at him in wonder. "Aunt Hermia's jewels?"

He nodded. "It seems possible, but not likely to me he would have stolen them himself. It would have been dangerous for a gentleman guest to be discovered in the ladies' wing. Far safer for him to have pilfered something from another gentleman or from the public rooms. But if a lady were to try to lay hands on something small and valuable to meet the demands of a black-mailer, what better place to look than the bedchamber of an absent hostess?"

I sat back, marvelling at the twisted little tangle of ideas he had just presented. "And if Lucy were engaging in an *affaire du coeur*, she might well cover the crimes of her lover by claiming sanctu-ary for a murder done by his hand."

"In which case she is in no danger, but still ought to be kept under watch so as to keep her near at hand," Brisbane put in.

"But she has been attacked, with malice prepense," I pointed out.

"Has she? What did the footman see but a sheet-draped figure drifting through the hall? You yourself pointed out the proximity of the vestry to the chapel. What if the footman nodded off and Miss Lucy or Miss Emma played the ghost? The footman went haring off after it, just as the miscreant planned. When he returned to his post, the brandy was there, supposedly by the hand of the phantom. The idiot footman passes it to them and they drink. It does not take much medical knowledge to know how much laudanum is fatal. And they might both have been pretending to be sicker than they were. We must keep them under guard for their possible culpability as well as their safety."

I shook my head to clear the cobwebs. It was a fantastic story, and the most fantastic part of all was that it might very possibly be true.

"Surely you do not think they would try to escape? To begin with, it would be impossible. The Abbey is entirely cut off from the outside," I argued.

"Not entirely." His tone was bland, but Father took his meaning at once.

"The passage from the priory vault to the family crypt in the churchyard," Father murmured, shaking his head. "So that is how you got the old fright out of here last night, is it not?"

Brisbane picked an imaginary bit of fluff from his sling. "It is, and though the mechanism was coming over rather thickly with ice by the time I returned, I imagine it would still function with a little persuasion."

I cursed my own stupidity. I had thought enough about hidden passageways in the last few days. I ought to have remembered that one. As children we had never been permitted to play there, but we had heard it spoken of from time to time. Originally built to provide dry, easy passage to the village for the monks, it had been just as useful as a means of egress for mischief-minded Marches for centuries. My grandfather had locked the passage during Father's boyhood, claiming it was unsafe for the children. But Aunt Dorcas would remember it well from her own youth; doubtless she even recalled that the key had been thrown into a great Chinese pot on the mantel of the dining room. It would have been a child's trick to find it. Why she had left the Abbey, and why Brisbane had seen to her passage were puzzles I burned to solve. But the murder of Lucian Snow was more pressing.

I turned to Brisbane.

"If Lucy even knows of that passage," I countered. "I had entirely forgotten it myself. It has not been used in years. Grandfather had it locked ages ago. I can't imagine it has been opened since."

"It has not, insomuch as I could determine," Brisbane confirmed, his handsome upper lip curling in distaste. "A fair bit of it has collapsed, and I saw distinct evidence of rats."

I shuddered. "How in the name of heaven did you persuade Aunt Dorcas through that passage?"

Brisbane gave me a deliciously wicked look. "My dear lady, I did not coax. I was *led*. Lady Dorcas was thoroughly acquainted with the passage and showed no hesitation in scrambling over broken stones and splashing through puddles."

"The maid said she took no coat. She must have been freezing," I remarked.

"Not at all. She sent me to the lumber rooms for some furs and was warm as toast."

Father and I were silent a moment. I was having a difficult time imagining Aunt Dorcas, wrapped in furs, leading the charge down the rock-strewn, rat-infested passage. I suspected Father was as well.

"And you say she is in good health?" Father asked finally.

Brisbane gave a short nod. "Quite. Now, on to other matters. I discovered nothing of interest in Sir Cedric's room," Brisbane reported. "There was a good deal of correspondence from his agent in London, but nothing unusual. The letters confirm he is what he presents himself to be—a successful man of industry. I took the opportunity of searching Henry Ludlow's room, as well as that of Alessandro Fornacci," he finished smoothly.

"Tell me you did not," I said, levelling my gaze at him.

He returned my stare with a coolly appraising look of his own. "Oh, but I did. Fornacci is the only other gentleman of the party not connected with this family. That fact makes him suspect. Am I to infer you did not search his trunk?"

I opened my mouth to speak, then snapped my teeth together. "Blast," I muttered between them.

"From that delicate expression I will conclude you put sentiment aside and searched it. I will further presume you found nothing to incriminate him. You will be pleased to hear I found nothing in his room pertaining to this investigation."

Father raised a hand. "No sparring, I beg you. Now, what will you be about, Brisbane?"

"I have other matters to attend to at present. When Lady Julia has something relevant to report, I will listen."

He rose, nodded sharply once to Father and once to me. He

clicked his fingers at Grim, who responded with a happy *quork* and a flap of glossy black wings. I waited until the door had closed behind him before turning to Father.

"If the passage to the churchyard is navigable, why can we not remove Mr. Snow now?"

Father flicked the snuffbox open, then snapped it shut again. "You heard Brisbane. It is collapsed in places. Fallen stone, icy puddles, rats. It would be madness to attempt it."

"Surely not. If Aunt Dorcas could manage it, I daresay a few footmen could maneuver Mr. Snow quite handily."

Flick. Snap. It was rather hypnotic, the slow, even movements of his fingers on the snuffbox. Father scorned modern instruments, but played the lute quite beautifully. He had taken it up as part of his homage to Shakespeare. I had not heard him play in years, but there was still a musician's suppleness to his reflexes.

"It is a trifle unseemly, don't you think? One ought to treat the dead with dignity."

Still his hands moved, and as I watched them, it did not seem entirely fanciful to imagine them laced about Snow's throat, closing tighter and tighter, choking the life out of him.

"Julia."

I jumped in my chair. "Yes, Father?"

He laid the snuffbox onto the desk and gave me an apologetic smile. "Your aunt deplores my little habit as well. I shall endeavour not to fidget."

His eyes were warm over his little half-moon spectacles and I felt instantly flooded with shame. How could I have suspected, even for a moment, my beloved parent had had any role in Snow's murder?

But the greatest danger of evil is that it is insidious. It had crept into my home on cloven feet, and would not leave until the murderer was brought to justice. Until then I knew I would be doomed to view every man around me, even my father, my brothers—Plum with his broad palms calloused from chiselling marble, Lysander with hands stronger than a labourer's from spanning a violin and keyboard for hours every day—as potential murderers. I stiffened my resolve to unmask the villain and put an end to this hateful charade. I rose to leave then, but one last thought intruded.

"Father, I understand you do not wish to remove Mr. Snow until it can be done in a dignified fashion," I began, tactfully ignoring the fact that the poor man was laid out in the game larder. One can hardly imagine a more undignified place of repose. "But I wondered if you had sent a note to Uncle Fly yet. He will know how to find Mr. Snow's family. They ought to know."

Father took in a great breath, then expelled it slowly in a soft, sorrowful sigh. "When a member of the family passes we stop the clocks, to show that time itself has stood still. We do not observe this custom for Lucian Snow, but so long as the Abbey remains snowbound, time *does* stand still. Out there, life carries on its usual pace. No one knows what transpires here, we are an island unto ourselves. For this little time, there is nothing for anyone to know. When the snow melts and the ice runs to water, then we must tell the world what has happened."

This was a mood I recognised well. Whenever he felt particularly gloomy, he was inclined to talk like Prospero. It was an affectation, of course, but a harmless one, and I looked past his words to the sentiment behind them. So long as we were housebound, no one knew of Snow's murder, and no one could speculate about the crime or its author. Once word of the murder spread, nothing would be quite the same. The newspapers, ravenous for scandal, would use this story to slake their appetite. From Dover to Orkney, our names would be bandied in every household. It was enough to make me long for Italy and anonymity. It would be so easy to pack my bags and board the first steamer across the Channel.

But for Father there would be no escape. His name was already well-known for his radical politics, the antics of his scampish youth, his charming eccentricities. And when folks tired of gossiping about him, they would cheerfully savage the rest of us. I shuddered to think what my brother Bellmont would make of this. Elected as a Tory, Bellmont was frightfully conservative, and more mindful of his dignity than the queen. As soon as the merest scrap of this reached the papers, he would descend upon us with all the wrath of a Biblical plague, blaming us for dragging the family name into disgrace once again. When he discovered my husband had been murdered, he had stopped speaking to me for two months. It was actually something of a relief, but I did not like to be at cross purposes with any of my family, no matter how maddening they could be.

"I have made a terrible mistake, I fear," he said softly. "I ought to have left you in Italy. You were happy there."

"You sent for us because Lysander married without permission. It had nothing to do with me," I reminded him.

He waved a hand. "Do you imagine I have nothing better to do than meddle in my children's romantic entanglements? It's a fool's game, and one never wins."

He was pensive, fretting now, talking more to the fire than to me.

"Then why did you send for us if not for Lysander's sake?"

He hesitated, as if weighing his words. "I knew Brisbane would be here. For weeks. I thought if I brought you home, he might declare himself."

"Oh, Father." His expression was apologetic, and a little of the spirit seemed to have gone out of him. "You just said you do not meddle in your children's romantic entanglements."

He beetled his heavy white brows at me. "I also said it was a fool's game and I am nothing if not a fool. A very great fool."

I started to rise, then sat back down, thinking swiftly. "Brisbane was betrothed to Charlotte. Why would you expect him to declare himself to me?"

"Bah. That engagement was a farce. It is you he loves."

My heart lurched a little. "He does not love me," I said flatly, remembering Brisbane's insistence on never taking a wealthy wife.

"He is far enough down the path, my dear," Father returned sharply, "and when he gets there, it will be the devil to pay. I ought to have left you in Italy," he repeated. "If only I had seen him for what he was."

I stared at him, my fingers tight around the arms of the chair. "What is he?" I asked, my voice barely above a whisper.

"A buccaneer," Father said harshly, "of the worst sort. He will think nothing of you, only himself and what serves his investigations."

I relaxed my grip on the chair and blew out a sigh of frustration.

"This is not about me. This is about you, resenting the fact that you brought him here and he has acted as lord and master in your home," I told him waspishly. "You thought you could put the bit between his teeth and guide him where you liked, and it nettles you that he cannot be mastered. He is not like your sons, Father. He doesn't give a tuppence for your great house or your lofty titles. He accepts you as an equal, but you will not do the same for him. You are a terrible snob, do you know that?"

Father's lips went very thin. "I am no such thing."

"Yes, you are." I rose, smoothing my skirts. "You always taught us that we should value a man according to his merit, his competence. Do you know a man more competent than Brisbane?"

He said nothing, his mouth set mulishly.

"I thought so. You are behaving very badly, Father. Very badly indeed."

I reached out and took up the little cache of Aunt Hermia's jewels, pocketing the bundle. "That is why you would not let him take these. You simply wanted to prove you could impose your will. He would never do anything to harm this family, Father."

Father lowered his head, peering peevishly at me over his spectacles. "I think I may know better than you what that man is capable of, child. There are depths there you cannot begin to plumb."

I smiled maliciously. "I seem to remember a time when you thought a dalliance with him might be advisable. Have you changed your opinion of him so much then?"

He did not reply to that, and I knew better than to push him further.

"I shall take Grim with me for a bit of exercise," I told him. If he heard me, he gave no sign of it. He simply reached for his snuffbox again and flicked it open as I left him to his thoughts.

THE TWENTY-FIRST CHAPTER

O, how bitter a thing it is to look into happiness through
another man's eyes.
—AS YOU LIKE IT

I found Sir Cedric in the smoking room, alone with his thoughts and a thoroughly vile cigar. He rose when I entered and made to crush it out, but I stopped him.

"You must not on my account. I do love a good cigar," I told him with a smile. It was not entirely a lie. I did love the scent of Brisbane's thin Spanish cigars. The aroma of them clung to his fingers and clothes, cloaking him in mystery and a bit of a glamoury, conjuring thoughts of smoky campfires and the sharp-blooded dances of Andalusia. Sir Cedric's cigar, an enormous fat sausage of a thing, smelled of mould and old dog.

I took the chair opposite and he resumed his, watching me with an appraising glance. Grim had wandered off in the direction of a rather fine bust of Caesar, quorking softly to himself.

"An interesting pet, my lady," Sir Cedric commented.

"He is, rather. Some people find him too morbid, but I am very fond of him." I sat a little forward in my chair, hands clasped on my lap, smiling at him winsomely. "Sir Cedric, I believe you must know by now we are an unconventional family. We observe society's customs when it suits us, and cast them to the winds when it does not."

"I had noticed," he replied acidly. He flicked a bit of ash into a china dish at his elbow, and I noticed his mouth had settled into lines of discontent. As well they might, I thought. His beloved fiancée enmeshed in a terrible crime, his temper worn to the thinnest edge. He had not as yet been told of the attack upon Lucy and her sister, but I thought it would take very little to push him to the brink of violence. I realised, repressing a little shudder, that he might well have already done violence. I thought of poor Mr. Snow, lying broken and bloody on the floor of the chapel, and the memory of it stiffened my resolve. I would use whatever means I held at my disposal to unmask his murderer, even if it was the man before me.

And the strongest weapon in my arsenal was surprise. I pitched my voice low and gentle. "I am worried for Lucy, and it is this cousinly concern that prompts me to speak freely to you. She has confessed to a terrible crime, which I believe she did not commit. I will ask you, sir, if my cousin is proved innocent, as I believe she must be, will you marry her still?"

His teeth ground together as he crushed out the glowing tip of the cigar, with rage or some other emotion I could not decide. He rose, looming over me in a fashion I could not help but find a little threatening.

"I cannot see that it is any business of yours. Your father ought to find you another husband, one who will mend your meddle-some ways." He turned to go, and for what happened next I can only credit instinct. I reached out to him, laying a gentle hand on his sleeve, and when I spoke, it was with a kindliness I feigned.

"She has broken your heart, has she not?"

He paused, his entire body stiffening like a pointer's. Then he collapsed into the chair with a groan, burying his face in his hands. It was some minutes before he dropped them, and when he did, I saw they shook a little.

"Did you hear the story of how we met, Lucy and me?" he began. I shook my head, concealing my surprise at the turn of events. Instead of being rather sternly lectured, it seemed I was to be treated to a story. "It was Ludlow's doing. His side of the family put great stock in education, refinement. My father thought solely of money. We lived in the poorest slums, not because my father could not afford better, but because he would not spend a tuppence more than he must for anything. He was a grim, miserly man who lived by one creed—if it could not put a penny in his pocket, he cared nothing for it. But I was a smart lad, and when Father put me to work as a bootmaker's apprentice, I learned the trade faster than any other boy in East London. I could cut a sole as quick and pretty as you please, and not one of the other lads could touch me for the stitches I used to make, so small you would need a magnifying glass just to see them."

Sir Cedric paused, his tawny eyes glazing slightly out of focus as he looked beyond me into his past. "One day the bootmaker's son was sick abed, and he shouted to me to come and help him fit a gentleman who had called at the shop. I had never seen a person of quality before, not like that. He was straight as a ramrod, a spine of steel and a nose like a whippet's. He looked down at me with that nose, and why not? I was scruffy and ill-fed. I slept with the beetles under the stairs, and I washed only when forced to it. But I forgot myself, my worn clothes and ill-kempt hair. I made so bold as to stare at the gentleman, and when he took a book from his pocket and began to read, it was like he was doing magic in front of my very eyes. I was eight years old and I had never seen anyone read a book, can you imagine that?"

I could not, but I knew to comment at this point might be disastrous. He was lost in his reminiscences, and I dared not call him back.

"The gentleman noticed my interest, my obsession, and as he left, he *gave me the book*. I have read a thousand books since, but not one of them ever taught me a word to describe the feeling I had in that moment. *Joy, euphoria, ecstasy,* they are pale and feeble ghosts of the word I want. I thought the feeling would consume me. I might have gone up in a pillar of flame in that moment, and done so happily. The feeling lasted until I opened the book and realised I could not understand a letter of it," he added with a wry smile. "But I did not let that stop me. I begged the bootmaker's daughter to teach me my letters, and she did, *a* to *zed,* right the way through, and by the end of that autumn, I could read the first line of the book the gentleman had given me. *'If music be the food of love, play on'.*"

"*Twelfth Night!*" I exclaimed, forgetting myself. But Sir Cedric merely smiled indulgently.

"Indeed it was. I thought it was the most magical thing I had ever heard, a shipwreck, false identities, love that could not be satisfied. My contentment never waned, no matter how many times I read it. Until I went home on Christmas Day, and my father threw it into the fireplace and burnt it before my eyes."

I drew in a sharp breath, expelling it slowly. Sir Cedric curled a lip in derision.

"Do not pity me, lady. He burnt it because he thought I had wasted my wages on it instead of handing them over as I ought. But I got my own back, I did," he said, his eyes snapping with a hellish mischief. "I burnt his only suit of clothes. The house stank of charred cloth for weeks—as long as I carried bruises on my back from the beating he gave me—but I did not care. He took ill that winter and was buried by Easter. I came home to live with my mother, and I promised her I would care for her. I did. By the time I was fourteen I had earned enough, coupled with what my father left us, to start my own business, selling cheap shoes out of a cart for four times what they cost to make. They fell apart the first time they got wet, but no matter. By the time I was sixteen I had enough money to buy a pub. My mother signed the papers as I was not old enough, and I hired a rough-looking fellow to water the gin and look the other way when the doxies brought clients upstairs. Ah, you are shocked at that, I think. Not many know I made a tidy profit from the whores in Whitechapel, turning a blind eye to their doings, taking a share of their earnings in exchange for a private room and a bed. And with that profit, I bought my first factory, a textile mill in the Midlands, where I made my first millions on the backs of women and children."

I did not speak. His story had clearly been told to offend me, and I refused to give him the satisfaction. I had thought him capable of real tenderness, but as he related the events of his youth, I began to doubt it.

"Now I owned copper mines and steamships, paper mills and even a small railway in Scotland. But still I lacked something. It was Ludlow who told me what it was. Civility, he said, education, polish. I had not read a book since the one my father burnt. No time for such foolishness, but Ludlow convinced me it was foolish not to. He said no lady of quality would marry a ruffian like me. So I hired a teacher of etiquette to smooth out my edges. I bought the entire library of a country house at auction and read every book in it. I attended plays and operas and exhibitions of the greatest paintings. And I went to lectures, everything from Darwin to the Dolomites, and it was at a lecture I met Lucy. Your father spoke two hours that night, and I heard not a word of it. I could not take my eyes from her."

Sir Cedric seemed to recollect my presence then. He slanted me a look from under his thick brows. "Doubtless you think me a fool, but I tell you I looked at her and I understood every poem I had ever read about love. It was that quick, that irrevocable. One minute, I was myself, as I had ever been. The next, I was consumed with her. I decided then that I must have her, and the rest you know. I wooed and won her in a fortnight. I care not for the particulars of how it happens. I left the planning of the wedding entirely to Lucy." His features, so changeable and so reflective of his mood, altered then. His lips thinned, his brows drew together, and the colour of his complexion rose. "And now she has done this, ruined it all with her foolishness," he said, spitting out the words as if they lay bitter on his tongue.

"Then you do not mean to marry her?" I ventured softly.

He raised his chin, curling his lip in scorn. "I made a promise to wed her and I am a man of my word. But do not think I am unaware of what it will mean. She has made us a laughingstock, figures of fun for all the world to jeer at. I shall be mocked for it, but I will marry her."

And make her pay for it the rest of her life, I imagined. Poor Lucy. Whatever part she had played in the aftermath of the murder, she did not deserve Sir Cedric's resentful affections. He did not appear to be a man who easily relinquished his grudges, and I felt certain Lucy would bear the lash of his grievances the whole of their marriage.

"I am sure there are those who will think it laudable you stood beside her when she most needed your support," I commented. Sir Cedric blasted me with a look.

"Surely you must understand what it means to be ridiculous in the eyes of society," he said. "There is not a month goes by some fresh gossip about the Marches doesn't find its way into the newspapers. I thought Lucy was far enough removed from that. She assured me after that business with your father—"

"My father? What of him?" To my knowledge, Father had been remarkably well-behaved of late. I had credited it to Hortense's influence, but perhaps I had been too generous.

Sir Cedric shifted in his chair. He was the sort of man who

liked always to be in the right, I suspected. If he knew something of Father's exploits and had been instructed to keep his counsel, breaking that trust would put him squarely in the wrong. But I had not anticipated the streak of malice running like an ugly flaw through the fabric of his character.

"Your father was very nearly arrested a fortnight ago," he told me, his eyes sharp with spite.

Thoughts spun past and I snatched at one. "The riot in Trafalgar Square?"

"That's right. He went to support his friend, that treacherous Irish bastard."

"You mean William O'Brien." An Irish member of Parliament, he was at present languishing in prison, where his ill-treatment had been cause for the outrage in Trafalgar Square.

"I do indeed," he spat.

"What happened?"

Sir Cedric shrugged. "March very nearly got shot for his troubles. If it had not been for that Brisbane fellow watching his back, your father would be lying next to Snow in the game larder." He chuckled at his own joke and reached into his pocket for another vile cigar. I could not make sense of this. I had suspected Brisbane had been in Trafalgar Square on the fateful day and sustained his injury in the process. But that Father had been there as well was something I could not entirely take in.

"I am sorry, Sir Cedric, but I do not follow you. Do you mean to say that Lord Wargrave went to Trafalgar Square to protect my father?"

He clipped the end of his cigar, lit the tip, and pulled deeply from it, the end glowing like a ruby.

"I do not know how he came to be there. I only know that someone in that square fired a shot at your father, and *Wargrave*," he said, spreading the title thickly with sarcasm, "stepped in front of the bullet. He and his man hurried your father out of the square before he was recognised, and them with a bullet wound and a broken leg between them." He drew in a great lungful of smoke, then expelled it slowly through his nose. "If it were not for your friend, your father's name would have been all over the newspapers, and he would have likely been accountable to Parliament for his treasonous actions."

I bristled. "Father is no traitor. He merely has unconventional friends."

Sir Cedric waved his cigar. "His friends are traitors, and as far as I am concerned, he is cut from the same cloth."

"Then I must wonder that you are so willing to marry into his family," I retorted.

Sir Cedric paused, puffing away at his cigar, clouding the atmosphere of the room with its poisonous aroma. Grim made a sound in his throat and rose to the top of the bust of Caesar where the air was clearer.

"I want the girl," he said simply. "I want her, and what I want, I have. But she is soiled goods to me now, and I do not think I will ever look on her without thinking I have been got the better of."

I stared at him, scarcely believing he was serious, but his countenance betrayed no sign of levity, and I knew he spoke the truth.

"Lucy is not responsible for the actions of her family," I said, rising from my chair. He did not offer me the courtesy of rising as well, but merely sat, drawing deeply from his cigar and watching me with his tawny predator's eyes. "Any more than we are responsible for her choice of husband," I concluded with a fatuous smile.

I whistled for Grim and took my leave, my raven bobbing along in my wake. I had much to think on.

THE TWENTY-SECOND CHAPTER

He gave you such a mastery report
For art and exercise in your defense,
And for your rapier most especially.
—HAMLET

reunted Grim to his cage in Father's study, pleased to find the room deserted. He had likely gone elsewhere to sulk, and he was welcome to it. I took the chance to sit a moment, deeply occupied with the thoughts that were tumbling through my head like bits of glass in a kaleidoscope. The difficulty was none of these bits seemed to make any nice, pretty patterns. There were dozens of snippets of conversation, impressions, facts, theories, all whirling madly, none pausing long enough for me to make sense of them. This would never do, I told myself severely. The only way to fit the pieces together was to first make them orderly.

With a brisk step I went to my room, banishing Morag and the dog as I retrieved paper and pen. I arranged them on the blotter, remembering the maxim one of my governesses had always chanted, "A tidy desk is the reflection of a tidy mind." Of course, this particular governess had been discharged when Aunt Hermia discovered her dancing naked on the front lawn in celebration of the summer solstice. Perhaps it was best not to put much confidence in her little philosophies, but I had nothing to lose.

Writing swiftly, I put down everything I could think of pertaining to the murder, the theft of the pearls, and any other curious behaviours I had witnessed—the drugging of Lucy and Emma, the flirtation between Plum and Charlotte, the antipathy Snow held toward the Gypsies, the ghosts—I noted it all. And written down in a neat and orderly fashion, it was as tremendous a mess as it had been in my head.

I sat back in my chair and closed my eyes, thinking hard. Nothing made any sense at all; the pieces were too tenuous, the connections between them too vague and shadowy as yet. I groaned and threw the paper into the fire, deriving a very little satisfaction in watching it burn. "How Brisbane does this every day I shall never know," I grumbled.

But if I were to be entirely honest, I must admit I felt more alive, more *necessary,* than I had in half a year. My wanderings around Italy had been pleasant beyond description, but *pleasant* is a very little word. And I realised, as I sat watching my efforts at deduction smoulder to ash, I wanted a larger life than the one I had led. I wanted adventure and passion and romance, and all the other things I had scorned. More than seven hundred years of wild March blood had told at last, I thought with a smile. I had done a mighty job of suppressing it for the first thirty years of my life, but it simply would not do anymore.

* * *

With a newfound vigour, I left my room and made my way downstairs. Just as I reached the bottom of the staircase, Hortense appeared, coaxing a moody Violante along. My sister-in-law was dabbing her eyes with a handkerchief and Hortense looked at me over the girl's head, her eyes warm with sympathy and perhaps a touch of relief.

"Ah, Julia. Just the friendly face we hoped to find. Violante is a trifle upset, and perhaps you can cheer her better than I. I think she grows weary of me," Hortense said, hugging Violante close to her side and giving her a wink.

Violante hugged her back, watering the silk of her gown with her tears.

I put out my hand. "Come, walk with me, Violante. We will be very naughty and steal cakes from Cook and eat them on the stairs as Portia and I used to do as children."

Violante pulled a face and put a hand to her stomach. "I do not think the cakes I would like very much."

"Perhaps not, but you will like being with me. I am far nicer than Lysander and much prettier than Plum."

She laughed at this and took my hand, giving Hortense a quick kiss in farewell. I was astonished at how quickly they had become intimate, but it ought not to have surprised me. I knew only too well how kind Hortense could be. Compassion was the brightest treasure in her jewel box of virtues.

Violante and I strolled down the corridor, arm in arm. I felt a little ashamed of myself. The poor child was in a foreign country, with an imperfect grasp of the language, struggling to accommodate herself to her new family, and had endured a murder in her home, as well. And one could only imagine how the knowledge of her pregnancy had affected her. Doubtless she was pleased, but she had not had an easy time of it thus far, and I noticed her mouth was drawn down with sadness.

Impulsively I patted her hand, sorry I had not remembered earlier how affectionate she was. She must have missed the easy intimacies of her sisters and cousins in Italy. I brushed the hair back from her brow. "You are a little homesick, I think."

She nodded. "Si. I miss the sunshine, the flowers, the good foods of Napoli." I raised my brows and she hurried on. "England is very nice, of course. But it is not my home. There are no dead people at home."

I blinked at her. "Of course there are dead people in Italy, Violante. Some of them are still lying out in the churches for people to look at. I have seen the guidebooks." They were gruesome too, those decaying old saints, preserved under glass like so many specimens in a museum of natural history. I had made a point of visiting as many as possible during my travels.

"They are not in my house," she corrected, and I had to concede the point. To my understanding, her upbringing had been a conventional one. Her family might be passionately Italian, but at least murder had never broken out at one of their house parties.

"Please believe me when I tell you that they are not usually in this house either. This is a very strange turn of events, my dear, and not at all the welcome we had planned for you," I said consolingly.

404

She smiled at me, but doubtfully so. I changed the subject. "What do you think of Father?"

Her smile deepened. "He is very nice." *Verra nice.* "His Italian, it is not so good as my English, but we understand each other."

"Good," I told her. "It is good when family understand one another."

She leaned toward me conspiratorially. "I am making him a waistcoat—it is a surprise, tell no one."

I blinked at her. "Of course not. What a charming idea. Father will be delighted."

She smiled, clearly pleased with herself. "It was Lysander's idea. He thought if I made something for Papa with my own hands, it would show how much I est—est—"

"Esteem?" I suggested.

"Esteem him," she finished happily. "I want to be the good daughter to him."

I resisted the little dart of annoyance I felt when she said that. Father had five daughters, he scarcely needed another. But I reminded myself that Violante was a stranger in our country, and that we were her family now.

I patted her hand. "That is a noble idea, Violante. I am sure he will be very pleased."

She brightened and tucked her handkerchief into her pocket. "I will go and work on it now. Tell me, does he like best the purples or the oranges?"

I tipped my head, considering carefully. Father's wardrobe was usually an excellent barometer of his mental state. When he was feeling melancholy and sulky, he wore his decaying old tweeds and shirts made for him in Savile Row thirty years ago. When he was in fine fettle, he dressed like a maharajah with just a dash of circus performer, all colour and light. It had not escaped my attention that he had worn his threadbare tweeds with a pair of disgusting old gaiters since our arrival at the Abbey. Perhaps a fine new waistcoat would be just the thing to raise his spirits.

"He loves them both, Violante. He loves them both so much you ought to make him a striped waistcoat, orange and purple together. Perhaps with some nice red taffeta for the back," I told her firmly. "And great buttons all down the front, green ones."

She beamed at me, and I beamed back at her, baring my teeth in a fond smile. I was quite beginning to like the girl.

Violante and I chatted haltingly for some little while as we paced the length of the ground floor. She told me about the baby and I pretended to be surprised, and by the time we finished, she seemed much more cheerful than she had been when I found her with Hortense. At one point she threw her arms around me, kissing me soundly on the cheek.

I patted her shoulder a little awkwardly. "How very sweet you are, Violante. Now, why don't we go and find Lysander? It is almost time for tea."

She nodded enthusiastically. "I like tea. It is very nice." *Verra nice.*

She looped her arm through mine while we walked like two schoolgirls on holiday, searching for Lysander. The library and music room—his likeliest haunts—were quite empty, but as we quitted the latter I detected a faint roar. I turned to Violante.

"Did you hear that?"

She cocked her head, jetty curls spilling over one shoulder. "The growl? Like the boar?"

"Bear," I corrected. "Yes, that is precisely what I meant."

I led the way down the corridor, and as we moved closer I distinctly heard another muffled growl and an unmistakable metallic clang. I groaned.

"What is it?" Violante demanded, her eyes wide as she clutched at my arm.

"A prime display of male conceit is what it is," I muttered.

We had reached the door of the billiard room. It was closed, but I did not need to see inside to know what mischief was afoot. Carved from the great width of the south transept, the billiard room was a vast open space. Previous earls had found it a useful place to store weapons. The walls were studded with every conceivable variety of blade and bow, axe and arquebus. It was also the room where all of my brothers had received their fencing instruction. Father had shoved a billiard table into a corner and renamed the place, but to us it would always hold fond memories as the armoury.

I threw open the door and crossed my arms over my chest. As I expected, mock combat was under way. Lysander and Plum were engaged, while Ludlow sat at a safe distance, instructing Charlotte in the finer points of swordsmanship. To my shock, I saw another pair of duelists, Alessandro and Brisbane.

"This cannot end well," I said, more to myself than Violante. I motioned for her to follow me and we skirted the fencers, making our way to where Ludlow and Charlotte sat on a bench of polished oak. They greeted us, Charlotte rather more coolly than Ludlow. Violante took no note of the snub, and I welcomed it. It saved me the trouble of being nice to her. Violante and I seated ourselves and I turned my attention eagerly to the bouts already engaged.

The gentlemen combatants sported various states of undress. Plum had removed only his coat, while Alessandro and Ly had discarded their waistcoats as well. Brisbane had retained his waistcoat, but lost his neckcloth at some juncture, and his shirt was open at the throat.

"It is a friendly bout," I told Violante. "Do you see that each of the swords wears a blunt tip? And none of the gentlemen wear a mask. That means they agree to direct their thrusts away from the face."

I had thought to reassure Violante, but in truth I was the one heaving a sigh of relief. For one mad moment when I had spotted Brisbane parrying a thrust of Alessandro's, I had feared the worst.

Violante asked a few questions then, and I answered her as best I could. What facts I forgot, Ludlow was prevailed upon to supply, and he pointed out a particularly nice bit of footwork on Plum's part.

Charlotte gave an ecstatic little sigh and looked at him worshipfully.

"Beh," Violante said. "Lysander, he is faster than Plum, and his sword is much nicer. See how pretty," she said, pointing toward the finely etched hilt of Lysander's weapon.

Charlotte set her mouth in irritation, and Ludlow suppressed a smile.

"I believe the quality of the blade, not the beauty of the hilt, is of primary importance, Mrs. Lysander," he said kindly.

Violante, utterly unconcerned, shrugged and watched the fencers with interest, clapping and cheering for Lysander, booing Plum with enthusiasm. I did not have the heart to tell her such things were not done, and as I watched her face, shining with pleasure, it occurred to me Ly had done rather well in finding a bride to fit into our family.

"You seem to know a great deal about swordsmanship, Mr. Ludlow," I remarked during a lull in the bouts. "Did you have a go with the others?"

Ludlow smiled. "I did. I believe Mr. Lysander thought it an unfair advantage that I wield a sword in my left hand, but Lord Wargrave fought me right-handed and thrashed me soundly. It did not seem to confound him in the least."

Just then Lysander and Plum executed a series of complicated maneuvers, each of them moving smoothly, although Ly seemed a little off his footing. Plum was attacking rather aggressively, and Ly was determined not to let him land a blow. They seemed likely to resort to fisticuffs soon, and as I watched them I realised what Ludlow had just told me. Ludlow was left-handed. He and I had been seated next to one another at the luncheon at Uncle Fly's. We had spent half the interval apologising to one another for our colliding elbows. I had known it, but I had not translated it within the context of our murder. The syllogism was a simple one: the murderer was right-handed. Ludlow was not right-handed, ergo Ludlow was not the murderer.

Lysander rallied then, posting a series of deft attacks that left Plum breathless. After another bold maneuver, Ly had the tip of his sword at Plum's chest. Violante cheered loudly, and Plum stepped forward, slapping Lysander's sword aside to punch him soundly on the jaw.

Lysander staggered back, then dropped his sword and came back at Plum, fists swinging.

"Well, honestly," I muttered. The scuffle was over as quickly as it had begun. Plum was bleeding profusely from his nose, and Lysander's lip was split open cleanly. They circled each other warily as they moved apart, each of them mouthing profanities.

Violante was shaking her head. "Lysander must learn to move his head to the side. He should have ducked and hit Plum in the— what do you call this?" she asked, pointing to the small of her back.

"Kidneys?" I hazarded.

She nodded. "*Si,* the kidneys. That is how to hurt a man," she concluded sagely.

Charlotte stared at her in horror, then rose to go to Plum, clucking and fussing as she handed him her handkerchief to stem the flow of blood welling from his nose.

"And how do you come to know so much about the finer points of grappling, Mrs. Lysander?" Ludlow inquired politely.

"I have eight brothers."

I gestured toward Lysander. "Should you not go to him?"

She waved a hand. "It is only the lip, he be fine. I only worry if there is enough blood to need the mop."

She called encouragement to her husband who blew her a kiss.

Brisbane and Alessandro had halted, swords at their sides, when Plum and Ly had sunk to brawling, but they resumed their bout. Lysander came to sit with Violante, while Plum and Charlotte took chairs on the opposite side of the room, both of them casting dark looks toward Lysander. Lysander made a few jests as he took his seat, but I noticed his eyes strayed more than once to our brother, and when they rested on Plum, his expression was thoughtful.

Like Plum and Ly, Alessandro and Brisbane fought with blunted tips, but one would never have guessed from their expressions that this was a friendly duel. Alessandro's eyes gleamed with ferocity, and Brisbane's face was a study in concentration, his eyes fixed upon the younger man's sword hand.

"He is hurt. Why does he fight?" Violante inquired, pointing at Brisbane.

"Because, like all men, he is proud," I returned.

"And stupid," she added. Lysander bristled, but Violante and I exchanged knowing nods. I could piece together well enough what had transpired. Alessandro, perhaps feeling a trifle neglected and perhaps a little jealous of my friendship with Brisbane, had challenged. Brisbane, proud as an emperor, would sooner have cut his own arm completely off than admit he could not spar with a younger opponent. And Alessandro, who ought to have taken Brisbane's injury into consideration, was instead taking advantage of the situation, attacking with all the ferocity of a lion cub pouncing on his first prey.

"Poor Alessandro," I murmured. "He will regret this."

But if Alessandro had thought the inability to use his left arm would hinder Brisbane, he had underestimated him badly. They had chosen smallswords, and these lighter weapons needed less of a counterbalance than a heavier rapier would require. The technique lay in the footwork and the dexterity of the wrists, both of which Brisbane possessed in abundance. But even I could see that for all his excellent defensive maneuvers, he was holding something in check, refusing to mount an attack. No matter what devilish move Alessandro threw at him, Brisbane countered coolly and withdrew, never engaging further than necessity demanded. It was a deliberate strategy, and one that was rattling Alessandro badly. His face was flushed, his hair curling damply at the temples, and he was breathing quite quickly, tiring himself on his endless assaults but never gaining the advantage. He was quickly growing fatigued while Brisbane looked as though he could carry on for days.

It was not long before Alessandro's mounting fatigue turned to outright frustration. His lunges became more desperate, his footing more uncertain.

Suddenly, he took a deep breath as if to rally himself and thrust deeply, a well-placed stroke that a lesser opponent would have been at great pains to meet. But Brisbane parried and riposted; their swords connected in a great clash of steel, and in a swift glissade, Alessandro's blade rode up the end of Brisbane's weapon. Without warning, Alessandro flicked his wrist, circling the tip of his blade around Brisbane's, aiming directly for Brisbane's face.

One of the ladies—it may have been Charlotte—screamed, and with a roar of pain, in a movement so swift the eye could scarcely follow it, Brisbane thrust his left hand up and out of the sling, gripping Alessandro's blade in his bare palm. Brisbane's face was white with fury as he jerked Alessandro's sword toward him, bringing the younger man's face within inches of his own.

Instantly, Alessandro's face drained of colour as he realised what he had done. "*Signore,* you must accept my apologies, I am most abjectly sorry."

Brisbane said nothing for a long moment. Then, with infinite slowness and perfect disdain, he pulled Alessandro's sword from his hand and dropped it to the floor. Alessandro winced as it clattered on the stones, and it was still echoing when Brisbane stalked from the room, closing the door softly behind him. I think I would have preferred if he had slammed it.

Violante put a tentative hand to my shoulder. "Giulia, are you all right?"

"Of course. I am perfectly all right. Should I not be?"

She shrugged. "You screamed, very loud."

"I most certainly did not."

Violante gave me a little push. "You did."

I drew myself up to my full height and smoothed my skirts. "I most certainly did not. Now, if you will excuse me, Brisbane seems to have left his coat behind. I will make certain it is returned to him."

As I gathered up Brisbane's coat, I noticed Alessandro, still standing where Brisbane had left him, defeated and a little shocked. I ought to have said something encouraging to him, but Ludlow and Plum had already taken him in hand, and I wondered if perhaps this was one time the company of other men was preferable to a lady's society.

I gave a quick backward glance as I left. Alessandro was staring after me, his expression anguished. It would have been a kindness to offer him a smile of absolution, but I did not. I was not feeling particularly kind, I reflected sourly. And Alessandro had just revealed a little too much of what mettle he was made of.

THE TWENTY-THIRD CHAPTER

Things without all remedy should be done without regard.
What's done is done.
—MACBETH

made directly for Brisbane's room in the Galilee Tower. It seemed likely he had withdrawn there to attend to his shoulder. I mounted the staircase slowly. It was possible the violent movement of his left arm had opened the wound, and I was no Nightingale to look easily on blood. Better to let him see to that himself in privacy, I decided, and not suffer distraction when I informed him of my revelation regarding Henry Ludlow.

As I rounded the corner into the bachelors' wing, I heard a door close and saw Aquinas coming my way carrying a tray.

I gestured toward the tray. "I presume you have been playing nursemaid to the patient?"

Aquinas gave me a short nod. "I believe his lordship is in considerable pain, but the wound opened only a little. He refused to permit me to put in a stitch, so I packed it with Lady Hermia's green salve and bandaged it."

I glanced down at the tray and saw a pile of cotton strips, streaked with blood.

"Very good of you, I'm sure." I looked up at Aquinas, but his face swam out of focus.

"My lady, are you quite all right? You have gone very pale."

I blinked hard and swallowed. "Quite well, thank you. Brisbane left without his coat. I will return it to him now."

If he thought it unseemly I would visit a bachelor in his rooms, he betrayed no sign of it. He merely inclined his head and went about his business. Portia had told me before that whatever I paid him was undoubtedly not enough, and once again I was forced to believe her. Discretion is an invaluable commodity in a servant.

I tapped at Brisbane's door and waited a moment. When there was no reply I knocked, quite loudly, and he growled for me to enter.

I was not surprised to find he had flung himself into an armchair. He was sucking hard at the mouthpiece of his hookah pipe, drawing in great choking lungfuls of smouldering hashish.

I waved a hand, clearing the atmosphere just a little.

"Good heavens, Brisbane, you are as bad as Sir Cedric. I thought I would choke on the stench of his cigars this afternoon."

Too late I realised I had betrayed myself. In spite of the narcotic fog, Brisbane's wits were undulled. He looked up at me inquiringly.

"Sir Cedric indulges only in the smoking room," he said slowly. "When were you there? And more to the point, why?"

I thrust his coat at him irritably. "I went to ask him about Lucy. I learned nothing of importance, save that he is a thoroughly nasty man. Here is your coat. You left it in the billiard room after that revolting display."

He blew out a great exhalation of smoke. "Am I to deduce you blame me for what happened?"

I took the chair opposite, flopping gracelessly with my elbows on the padded arms. "I do. I do not believe for a moment you challenged Alessandro. It was entirely within your power to avoid such a confrontation by not accepting his challenge. And then to bait him—"

"I did no such thing."

"You most certainly did. You pranced about, refusing to engage him. It was insulting. You patronized him and deliberately frustrated him to the point of rashness."

Brisbane lowered the mouthpiece. "I never prance. I would not know how to begin to prance. And you are quite wrong in any event. I did challenge him."

I sat up, staring in disbelief. "I do not believe it. Even you could not be so willfully stupid. That shoulder is not healed. You have a bullet wound scarcely a fortnight old—"

"I fell off my horse."

"You do not ride! For the love of heaven, can we not have the truth between us?" I cried. "You were in Trafalgar Square during the riot and you were shot!"

Brisbane leaned forward, his pupils indistinguishable from the rest of his piercingly black eyes. "I. Fell. Off. My. Horse."

"Oh, you are the most maddening man I have ever known. If stubbornness were water, I could sail on you to the ends of the earth."

Brisbane resumed his pipe, giving me a sardonic smile. "Well, we have that in common at least."

"Whatever do you mean? I am the most amiable of women."
I felt a little insulted. I had never thought of myself as stubborn,
and it was hurtful of him to say so.

He laughed. "You might have been, a year or two ago. Now
you are unmanageable as any March."

"Then we ought to both be grateful it is not your task to manage me," I retorted hotly.

An uncomfortable silence fell between us. I do not know what
thoughts ran through his head in those moments, but I would
have given my last farthing to know. He merely sat smoking, inscrutable as a pharaoh, while I hated myself only a little less than
I hated him.

"Why did you challenge Alessandro?" I asked finally.

"I wanted to take the measure of him. Your brothers were feeling restless, so Lysander suggested a friendly bit of exercise with
swords. And for my purposes, fencing is as useful as chess in
learning one's opponent."

"And what did you learn of Alessandro?"

Brisbane shrugged, then winced sharply as he eased his
wounded shoulder back into place. He made no sound, but he
had gone pale under the deep olive of his complexion.

"I learned he wishes to be taken seriously. He is a man, but
not yet respected as such. He feels any slight to his dignity deeply,
and when he is frustrated, he is apt to strike without thinking."

I felt my blood running cold in my veins. "You think he murdered Lucian Snow."

Brisbane took another deep draw of the pipe, exhaling slowly through his nose. Sir Cedric had done something similar with his cigar, but from him it was faintly grotesque. On Brisbane, the gesture was suggestive of something altogether more sensual.

"I do not know. What possible motive would he have? He seems to have no ties to Lucy, no reason to bear a grudge against Snow. He may have the temperament to do murder, even a murder of this variety, but whether he did or not, I cannot say. There is simply no motive, though God knows I have looked for one."

I shook my head. "I wonder at you. How can you be so determined to lay this crime at the feet of a young man who has given you no cause to think ill of him, save one impulsive moment that was completely provoked?"

"And I wonder you cannot see it for yourself," he said softly.

I paused. Surely Brisbane could not wish Alessandro to be guilty simply because of his affection for me. That would demonstrate a possessiveness, an attachment to me on Brisbane's behalf that I could scarcely credit. It was astonishing. I felt my breath catch in my throat. My lips trembled as I parted them.

"Brisbane," I murmured.

"It is quite simple," he said, smiling slowly, triumphantly. "If Alessandro is the murderer, then no member of your family is implicated, Lucy will go free, and I can return to London and put this case behind me."

If there had been a vase at hand I would have thrown it at his head. Instead I summoned a smile of my own. "How succinctly you put it. If you will excuse me now, it is time for tea, and I have things to attend to."

I took my leave, remembering only when I reached the gallery I had forgotten to tell him about Henry Ludlow. I shrugged and dismissed the thought. Brisbane was stalking his own game. I would give chase myself and see what the hunt turned up.

I hurried down to tea, nearly colliding with Portia on the staircase.

"Heavens, Julia, have a care. You nearly upset Puggy," she chided. She was carrying her loathsome pet in her arms. He snuffled wetly at me and I curled a lip at him in return.

"It would be no very great crime to upset Puggy," I remarked peevishly.

Portia gave me a dark look. "Do not think of joking with me. I have had a vile afternoon, and my head is throbbing again."

"I am sorry, dearest. What is the trouble?"

She adjusted Puggy in her arms and we started slowly down the stairs. "Another one of the cats has delivered a litter, this one in the fireplace in the dining room, so we cannot light the fire."

"Which cat?"

"Peter Simple."

I paused on the stairs. "A moment, Portia. You mean to say both of Father's toms have thrown litters this week?"

Her lips thinned in annoyance. "I do. And in the most inconvenient places. None of us has had clean linen on our beds because Christopher Sly scratches anyone who comes near her babies, and now we shall have to dress like Esquimaux at dinner or risk slowly freezing to death over the pheasant."

"Oooh, I do love a nice pheasant. Normandy sauce, I hope?"

"Puggy, darling, do try not to drool on Mama. What? Yes, of course Normandy sauce. You know it is Father's favourite. But when I ordered the pheasant for dinner, Cook nearly had an apoplexy and I had to spend almost an hour soothing her."

"I thought Cook prided herself on her pheasant," I put in. I was trying to pay attention for Portia's sake, but the domestic dramas were all a bit tedious to me. Aquinas had ordered my household in London, and since the fire I had been without a home of my own. I felt a little adrift without a proper home. If nothing else, it would be lovely to have a place to keep Aquinas. I had never enjoyed the homekeeping aspects of marriage, but now I was on my own, I thought I might rather like to set up a little household. Whatever mess I made of it, Aquinas would soon sort out.

Portia, on the other hand, was alarmingly competent at that sort of thing. She had organised her husband's household in a matter of days, overthrowing a century's worth of poor management and turning the country house into something of a showplace. Her house in London was equally fabulous, and she was renowned for her elegant dinners.

"She does an excellent pheasant," Portia said patiently, "but she did not want to cook *these* birds because they were in the game larder when Lucian Snow was brought in."

My stomach lurched a little. "Oh, dear."

"Indeed. They were cleared out quickly enough, and it isn't as though they *touched* him, but she still kicked up a tremendous fuss. And then of course she was quite bitter about the laudanum."

We had reached the bottom of the stairs and I knew I had but a moment to extract the rest of the story from Portia. I laid a hand on her arm.

"What laudanum?"

Puggy leaned over and sniffed at my hand, then gave a great sneeze. "Julia, honestly. You haven't been into any lavender, have you? Puggy suffers so from lavender."

I pulled a handkerchief from my pocket and wiped at the moistness on my hand, feeling slightly queasy. "No. Now tell me, what laudanum?"

"Cook keeps a bottle in the water closet belowstairs, for medicinal purposes," she said, raising a brow significantly.

"That is ludicrous. Why, any one of the scullery maids or boot-boys could have at it. What possible reason could she have for keeping laudanum so near at hand?"

Portia raised the brow even higher and said nothing.

"Oh. You mean she doses herself, and quite often I imagine if she must needs keep it so close."

"Precisely. She claims it helps the rheumatism in her knees, and who am I to contradict her? She said there was but a drop left in the bottle. But the fact remains it is gone, and it took me another quarter of an hour to settle her feathers about that." I thought feverishly. A drop would never have been sufficient to account for the poisoning of the brandy bottle. But it might be just enough to put a small dog entirely unconscious.

I patted Portia's arm. "Poor dear. No wonder you have a headache. Have you had something for it?"

"I would have done, but the laudanum is missing," she replied sourly.

As we started toward the drawing room, my mind was working rapidly. The water closet belowstairs was actually located in a back passage, quite removed from the kitchens and sculleries of the Abbey, and readily accessible from the back stairs. It would have been an easy matter for anyone to have slipped down that way and helped themselves.

Just as we reached the door of the drawing room, I glanced at Puggy and noticed an embellishment.

"Portia, is Puggy wearing a ruff of black crêpe?"

She paused and looked down at Puggy, then up at me, her eyes wide. "Yes. I thought it proper in light of the events of late."

"You put mourning on a dog."

"The fact that Mr. Pugglesworth is a dog is no reason for him to fail to pay his respects, Julia. I saw Morag leading that creature of yours out earlier in an orange taffeta coat. *Most* inappropriate."

She gave me a severe look and left me standing in the corridor, mouth agape. Just then Henry Ludlow appeared, hurrying a little.

"Ah, Lady Julia. If you are still lingering in the corridor, I must not be as late as I feared," he said, favouring me with a smile.

"Mr. Ludlow, do you think it peculiar to dress a dog in mourning?"

He considered the matter, or at least gave the appearance of considering it. "I do not," he said finally. "The dog would not choose to dress itself in mourning, so we must look to the motives of its master or mistress. And it exhibits a very fine feeling of respect to the deceased."

I smiled at him, suddenly terribly glad that he could not be our murderer. "Well spoken, Mr. Ludlow. But we must not dally here. I have it on very good authority that Cook has sent up violet faery cakes for tea today, and I for one should be very sorry to miss them."

With a gallant inclination of his head, he offered me his arm and we proceeded into the drawing room. The tea things and most of the company had already been assembled. Brisbane remained absent, no doubt choosing to drown his sorrows in hookah smoke rather than a nice cup of tea, and Emma and Lucy were still recuperating in their room. The rest of the party had gathered, and if one had not known of the corpse lying in the game larder, one might have thought it a very pleasant interlude.

A very pleasant interlude on the surface, at least. But underneath dangerous currents swirled, threatening at any moment to drown the lot of us. Sir Cedric sat next to Portia, saying almost nothing but helping himself liberally to the plates of cakes and sandwiches Cook had prepared. Charlotte and Plum were engaged in a tête-à-tête, much to Father's interest. More than once I noted his attention resting on the pair, and from his expression, it was apparent he was not pleased.

Hortense, freed from the constraints of dancing attendance on Aunt Dorcas, exerted herself to charm Sir Cedric, chatting amiably with him in spite of his gruff, monosyllabic replies. Lysander and Violante were speaking in low tones, but I caught a few snatches of their conversation and it was not a happy one. They were carping again, about what I could not determine. Alessandro was seated on Portia's other side, and my sister did a masterful job of diverting him from his sulky mood. Once or twice I heard him laugh aloud, and I was able to savour my tea without fretting over him.

For my part, I nibbled at a scone and dripped butter on my skirts and sipped a scalding cup of tea. Ludlow had taken a chair next to mine and we talked in a desultory fashion, neither of us caring very much about the subjects, but both of us enjoying it thoroughly, I believe. We had just moved from the relative merits of Bach versus Haydn when I happened to look across the tea table. I do not know why the scene should have caught my attention, but it did, and for the merest moment everything froze as if in tableau.

Portia was pouring another cup for Alessandro, giving him an excellent view of her décolletage as she reached for his cup. Hortense was facing Sir Cedric, regaling him with some merry tale as he buttered his scone. And Sir Cedric was deftly wielding a butter knife, in his left hand.

Instantly I turned to Henry Ludlow. "Do you know, something has just struck me. Is your cousin left-handed?"

Ludlow finished chewing his faery cake and swallowed, nodding. "Yes. As am I. It does tend to run in families, you know. The mighty Kerr clan of Scotland boasts a great number of left-handed members. That is why the staircases in their castles are built to spiral counter-clockwise, so that a swordsman who carries his weapon in his left hand may fight unimpeded."

He reached for another faery cake, making the appropriate

noises of delight, but I scarcely heard him. I had been so certain of Sir Cedric's villainy. It seemed a pity to discard him now, but it was impossible to reconcile his guilt with the evidence. If there was one thing I had learned under Brisbane's tuition, it was that the evidence, however improbable, does not lie.

Blast, I thought irritably. It seemed a terrible waste to have such a lovely villain right in front of me and not be able to connect him to the murder. I could not think of a man in the Abbey more suited to murderous pursuits than Sir Cedric.

But as I sipped at my tea and made polite faces at Ludlow, I realised it was much more than a pity. If Ludlow and Sir Cedric must be eliminated, then that left only the members of my own family as suspects. Members of my own family, I thought, lifting my gaze to the man at Portia's side, and Alessandro.

Just then he raised his head and returned my stare. I gave him a tentative smile, but he simply looked at me in return with the same detachment one might offer any stranger in the street. It was oddly chilling, and after a moment I dropped my eyes.

"My lady," Ludlow asked suddenly. "Is everything quite all right?"

I rallied and gave him what I hoped was a convincing smile. "Perfectly, thank you. I was merely woolgathering."

Ludlow smiled in return. "I think I have bored you with my talk of music. We must speak of something else, something that interests you."

"Not at all. I am very fond of music. Tell me more of the recital at Covent Garden," I encouraged, grateful I had collected at least that little snippet from his conversation.

He obliged, and with a few artful questions I was able to pass the rest of the tea hour peacefully, my thoughts running away with themselves while Ludlow talked on, his voice a gentle monotone in the background.

When the teapots were emptied at last and all that remained on the plates were buttery crumbs and puddles of cream, the party slowly broke up. We left to follow our own pursuits, some to rest, others to read. I had correspondence to answer, some of it long overdue, but I knew my letters would have to wait another day. I had laid plans for later that night, and a nap was just the thing to ensure I remained wakeful.

As I left the drawing room, Charlotte fell into step beside me, and if it was intentional it was skillfully done. She seemed pleased to have me alone and wasted not a moment in speaking her piece.

"Lady Julia, forgive my presumption, but I must wonder if you are angry with me?"

I kept walking but turned to look at her, taking in her widely innocent eyes, the powdered freshness of her complexion. "Why-ever should I be?"

She spread her hands and looked demurely away. "I know you are friends with Lord Wargrave. And I believe you must know by now our betrothal is at an end."

"Oh, that." I waved a hand in dismissal. "Think nothing of it, my dear. I assure you I have not."

"But I would not have you think ill of me for breaking our engagement," she persisted. "Particularly in light of recent developments."

"You mean your flirtation with my brother?"

She gasped. "My lady, such a common term! I would never have thought to phrase it thus. Mr. Eglamour is a good friend, an amiable gentleman whose many kindnesses have been a balm to my wounded spirit in these dark hours."

I snorted and coughed behind my hand to cover it. "Yes, Plum is famous in the family for his balmlike qualities. We have often told him so."

Charlotte lowered her chin, looking at me from beneath a fringe of dark lashes, her lower lip thrust ever so delicately outward. "You mock me, my lady. And I cannot even fault you for it. I know my own conduct has been grossly unladylike. My dearest mama would spin in her grave could she but see what a mockery I have made of the womanly virtues she tried so desperately to instill within me."

I paused and turned to her. "My dear Charlotte, I have very little interest in virtues, particularly those of the womanly variety. Marry Brisbane, do not marry him, it is of no consequence to me. But since you pay me the compliment of your confidence, I will offer you this piece of advice—do not look to my brother to play Galahad to your distressed damsel. He has told a hundred ladies he loved them, and never once did he mean it. Plum is a lovely boy, and I am delighted he is my brother. But do not put your hope in him. He is altogether too fragile a vessel."

With that I left her gaping after me. I was perfectly aware my words would be of no consequence to her if she really harboured a *tendresse* for him. But the chance that a bit of plain speaking

430

might dampen her ardour was not to be missed. I knew Plum well enough to know when he was merely playing at being a lover. His romantic imagination had been roused by Charlotte's plight, and her chocolate-box prettiness had only heightened the effect. Plum, however, was not the sort of man to be captured for long by a pretty face with a penchant for ruffles and bonbons. He craved exoticism, mystery, the unknown. Charlotte was a departure for him simply because he had travelled so long abroad, sating his appetite for dusky *signorinas*. He would tire of her as soon as he realised she was uneducated and uninteresting, precisely the sort of bland Englishwoman he had scorned for so long. I only hoped he realised his mistake before they married and I was made an aunt again.

Morag was out when I reached my bedchamber, but Florence was fully awake, inspecting the room and wreaking destruction. She had savaged a cushion and a book, eaten the better part of a candle, and was trotting about with a slipper clamped firmly between her tiny jaws when I found her.

"You are a vile little monster," I told her, wrestling the slipper out of her mouth. She growled and retreated to her basket to sulk. I looked at the ruined slipper in my hand, not entirely surprised to find its mate, damp and missing half its embroidery, already tucked in her basket.

"Go on then," I told her. "Keep them both. But no more or I will give you to the cats for a plaything."

She turned her back to me and settled down with her new slippers. I lay on my bed, fully dressed, and read for a while. At some point I must have slept, for I know I dreamed. I was moving through the hidden passages of the Abbey, up the winding stair to the lumber rooms. But they were not lumber rooms. They were scriptoria again, as they had been so long ago. Robed and sandaled monks sat at their small desks, dipping their quills into bottles of ink, frozen with the cold. They blew clouds of breath at me, breath that smelled of hashish until I fled to the darkened priory vault and down into the stone-strewn passage to the churchyard. I was running as fast as I could, one hand holding a candle aloft. By the inexplicable alchemy of dreams, it did not gutter but shone brightly, lighting the way ahead.

And as I ran I heard the echo of my own footsteps, and those of another. I turned, many times, raising the candle to peer behind me. But I saw nothing and still I ran, the passageways much longer than I remembered, and narrower, twisting and tightening until I became stuck fast and screamed for help. I heard a deep metallic sound, like the striking of the sanctuary bell. Then, horrified, I heard the second set of footsteps approaching and a quick, sharp exhalation of breath as someone blew out my candle.

I woke trembling then, to find my limbs twisted in the bedclothes. I must not have cried out, for Florence still slept peacefully in her basket. I heard the bell strike again, and I realised then it was the signal to dress for dinner. I looked at the clock, surprised to find how long I had slept.

Slowly, I untangled myself from the bedclothes and rose. I rang for Morag, and for once was glad of her idle chatter as she dressed me. I wore black again out of respect for Mr. Snow—if Portia's dog must wear mourning, so must we all, I decided sourly—and left off my jewels, except for the pendant Brisbane had given me. I had not expected to wear it again, but the dream had left me badly shaken. It seemed almost a presentiment of something frightening to come, and though I did not stop to think of it then, the little silver coin struck with the head of Medusa had become something of an amulet. I would admit it to no one, but I believed firmly and unaccountably that so long as I wore it, no harm would befall me.

THE TWENTY-FOURTH CHAPTER

*The most peaceable way for you, if you do take a thief, is
to let him show himself for what he is, and steal out of your company.*
—MUCH ADO ABOUT NOTHING

At dinner I was mightily put out to find Brisbane absent. The pheasant was delicious, but the dish was hotly peppered with my pique. He might have been in a bit of pain from the bout of fencing, but it had been his own notion to engage Alessandro, and he had only himself to blame. He had a responsibility to Father, to this investigation, to *me*, to follow through with his inquiries. And as I sat at table, glancing surreptitiously at my companions, it occurred to me our time together was drawing to a close. This grim thought was borne out by Father, who rose after dessert and addressed the company.

"I thought it appropriate to take this opportunity to speak to you all. This chance may not come again. A westerly wind has blown in, and the snow is nearly melted. I am assured by tomorrow morning the roads will be muddy and slow, but passable. If that is indeed the case, Lord Wargrave will leave us then to bring a detective inspector from Scotland Yard. If the telegraph is still inoperable, he will travel up to London personally and then the investigation into the death of Mr. Snow will be taken out of my hands, and what has transpired here will be known to all." He paused here for dramatic effect. It was a gesture I had seen often enough when he played Lear in our amateur theatricals, but it was highly effective. He looked slowly from one face to another, giving nothing away. Some squirmed a little under his scrutiny, some dropped their eyes, and some met his gaze squarely with their own.

"I should also make you aware of a murderous attack perpetrated upon my nieces, Emma and Lucy, last night," he said, his voice ringing out in tones a thespian would have envied. Sir Cedric made to rise, but Father waved him back to his chair. I bit back a groan. Brisbane had specifically instructed him to tell no one of the attack. He would take Father apart with his bare hands when he heard what he had done. The rest of the company sat in mute horror as Father continued.

"Thanks to timely intervention, they are both quite well, but I have ordered them kept under watch of my own staff in the ladies' wing. This matter will also be given over to the detective inspector. But as this place has proven dangerous for members of my own family, so it may be so for the rest of us. Therefore, when you rise from table, you will go directly to your rooms and remain there until morning."

He paused again, pitching his voice lower for effect.

"I think tonight would best be spent in contemplation. If you are the sort of person given to prayer, then do so. Pray for us all, pray for the soul of Lucian Snow, and pray for the murderer who walks among us."

Charlotte gave a little sob and buried her face in her hands, but the rest of the company made no reaction. For my part, I thought it a masterful bit of rhetoric on Father's part. I had never heard him speak of prayer before, for he was not a religious man. He believed in the repose of one's mind, of solitude taken in regular doses to quiet the spirit. But in this place, this Abbey once consecrated to the service of God, the very stones still echoed with the chants of holy men.

Perhaps he hoped it would be enough to prick the conscience of the guilty to confession. Or perhaps he simply wanted an evening free of all of us. If the latter, his aim was true. We left the chilly dining room then—dinner had been a frigid affair, marked with the mewling of infant cats and an occasional hiss from their irritated mother—and went our separate ways, bidding one another good-night in subdued voices. Portia and I made our way slowly upstairs, and I noticed anew the marks of fatigue upon her lovely face.

"I am glad Father has banished us to our rooms tonight," I told her. "You look a fright."

"I feel one as well. You cannot imagine how difficult it is to entertain properly when there is a dead man in the game larder."

I patted her shoulder. "I am sorry for it. Rest is what you need now. Take a nice, dull book to bed and you will be asleep before you know it."

"I must look in on Brisbane first. He sent his regrets for dinner by way of Aquinas, but I would like to make certain he is quite all right."

That Brisbane was perfectly fine, I had no doubt. He was simply being mysterious, holed up in his room like a wintering bear, nursing at his hookah pipe and cogitating, instead of actively investigating as he ought to be.

"I am sure he is entirely well," I told her acidly. "I think you need not bother."

She waved an airy hand. "Oh, I do not mind. Besides, I wish to speak with him about another matter we have been discussing. A bit of business between friends," she finished with a maddening air of vagueness.

Portia had the nasty habit common to all elder sisters of sometimes pretending to knowledge I did not have in order to provoke me to irritation. I would not be provoked. Instead I lifted my chin, gave her a sweetly sticky smile, and simply replied, "Then I will leave you here. Good-night, dearest."

She continued on to Brisbane's room, leaving me seething with annoyance. "A bit of business between friends," I muttered. "Bit of business indeed. And what friends? They hardly know one another."

I continued on in this fashion until I reached my room where Morag was dozing over her knitting. I poked her with a finger.

"Get up and go to bed. I shall not want you this evening. And take the dog with you." My plans did not include Florence. Morag yawned and stretched, an elaborate production that took a few minutes. She made a great show of packing up her knitting and collecting the dog whilst I waited.

"You needn't tap your foot at me," she warned. "I am going as fast as I can."

"Feathers. You are slow as treacle because you want to know what I am about. And what I am about is none of your business."

"Oooh, you are in a right nasty mood, you are. Come, Florence. We've no call to be spoken to like that."

Nose in the air, she stuffed the dog under one arm, the knitting under the other, and retreated to her room. I paced the room after she left, working off my impatience. I was anxious about the night to come, worried my plan would work, and terrified it would not. Restless, I picked things up and put them down again, tried to read for a while, and even attempted to answer a few letters with little success.

At last the clock struck midnight, the earliest hour at which I thought my plan might be put into play. I rose from my chair and threw a black dressing gown over my clothes, changing my evening shoes for a pair of slippers with soft felt soles. If I were seen, I could easily claim I was wakeful and in need of a book or some refreshment. But I did not mean to be seen.

I crept from my room, careful to keep to the interior wall. The gallery was flooded with shifting moonlight. The moon had waxed full, shedding soft pearly light through the great windows. The light shifted as ragged bits of clouds, torn by the warm west wind, dragged over the moon's face like bits of veiling. I made no sound as I slipped behind the tapestry and depressed the mechanism. I had brought no candle with me. I could not risk being betrayed by the feeble light, and I knew the passage well enough to traverse it by feel. If I climbed slowly and kept my hands in front of me, I should be quite all right, I reasoned. But

I will admit to heaving a great sigh of relief when I gained the lumber rooms. Though the moonlight was even brighter here, it took me some minutes to arrange a place of concealment. Finally, I hauled a small trunk onto a larger one and topped them both with a hat form, tucking myself neatly behind. And then I waited.

It was bitterly cold in the lumber rooms, even with my dressing gown over my clothes, and I wished more than once I had been clever enough to have dragged out a few of the moth-eaten old furs to line my little den. I dozed in spite of the cold, but jerked myself awake, occasionally resorting to little pinches and pokes to keep alert. I waited, thinking of all the things I would rather be doing at that moment. I must have fallen asleep, for the next thing I knew I heard a softly muttered curse. Carefully, I stretched my stiffened limbs and dared a peek over the trunk.

A woman was standing with her back to me, scarcely a dozen feet away. She must have been there a few minutes at least for she had nearly finished assuming her costume. Her hair was obscured by the thick white veiling, and she was already dressed in the ghost's attire, completely concealing her identity. She was fumbling at her feet, doubtless attaching the pattens to her shoes.

"Blast," I mouthed silently. She must have entered whilst I was asleep and I had nearly missed her altogether. It was little wonder Brisbane's faith in my abilities as a detective was so feeble.

The woman straightened then, and I had to admit, even at so close a distance, the moonlight lent an eerie effect. I had just watched a mortal woman dress herself in these bits of theatrical garb, and yet I could not suppress a shiver as she glided toward the door, seeming to float above the stone floor like a phantom in a Gothic tale.

I counted slowly to fifty after she left, then eased from my hiding place. Since I had seen her make use of the hidden stair before, it seemed reasonable she would do so again. I followed, straining my eyes for a glimpse of her flowing white draperies, careful to keep myself in the shadows.

There was no trace of her on the hidden stair, but when I emerged into the gallery of the ladies' wing, I saw her at the far end, hovering above the floor, moving slowly toward the staircase. I moved at a pace faster than a walk, but not quite a run, concealing myself behind statues and potted palms. I dashed from one to another, always pausing to make certain she was still within my sights. I followed her from the ladies' wing and onto the landing. I had a great fright then, for just as I reached the landing she turned back and I was forced to dart behind a suit of armour. I counted to fifty again and dared a peek. She had disappeared, and I had a bad moment or two until I realised she must be on the staircase. There was no possible way to descend while she was still on the stairs, so I waited, marking which way she turned at the bottom, then flying down as fast as silence would permit.

She had just reached the end of the transept corridor and turned right toward the drawing room. I followed her progress mentally. If I did not see her when I reached the bottom of the stairs, she must have gone into the great drawing room, in which case the little alcove behind Maurice the bear would make a splendid vantage point to watch for her return. And if she was still gliding down the corridor, Maurice would also be an excellent place from which to monitor her progress.

At least, that was my plan. Over what happened next, I would like very much to draw a veil. It was not my finest moment.

Just as I turned to the left I saw the ghost, stock still, squarely in the middle of the corridor, and not five feet from me. For an instant I forgot the trick of the black veiling and saw only a faceless phantom, floating above the floor. It lifted its featureless head and raised a spectral hand, pointing at my heart. It gave a low, anguished moan of despair, and with that tormented sound, the illusion was complete.

I gave a scream, a very little one, and stumbled backward, stepping hard on the hem of my dressing gown. Just as I fell to the floor, a shadow vaulted over me. It was Brisbane, moving like something out of myth. The moonlight sharpened the angry planes of his face, lending him the aspect of an avenging angel. I sat up just in time to see him rush headlong into the ghost, knocking her soundly to the floor. I struggled to my feet, remembering the candle always kept burning in this corridor at night. The ghost must have blown it out to show herself to best advantage in the gloom. It took but a moment to light it again, and by the time the little flame flared up, illuminating the scene, Brisbane had hauled the ghost to her feet, her black veiling dangling free.

"Charlotte!" I cried.

She made to wrench her arm free, but Brisbane held her fast

with his good arm. "Charlotte, do not give me a reason to slap you, I beg you," he said pleasantly.

"Bastard," she spat.

"What the devil is this about? I want the truth, and I think I deserve it," I stated, folding my arms over my chest.

"She does deserve that much at least, Brisbane. Let us go into the study and discuss this like rational creatures," Father said. I whirled to find him standing on the last stair.

"You as well?" I demanded. Father had the grace to look abashed, but he said nothing. He turned to Brisbane in appeal. Brisbane gave him a curt nod and prodded Charlotte toward the study. I hurried after them, and Father followed. We were an unlikely quartet, I thought as Father closed the door carefully behind us and I hurried to light lamps and put a candle to the fire. It blazed up quickly and cheerfully, a counterpoint to our solemn faces. Brisbane was angry, Father was aggrieved, and Charlotte seemed broken, the hot flash of her anger now burnt to resignation. I was frankly bewildered, and after we had taken chairs and accepted the whiskey Father poured out, I settled back to await an explanation.

"Charlotte King is a jewel thief," Brisbane said flatly. "A rather exclusive one, to be sure, but a jewel thief nonetheless. I have been engaged to retrieve something she has stolen."

"I am *not* a thief," she said quietly.

"Mrs. King, do not speak," Father advised. "We shall all of us remember what you say, and perhaps we may one day be prevailed upon to repeat it, under oath and to your detriment."

Charlotte fell silent and sipped at her whiskey, her eyes downcast.

"I presume that was the reason for the fictitious engagement?" I asked Brisbane.

"It was. I needed to spend time with her, to search her place of residence, to follow her to her boltholes and bribe her confederates."

Charlotte gave a short laugh, nothing like the silly giggle she had affected. Her façade of sweetness cracked, she seemed a dozen years older. "Confederates, my lord? I must remember that."

Brisbane ignored her, as did I. "Why bring her here? To my father's house?"

"I had information, from one of her *confederates,*" he said, drawling the word, "that she was planning to leave the country soon. It seemed logical she would take this particular item with her. I had had no success in recovering the jewel, and time was growing short. It was necessary to isolate her in a place without friends or accomplices and in possession of the stolen property. His lordship volunteered to invite her here."

"Father?" I gave him a stern look and he nodded, a trifle sheepishly.

"I did. I owed Brisbane a rather significant favour," he said shortly. His jaw was set, and I knew he regretted bringing the sordidness of an investigation into his home. I cocked my head, wondering if either of them would admit to Brisbane's daring deed in Trafalgar Square.

"What sort of favour?"

Father's eyes slid from mine. He was suddenly terribly interested in the state of his blotter.

"It does not signify," Brisbane cut in smoothly. "The fact remains, his lordship offered the use of this house party as a suitable setting to apprehend her."

Charlotte gave a harsh laugh. The colour had risen in her cheeks, whether from her predicament or the whiskey, I could not say.

"Apprehend me! And what have you got, my lord? A handful of tatty old rags and a girl out of bed when she oughtn't be," she said to Brisbane, her voice shrill, very near to hysteria, I thought.

"Is that true?" I asked him. "You have no proof of her crimes?"

Brisbane's jaw tightened. "I do not. She has been clever enough to secure the item in question somewhere other than her room or her trunk. I had a strong suspicion she was going to move it tonight. I hid myself in the gallery of the ladies' wing and followed her when she entered the hidden passage. Once I realised she was assuming her disguise, I retraced my steps and resumed my hiding place in the corridor. From there, I knew once she was garbed in her ghostly costume, she would lead me directly to her cache."

I felt a cold chill creep over my limbs that had nothing to do with the temperature of the room. Brisbane was regarding me with an icy stare, and I understood with a thrill of horror what I had just done.

"You mean I ruined—" I could not bear to finish the thought.

"You did," he put in brutally. I had thought him angry with Charlotte. I should have known better. Brisbane was a professional. He did not permit his emotions to become entangled with the criminals he pursued. My interference, however, could be viewed in a very different light.

"Oh, *no,*" I groaned, burying my face in my hands.

Charlotte laughed again, mirthlessly. "I suppose I ought to thank you, my lady. Brisbane has nothing to charge me with except the wearing of old clothes I found in the lumber room, and there is no crime in that." Old clothes she had likely discovered when Aunt Hermia had led a party of chattering ladies to the lumber rooms to choose Lucy's wedding finery. How simple it must have been for Charlotte to mark those few articles, then return later to fashion them into her ghostly garb. Under different circumstances, I might have admired her ingenuity.

I raised my head. "But clearly you were abroad for some nefarious purpose," I argued, desperate to salvage this calamity I had wrought.

Charlotte smiled at me and took a sip of her whiskey. "Or was I creeping around in this disguise to preserve my reputation? Perhaps I was seeking an assignation?"

There was no malice in her eyes, only the calm certainty of a woman who has taken every precaution in a dangerous game. This was why she had courted Plum's attentions, then. She had earned herself a stalwart defender should she have need of one, and an alibi as well.

She rose and placed her glass on the table, patting her hair to smoothness. "I do hope you will excuse me. I am very tired, and it is quite late. I will of course return these things to the lumber rooms, my lord," she said with an arch smile at Father. "I should not like to have it said I took anything that did not belong to me."

She dropped a deep curtsey and left us then. I sank further into my chair, wishing I could escape as easily as that.

"I am sorry," I murmured. "I had no idea."

"Yes, you did," Brisbane said bitterly. "You knew I would never seriously consider marrying a woman like that. You taunted me with it that day by the river. But you could not reason further to realise I was engaged upon an investigation?"

I spread my hands helplessly, wishing Father would say something, anything at all. "I did realise it, but I never took her for a villainess. You even implied someone else might use her as a scapegoat, if you will remember. You said someone else might cache jewels in her room to throw suspicion upon her. And even if I were inclined to believe the worst of her, two minutes in her company would have cured my doubts. She looks like a Dresden shepherdess and she talks like a milkmaid!"

Brisbane's mouth twisted. "Well, your little Dresden shepherdess managed to steal one of the single most valuable jewels in the entire kingdom, and if I do not recover it…"

His voice dropped off as if he could not bear to give voice to the magnitude of his ruin if he failed. "What did she steal?" I dared to ask in a very tiny voice.

"The Tear of Jaipur," Father said softly. "I have only seen it once, but it was the most magnificent thing I have ever laid eyes upon."

"A diamond?"

"Not a diamond," Brisbane corrected, his voice thick with sarcasm. "*The* diamond. The largest one in the queen's personal collection. It was a gift from an Indian potentate when she became their Empress."

I nearly laughed aloud. The very idea was preposterous, another one of Brisbane's nursery stories to keep me in the dark. "The queen? Charlotte stole the queen's diamond? How? Did she scale the walls of Buckingham Palace? Or did she overpower the guards like Colonel Blood?"

Father winced and Brisbane looked grimly at the glass in his hands. He rolled it between his palms, the flames on the hearth flickering in the reflected depths of the whiskey. Too late I realised he had told the truth.

"The queen had given the jewel to her daughter-in-law. No, I will not say which," he said sternly as I opened my mouth to ask. "But she gave it as a mark of extreme favour. And the stupid woman gave it away."

I blinked at him. "To whom?"

"A lover," Father said, pulling a face. It might have been a deliciously scandalous story if matters had not turned out so disastrously for Brisbane, I thought.

"How could she possibly expect the absence of such a thing would not be noted?" I demanded.

Brisbane shrugged. He did not grimace, and I wondered if the aftereffects of the hashish were still allaying the pain of his injury. "He spun her a tale. He told her he wanted to keep it, just for one night, a pledge of her faith and devotion."

"And she believed him?" I scoffed, but Father gave me a world-weary shake of the head.

"Never underestimate the stupidity of a woman in love," he said. "Or a man," he hastened to add.

"The lady did believe him," Brisbane continued. "She gave him the jewel for one night and never saw him again. His name was Edwin Campbell. He is Charlotte's husband, or rather, the man she acknowledges as her husband. I have found no evidence they were ever wed. She took the diamond from him and he has not seen her since."

I shook my head. The tale hung together, but loosely, like cobweb lace. "Why would she move openly in society if she were hiding from her husband?"

"He was taken to gaol shortly after the theft for other crimes. He refuses to speak against her. Poor devil still believes she will come back to him, with the diamond."

"But she is leaving the country? You are certain?"

"As certain as one may be of information one has bought. But it seems the only possible course for her. She has the diamond. She cannot hope to sell it here, but on the Continent, in the Americas even, she could make a tidy fortune and live quite comfortably."

I shook my head. I could not quite take it all in. "I cannot believe she is a thief. I thought her so refined, so feminine."

"Make no mistake, she is the daughter of a gentleman, and she has been educated as a lady. Presenting herself as a genteel society widow was no great difficulty for her. And Campbell was a rather talented forger. He wrote letters of introduction for her, and with those she wormed her way into the highest circles. She was invited to parties at the wealthiest houses. She was quick and careful, and if the hostess noticed some time later a valuable trinket was missing, she would never connect the theft with the charming and garrulous Mrs. King."

"Clever," I said, admiring her just a little in spite of myself. She was thoroughly amoral, and her lifestyle was utterly reprehensible, but there was still something, some elusive quality about her that drew one in. Perhaps it was charm, or a vulnerability she thought she had masked with her deceit.

"Clever and vicious. She was nearly apprehended once by a lady's maid. She bashed the woman over the head with a candlestick and nearly killed her."

I caught my breath. The implication was horrifying. "Brisbane, you do not think, I mean, it is not possible. Not Mr. Snow."

"No," he said slowly. "She could not have killed him. Her hands are smaller than yours. If Edwin Campbell were a free man, I would have suspected him instantly, particularly as Snow had jewels in his pocket. But he is a guest of Her Majesty's, enjoying the hospitality of Wandsworth Prison at present. And the jewels Lucian Snow had in his pocket were not of the variety to tempt the lady. The Grey Pearls would have been much more in her line."

"You think she stole my pearls?"

"I know she did, I can feel it in my bones. But without a witness, without the pearls, without a confession, I have nothing. Less than nothing," he said, his mouth thin with bitterness. "I do not even have the Tear of Jaipur."

I said nothing for a long moment. Father remained silent, and the only sounds were the ticking of the mantel clock and the rustling of the fire.

"The princess herself retained you to recover it?" I ventured finally, afraid of his answer.

"Through the prime minister," he said calmly. It was even worse than I had feared.

"And now you will have to go to them and admit you have failed," I said wretchedly.

"The letters patent," Father began. The letters patent, drawn up to bestow Brisbane's viscountcy, a viscountcy that would not be his until the letters had been published.

"Useless," Brisbane cut in, his voice clipped.

I looked from one to the other. "The letters patent? For your title? What do you mean they are useless?"

Brisbane looked into his whiskey glass, studying the amber depths. "The letters were drafted by Lord Salisbury. He approached me about recovering the jewel for Her Royal Highness after some success I had on behalf of the Prince of Wales in the autumn. The letters were to be held until the diamond was recovered. If I fail, he will burn them."

Puzzled, I turned to Father. "But you have already been addressing him by the title of viscount."

Father shrugged. "A ruse to sweeten the honeypot for Charlotte King. Jewel thieves are terrible snobs."

I shook my head, feeling suddenly sick. "Because I interfered, you will lose a title? And an estate?"

Brisbane drank off his whiskey and put the glass carefully onto Father's desk. "It does not matter, my lady. I was not born to it. The loss of it does not grieve me."

The words should have been comforting, but somewhere underneath them was a current of some indefinable emotion in his voice that made me ache. Was it longing? Did he care so much for what he had never had? I thought of the life he might have led, lord of the country manor, perhaps a husband and father, caring for his stock and his tenants, managing them all with fairness and generosity. I could have wept for him. But something in his face, his implacable, unyielding face, warned me not to.

I rose, a trifle unsteady after the shocks I had endured and the whiskey I had drunk. "There is no possible method by which I may apologise as profoundly as you deserve. I can only tell you I will regret my thoughtlessness, my impetuosity, every day of my life."

I left them then. I heard the low rumble of voices as I closed the door. I did not stay to eavesdrop on what they might have said. They had their own differences to sort between them. I had interfered enough for one night.

Or so I thought. There was one last bit of meddling yet to come. It was a silly thing, really, that finally revealed to me the murderer of Lucian Snow. It happened when I tripped on my slipper on the stair. I was tired and stumbled a little, catching the sole. I looked back to find the slipper sitting on the stair, the toe facing backward, and when I went to pick it up, I understood what we ought to have seen before.

When I reached for the slipper, I instinctively turned my hand, thumb facing back, so that when I straightened and brought the slipper up, the toe would face forward. A simple, stupid detail one would never think on in the course of an ordinary day. But this had been no ordinary day. A man lay murdered under my father's roof, strangled by a right-handed man.

Unless the murderer was upside down. No, that was ridiculous. It was *Snow* who had to be upside down, and once I knew that, the rest of it fell tidily into place. I sank down onto the stair, closing my eyes to better imagine it.

I saw the two men in the chapel, perhaps by arrangement, perhaps by accident. Snow turns his back. Was he caused to do so? He could have been. The little bundle of jewels would have been a pretty lure. He could pocket them and then, his back still turned, he is struck down by a single vicious blow from the candelabrum.

Stunned, perhaps dying already, he slumps unconscious to the floor. His murderer turns him onto his back, and standing at Snow's head, reaches over his face to strangle him. The bruises would speak eloquently of a right-handed man, the perfect alibi for a left-handed murderer.

I opened my eyes, surprised to find myself still on the stair. I had seen it so clearly in my mind's eye. All but the face of the killer, and it did not require much imagination to supply that.

I rose and put on my slipper, determined not to waste a moment. I sped to the gentlemen's wing and knocked softly at one of the doors. It took an agonisingly long time before he replied, but at length he did. I had expected I would rouse him from sleep, but his hair was neatly combed, and his eyes, though shadowed with anguish, were clear and alert.

"My lady," he began, his expression one of naked astonishment. But I gave him no opportunity to say more. I pushed him into the room and closed the door behind us.

He recovered from his surprise and quickly gestured toward the chairs by the fire. I took one, schooling my expression carefully. I must not seem accusatory if I hoped to win his confidence. I must be gentle, sympathetic even.

With that in mind, I reached out when he had seated himself and I took his hand in mine. He started, but did not remove his hand, and after a moment I felt it relax in mine.

"I think you know why I have come. You are burdened. Would it not ease you to speak?"

He sighed then, a great exhalation carrying all the weight of the world with it, but he did not speak. His hand was warm and smooth in mine, and larger than I had expected. I had thought it would feel less substantial somehow, but there was a solid, sinewy strength in his fingers.

"It weighs on you, does it not? You should not carry this burden alone."

He gave a little groan and started to pull his hand away, but I held it fast and courtesy would not permit him to push me away.

"I shall not leave until you talk to me. Believe me when I say I am your friend, and I can help you. My family has a great deal of influence, and if you confide in me, I will do everything in my power to see justice is done. You believe that, do you not?"

He nodded, closing his eyes. His hand was now clasping mine, and I knew he was very nearly there. Just one last push…a shot in the dark, but my only chance to reach him.

"I think that she would want you to tell me."

His eyes flew open. "She said I must never," he whispered hoarsely.

I tightened my grasp on his hand. "She is overwrought. If she were thinking clearly, she would never want you to suffer, I am certain of it. And you are suffering now. It is written plainly on your face."

His expression did not change, but I noticed a sudden brilliance to his eyes, the shimmer of unshed tears. I had found his most vulnerable spot. And like Paris bringing down Achilles, my aim must be true.

"It is not right you should suffer. All you have to do is tell me, and it will be over."

For an instant I thought I had pushed him too far. But then his body sagged and his other hand reached out to cover mine.

"Yes. That is what I want, for it to be over," he murmured.

"Then tell me. I will not abandon you. I swear it."

"I believe you," he said simply.

And I settled in my chair and waited for Henry Ludlow to tell me everything he knew.

THE TWENTY-FIFTH CHAPTER

Smooth runs the water where the brook is deep,
And in his simple show he harbours treason.
—II Henry VI

*I*t was not his fault. He was Sir Cedric's employee and cousin, poor relation to a monster who held the purse strings. Whatever crimes Sir Cedric had committed, Ludlow must fear being charged as an accomplice. I could well understand why he had kept silent. But as his kinsman he must know Sir Cedric better than most, witnessed the ferocity of his temper, his obstinance. And he must have drawn his own conclusion about the author of the murder in the chapel. Lucy's claim to sanctuary must have cemented the conviction that Sir Cedric had murdered Lucian. A woman knows the heart of her beloved, and what she does not know, she intuits. Even if Lucy had not been privy to his plans, she had looked at the broken body on the floor of the chapel and known the handiwork of her beloved.

"His arrogance," Henry began softly, "was deplorable. I have rarely ever encountered a man so replete with it, and for so little cause. I would have hated him on his own merit, even if she had not revealed to me exactly what he was."

I felt the niggle of a question, but did not ask. Now that Henry was talking, I was reluctant to interrupt him.

"I have known other men like him—that bluff, hearty sort. Think they own the world, and they very often do. They stand astride the world like Colossus and they never see what they crush beneath their feet. I hated him from the moment I first made his acquaintance."

I had no choice but to break in. "Why did you accept a position in his employ?" I ventured softly.

Henry blinked at me. "Employ? I was not speaking of Sir Cedric. I was talking about Lucian Snow."

"Ah, yes, of course. I do apologise. Go on," I said with an encouraging smile, but inwardly I was thinking feverishly.

"His inhumanity, his impiety, characteristics to be deplored in a clergyman. To listen to him expounding his plan to reform the Gypsies did not improve my opinion of him," he said angrily. "And when I heard how he had left the army and taken a living so blithely, as a means of keeping himself with little effort and no care whatsoever for his parishioners, it made me quite physically ill."

He looked intently at me, his eyes alight with passion. "Do you know what I would have given for a living of my own? My very heart's blood. It was all I ever wanted. A small country parish where I could do some good. That was my entire life's ambition. To shepherd a flock. To guide, to help, to protect, to inspire. That is all I wanted. It was my dearest dream, and it was taken from me. And given to a man like that—no, not a man. A child. He looked at it as if it were a plaything, to be picked up and cast aside when it suited him, with no care for the needs of his parishioners, no interest in them save whether they had pretty daughters," he said, with real bitterness.

His hands were holding mine very tightly, and even if I had wanted to remove them, I doubt I could have done so.

"But I was cordial to him, because it is my job to be cordial to everyone with whom Sir Cedric chooses to associate. I told myself I should not have to bear him long. He would only be here until the wedding was celebrated. After that he would return to his lodgings in the village, and I would see him no more. I would think on him no more."

Henry's eyes slid away from mine then, and I knew he was seeing it all again in his mind's eye.

"And then she came to me, in tears. He was blackmailing her, demanding payment for his silence over some youthful transgression he had discovered through mutual acquaintances. She would not tell me what it was, only that he had misunderstood something quite terribly, had twisted an innocent mistake into something ugly and untrue. She had no money, and she faced utter ruin if he was not silenced."

The room was quite warm, I decided, or perhaps it was just that we were sitting too near the fire. But I dared not move and draw attention to myself. Henry seemed not to notice. A drop of perspiration trickled down his hairline, but he did not dash it away.

"You must not think we are friends. I would not presume such a thing—but we are confidants after a fashion. I told her of my disappointed hopes, and she told me of hers. She trusted me."

My mind raced on, piecing the snippets he dropped in my lap. I had never heard any scandal attached to Lucy's name, but she had lived quietly. And if the youthful transgression was an innocent mistake as she claimed, it seemed reasonable we would not have heard talk of it. As for her relationship with Ludlow himself, it was entirely understandable. A young, romantic girl betrothed to a much older man of stern temperament—what other gentleman would serve so well as a confidant than her husband's cousin, her own future kinsman?

I turned my attention back to Ludlow. He picked up the thread of his tale, his voice lower. The perspiration was beading freely on his brow now, but still he did not move.

"She came to me, that first night we were here in the Abbey, when we were introduced to Lucian Snow at dinner. She was in tears. I have never seen her so distraught. It was half an hour before she could speak and tell me what he had done."

Here he broke off and, coming to himself a little, he wiped the sweat off of his brow. His other hand still clutched mine.

"What had he done?" I prompted softly.

"He threatened to reveal all to Cedric and the earl if she did not offer him payment. He said he would see her ruined if she failed."

He leaned a little closer, his expressive eyes dark with anguish. "Can you imagine what that meant to her? To see that monster here? In polite company, received by his lordship as an honoured guest? Sitting at table and making polite conversation with her? She was shattered by it, wholly. I could not believe that a man of God could be so foul. But I heard with my own ears when that man would talk so lightly of worldly things. I realised the picture she painted of him was a true one. And I knew he must be prevented from ever hurting anyone else."

I swallowed hard, sickeningly conscious of the fact that I was holding hands with a murderer. How had I gotten it so profoundly wrong?

"So you determined you must stop him," I said evenly. It would not do to alarm him now. There was nothing else to do but encourage him calmly to tell his tale.

"You must see that I had no choice," he said, a touch of anger sharpening his words.

"Of course," I told him, my tone soothing. "It had to be done."

His expression lightened at once. "Yes, that is it. It had to be done. You do understand. I did what must be done. And I am not repentant of it, save for the burden of guilt upon my immortal soul. It was no different than hunting a fox. He was predatory and destructive and he had to be stopped. So I took the jewels from Lady Hermia's room and while he was turned with his back to me, gloating over them, as trusting as a lamb, I struck him down. It was an easy thing, so much easier than I thought to put my hand to his neck and finish it. He did not even struggle. He simply opened his mouth and gave one great sigh and his eyes rolled over white. I had a bad moment when he would not turn loose of the jewels," he said, almost apologetically. "I thought I would have to force his hand open, but there was one last shudder and his fingers relaxed. I did not know the dead would do such a thing. I put them into my pocket, and later I left them with his things. I thought someone might find them there, and in death know him for what he was."

He bowed his head, raising our clasped hands until they touched his damp brow. We were silent for a long while; he seemed spent, and yet somehow cleansed, as if talking of the deed had washed him free of the stain of it. For my part, I knew I should never be clean of it, but still questions lingered.

"I am curious about something," I said softly. "When we entered the chapel and Lucy was discovered, standing over the body, why did you cry out and ask her what she had done? You as much as accused her of murdering Snow herself."

He flushed painfully. "That grieves me more than taking the life of Lucian Snow. Snow was a devil, and devils must be cast out. But implicating Miss Lucy was a sin I cannot forgive in myself." His expression was rueful. "I was tempted, my lady. I saw in that instant she might be blamed for it, just for a little while, and Cedric might break with her."

"And if he did not marry, you might inherit his millions," I finished.

He nodded, the flush ebbing to leave him white-lipped. "So much money, so much good might be done with it. But it was unworthy of me to covet what is not mine, and I am wholly repentant."

"But why did you attack Miss Lucy and Miss Emma with the brandy?"

His eyes widened. "I would never—that is, I could not. Not a lady. Least of all so good, so deserving a lady, nor her sister. I could never raise my hand against an innocent. I promise you, I have confessed my sins. Do not lay that one at my door as well."

His back drooped a little, and the spirit seemed to go out of him, but I was still wary. He was a changeable creature. His manner might be soft and gentle with me, but he had killed in cold blood, and I was deeply conscious of the fact that we were alone together.

"Lady Julia, you must believe I did what I did because it had to be done. And I have paid for it every moment since. I cannot close my eyes that I do not see his, staring up at me as I pressed the life out of him. I am not accustomed to such dark deeds. I am a clergyman's son from Kent," he said with a small, mirthless laugh. "What do I know of such things?"

Tears gathered in his eyes again. "My father was right, you know. He always told me that of the seven deadly sins, envy was the deadliest. I was envious of Lucian Snow. It was not just that he was a monster. It was that he had everything I had not. And he did not deserve it."

"That was not for you to decide, Henry."

"I wanted to believe I was an instrument of justice. At least that is what I told myself when I thought of taking his life. But when the moment came, there in the chapel, when my hand tightened at his throat, all I felt was that cursed envy. I knew I was taking away from him everything he had that I did not, and I delighted in it. Tell me, Lady Julia," he said, his voice cracking on a sob, "who is the monster?"

He fell into me then, and I shied from him. But he meant me

no harm. He was sobbing, the great, racking sobs of a child whose heart has been irreparably broken, and all he looked for in me was comfort. Without thinking, I put a hand on his back and petted him. He slid from the chair to his knees and stayed there, weeping into my lap for some time. Finally he recovered himself and drew back, wiping his face with a handkerchief.

"I am sorry. More than that, I am penitent. I know justice must be served, Lady Julia. I am content you should go and tell his lordship. I give you my word I will not try to escape," he said, straightening his shoulders and looking me squarely in the eye.

I rose and edged my way to the door. I did not truly believe he would harm me, but I had been wrong about such things before. It seemed to me a little caution, even at this late juncture, would be prudent.

"Will you grant me one thing before you go?" he asked. He had command of himself now, but only lightly. His shoulders were trembling and his tone was plaintive.

"If I can," I told him, my fingers wrapped about the doorknob.

He raised his chin, summoning his dignity. "Will you promise not to think too badly of me? I would not like to think that I was entirely friendless in this world, although God knows I do not deserve your regard."

I paused a moment, my instincts warring. Then I released the doorknob, and with cool deliberation walked to where he stood. I put out my hand.

"You are not friendless, Henry. It is not in my power to forgive you, but neither is it in my power to condemn you."

Solemnly as a judge, he shook my hand and the ghost of a smile touched his mouth.

"Thank you for that. Your kindness means more to me than you can possibly comprehend."

I nodded and hurried out, stopping only when there was a stout door between us. I took a few deep breaths, not surprised to find my legs could barely hold me up. I was shaking, and cursing myself for a fool. But there was no time for recrimination. I hastened to Father's room and banged upon the door. He must have returned to his room whilst I had been hearing Henry Ludlow's confession, for he had already retired to bed; he was half-buried in a pile of mastiff pups, dear Crab snuffling in her sleep on the floor.

"What the devil is it now?" he growled, sitting up and straightening his nightcap.

"Father, you must come. Ludlow has just confessed to the murder of Lucian Snow."

It took several minutes before I could make him understand what I had just learned, his expression growing more ominous by the minute.

"You mean to say you went to this man's room alone to accuse him of murder?"

"Not precisely, no," I temporised. "But he has confessed it, and you must come."

It took three more tries to coax him out of bed, and by that time he was scolding me bitterly.

"For an intelligent woman, Julia, you are by far the most headstrong, reckless, thoughtless, *feckless* of my children. And *that* is quite saying something," he grumbled, tumbling the puppies as he threw aside his bedclothes.

I retreated hastily to the corridor and paced, waiting for him to appear. He had dressed himself quickly, not bothering with collar and cuffs.

"You might want to remove, er—" I pointed to his nightcap. "It lacks a certain gravitas."

He gave me a filthy look, then yanked off the offending garment and stuffed it into his pocket. "Get Brisbane," he ordered. "I will take Aquinas to Ludlow's room and we shall take him into custody. God only knows where we will put him. I suppose we must lock him in the wine cellar," he trailed off, more to himself than to me.

"Father, let me find Aquinas. Brisbane's room is quite near Ludlow's. You could fetch him on the way," I suggested.

Father regarded me coldly. "I have no wish to speak to him at present. *Words* were exchanged this evening. No, you go and tell him what you were about, and I will deal with the matter of Henry Ludlow."

I whirled and left the room, thoroughly put out with his peremptory attitude. I stalked to the Galilee Tower and rapped sharply, my temper rising. Brisbane answered the door on the first knock, still dressed in trousers and shirt, his dressing gown thrown over his shoulders. "What has happened?" he demanded without preliminaries.

"Henry Ludlow has confessed to murdering Mr. Snow. Father

has gone to fetch Aquinas to lock Ludlow in the wine cellar," I said. His eyes narrowed in suspicion and I retreated a step.

"And how exactly do you come to know all of this?" he asked, his jaw tight.

I could sense his anger simmering and I thought of Father, ordering me about as if I were still a child. I thought of Brisbane, beckoning me toward him with one hand and shoving me back with the other. And I decided I had had enough of overbearing men.

I stepped forward, drawing myself to my full height and lifting my chin. "I know because I went to his room to continue this investigation, the investigation I was charged by my father to undertake. And because of my actions, a murderer has confessed and justice will be satisfied." I put my hands on my hips, not caring if I sounded like a Billingsgate fishwife. "Yes, it was a dangerous thing to do, but as it seems to have escaped your attention, I will remind you I am above thirty years of age, of sound body and mind, and in control of my own fortune. That means," I said, moving closer still, poking his chest for emphasis, "I am mistress of myself and I answer to *no one*. Not you, not even Father. I am fed up to the back teeth with being wrapped in cotton wool and treated like an invalid."

He opened his mouth to speak, but I shouted him down. The floodgates were opened now, and nothing would stem the flow of my indignation. "I spent more than five years in a marriage that smothered me. I was buried alive in that house, dying slowly, and I did not even know it. And just when I thought I might learn to really live, I nearly lost my life." His expression changed; something flickered in the depths of his eyes. "I know you blame yourself for that, and so long as you do, there will never be anything between us except regret. Well, I do not mean to live my life haunted by the ghosts of what might have been. I intend to live every day just as I please, and right now it pleases me to do this."

Before he could utter a word I reached up, took his head between my hands and pulled him to me. He had kissed me twice before, both times at his behest, and I had been merely a willing participant. But this embrace was mine, and from the moment I touched him I made certain he knew it. I pushed him back against his door, using him as I liked. I was insistent, demanding, taking more than I gave. But when he made to circle me with his good arm, I broke away, holding him at bay.

I straightened my dressing gown and looked at him coolly, lofty as a duchess. "There. Now you have been used at *my* whim."

He put out a hand to me, but I stepped sharply out of his reach. "No. I want you to think on what I have said. And if we meet again, it must be on equal ground, or I will have none of it."

I gestured toward the carpet at his feet. "You will want to leave that shirt for the maid to mend. I am sure the sleeve can be put back on."

He said nothing, did not even incline his head. He merely stood, staring after me as I left, his expression inscrutable. I could not imagine what he was thinking, and for the first time, I did not care. I was determined, well and truly, to be my own woman, to stand on my own two feet and to employ whatever talents and abilities I possessed in some useful occupation.

And I would be treated as an equal, or not at all, I told myself fiercely as I made my way back to my bedchamber. I threw myself onto the bed, astonished at my own ferocious will and my resolve to be mistress of myself. But even this new determination was not enough to stop the slow slide of tears onto my pillow.

I woke early the next morning, having slept a scant few hours, and badly, as well. A dull headache lurked behind my eyes and I snapped at Morag more than once as she performed my toilette. She got her own back by yanking at my hair with the brushes and muttering under her breath about what a trial her life was.

"Not a word of appreciation," she grumbled, jerking the brush through a snarl of hair. She twisted and pinned ruthlessly, jabbing pins into my head. "And does not even look behind herself to see what a mess she's made, leaving her dressing table a right disaster and her pockets full of rubbish."

I twisted round in the chair to look at her. "What rubbish?"

She pulled my head back around and shoved in another pin. "There. You still look a horror, but at least you're a tidy horror." She reached into her pocket and pulled out Aunt Hermia's bundle of jewels. "I found these in your pocket yesterday. Would have served you proper if I'd kept them, it would."

I took them from her and made a note to return the jewels to Aunt Hermia's room before breakfast. There would be little enough else to do, I thought ruefully. Before dawn I had risen to push aside the draperies and watched Father and Brisbane depart in a closed carriage, Henry Ludlow positioned firmly between them. With the murderer confessed, Father had decided to present the matter to Scotland Yard as a *fait accompli*. He meant to call at the vicarage en route to the station to break the news to Uncle Fly himself. It would be an unpleasant task, but no worse than Uncle Fly's. He must write Snow's sisters and tell them of their loss. I hoped they would grieve for him. I did not like to think of him unmourned.

The body of Lucian Snow followed the carriage on a farm wagon, stowed in a makeshift coffin draped with a length of blue fabric. Someone, perhaps Aquinas, had fashioned a wreath to pin to the fabric. With a shudder, I realised it was the white heather intended for Lucy's wedding flowers. I had turned away then, desperately sad, my heart feeling too full to sit within my chest.

The rest of the household felt the same, if the faces at the breakfast table were anything to judge. Charlotte was absent, doubtless sulking in her rooms, but the rest of the party had assembled, a sad, dwindled little group after the events of the past few days. Hortense attempted to make conversation, but no one was terribly interested and eventually she lapsed into silence, probably relieved. Emma and Lucy, looking a good deal stronger than the previous day, were quietly picking at their eggs, while Cedric looked utterly bewildered. I felt rather sorry for him. All this time, harbouring a cousin in his employ who was capable of such viciousness. Lucy rose to the occasion, bringing a plate of eggs and kidneys from the sideboard and coaxing him to eat. I had wondered how their betrothal would stand after Ludlow's revelations, but as I watched them, noting her gentle ministrations,

I wondered if Ludlow had not told the whole truth to my father and Brisbane.

I pulled a piece of toast to bits, thinking quickly. Without me present to question him, he might well have omitted any reference to Lucy at all in his motive for killing Snow. His envy would have provided motive enough, and with a confessed murderer in custody, no one would question him too closely. The authorities, and Father as well, would be grateful enough to have the matter closed before it was even officially investigated. I would not be asked to provide any sort of statement under oath so long as he confessed before other witnesses, an eventuality I was certain Father would ensure. Considering Ludlow's fondness for Lucy and his chivalrous nature, it made sense he would hold his tongue. He had deplored Snow's blackmailing of her. By going to the gallows without disclosing her role in the affair, he ensured she would live out her life unmarred by scandal, her prosperity and happiness providing an expiation for his guilt. I still wondered about the poisoned brandy, but no one spoke of it. I heard from Aquinas that Father had decided Ludlow must be responsible, and since the fellow had refused to speak further, that crime would likely be attributed to him as well, and all but forgot in the greater horror of a clergyman's murder.

Sir Cedric interrupted my musings then, rousing himself to demand coffee. It was Aquinas' duty, but he was absent, retrieving another rack of toast from the kitchens. In his place, Lucy sprang to her feet, fetching the coffeepot and pouring out. She was smiling, but there was a new anxiety I had not seen in her eyes before, and I knew in that moment I had just had a glimpse into what the rest of her life would be: catering to the demands of a capricious, temperamental man who would always keep her firmly in his debt because he had married her in spite of the scandal that was sure to break over our heads like a thunderstorm.

Lucy's hand shook a little and a drop spilled on the saucer. She darted a quick glance at Cedric, who sighed deeply.

"You are clumsy this morning, my dear," he commented. He smiled a little, but there was no blunting the barb. She flinched and apologised, using her own napkin to wipe the saucer clean. No one else at the table seemed concerned with their little drama, but as I glanced about I noticed Emma's eyes were too firmly fixed on her plate, two harsh spots of colour high on her cheeks, a clear sign she was angry. She must have heard every word, and she must see as clearly as I did what the future held for her sister.

Perhaps she felt my gaze upon her, for she looked across the table at me then; our eyes met and held a moment. I gave her a small, sympathetic smile. She pressed her lips together and dropped her eyes immediately. I returned to my breakfast, chatting quietly with Hortense as she sampled her hot fruit compote. And every time I glanced back at Emma, she was staring at her plate, cutting her ham into tiny shreds.

THE TWENTY-SIXTH CHAPTER

*Unbidden guests
Are often welcomest when they are gone.*
—I Henry VI

fter breakfast I returned to my room to look in on Florence. She was busy savaging my favourite set of hairbrushes while Morag knitted by the fire. I left them to it and decided to take a turn about the Abbey, walking slowly from wing to wing. Everyone had scattered to their own pursuits and I was glad of it. I was dreadful enough company for myself; I should have been worse if I had been forced to make polite conversation. Just as I passed the lesser drawing room Plum came barrelling through the doors, his complexion high. He brushed past me, so closely that he dropped his sketchbook.

"Plum, you will want this," I called after him, but he did not turn. He simply strode off in the direction of his room, and when I glanced into the chamber he had just quitted, I understood why.

Charlotte was sitting alone by the fire, pensive. I stooped to retrieve the sketchbook, then rapped lightly at the open door. Charlotte nodded at me to enter and I took the chair next to her.

"You have an animal's instincts for survival," I commented

archly. "This room is the warmest in the Abbey. The monks piped hot water under the stones. Astonishing that the system still works, isn't it?"

Charlotte gave me a sideways smile. "I meant what I told you in the inner ward, about how wonderful it is here. It makes it a little harder to hate you."

I stretched my feet toward the fire. "Heavens, why should you hate me? I have troubles enough of my own."

She laughed, a short, sharp bark of laughter. "I should like to have your troubles. Which dress to choose, which noble lord to marry, which country to spend the winter? Yes, those are troubles indeed."

There was mockery in her voice, but it was not malicious, and I knew we understood one another after a fashion. Under other circumstances, I might have been friends with this woman. The silly, prattling widow she had pretended to held no interest for me at all.

"I never meant to turn to thieving," she said, leaning her head back against the chair. "Oh, yes, I will tell you of it now. It does not matter. And I think I would like to tell someone."

I settled more comfortably into my chair and awaited her tale.

"My mother was an actress. You would not have heard of her. She toured provincial theatres, giving second-rate performances to third-rate audiences. My father was a gentleman, and I think I need not tell you my birth was not blessed by the church. My father paid for my education. He thought to put me into service, as a lady's maid or companion, but I am my mother's child. I left school and took to the stage, a conjurer's assistant, smiling prettily and showing my legs."

She turned her head to look at me. "Did Brisbane tell you about Edwin?"

"Your husband?"

Charlotte smiled a tired, hollow smile. "My life. Edwin cannot marry me, and I do not care. He was the conjurer who took me onto the stage and into his bed when I was fifteen. He is, quite simply, the most beautiful man I have ever seen. White-gold hair, and eyes bluer than the sea. His skin is so pale, you could almost see the wine move down his throat as he drinks."

"So Brisbane was not the sort of man to attract you in any event," I hazarded.

She laughed again. "Absolutely not. Who would want the dark of the moon when you have been dazzled by the sun? But for all his beauty, Edwin is not a gifted magician. You cannot imagine how many birds he has smothered in his pockets or rabbits he has let wander off because he forgot to shut the cage. But he is glorious, and I am not the only lady to think so. There have always been others, others willing to pay for the privilege of what he gives freely to me."

I said nothing, but the room had gone suddenly chill and I shuddered a little. Charlotte's watchful eyes missed nothing.

"I have shocked you, my lady. You cannot imagine sharing a man you loved."

"Indeed not," I agreed. "I should sooner cut out his heart and serve it to him on toast."

Her pretty mouth curved into a sneer. "You think you would. But you have the luxury of food in your belly and a roof above your head. What if all you had was that man? Would he be feast enough for you? Could you not simply gorge yourself on him and let other women have the crumbs? Oh, I think you ought not to judge, my lady, until you have lain awake at night, the hunger pains in your belly so sharp you cannot sleep, the rain soaking your thin bed as the wind shrieks into the room, chilling you to sickness. Then you will have trod a mile or two in my shoes, and then you would understand."

She turned away again and resumed the thread of her tale. "Edwin sometimes took things, little trinkets usually, something grander upon occasion. We lived on what he earned on his back and what he stole from the women who used him. It was his idea to take the Tear of Jaipur, and a grand idea it was. The princess used to come, incognita, to see friends of Edwin's perform. Acrobats, they were, and she would clap and smile like a child as she watched them. But Edwin was often seated in a box near the stage, and it was not long before her eyes strayed to him and lingered. He can read the need in a woman like some men can read a newspaper. He knew what she wanted of him, and he knew she owned the Tear. It was simple enough to arrange. He took the jewel, pledging to return it the next day. She was nervous, but she trusted him. That's the trouble with women," she said wonderingly. "We know what we oughtn't do, and yet we do it anyway. Nature has given us instincts, but when a man comes along, we hear only his voice, and not our own."

She shook herself out of her reverie. "We would have left England that very night, but I had fallen ill and Edwin would not go without me. It was dangerous to keep the Tear in our lodgings, so Edward hid it in a piece of furniture and gave it to a friend for safekeeping. He was taken the next day for some jewels he had sold the week before. It wasn't like him to be careless. I think he was so taken with the idea of the Tear and all it promised that he made a mistake. He sold the jewels to a pawnbroker he had used before, and the man marked him well. Edwin was taken, and I had no money, no means of living. It was too dangerous to sell the Tear, but I was desperate. Edwin penned letters of introduction, and within a week, I was the houseguest of Lady Hester Millar. From there, I moved in only the most exclusive circles. I took what I needed, discreetly."

"There is a lady's maid with a cracked skull who might disagree," I commented dryly.

Charlotte shrugged. "A cornered animal fights, and as you observed, my lady, I have an animal's instinct for survival. It was not long before Brisbane appeared, trailing me like a hound. I visited Edwin in prison. I told him I was frightened, but he only laughed. He told me to be bold, that I must throw myself into Brisbane's path to divert suspicion. In the meanwhile, I would plot my escape from England, and establish myself abroad when it was safe to move. I would sell the diamond and buy land, acres and acres of it where we would be our own lords of the manor. The charges against Edwin will be difficult to prove. He will be released in a matter of months and we will be together."

"But without the Tear," I reminded her. "Your things have been searched." Even as I said it, I realised she might well have hidden the jewel anywhere in the Abbey, along with my pearls. But she could not hope to recover them.

She gave me a lazy smile. "Then I will go without it. I will make a future for myself and for Edwin." There was something I did not like in her manner, some smugness that she was unable to conceal.

"And my pearls?"

"Have not left the Abbey. I leave you to find them since you love a good mystery," she said, slanting me a challenging look.

My tolerance for her was moving rapidly into hatred. "And my dog? I suppose you were the one who poisoned her?"

Charlotte's eyes widened in mock horror. "My lady, you shock me. I would never poison a dog. I merely drugged her with a tasty bit of venison soaked in a drop of Cook's laudanum. I discovered it when I was stirring up the Christmas puddings, and I thought it might be useful."

There seemed nothing else to say. She had admitted to her crimes, but without either the jewels or the authority to hold her, I was powerless. She gave me a fond smile.

"I have actually quite enjoyed myself, you know," she told me. She stretched, lissome as a cat. "I shall be sorry to leave Bellmont Abbey."

"Do forgive me if I say that we shall not be sorry to see you go," I returned.

I left her then, her laughter echoing in my ears.

When I moved into the nave, I was astonished to find Sir Cedric there with Emma and Lucy, dressed in travelling clothes and surrounded by their baggage. Sir Cedric was quite purple in the face and yelling at Aquinas.

"Sir Cedric, contain yourself," I said crisply. "There is no call for that sort of behaviour. Now, what is the trouble?"

Sir Cedric was sputtering too much to speak, so Aquinas stepped in. "Sir Cedric and his party wish to leave and have requested a carriage and baggage wagon to take them to the station in Blessingstoke. I have had no instructions from his lordship on the matter, and I am uncertain of his wishes."

I looked at the little trio of travellers. Sir Cedric had lapsed into furious muttering under his breath. Lucy and Emma stood a little apart, Lucy biting at her lip while Emma stood so straight I thought her back would snap from the strain of it. Their faces were white and nervous, and I pitied them thoroughly.

"Aquinas, order the conveyances." Father had taken the coachman to London, but Whittle, the gardener, was a fair hand at the whip when necessary, and one of the footmen could manage a baggage wagon as far as Blessingstoke.

Aquinas bowed and withdrew to make arrangements. Sir Cedric pulled his greatcoat tighter about his girth, his expression almost, but not quite, mollified. Lucy shot me a look of pure gratitude before sinking down to sit on one of Cedric's trunks. Emma laid a hand on her shoulder, and it occurred to me then she would also have to tread on eggshells if she hoped to stay in her future brother-in-law's good graces.

"Sir Cedric, I presume you are returning to town? Father must give your direction to Scotland Yard. They will want to speak with you about this business with Mr. Ludlow."

"Do not speak his name to me," he thundered, his face purpling again. "No, I do not mean to return to town. We leave for Southampton. I mean to be aboard ship tonight."

It took me a moment to grasp what he was saying. "You are leaving the country? Tonight? But Mr. Ludlow will need you. He must present a defence to the charges of willful murder, as well as the attack against Emma and Lucy. Statements must be given, and references to his character. I grant they will not weigh heavily as he has confessed, but you must help him."

"Must I?" His tawny lion's eyes narrowed to something small and mean. "He has disgraced himself, and me by association. I do not mean to stay here whilst I am made sport of by the newspapers. He will be tried for the murder. To have the attack upon Lucy and Emma made public would be unacceptable. We leave for India tonight. Lucy and I will be married on board the ship, and we will remain in India until this is all quite finished."

"You mean until Henry hangs for what he did?" I asked brutally.

Sir Cedric looked at me appraisingly. "I was quite right about you. You need a husband. Someone with a firm hand to keep you in line. You are far too forward and mannish."

I inclined my head graciously. "How kind of you to notice. In that case, permit me to wish you as pleasant a journey as you deserve."

I exchanged pecks on the cheek with Emma and Lucy. Emma was in complete command of herself, although her manner seemed brittle, as if her nerves were stretched taut as a bowstring. I did not envy her future in Sir Cedric's employ.

"Thank you, dearest Julia," she murmured into my ear. "You helped to save my darling girl, and I cannot ever repay such a debt."

She squeezed my hand and turned away, blinking furiously. Lucy was inclined to cling. Her lips were bleeding a little where she had chewed them, and her nails were bitten to the quick. Eventually, I detached her from my neck and patted her arm. I took my leave then, but as I mounted the stairs I took one last look over my shoulder. Sir Cedric was fussing over some imaginary scuff Lucy had left on his bag. Lucy was on her knees, buffing at it. And behind them stood Emma, her expression blank as a marionette's as she watched them both.

I met Portia at the top of the stairs and quickly related the news that Cedric was leaving his cousin to the mercy of the law, without recourse to money or influence to help his defence.

"I never liked him," Portia said stoutly. "I wonder if Lucy knows what she is doing?"

I tipped my head thoughtfully. "I think she begins to see it, and to worry. But it is too late. If she puts a foot on the deck of that ship, she has as good as married him. What is that you are carrying?"

Portia unrolled the bundle of white linen. "A ghost," she told me, pointing to the two charred spots where the holes for eyes had been burnt. "The maid found it in the linen cupboard this morning. Christopher Sly has decided at last to admit people to her nursery."

I held it up, touching the blackened holes lightly. "But I thought Charlotte was our only ghost," I murmured.

Portia shrugged. "I could not care less, my heart. I only know I have to explain to Aunt Hermia why one of Grandmama's prized sheets from France is ruined." She put a finger through the hole and waggled it at me. "I do not suppose you would like to break the news?"

I took the sheet and gave her a quick kiss on the cheek. "I would be happy to do it."

Portia peered at me. "Are you starting a fever? You are unnaturally decent this morning."

I smiled at her, thinking of Lucy and Emma and the lives they would lead. "I am merely exceedingly grateful that we are ladies of independent fortune," I told her. And I left her, staring after me in puzzlement.

THE TWENTY-SEVENTH CHAPTER

Love looks not with the eyes, but with the mind.
—A MIDSUMMER NIGHT'S DREAM

After I left Charlotte, I had no desire for company. But I still carried Plum's sketchbook, and I knew he would want it back. A page had come askew when it fell, its corner poking out from between the thin morocco covers. I opened the book to put it to rights, and suddenly realised the page was not part of the sketchbook at all. In fact, it was not even a page. It was the corner of an envelope, a thick, creamy envelope stamped several times over with Italian postmarks. There was a letter inside, written in formal Italian and penned in a thin, ornately spidery script. The paper bore the cipher of the Palazzo Fornacci in Florence.

For what I did next, I do not apologise. Too many secrets had been kept in our house already. I went straight to Father's study, closing the door softly behind me. Grim *quorked* at me from his cage and I let him out. With a whirr of black wings, he came to settle himself on Father's desk, watching me with great interest. I took the letter from Plum's book and retrieved Father's Italian dictionary. It was slow going. My command of the written language was poor, and for all the purity of the Florentine dialect, the letter was liberally sprinkled with colloquialisms I could only guess at.

When I had at last deciphered it, I sat back in Father's chair, musing.

"Sweeties," Grim demanded, bobbing his glossy dark head at me. I gave him a pat and tossed him a sweetmeat. He devoured it happily, then toddled across the desk, looking for more.

"No, you shall get fat," I scolded him, pushing the box out of reach. He cocked his head at me, then lowered his beak and began to peck at Plum's sketchbook.

"Don't do that, Grim." But ravens are somewhat less obedient than dogs, and he did not listen. He worried at the cover until he managed to open it.

"That is quite enough," I told him, pulling the book onto my lap. He gave me an irritable *quork* and withdrew to his cage, turning his back to me.

"You needn't sulk," I began, but then my eyes fell to the open book. Something about the image Plum had sketched there caught my attention. I ruffled through the rest of the book. There were a few sketches of me, one of Charlotte, an assortment of Italian *signorinas,* and one form in particular, rendered in a variety of poses. He had caught her unawares, it seems, for most of the sketches were of her profile, sometimes laughing, once in tears. But for one sketch, she must have sat for him. She looked out from the page, her expression at once both apologetic and triumphant.

I snapped the book closed, sorry I had seen it. But now that I had, those few lines of charcoal had changed everything.

I went directly to Plum's room. He called irritably for me to enter when I knocked. He was sitting in the window embrasure, looking out at the melting snows, scratching at the glass with a fingernail. He glanced up when I entered, then turned back to the window.

"If you've come to call me a fool, be content. I've done it a hundred times. I understand she stole your pearls?"

I crossed the room and levered myself up into the embrasure to sit next to him. It was cool there, and I wrapped my skirts about my legs as I gathered them under me.

"Apparently, she did. But she will not say where she has them hid, and the Abbey is simply too massive to search. She cannot leave with them, and I am sure they will turn up one day."

He rested his head on the stone wall behind him, one hand draped over his knee, the fingertips smudged softly black with charcoal. "I ought to have known better. I ought to have *behaved* better. It was bad form to dally with Brisbane's fiancée, even if the engagement was a sham."

I shrugged. "We are all of us stupid at times. Perfection is dull, my love." I brandished the sketchbook. "You dropped this outside the drawing room. I thought you might go looking for it."

I laid it on the bit of window seat between us. He made no move to touch it but simply looked at me, his eyes half-lidded in pain.

"I suppose you looked through it."

I nodded slowly. "I did. And I'm sorry. Perhaps that is why you behaved so badly with Charlotte. Because you cannot have *her*."

He made a little sound that was halfway between a laugh and a sob. "No. And now that she carries my brother's child, I never will."

He thumped a fist against the windowpane, the glass shudder-ing lightly under his hand.

"Plum, you would never have had her in any case. She loves Lysander. She married him," I said, my voice low and soothing.

He looked at me with something like pity. "You still do not understand. I saw her first, I loved her first."

I blinked at him. "But how? Lysander came back to Florence already married to her."

Plum stared out at the winter landscape, but I knew he was seeing another place and another time. "It was last summer. Lysander and I were in Rome, awaiting your arrival. We went to a church, something about a new organ Lysander wished to hear. She was there, just across the aisle, her head draped in a veil of Venetian lace. I saw only her profile, but it was enough. I sat and listened to the music and worshipped her for an hour. And when it was done, Lysander simply rose and left, complaining about the organist's sense of timing. He never sensed her, never realised that she was there, like a goddess stepped from Olympus to grace mere mortals with a glance."

I suppressed a sigh. It was very like Plum to romanticise his feelings for Violante, and I knew it would be fatal to remind him that she was simply a pretty girl with lovely eyes and indigestion.

He went on, dreamily. "You cannot imagine what a shock it was to me when Lysander brought her into the room that first night and made his announcement. *I have taken a wife, Plum. Come and kiss your sister.* And I had to press my lips for the first and only time to that alabaster cheek, knowing she would never be mine." He roused then, smiling from faraway. "Lysander has always been generous with me. Anything I admired, he gave me freely. But she is the only thing of his I have ever envied, and the only thing I cannot have."

"And that is why you have been beastly to him? And cold to Violante? This is what was behind that ludicrous display in the billiard room when you punched him on the nose, is it not?"

"Julia, you do not know. You cannot imagine the torment—"

"Eglamour Tarquin Deiphobus March, don't you *dare* tell me what I do not know," I began, rising from my perch. "I know a very great deal about eating your own heart out over someone you cannot have. And do you know what I have learned? It is pathetic and sad. You are a strong, healthy, passably handsome man with a reasonably good intellect, if you would care to use it, and a talent for drawing that Michelangelo himself would have approved. And what do you do with all those virtues? You flirt with betrothed women and moon about over your own sister-in-law. You are maudlin and sentimental, and it is high time you took a rather hard look at yourself and realised you are in danger of becoming ridiculous."

He gaped at me, open-mouthed. He did not even attempt to speak.

"Now, I am about to go and bruise the heart of your friend. If you can have a care for anyone other than yourself, you should make preparations to take him back to Italy. It would be the best thing for the both of you. Alessandro can get on with the business of his life, and you can do something with yourself."

He slumped against the window, his brows drawn together. "Like what?"

I spread my hands. "Restore a church. Learn to quarry marble in Carrara. Go to Greece and build boats. Only for heaven's sake, do not let this destroy you. You love her now, but in a year or two, when she has had a child and grown fat and content, you will not. You will have replaced the memory of her with a hundred more precious. But you must try."

For a long moment he did not move. Then, by way of reply, he held the sketchbook out to me. "Burn it."

I took it from him, noting how his fingers trailed over the cover as if to memorise the pages that lay beneath.

"Are you quite certain?"

He nodded. "You are right, of course. I must cut her out, painful as that may be. And who knows, perhaps something else may grow there."

"And what of Alessandro's letter?" I ventured.

He gave a tiny smile. "You were thorough. I ought to give that back to him. He wanted me to read it, to advise him how best to handle his father. A moot point now, if you mean to send him away."

I shrugged. "It is better this way. For everyone." I handed him the letter and took the book away with me. He had been brave enough to ask me to burn it. I was not cruel enough to make him watch.

After I had burned the sketchbook, waiting until it fell to thin, grey ash, I retrieved a Kashmir shawl from my room and went in search of Alessandro. I finally ran him to ground in the library, gamely working his way through *Pride and Prejudice*. He sprang to his feet when I entered, smiling broadly.

I nodded to the book. "How are you enjoying Jane Austen?"

He waggled his hand from side to side. "She is a little silly, I think."

Now I was more certain than ever of my decision. I could not love a man who did not love Jane Austen. "The great Duke of Wellington thought her the greatest literary talent in all of England."

He smiled politely. "Perhaps she improves upon second reading."

"Hmm. Perhaps. I wanted to speak with you."

His smile froze, his lips suddenly quite stiff. He swallowed hard and laid down the book. "You are refusing me."

I put out my hand to him and he took it. His was warm and firm in mine. "I am. Walk with me in the courtyard and I will try to explain."

It was characteristic of his youth that he did so. An older man would have armoured himself in his pride and refused an explanation. Only the young have such a gift for self-torture.

We moved out into the courtyard arm in arm. The sunshine, after days of mournful grey, was a revelation. The warmer air had melted off most of the snow and what remained was slowly dripping away against the stone. It was cold to be sure, but nothing like what it had been, and I stopped to raise my face to the sun.

"You are sure you do not wish to come to Italy?" he joked bravely. "We have the sun almost the whole of the year. You do not have to search for it as you do in England."

I opened my eyes and smiled at him, taking a moment to

memorise the soft black hair touched with bronze, the noble profile, the gentle eyes staring into mine with such sadness, and perhaps the merest touch of relief.

The wind rose a little just then, scudding a cloud over the face of the sun and throwing the courtyard into shadow.

"You are shivering. Take my coat," he insisted, draping the garment over my shoulders. I murmured my thanks and took his arm, leading him toward the iron gate that led to the gardens.

"You see, Alessandro," I began slowly, "you come from an old and proud and very dignified family. I too come from an old and proud family, but I am afraid we are a little short on dignity."

He opened his mouth to make a polite protest, but I held up a hand. "Oh, do not, I beg you. I know my family for what we are. From the manner of our dress, our speech, our small eccentricities and our grand follies, we are odd. We do not fit the pattern of society, and as a result we are often talked of."

He said nothing and I pressed on, gently.

"I should not suit you, Alessandro, not truly. I keep a pet raven and I speak my mind and I associate with those who are beyond the pale of society, and yet I am very nearly the most conventional member of my family. People are still talking about my cousin Charles' appearance at a house party last month. He wore his wife's gown and demanded to be addressed as Carlotta."

Alessandro choked back a laugh and I squeezed his arm. "You may think it amusing, but to us, he is family. We will not hide him in the cellars and pretend he does not exist. We will welcome him with open arms, and very likely give him the names of our dressmakers," I finished, smiling at my own little jest.

Alessandro's brow puckered. "But surely such things are better left unknown. I too have the curious cousins, but we do not speak of them."

"That is the difficulty, my dear. In your family you do not speak of them. In my family, we celebrate them. In Italy, one must always be conscious of *la bella figura,* of presenting one's best self. Among the Marches, we please ourselves and the devil take the rest."

His brows lifted slightly and I patted his hand. "You see? I even shock you with my language. We would be very badly suited indeed. Besides," I said carefully, "I believe your father has plans for you. Exalted ones."

There was a sharp intake of breath. "How did you know that?"

I smiled, not looking into his eyes. His father's letter had been idiomatic and excessively difficult to translate. I had deciphered perhaps one word in five. But those words were enough. "It is not difficult to guess," I temporised. "Your father is a judge, is he not?" I hoped I had gotten the translation correct from the letter. Father's dictionary had been printed two centuries back and mice had nibbled a fair number of holes through the most useful words.

Alessandro nodded, his lovely mouth turning sulky. "*Sì.* He is an important man in Firenze, with much influence and power."

"And he wishes you to be the same, in your time. A very natural ambition for a father, I think."

Alessandro scuffed his shoe against a paving stone. "But should a man not be ambitious for himself?"

"Of course. What is it you would like to do?"

He dropped my arm then to spread his hands. Like most Italians he was incapable of speaking for any length of time without gesturing.

"I also want to be a judge, to give justice, to have the power to influence people. But I want to want such things for myself. Why are you smiling at me?"

"My dear Alessandro, what difference does it make if your father wants these things for you as well? If you want them, take them, and be happy. Life is either far too short or far too long to make yourself miserable."

He said nothing as he considered this. I looked through the garden gate, marking the withered vines, the blind stone eyes of the statues, the sharp angles of the hedge maze. It was not grand or even particularly beautiful, but it was my home and I felt a rush of love for the old place so acute, so complete, I nearly wept.

"Perhaps you are right," he said slowly.

I turned back to him and assumed a brisk, governessy tone. It was time for the *coup de grâce*. "Of course I am. And I will tell you something else I am quite right about—you will need a wife who will understand you, who will present *la bella figura* and make you proud. I would imagine your father already has someone in mind," I said, widening my eyes innocently.

"You are a witch," he grumbled. "How could you know this?"

I gave a modest shrug, remembering how his father had described the girl in question. *Una belleza perfetta.* I wished Alessandro a lifetime of happiness with her. "It is only logical."

He rallied, and attempted once more to change my mind. He seized my hands, drawing them to his heart. "I would give up everything for you, Giulia."

I smiled at him gently. "But you must understand. I should never want a man to give up anything for me. I should want him to feel in winning me he has won the whole world. Now, go back to Italy, marry your lovely *signorina,* and have a good life. And when you are quite old and sitting on the terrace of your *palazzo,* sipping a fine *chianti* you have grown in your very own vineyards, I want you to think of me sometimes and smile mysteriously so that your grandchildren will demand to know what you are thinking of."

He laughed then and reached out, as if to embrace me, then thought better of it and took my hand. "It was a beautiful dream," he said, his voice laced with resignation.

"It was a beautiful dream indeed," I agreed.

He raised my hand to his lips and kissed it, and when he had done, I pressed it to his cheek. Then, slowly, we made our way into the Abbey and went our separate ways.

It was destined to be a day of partings. I left Alessandro in the library, meaning to retire to my room to repair my toilette before luncheon. The wind had risen at the last minute, loosening hairpins and whipping colour into my cheeks. A few moments with my hairbrush and a pot of face cream were all I needed, but just as I set foot on the staircase I noticed Charlotte descending. She was dressed for travel and carrying her small portmanteau. She saw me and lifted her pointed little chin.

"I mean to go," she warned. I blinked at her and she skirted around me, never slowing her pace. I followed her through the cloister and out to the inner ward, arriving just in time to see Aquinas appear.

"The carriage is ready, Mrs. King," he informed her.

"Good. The sooner I am quit of this bloody place the better," she muttered.

Aquinas caught sight of me then and hurried to my side. "My lady, Mrs. King requested transportation to Blessingstoke. You were not to be found, and since the carriage was placed at Sir Cedric's disposal earlier, I thought it acceptable to extend the same courtesy to Mrs. King. His lordship left no instructions."

I sighed. It was bad enough Cedric had left with Lucy and Emma. What would Father say when he learned I had let Charlotte go as well? Still, I was rather inclined to view the situation as one of his own making. "If Father wanted anyone detained, he ought to have said so. Besides, we have no right to hold anyone against their will. We are not the law."

I had spoken softly, but Charlotte overheard this last part. She gave me a broad smile and extended her hand.

I shook it, not quite willingly. Charlotte could be a likeable rogue, but she was insubstantial. She had re-created herself so many times I was not certain where her fictions left off and the woman began.

Her smile deepened to one of genuine warmth. "Do not be like that. We got on well enough, didn't we? I am fond of you, my lady, for all your money and fancy ways," she said pertly.

I returned her smile and inclined my head. "Mrs. King, I will wish you a pleasant journey."

She gave a short, sharp bark of a laugh. "I am sure. But go I must. I would rather not meet your lover again."

Her expression was bland, but her eyes were sharp with malice and anticipation. She was waiting for me to sputter in outrage, to deny, to throw her out of the house in my fury.

And in a flash of blessed inspiration, I realised why. The Tear of Jaipur.

I turned to Aquinas. "Fetch Morag. Tell her to come at once." He withdrew and I smiled sweetly at Charlotte. "I shall be only too happy to permit you to leave, as soon as your bag and your person have been searched."

The following minutes were not wholly pleasant. In spite of her ladylike demeanour and her delicate looks, she raged, she spluttered and cursed us all. She scratched and kicked and Aquinas sustained a rather nasty bite on his thumb. But at last we managed to lock her in the boot room with Morag. There were ominous sounds, bumps and thumps and all manner of swearing. After a very long interlude, Charlotte emerged, hair straggling down her back, clothes askew, clutching her portmanteau.

"Nothing, my lady," Morag advised me, rolling down her cuffs and pinning them neatly into place. It was a testament to her efficiency and her brutality that she had not a hair out of place.

"In that case, you are free to leave, Mrs. King. Farewell," I told her pleasantly.

By way of reply she turned on her heel and fairly ran from the

Abbey. Aquinas slammed the door behind her and the three of us stared at one another in bemusement.

I glanced at the tall case clock. "Lord, I must fly. I shall be late for luncheon as it is. Thank you both. I know Mrs. King was a trial, but she is gone now and we need not think on her again. She is a thief and a liar and we are well rid of her."

"And she didn't even leave a tip," Morag put in bitterly.

THE TWENTY-EIGHTH CHAPTER

And so, from hour to hour, we ripe and ripe,
And then, from hour to hour, we rot and rot,
And thereby hangs a tale.
—As You Like It

*I*f that day was one of partings, the following was one of homecomings. Father and Brisbane returned just after tea, exhausted and in identically vile moods, although they seemed to have made up their quarrel after a fashion. They made straight for Father's study and the whiskey bottle in spite of the hour. Father poured out a large measure for them both, a daintier portion for me.

"Aquinas informs me we have lost four guests," Father said mildly.

I bristled a little at the implied criticism. "They were determined to go, Father. I had no authority to hold them." Brisbane's mouth opened and I held up a hand. "And I took the precaution of having Charlotte searched. The Tear of Jaipur was nowhere to be found, and I am certain Morag was painfully thorough. She must have cached the stone somewhere before she came to the Abbey."

"And now I have missed the opportunity to follow her whilst she retrieves it," he said sourly.

"Then you ought to have stayed with her," I returned. He raised a brow at the tartness of my tone, but said nothing.

Father wagged a finger. "Enough. The fault is indeed ours, Brisbane. If we meant to keep everyone here, we ought to have seen to it before we went haring off to London."

Brisbane's only reply was to take another deep draught of his whiskey. I turned to Father.

"Where is the inspector? I thought he would return with you."

Father smiled thinly. "He is warming his bottom by his own hearthside, my dear. He was pleased enough to take the body and the villain into custody and to take our word for which was which."

"That cannot possibly be right. He ought to have come here, investigated properly, taken statements, asked questions," I trailed off, too indignant to finish.

"Yes, he ought," Father agreed, draining the last of his whiskey. "But he did not. He is content to accept what Brisbane and I told him and leave matters at that. Ludlow confessed again, this time to the inspector. Our involvement is not required. The boy will swing for it at his own request."

I said nothing. Father was pleased because it meant there would be little in the way of repercussion as far as the family were concerned. But it seemed deeply unsatisfying to me that it should all end thus. Ludlow was a murderer and deserved to be punished to be sure, but to be dispatched with so much haste and so little concern for his motives struck me as unjust. I could not like that Lucy had escaped so easily from bearing the consequences of her role in this tragedy. Then I thought of her life with Cedric and realised the consequences to her could hardly be worse.

I left them then with their black moods and whiskey. They would be drunk as lords by dinner, I thought, and appropriately so. I turned the corner toward the staircase and nearly collided with Aquinas. He was coming from the direction of the kitchens, holding a festively wrapped box in his hands.

"What have you there?" I teased. "My Christmas present?"

He smiled. "No, my lady. It is a Christmas pudding. When Mrs. King stirred up the puddings for the family, she made one for each member of the house party, including herself. Before she left she asked Cook to send hers on."

I felt a prickle along the back of my neck. It could not be so simple. "Why did she not take it with her?"

"Mrs. King took only her portmanteau. She asked that her trunk be sent directly to her hotel and told Cook to tuck the pudding into her trunk before it was sent on. I have her direction. The maid has nearly finished packing her trunk. I meant to dispatch it today."

I took the parcel from him, pricking my finger on the little sprig of holly Cook had tied neatly to the top. I ripped through ribbons and brown paper until I reached the pudding itself, firm and glistening, a masterpiece of the confectionary arts. The smell of fruit and spices rose from it, perfuming the air with Christmas.

I took a deep breath and plunged my hand into the pudding.

Nothing. I pushed further. My heart gave a great lurch when I pulled out a trinket, but it was only a coin, stirred in for luck and prosperity in the coming year. I pushed my fingers into the sticky mess one more time, willing it to be there.

Aquinas said nothing through all of this. He merely stood, serenely, behaving as though it were the most natural thing in the world for his mistress to destroy Christmas puddings.

I pulled out my hand.

"My lady?" he asked. "Did you find what you sought?"

I turned my hand over and opened my fingers. There on my palm lay the largest diamond I had ever seen, winking up at me through spiced crumbs and bits of currant.

"I have indeed, Aquinas. May I introduce the Tear of Jaipur?"

Had I a better sense of the theatrical, I would have cleaned the jewel carefully and presented it to Brisbane with a flourish and a fanfare. But I knew time was of the essence. No sooner had I shown it to Aquinas than I gathered my skirts in my sticky free hand and dashed down the hall, cursing my corset as I ran, Aquinas hard on my heels. I flung open the door to the study.

"I have it!" I cried. "And her direction as well."

Father stared owlishly at me over his spectacles, but Brisbane surged from his chair, at my side in a heartbeat. He took the diamond, rubbing at the traces of pudding with his thumb. He sniffed at it, then poked a tentative tongue at the mess.

"Pudding? She had it cooked in a Christmas pudding?" he

asked. Emotions warred on his face, disbelief, elation, and a deeply felt satisfaction, I think. Father rose and came to look at the stone, clucking under his tongue.

"It is a very fine thing, when it isn't covered in muck," he observed.

I looked at Brisbane. "She told Cook to make certain it was packed in her trunk and sent on to her. Aquinas has the direction. She will not move without the Tear."

"Unless she feels cornered," Brisbane said, taking out a handkerchief and carefully pocketing the diamond. "Aquinas?"

Aquinas retrieved a slip of paper from the pocket of his coat. "A hotel in Southampton, my lord."

"Southampton!" I exclaimed. "She has taken a page from Sir Cedric's book. She must mean to quit the country as soon as she has the jewel."

"She will not have the chance," Brisbane said grimly.

"I will summon the carriage, although I believe the last train to Southampton has already left Blessingstoke station, my lord," Aquinas put in.

"I need a train to London," Brisbane corrected. "I must return the jewel for safekeeping before I pursue her."

I shuddered at his tone. There was a grim determination there I had not seen in him before, and I felt suddenly rather sorry for Charlotte King.

"Ah, in that case, if we make haste, it should just be possible," Aquinas said, withdrawing quickly to make the arrangements.

"I shall go with you as far as the station," Father offered. "I must pay a call upon Fly in any event. He will want to know what Scotland Yard has said about the murder of Mr. Snow." His expression was doleful as he left us.

When we were alone, Brisbane turned to me, his eyes bright with anticipation. "Well done," he said softly.

The words were simple enough, but in that moment I was acutely aware of his physical presence.

"Yes, well, if I hadn't happened to fairly run Aquinas down in the hall, I might never have discovered the jewel," I told him.

He said nothing for a long moment. He merely stared at me, his dark gaze roving restlessly over my face as if memorising every feature. Time stretched out between us, and everything else, the sounds of the Abbey, the urgent knowledge that he must hurry to leave, all of it fell away. I felt stripped somehow. The moment was far more intimate than any of the kisses we had yet shared. I dropped my eyes, breaking the spell.

He stepped closer. "I must go," he murmured. "I do not know when I will return."

He was mere inches from me, so close I caught the scent of his skin.

"Of course," I replied. With every word we moved closer to one another, not quite touching, but with only a breath between us. I stared at the buttons on his waistcoat.

"Thank you," I said faintly.

He bent his head toward mine, brushing his cheek against my hair. I heard him inhale deeply. "For what?"

"Saving Father in Trafalgar Square."

I knew in this moment he would not deny it. After a moment I felt him nod. I ran a finger along the silk of his sling. "I promise I shall not ask it again if you tell me the truth. Will you be quite all right?"

"The shot was a clean one," he replied, his voice muffled by my hair. "Another month and I will be right as rain."

"Thank God for that," I murmured.

The noises in the hall grew more frantic and I heard a footman announce to Aquinas that the carriage was drawing around to the door. Brisbane stepped back sharply. Once again he had assumed the unfathomable mask I knew so well. The moment between us, whatever it might have been, whatever might have been said, was lost.

I sighed and moved aside to let him pass. "Godspeed, Brisbane. I hope you find her."

He nodded and moved to the door, but paused with his hand on the knob. "You are wrong, you know."

I raised a brow. "About what?"

That fathomless black gaze held mine. "I think you are more my equal than any woman I have ever known."

And before I could reply he was gone.

I dressed for dinner that night with the deepest apathy. With Brisbane gone I felt oddly flat and out of sorts. I did not like to think I cared more for him than he did for me. I did not like to think I cared for him at all, truth be told. He was enigmatic and difficult, tricky as a cat and twice as sly. But care I did, I admitted, slipping his pendant into the décolletage of my gown. And I did not know when, if ever, I would see him again.

But if I was sulky at dinner, I was in better spirits than half the company. Father was preoccupied, grieved after his visit with Uncle Fly, who had been badly shaken by Snow's murder. Alessandro was quiet for reasons I did not like to think about. Ly and Violante had quarrelled again and were locked in silence, both of them pushing food around their plates and shooting each other nasty looks. And Plum looked pensive. He forgot to eat for long stretches, and more than once I glanced up to see him looking at a bit of food on his fork in bewilderment, as if wondering how it came to be there. Only Hortense and Portia made any pretense at normal conversation, and I was not entirely surprised when the subject turned to Charlotte.

"She was really a jewel thief?" Hortense asked. "I cannot believe it. She seemed so gauche, so unsophisticated, with her chattering and her silly mannerisms."

Plum flicked an irritated glance at her, but she did not notice. Portia shrugged. "She was thief enough to take Julia's pearls. They still have not been recovered, although how she would have gotten them past Morag, I do not like to imagine. Brisbane has gone after her, but she may have sold them by the time he reaches her. And that lot could get her halfway round the world and keep her in style for quite a long time," Portia finished.

I laid down my fork. The joint of pork that had been so delectable only a moment before sat like ashes in my mouth. Had Brisbane gone after her for my sake? He had been engaged to recover the Tear of Jaipur. He had the jewel; the princess and the prime minister would be happy. The letters patent would be published and he would have his title and his estate. Why then pursue Charlotte except for the pearls? I had seen him at work often enough to know he did not go beyond the terms set upon his employment. If he was asked to retrieve incriminating letters from a blackmailer, he did so. He did not destroy them, nor did he turn the evidence over to Scotland Yard. His clients invariably came from the cream of society, those who were desperate to avoid scandal. He investigated future husbands, restored runaway children, retrieved stolen property. But I had never once known him to embark on a chase once his objectives were satisfied. When his obligation to the client was fulfilled, the case was closed, whether the villain had been locked away or not. His business was justice, not retribution, and I nearly wept into my napkin to think of him, hounding Charlotte until she turned over my pearls. And I had not even asked him to do it.

Just then, a commotion arose from the hall. Servants yelling, dogs barking and, above it all, the high, penetrating voice of Aunt Dorcas. Before we could rise, the door was thrown back and Aunt Dorcas entered, flanked by two men. All three of them were garbed in Gypsy clothes, from the gold coins glittering at their belts to the scarves tied around their heads. Aunt Dorcas, who had stated loudly and with vigour her hatred of the race, linked her arms with those of her companions and raised her chin, her Roma finery clinking as she tossed her head and addressed Father.

"March! Bring food for my friends and wine as well. I am come home!"

* * *

In fact, the Gypsies did not sit down to table with us. In spite of Aunt Dorcas' insistence and Father's courteous invitation, they demurred, but agreed to take with them a hamper of hastily packed delicacies. Portia herded Aunt Dorcas upstairs for a bath and a change of clothes while the rest of us finished our meal in stunned silence. As soon as dessert was cleared I excused myself and made my way to Aunt Dorcas' room. I knocked and waited until she called for me to enter.

"Oh, it's you," she said. "Good. I rather thought it was that fool Portia again. Can you believe she's put me to bed? I am no invalid, but she was most resolute and unnaturally strong for so slight a woman."

I smiled and closed the door behind me. The room was a comfortable one, small, so the heat from the fireplace warmed it through. It was done in pinks and reds, with a cheerful view past the gardens to the village of Blessingstoke in the distance. The raspberry taffeta draperies were drawn now, but had they been open, she might have been just able to make out the campfires of her new friends.

But she had shed her Gypsy glamoury and was once more the quarrelsome old lady of my youth. Her nightdress, snugly buttoned at the throat, was edged in tasteful ruffles of lace to match the cap set tidily on her head. She looked up to see me eyeing it and snorted.

"I look like a muffin, do not deny it." I motioned for her to sit forward and I plumped a few of her pillows, smoothing the bedclothes when I was done.

"Do not fuss, Julia. Sit there and talk with me, but do not *fuss*."

I sat obediently, taking the chair she had indicated. It was a pretty thing, but the seat was hard and slippery.

"And do not fidget," she scolded. "I do not trust a fidgeter."

We sat for some minutes in silence. I looked about the room, memorising the paintings and mentally moving the shepherdess from the landscape into the still life of apples and cheese.

"Julia, do not furrow your brow like that. It will give wrinkles and it makes you look simple."

I widened my eyes. "I am sorry, Aunt Dorcas. Would you like for me to read to you?"

I reached for a book on the night table, but she flapped an irritable hand at me, shooing me away.

"I am in no mood for reading," she said.

"Then why don't you tell me about your adventures?" I coaxed. "I think you enjoyed yourself whilst you were away."

She fixed me with a cold stare, her bosom quivering with indignation. "I was in fear for my life, and you think I *enjoyed* myself?"

I blinked at her. "In fear of your life? From whom?"

Aunt Dorcas clamped her lips shut and shook her head. "I must say no more," she murmured, her lips still tightly closed.

I shrugged. "Very well. I will leave you then. Good night," I said, rising.

"It was that boy, Ludlow," she said, and I turned back, assuming my chair once more.

"The murderer? Yes, it was. He confessed, more than once, in fact."

She took the edge of the sheet in her fingers, worrying the lace like prayer beads. "He did not work alone," she said, more to herself than to me. "It was her."

I froze in my chair, uncertain of how to proceed. She was entirely correct, a woman had been involved. But Ludlow had not chosen to expose Lucy, and the girl was on her way to be married to a man who would make her life agony. Most would say justice had already been satisfied.

"You need not confirm it," she said, nodding. "Your face is an eloquent one, Julia. It was always thus, even as a child."

"Very well," I admitted. "He did say he murdered Snow because of a woman. Snow was blackmailing her for some wrongdoing she had committed in her youth."

Aunt Dorcas gave a little groan and covered her mouth.

I half-rose from my chair. "Aunt Dorcas, are you quite all right? Shall I ring for a maid?"

She shook her head, almost violently. "No, sit. And what we speak of in this room tonight must never be repeated," she told me, fixing me with those dark toadlike eyes. "Swear it."

"I swear."

She relaxed a little then, but resumed her twisting of the lace. I heard a tiny rip and made a note to tell Portia to have it mended. Poor Aunt Hermia. Yet another sheet damaged during this house party. Between the guests and the cats there would be nothing left to put on the beds.

"Did he tell you why she was being blackmailed?"

"No. He simply said it was a youthful peccadillo."

To my astonishment, she laughed. Not the tiny giggles she often affected, but great, heaving, gulping sobs of laughter that frightened me. After a moment the laughter turned to coughing and I was forced to intervene.

"Thank you," she said finally, recovering herself. "But it was not necessary to hit me so forcefully. I think you have bruised my back."

She gave me a reproachful look as I resumed my chair again. I said nothing and she paused, her expression faraway and touched with sorrow.

"This was no youthful peccadillo," she said finally. "Emma was being blackmailed because she murdered my sister."

I stared at her, gripping the arms of the chair so tightly I could not feel my hands. "No, it was Lucy he killed for, Lucy who was being blackmailed by Mr. Snow."

Aunt Dorcas looked at me pityingly. "Are you so certain?"

I rose and paced the room, putting the pieces together again. I went over every word of the conversation with Ludlow and realised with a cold shudder that he had not spoken Lucy's name. I had assumed it, but what if he had meant Emma? *And then she came to me in tears*…those had been his words, but he had never said a name. And when I asked him about the discovery of Lucy with the bloody candelabrum in her hand, he had referred to her quite clearly as Miss Lucy.

"Sit down, you make me quite dizzy," Aunt Dorcas ordered. I did, marvelling at the wickedness. Snow was blackmailing Emma, and out of his chivalry and his envy, Ludlow had killed the man for her. Then, when her sister had happened on the scene, he had succumbed to the temptation to blame Lucy, if only for a little while, in hopes of breaking her engagement to Sir Cedric. And all the while, Emma had stood silently by, letting Lucy twist in the wind for her villainy.

And yet, I realised with a shudder, Lucy must have known. Perhaps she had not been able to look squarely at the truth, but somewhere, deep within, she must have known. Whether she saw her sister steal out of the chapel when the deed was done, or whether she merely feared Emma's involvement, her first instinct had been to call blame down upon herself, to shield the sister who had been a mother to her during their long years of poverty and despair. No one would ever know what they spoke of during those dreary, cold hours in the chapel, or huddled in the bed behind locked doors after the attack upon them. Or whether they spoke of it now. But the murder of Lucian Snow would lie between them for the rest of their days, I was certain of it.

I felt suddenly queasy. "If you mean to be sick, do it elsewhere," Aunt Dorcas said sternly. I took a deep breath and blew it out slowly.

"I will not be sick. But I am forced to believe you. Ludlow said there was a lady involved, but he never spoke her name. I assumed it was Lucy."

Aunt Dorcas gave a little snort. "Lucy would not say boo to a goose. Emma would fatten the goose, invite it to tea and slice out its liver for pâté."

The image was not a pretty one. "What did you mean about your sister?"

Her lips worked furiously for a moment, and I realised she was fighting back tears. When she spoke, the words came fast and harsh. "India. Gertrude took Emma out to find a husband." Her thin lips curled into a sneer. "She found something else. A native man she wanted to marry, far above her station in India. His family were connected to the *nazim*. Gertie tried to tell her the man would never marry her, but she would not hear anything against him. Finally, it came out that Emma was pregnant by him. He offered her money, but nothing more. Can you imagine that? Offering her money like a common whore? And that's all she was, giving herself away like that."

I maintained a tactful silence. Emma might have chosen her lover unwisely, but taking a solitary lover hardly made her a whore.

"Gertie told her they were leaving India. Emma cried and screamed and threw such a fit she miscarried, thank God. Gertie tried to explain the child was malformed, she had seen it herself, but Emma never believed her. She thought Gertie had caused it somehow. She blamed her for the loss of her lover and her child. Gertie hushed it all up the best she could, but there were still many who knew. It was impossible to hide it, the tantrums, the dead baby. Your Mr. Snow was one of them. He served in India. And Emma recognised him, I saw it in her face the first night she met him here in the Abbey. I watched him watching her. It took him the better part of the evening to place her, but he finally did. There was an air of triumph about him, and Emma looked sick as a cat. She knew he remembered her from India and that he knew about the baby. Poor Gertie. She tried so hard to keep it all quiet, to protect Emma. In the end, she did the only thing she could. She packed Emma up and boarded the next ship home."

Aunt Dorcas looked away then, her lips working even faster now. "Gertie never saw England again. She died on board that ship and they buried her at sea. Word got back to her friends in India, and there was talk. Not openly, no one would dare. But there was speculation. It was whispered Emma had exacted her revenge."

I nodded slowly. "I remember now. Not about Emma, but about Aunt Gertie dying during a sea voyage. I had just come out into society and someone asked me at a ball if the lady buried at sea was a relation of mine. The newspapers mentioned it."

"Emma told the captain and the ship's doctor it was her heart," Aunt Dorcas said bitterly, "but Gertie was never sick a day in her life. She was the strongest of us all. No, that girl poisoned her, I know it, though it can never be proved. She saw to that. A body buried at sea cannot be examined. She got right away with murder. And when there was murder done in this house, I knew her handiwork for what it was. And I knew I should be next."

For the first time I saw her for the frightened old woman she was. "And you left that night? With Brisbane?"

She nodded. "The maid who brought my hot milk that night told me what had happened. I knew it was Emma, and that I had to get right away. We had never spoken of what happened to Gertie, but once or twice in the years since I have seen her eyes on me, *thinking,* as if she wondered what I knew. If she thought I believed her guilty of Gertie's death, she would not have hesitated to put me out of the way, I know it."

I thought of Emma, so solicitous of Aunt Dorcas, wanting to know if there was any news of her whereabouts. My stomach ached to think of it.

"What did you tell Brisbane?"

She shrugged. "Nothing of substance. I told him I would not stay in a house where murder had been done, and that I must speak with the Gypsies, for the spirits would reveal all to them. I told him I knew of a passageway that would lead to the churchyard."

I shook my head. "I cannot believe he would take you there on so flimsy a pretext."

"It was not flimsy," she said stoutly. "It was the truth, at least part of it. I could not tell him more. He is not family. I have spent the better part of a dozen years crushing that scandal. Do you think I was going to resurrect it with my own hands? I had no proof, only my suspicions, and you know as well as I, my dear, the ramblings of an old lady carry little weight. What would have happened if I had pointed the finger at her? Eh? The lot of you would have dismissed me—mad old Aunt Dorcas is at her tricks again."

I remembered Emma then, slyly insinuating about Aunt Dorcas and her "odd turns", all the while watering her villainy with crocodile tears. It was diabolical.

"I prefer to think we would have listened," I told Aunt Dorcas.

"And you might have. But I was not about to gamble my life on it."

We fell silent then, both of us stubbornly certain we were right. But as I thought on it, I realised how brave she was. She

523

had taken matters into her own hands when she felt threatened, and had gone to live among the Gypsies, an intrepid thing indeed at her age.

I smiled at her. "How did you like the Gypsy camp?"

She pulled a face. "No proper sanitation, and do not even ask me about the food," she complained. But even as she spoke I saw the corners of her mouth turn up a little. It had been the adventure of a lifetime, I would wager, and the memories would warm her for a long time to come.

I rose then and dropped a kiss to her cap. She scrubbed at her cheek and scowled at me. "I do not like displays of emotion, Julia. It comes from having all these Italians in the house. I feel a headache coming on. Go and fetch me my lavender salts."

She gestured toward her travelling case, a kidskin affair, fitted with a dozen bottles, all stoppered tightly and labelled with her spindly script. I reached for the lavender, surprised to find it empty. I turned it over and read the label. And as soon as I saw the word lettered there, I knew what she had done. I slipped the bottle into my pocket, then reached for the one slotted in the next compartment.

"Here are your salts," I told her evenly. She took them and began to sniff, waving a handkerchief in front of her face to waft the fumes to her nose.

I drew the other bottle out of my pocket. "And you will want to restore your supply of laudanum. The bottle is quite empty. You ought to be careful with such things, you know. That much laudanum could kill a person."

I held the bottle out to her and she averted her face, her mouth working furiously. "You were in too much of a hurry after you poisoned the bottle of brandy. You put the lavender and the laudanum in each other's place. It was careless of you, and worse still to ask me to go to your dispensary. I would never have thought it of you otherwise."

She raised her chin, staring me down with her great toad's eyes. "Emma had already done murder twice, once by her own hand and once by another's. If she died, God himself would call it justice."

"And Lucy?"

She clutched her handkerchief to her lips. "I have already told you, they are of a kind. Lucy would not harm another, but to save Emma, she would commit every sin and smile as she did it."

I shook my head, wonderingly. "I cannot quite believe it. How did you lure the footman from his post?"

She waved a hand at me. "I took the sheet from my bed. I burnt two holes for my eyes, and I was a phantom. A childish trick, but effective. I have forgotten more about this Abbey than you will ever know. How simple it was to show myself and let him follow me. It was the work of a moment to leave the brandy at his chair and remove the sheet. I was wearing a black gown. Even if he saw me leaving, I would have been but a shadow to him. I left the sheet in the linen cupboard when I sent Brisbane to the lumber rooms to fetch me a fur." Her eyes were gleaming now, and it occurred to me that she was rather proud of what she had done.

"It was not your decision," I told her. "You had no right to mete justice. You realise I must tell Father."

She scrabbled up against the cushions, her eyes wide with fear. "You dare not! He is grieved enough that a stranger has committed murder in this place. What would it do to him to learn of this? Think of the *scandal*. It is a different world now than the world of his youth, Julia. The story would make its way round the world, and everyone would know the shame of it. He would never recover from that."

I itched to slap her, elderly aunt or not. She was still staring fearfully over the edge of her handkerchief, but there was a touch of triumph in her. She had given me the one argument I could not fight.

I slid the bottle back into my pocket. "Very well. For Father, I will keep silent. But mind this—I am keeping this bottle. And if I ever hear that you have harmed anyone, in any fashion, I will produce it."

I spoke sharply, my voice ringing with conviction, but we both knew the threat was a hollow one. It would be my word against hers if ever I decided to tell my tale.

She gave a dry laugh. "I am old and I am tired, girl. My fangs are well and truly drawn. When I go back to Norfolk, it will be to die, and with me, so dies this story."

"That it will," I said. "Go tomorrow. I will not say farewell."

I left her then and went to my own room. In a very few minutes I was tucked into bed, warm and safe and so tired I thought I could sleep a month. But it was a long time before I slept, and every time I closed my eyes I saw Emma's face, watching from the shadows.

THE TWENTY-NINTH CHAPTER

Some say that ever 'gainst the season comes
Wherein our Saviour's birth is celebrated
This bird of dawning singeth all night long,
And then, they say, no spirit dare stir abroad.
—HAMLET

he days running up to Christmas were busy ones, and I kept myself too occupied to think much. Whenever I found my thoughts lingering on Brisbane or Emma or Henry Ludlow, I ruthlessly wrenched them away, turning instead to hanging mistletoe or poking cloves into oranges to make pomanders. I went for long walks in the gardens and attempted to train Florence to sit nicely. And I said goodbyes; some of them rose more easily to my lips than others. Aunt Dorcas left us the day after her return from the Gypsy camp, and in spite of my parting words to her the previous night, I did my duty and stood with my family to bid her farewell. She passed down the line of assorted relations, pausing when she reached me. She flicked me a cool glance, which I returned. Then she nodded, almost imperceptibly, proffering me a crumb of respect. I did not move, and she passed on. I was not sorry to see her go.

The following day, Plum and Alessandro, both of them nursing bruised hearts—and pride—took their leave as well. I regretted their leaving, but I was relieved, I realised with a guilty little pang. Alessandro had been a charming companion in Italy, but I had been mad to think even for a moment we might have been more than friends. And Plum was no companion at all at present. He was still sulking over his affairs, and Father had not been kind to him on the subject of Mrs. King, scolding him for taking up with such a creature. They were barely speaking by the time Plum and Alessandro departed, but I knew they would make it up eventually. Marches always did.

Still another parting made me quite nostalgic. My husband Edward's distant cousin, the nearest neighbour to the Abbey, had been forced to quit the manor house at Greymoor. The snowfall that had locked us in with a murderer had caused the weakened roof of the house to finally collapse. Thankfully none of his family or staff were injured, but the damage was too extensive. It was the perfect excuse for him to tear it down, and when he came to the Abbey to bid his farewells, he was full of building schemes for a property he had in Kent, near his wife's relations. So the last of the Greys moved out of Sussex, and the house was left to fall to ruin. It would not be long before the village children began to dare each other to run up and touch its sagging doors and peer into its broken windows, I fancied. Ghosts walked abroad at Greymoor, and I shuddered when I wondered if Edward might be one of them.

But the weeks before Christmas were happy ones, too. Aunt Hermia and Portia's beloved Jane came down from London, as well as a plentiful assortment of my brothers, sisters, spouses, nieces, and nephews. We were a full and merry party, and as the season ripened, I felt myself growing more relaxed. There had been no word from Brisbane, but I had not really expected one. I wore the pendant, as a charm for his safety, I suppose, and went about the business of Christmas. I wrapped presents and strung holly and ivy on the mantelpieces and played endless games of hunt-the-slipper with my nieces and nephews.

Christmas itself was Bedlam. The children were up at cock-crow, tearing into stockings and making a sweet nuisance of themselves. But in spite of the noise and frantic activity, the day was surprisingly pleasant. After breakfast we all bundled up and walked into the village for church. I had dreaded this, fearing that we would be met with stares and hostility. The shadow of murder still hung over our house, however normal we had tried to make things for the children. But I had underestimated either the power of the March name, or the affection with which the villagers regarded us. They were a trifle distant when we arrived, but after Uncle Fly's eloquent sermon on the subject of brotherly love, we were greeted much more kindly. We chatted politely, and Aunt Hermia even extended invitations to several families to come and take mince pies and wine with us. No one stammered or fled in fright, which I took as rather a heartening sign.

Once back at the Abbey, we feasted on a delectable Christmas lunch and then the children opened presents, a noisy and lengthy affair. Father, who could never bear to see anyone left out, gave each of his grown children a present as well. I presented Puggy with his finished cushion cover, which he received with an indelicate noise deep in his throat. I took that as an expression of gratitude. Florence looked exceedingly pretty in a collar fashioned of Venetian lace, and Grim bobbed his head in thanks for a tin of glacéed fruits from Paris. Then the children sang carols, and when they concluded—to tumultuous applause from their indulgent family—the tea things were brought in and we all gathered around as Father, preening in his garishly striped waistcoat from Violante, read out the Christmas letters from my absent brothers and sisters. There were few dry eyes when he was done, for we were all quite fond of each other and missed one another more than we would admit.

When he was finished, Father wiped his eyes and shooed us all to our rooms to prepare for the party that evening. Naturally it was to be a quieter affair than in years past. He had decided that dancing would be inappropriate, but Lysander had promised to play suitable music for our enjoyment. Everyone hurried to their rooms, the adults to change, the children to an early supper. Only Father remained behind, standing at the darkened window, and as I made to leave, he called me back.

I quirked a brow at him, and he waved toward the door.

"Close that, if you would. I do not mean to keep you long, but I should like to speak to you. Privately."

I obeyed, and then joined him at the window. It had long since fallen dark, but the landscape was dotted with lights—lanterns and bonfires and torches as folks moved from house to house in merry parties. Father nodded toward a light not far away, just at the edge of a small wood on the other side of the moat.

"There is the Rookery. Can you see it?"

"Of course." The Rookery was a tiny, quite mad-looking house. The Rookery had passed through several inhabitants since it was built in the eighteenth century. Each had left their mark, adding odd little staircases or pulling down façades and putting up new ones. What remained was a bizarrely charming confection with a pair of reception rooms and a few bedrooms, nothing more.

Father nodded again. "It is a sound little house. It was overgrown with ivy, and a few roof tiles were loose. Nothing that could not be mended. I had Benedick oversee the repairs before the snow fell. It is quite snug now, and perfectly in order, freshly painted, and not a bit of damp."

I was a bit mystified as to why he was telling me this, but I nodded encouragingly. "Oh, excellent. I have always thought it a darling house."

"I am glad to hear you say it," he said mildly. "It is yours now."

I blinked at him. "I did not hear you correctly, I am afraid."

"It is yours, Julia. I know I gave you a present with your brothers and sisters, but this is something else. Just for you."

I stammered a little in my confusion. "B-but, Father, surely there are others in the family who need a house."

"It is not a house," he corrected. "It is a home. Of your own, for so long as you shall live. I cannot give it to you outright. It is entailed with the estate, and when I am gone, it will belong to your brother, Bellmont. But I have arranged with the solicitor that it shall be yours to live in for the duration of your life, so long as you wish it. You may go and come back, as you like, but it will always be here for you to return to."

I shook my head. I could not quite take it in. "But why me, Father? Portia is a widow as well," I reminded him.

"Portia has a home, and Portia has Jane." He put out a hand and touched my shoulder. "I will not always be here, child. I do not know what the future holds for you, but I would have you cared for. You are my favourite."

I put a hand over his. "You have ten children, and five of them are under your roof right now. How many times have you said that today?"

"Five," he admitted ruefully. He leaned forward and pressed a kiss to the top of my head. "But I only meant it once."

He left me then and I was glad of it. I did not want him to see me weep.

Boxing Day was, in a word, noisy. The tradesmen called for their boxes and were quite civilly invited in for mince pies. We had a tremendous luncheon of the Christmas remains with far too much drink. By the afternoon, the children were rampant with sugar and excitement and the adults were sore-headed as bears. Father organised the children into a game of pirates, which entailed plundering the lumber room costume boxes and much shrieking and running about the Abbey. Raids were conducted and booty secured, and at one point I was even taken prisoner by my niece Perdita, and tied to my chair with a petticoat. She ran off as soon as she had secured me, waving a wooden sword and screaming threats in an alarming Irish accent. Portia had a great laugh at my expense. She had only been tied with a cravat and worked her way free very quickly. I quirked a brow at her loftily.

"You may well laugh, but I have just been captured by Grace O'Malley, the greatest pirate queen ever to sail the Seven Seas," I told her.

Portia snickered as I tried unsuccessfully to free myself. Eventually she was prevailed upon to untie my bonds. At that moment our niece returned and fixed me with a stern look.

"You were not supposed to free yourself. I must give you to Tarquin. He has ransomed you," she told me.

"Thank you, but I think not. I would rather be your prisoner than your brother's. He put spiders in my bed the last time I slept at the farmhouse."

Perdita's expression turned mulish. "But you *must,* Auntie Julia. He has paid the ransom," she insisted. "See?" She dug into her pocket and extracted a handful of plunder. There, on her grubby palm, lay a necklace of perfect grey pearls I had never thought to see again.

Portia and I gasped and lunged for them at the same time. Startled, Perdita shrieked and threw them into the air. Portia caught them neatly, while I took our niece by the shoulders.

"Perdita, dearest, where precisely did you get this necklace?"

She looked inclined to pout, but if Benedick's children were high-spirited, they were also well brought up.

"Tarquin gave it to me." Her expression darkened. "He would not agree to the bracelets as well, but I thought you were worth them."

"Indeed. And where is Tarquin now?"

"Mounting an attack on the kitchens. He means to take the larder. He wants cake."

I released her and patted her on the head. "Thank you, dearest. Play with Auntie Portia now. She will be your prisoner. I must have a word with your brother."

Portia shot me an evil look, and the last I saw, Perdita was lashing her ankles to a chair while Puggy danced around, snarling.

Tarquin was easy enough to find. I ran him to ground in the kitchens precisely where his sister said he would be. He must have been successful, for he was busily stuffing his pockets with ginger nuts and Cook was nowhere to be seen.

"Tarquin, my boy, may I have a word?" I asked him. He blinked at me, owlish in a pair of very smart spectacles. He was the cleverest of Benedick's children, and I suspected he would be the handsomest.

"You're my prisoner now," he informed me. "Did Perdita tell you? I paid an enormous ransom for you," he said, wrapping a striped scarf about my head. "I will release you and make you one of my crew if you promise to fight for me."

"Very tempting offer, I am sure," I said, removing the scarf. "But I wanted to ask you about that ransom. Where did you find the necklace?"

He pulled a disgusted face. "That bit of rubbish? You needn't worry, Auntie Julia. It is only a bit of glass. I found it stuffed in the bear."

I stared at him. "The bear? You mean Maurice?"

He nodded and tucked another ginger cake into his pocket. "There is a hole under his arm where the stuffing is coming out. I saw it when we were playing hide-and-go-seek earlier. I put my hand in, and I felt something I thought might be pebbles or some choice marbles. It was only those bits of trumpery. I found these as well—you can have them if you like."

He reached into his shirt pocket and pulled out my bracelets. I felt a little weak as I looked at them. Thousands of pounds' worth of perfectly matched pearls with diamond clasps, an empress' treasure, lying serenely on a boy's palm.

"Did you find earrings as well? And a great long rope of pearls?"

He shook his head. "But I did not have long to look. Grandfather was coming, and I had to hide."

I nodded knowledgeably. "Of course you did."

His face brightened. "Would you like for me to have a look round for you now? I know just where I found these bits. I daresay the others are there as well."

I nodded and he led the way, careful to take a circuitous route to avoid the scalawag ways of his uncle Ly, who was laying plans to board his ship and overthrow him, Tarquin told me solemnly.

At length we reached Maurice the bear, and Tarquin made a careful search. He retrieved every last piece of the Grey Pearls, presenting them to me with as much ceremony as the chancellor handing the crown jewels to the queen.

As my hands closed over them, he turned to me, his young face quizzical. "Aunt Julia, they aren't real, are they?"

I smiled at him. "Yes, they are, my dear boy. And I thought I would never see them again. Thank you."

He goggled at me, and in return for his aid I promised to return to serve as his crew once I had secured the pearls in my room. I put them away, nestling them onto their bed of black satin, and paused. I thought of Charlotte, the last person to touch them. Poor greedy Charlotte, clever and avaricious and dishonest. For all her sins, there was something almost likeable about her. I wondered where she was, and if she had eluded Brisbane, if he would believe her if she claimed not to have the pearls. Hiding them in the hole in Maurice's pelt had been a stroke of genius. It had been the merest accident they had been recovered. Perhaps she had thought to come back for them some day, or perhaps she had been happy enough to escape. It did not matter now.

I closed the lid with a snap. I was done with them.

The next day I left the Abbey directly after breakfast. It was a crisp, cold morning and I took care to wrap myself in my warmest clothes before setting out. I walked slowly, taking in deep draughts of fresh air and puffing them out in little clouds. The road was still muddy and my hems were deeply soiled by the time I reached my destination at the Gypsy camp. I lifted my nose, sniffing appreciatively at the little cooking fires kindled in the river meadow. Magda's brother, Jasper, raised a hand in greeting and disappeared into one of the caravans. A moment later Magda appeared, her unruly hair plaited with scarlet ribbons. The cold must have driven her into her caravan, for I did not see her tent and the tiny chimney of her caravan was smoking heavily. She smiled broadly as she approached, wrapping a heavy woollen shawl about her shoulders.

"Come to cross my palm with silver?" she asked, giving me a throaty laugh.

"I wanted to thank you for your hospitality to my father's aunt. She is not a very nice person. I am sure she did not express her appreciation for your kindness."

Magda tipped her head, her bright black eyes snapping as she looked me over from head to toe. "There is more. You want answers, do you not? Perhaps it is time you got them."

She turned and made for her caravan, never looking round to see if I followed. She led the way inside, and I paused on the threshold to admire her little home. It was compact and more orderly than I would have expected, all her possessions neatly stowed on pegs or in little cupboards fitted into the walls. There was a stove for warmth and a narrow bed snugged under the curved roof. A tiny table laid with a sprigged cloth and two chairs completed the furnishings, and yet there was no sense of meagreness about the place. The bed was spread with a yellow taffeta coverlet and curtains fashioned of flowered chintz covered the windows. The trim had been painted a bright blue, and the effect was one of exuberant high spirits.

She waved me to a chair and fussed a moment with the kettle and brightly patterned teacups. She arranged them on the table, careful to avoid the small crystal ball resting on its pedestal in the middle. When she had poured out and we had warmed our hands, she reached for mine, turning it over and stripping off the glove to read my palm. She peered closely at it, clucking once or twice, then released it. I pressed my hand against my teacup, but even through the warmth of the porcelain I could still feel the light stroke of her fingertips as she traced the lines.

"You want to know about him," she said finally. "Very well. Ask."

I did not stop to wonder why she was willing to speak now when she had never done so in the past. Perhaps she was in a generous mood, perhaps she felt badly for things that had been between us in the past. Or perhaps it was another means of making mischief for her. With Magda, there was simply no way to know.

"You spoke of a woman called Mariah Young," I began. "You told me about her months ago. You said she had died. Who was she?"

Magda took a deep swallow of her tea and settled back in her chair. She eased her feet out of her shoes, scratching one calf with the toes of the other foot. There was a hole in her stocking and it was badly worn at the heel. She scratched for a long moment. I knew better than to prod her. She had her own rhythms, and she would speak in her own time.

Finally, she put her shoes back on and put down her teacup. "Mariah Young was a Gypsy girl, known among the travellers of this isle for her gift. She had the second sight, and a powerful gift it was. But she had other gifts too. She was beautiful and lively, with a cloud of black hair down to her waist and the tiniest feet you ever saw. She danced for money and told fortunes and collected hearts. She broke them all too, all but one."

Magda's voice, accented by her native Romany tongue, was peculiarly suited to storytelling. It was low for a woman's, and she had a way of speaking that held the listener in thrall. I glanced down at the crystal ball on the table between us, and for an instant I could almost see a tiny figure with high-arched feet, dancing and snapping her fingers.

"The one man Mariah Young loved was not a Romany. He was a rogue, come from an old and proud Scottish family, and his people hated Mariah. But he must have loved her in spite of his wicked ways, for they married, and after seven full moons had passed, she gave birth to a child, a boy with his mother's witchcraft and his father's wildness."

Magda's eyes sharpened. "But blood will out, and the noble rogue left his wife and son. Mariah did not grieve for him. His love of drink and other women had killed her love, and when she saw she was rid of him she danced as she had not danced since she was wed. She took her boy to her people, tried to teach him the ways of the travellers. But the child was a halfling, born between two worlds, belonging to neither. When he was but ten years old he ran away, leaving his mother behind, and for the first time in her life, Mariah Young knew what it was to have a broken heart."

I took a sip of my tea and averted my eyes. The tea was bitter now, and I put it down again.

"Ah, the taste of regret," Magda said softly. "You wish you had not come. But you did, and you must let me finish the tale I have begun. After her son left her, Mariah Young would not dance, could not tell fortunes. Her gift failed her, and in its place came headaches, blinding ones. She took laudanum to ease them, and one day, when her little green bottle was as empty as her pockets, she stole a bottle from the chemist. She was discovered and put into gaol. Do you know what it means to a Gypsy to be locked up, lady? It means death to us. If we cannot breathe freely, we cannot breathe at all. And Mariah Young had no wish to live. She turned her face to the wall and died, but before she did, she cursed her gaolers. She cursed the chemist and the judge and anyone who could hear the sound of her voice. And before she died, she cursed her own son. She gave him the legacy of her sight, knowing he would fight against it, knowing it would destroy him slowly from within."

Magda's voice trailed off, a menacing, unearthly whisper. There was a scream of laughter from outside the caravan—one of the children, I think—and I jumped. I picked up my glove and yanked it on.

"That is a faery story for children. I wanted the truth."

Magda shrugged. "What is the truth? Mariah Young was Brisbane's mother. He ran away and she died in gaol for stealing a bottle of laudanum. Those are facts. Are they the truth? No, for they do not tell you of the heart, and that is where truth lives, lady."

"And I suppose it is the truth when you moan on about death in his shadow?" I asked, my voice thick with sarcasm.

"Did someone not die at the Abbey?" Her tone was even, but I saw the twitch of a smile at the corners of her mouth. "Come, lady, let us be friends. We have known each other too long to keep bad feelings between us. Give me your cup and I will tell you what I see."

Reluctantly I swallowed the rest of the tea and handed her the cup, the same Jubilee cup she always used for tasseomancy. She upended it on the saucer and turned it thrice, then picked it up and peered inside. After a moment she gave it to me. "There is an eye. You must be watchful."

I looked into the cup. Near the bottom was an oval shape, pointed at the ends with the sinister suggestion of a pupil. I thrust the cup back at her.

"Is that all? I must be watchful? Watchful of what?"

Magda shrugged again. "Sometimes the tea leaves do not have much to say. But I will tell you this—he fights with himself, he struggles, and to be with such a man, you will struggle as well."

"Did the tea leaves say that too? They've grown chatty."

She smiled, but this time there was no hint of the theatrics of the fortune-teller. It was a genuine smile, warm and sincere. "No, I say it as a woman who has lived a hundred lifetimes. He is a man beset by devils, and to be with him is to fight them too. But, oh, what a battle!" she finished with a wink.

"You have always warned me off of him. Why do you encourage me now?"

"Because I am growing old and sentimental." She waved a hand, imperious as a queen. "I see only a little, lady, but I know that your fortune is as twined with his as the ivy to the oak. Be happy. And do not forget to cross my palm," she admonished with a chuckle. She opened her hand for a coin.

I rose and reached into my pocket. "I have no silver, but I hope these will do."

I laid the Grey Pearls across her palm, spilling them into her lap.

"Lady," she began, her eyes round with wonder. I shook my head.

"They are real, and they are yours. Father can help you sell them for a fair price, if you like. Have Jasper arrange it."

I left her then, and we did not exchange another word. She did not thank me; I did not expect it. I had little doubt our paths would cross again some day.

THE THIRTIETH CHAPTER

Think you there was or might be such a man
As this I dreamt of?
—ANTONY AND CLEOPATRA

welfth Night marked the beginning of the end of that fateful house party. My brothers and sisters collected their children and returned to their homes, most of them on speaking terms for once. Plum had written to say he had been invited to stay in Florence for Alessandro's betrothal celebrations and would be leaving for Ireland as soon as the nuptials were concluded in the summer. Portia looked closely at me when she related the news, but I merely smiled and went on feeding Grim his sugared plums. Much to Father's delight, Lysander and Violante had decided to remain in England for the birth of their child, and Hortense—by now fast friends with Violante—had agreed to play companion to her. And in a small piece in the *Times* I learned that Scotland Yard was very pleased to report the apprehension of a jewel thief of some notoriety. Brisbane's name was not mentioned, nor was the Tear of Jaipur, though I knew they meant Charlotte King. But as closely as I read the columns, there was no word of letters patent or the viscountcy of Wargrave. There was, however, the smallest mention of an estate in Yorkshire changing hands into the possession of Nicholas Brisbane. It was no great estate, and no lofty title, but I was happy for him.

As for me, I went to London with Portia and Jane, accompanied by Florence and Grim, and of course Morag, grumbling as usual about the extra work. I had much shopping to do to outfit the Rookery, and I felt the need for the diversions of city life and the comforts of steam heat. Portia's house, a vast, modern place, was impossibly warm even in the dreariest months. We settled in companionably, and the dark days of January passed quickly away.

One wet afternoon late in January, Jane and I lolled by the fire, talking desultorily of things we might do once the weather improved. The butler entered with the tea things, and Portia followed him, flipping through the post. She had already opened one letter, and I caught the quickest glimpse of a bold black scrawl before she shoved it to the bottom of the stack.

"Jane, dearest, won't you pour? And Julia, you can hand round the cakes. Mind you take some of that sponge. Cook is quite proud of it."

Jane poured as Portia handed out the letters. Out of the tail of my eye, I saw her slip the opened one behind the cushion of her chair as she sorted through the rest. She lit on one from Aunt

Hermia, and exclaimed, reading it out to us as we sipped our tea and nibbled at sandwiches.

"Aunt Hermia says Hortense is well, and Violante is feeling quite strong now. She has put Father on a diet," she said with a smothered laugh. "Apparently he was a bit bilious, and she has decided he must not eat butter, gravy, or pastry. Poor Father!" We exchanged smiles. Father was the most powerful man of our acquaintance, but he was also the most susceptible to being fussed over. They might have begun rockily, but Violante was very likely in a fair way to becoming his favourite daughter-in-law.

Portia's expression sobered. "Father has received a letter from India. Oh, dear."

I took a bite of the slice of sponge. "What is it, dearest?"

Portia shook her head sadly. "It is Sir Cedric. He suffered a fatal attack on the voyage to India. He is dead."

The cake tasted dusty suddenly, and I put down the plate.

"How awful," Jane murmured. She refilled my cup, sweetening it heavily. "Drink this, Julia. You have gone quite pale."

I obeyed and felt marginally better. "What sort of attack?"

Portia shook her head. "She does not say. One imagines it must have been his heart. He was a rather florid sort of man."

"Perhaps an apoplexy," Jane suggested. She shook her head. "Poor Lucy Phipps."

I said nothing. I was thinking of Emma. Emma and her blind devotion to her sister, her jealous love. I thought of the slippery precipice of murder, and how much easier it must be to do the act again after you have raised your hand to it once.

"Not Lucy Phipps anymore," Portia corrected. "Aunt Hermia says that Sir Cedric died after they were wed. She is Lady Eastley now. She has inherited his entire fortune."

"How tragic," Jane went on. "To be so newly married, and to lose one's husband. I cannot imagine that the money is any great comfort to her. She must be utterly shattered."

"Oh, I don't know," I said faintly. "I think the money may be a very great comfort. She was always quite poor, you know."

"And now she and Emma will never want for a thing so long as she lives," Portia finished.

As we sipped our tea in silence, I was conscious of a deep unease, a vague dissatisfaction that something had gone quite gravely wrong and could never be mended.

When Jane had retired and Portia had left to bathe the repulsive Puggy, I poured myself another cup of tea and went to the chair where Portia had been sitting. The letter was still there, a little the worse for having been sat on. Doubtless she expected to retrieve it later. I sipped at my tea, holding the letter and debating with myself. It was a very short argument.

I slipped the letter from its envelope and read it quickly. There was no salutation, no endearment, and I felt a great deal more at ease when I read the brisk tone of the letter itself. I had not forgotten Portia's smug air when she informed me she had business with Brisbane.

By all means, come in April. The worst of the weather will be past, and I am told the spring is rather lovely here. I shall be vastly interested to see what you can do with the place. Do not think I am being modest when I say it is a ruin. It lacks every modern convenience, and I hope you are prepared for every possible discomfort. I can offer you only cold rooms, bad food, and lumpy beds.

As for your sister, I will not mention her again, except to say this: do not entertain the idea of bringing her. The estate is not fit for company. And since I flatter myself that I know you a little better than you might believe, I will repeat, DO NOT BRING YOUR SISTER TO YORKSHIRE.

The rest of the letter was a tangle of information about trains and schedules and domestic arrangements. I only skimmed it. I folded the letter and replaced it in the envelope and tucked the envelope behind the cushion. Portia would know soon enough I had read it, but there was no purpose to starting that quarrel just yet.

Instead, I busied myself making a list of everything I would need to pack for my trip to Yorkshire. I was keenly interested in seeing this ruin of an estate, and if Portia meant to put his household in order for him, she might well be glad of an extra pair of hands. Besides, April was three long, dreary, grey months away. After a winter in the city, I would be gasping for country air, and Yorkshire was reputed to be tremendously scenic. I had never been, but I had heard the moors were staggeringly lovely. Of course, I never expected Brisbane and I would find a body there. But that is a tale for another time.

THE EXTRAORDINARY DEBUT NOVEL BY
DEANNA RAYBOURN

A PSYCHOTIC MURDERER IS ABOUT TO MAKE HIS ONE MISTAKE: UNDERESTIMATING LADY JULIA

SILENT *in the* GRAVE

Available wherever hardcovers are sold.

A riveting novel by acclaimed author

DIANE CHAMBERLAIN

Twenty-eight years ago a North Carolina
governor's young, pregnant wife was
kidnapped. Now her remains have
been found and a man has been
charged with her murder. Only one
person—CeeCee Wilkes—can refute
the charges against him. But CeeCee
disappeared years ago....

Eve Elliot is a successful therapist
to troubled students, a loving wife,
a mother deeply invested in her
family. But her happiness is
built on a lie. Now, forced
to confront her past, she
must decide whether to
reveal to her family that
she is not who she seems,
or allow a man to take the
blame for a crime she
knows he did not commit.

the SECRET LIFE of CEECEE WILKES

"Diane Chamberlain is
a marvelously gifted author!
Every book she writes is a real gem!"
—*Literary Times*

Available wherever trade paperback books are sold!

MIRA®

A NEW THRILLER FROM THE AUTHOR OF *BODY COUNT*

P.D. MARTIN
THE MURDERERS' CLUB

THEY WATCH.
THEY WAIT.
THEY KILL.

Increasingly haunted by her ability to experience the minds of killers in the throes of heinous crimes, FBI profiler Sophie Anderson finds that her talent is uncontrollable and unpredictable. When bodies start showing up on a university campus, she and Tucson police detective Darren Carter are pulled into the case. However, Sophie is puzzled by the fact that certain signature elements are different in each killing. The FBI database has a record of many of the signatures—but they have been used by different serial killers.

As the bodies continue to appear, Sophie must hone her terrifying skills to try to track down the killer—or killers.

> **"Enough twists and turns to keep**
> **forensics fans turning the pages."**
> **—*Publishers Weekly* on *Body Count***

MIRA®

Available wherever
hardcover books are sold!

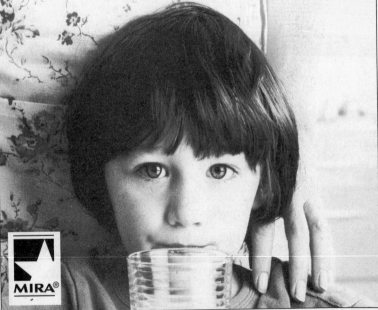